...a book...write a book...yes of course, why didn't I think of it before...I'll tell the whole fuckin' wide world about the injustices...about the needles and the strip-cells...the beatings...the kickings and the tears – but whoa, slow down baby, we don't want it all doom and gloom do we, no sir, leave a little space for some fun...oh yes, we will have some fun don't worry about that, lots of games maybe, and a riddle here an' there just to keep everyone on their toes, yes sir, I can't wait to get going and it'll be easy – just write about a thousand pages a day and then print 'em up on my own printing press, and sell 'em...ha...you send me a clean, crisp, five pound note and I'll send you a copy of my mind all printed out nice an' neat and when I've made two or three million I'll start giving it all away 'cos who needs all that much money baby, not me, no sir...

I lived it
I wrote it
All the errors are mine

Fumblemonkbox

D.B. Dunnit

– Anno Domino Press –

Published by Anno Domino Press

ISBN 0 9530435 0 9

Phototypeset, printed and bound in Great Britain by
Wace Burgess, Abingdon

I dedicate these pages to my beloved Christine,
and all the other Angels, both Earthbound and otherwise,
who must have struggled with me also.

These few words are for Allgolds and Dream-machines, who, after reading part one and part two, gave me such inspiration when part three became my own Mario chocolate island…

…and Fingleweed, though seemingly forlorn and in solitude, stood sentinel and remained steadfast throughout while those about him faltered and faded.

ACKNOWLEDGEMENT

I wish to offer profuse gratitude to the doctors and medical staff who tended me when I was in great pain. Had I not suffered their gross inhumanity, this book would not exist.

Special thankyous also to the Home Office, who seek out and employ such men who can stand and watch a man cry with pain and yet still be able to turn a key and walk...

PART ONE

1963

He moved the cabinet further into the passage, lifting it steadily over the lip of the carpet. He grabbed the blue money-bag and hoisted himself up until he could reach the wooden frame of the window-light, then climbed out onto the roof. He waited a few minutes, catching his breath. When he was sure nobody was in sight, he lowered himself from the roof and walked quickly away.

It was just after ten o'clock in the evening when he entered the small, grey-stoned building. It had previously been owned by the Church of England but was now in possession of Billy Seymour, a balding, middle-aged fat man who had converted it to a snooker hall. The three tables the hall boasted were old and worn, showing threadbare patches under the dim lighting. The high arched windows that ran down one side were blacked out and heavily barred, and a suspended ceiling had been fitted to reduce the echo. Brown industrial lino, impregnated with cigarette burns and tea stains, covered the floor. At one end of the hall was a make-shift sandwich bar and next to this stood a one-armed tic-tac-toe machine.

Jo Sullivan walked across to the bar and ordered a coffee and a cheese roll. The owner filled the order and placed it on the grimy counter, spilling half an inch of coffee in the saucer.

"Hey Bill, is that right you was a butler once?" said Jo, straightfaced.

"A butler? What d'ya mean, a butler?"

"Nothing, forget it – is anyone upstairs?"

"Yeah, a few of the boys are up there. Nice little game goin' on I reckon. Larry's winnin' a few bob an' they're callin' for plenty of teas as well."

"I'd better get up there then," said Jo, "and if I win I can give you back the tenner I owe ya."

Jo grabbed the coffee and roll, headed for the room at the top of the stairs, and went in.

The room was about twenty feet square with a small partition separating two poker tables. The flooring was covered with deep-pile carpet and the walls were decorated tastefully, in total contrast to the downstairs hall. One of the tables were empty but the other was occupied by four young men, smoking, playing cards, and oblivious to everything but the game and the escapism it brought.

Bob, the pot-man, gave Jo a nod as he came into the room. The pot-man played in the game sometimes but his real purpose was to take out the house money from each pot and fetch the teas when they were called for.

Being a regular to the hall, Jo was greeted by the players and invited to join the game.

"Hey Jo, how ya doin'?" asked Larry. Jo acknowledged the group and pulled up a chair.

"What's the limit?"

"Half the pot. It's a meaty game –"

"Deal me in," said Jo, cutting Bob short, "and I think we'll start with a nice new deck – if that's okay with you boys?"

Sure it would be okay. Nobody sitting round this table were going to argue with Jo Sullivan. Although only nineteen years old, Jo had earned his colours many times over with his ability to lay a man out, and, because of his many victories, others had bestowed on him the nickname, Jo Waterloo.

On his own since his fourteenth birthday, Jo soon became aware that being able to take care of oneself earned respect, and with respect came opportunities and open doors. An open door handed to Jo earlier in the evening had netted him more than £300. A friend had told him that a fair sum of cash could be had from an old firm of fruit and flower importers down on the docks. The cash was kept overnight on a Thursday so that it could be paid out early Friday mornings before the men went out on their rounds.

The information was good and getting hold of the money was easy to Jo as breaking in through a skylight.

"Hey Jo, come on man – pair of kings to bet," said Larry.

"Yeah," said Jo, getting his mind back on the game. "Make it eight pounds to play."

Larry threw £8 in the pot. So did Russel, a young, good-looker who was always cheating on his wife, and because of it, was known as Russel the Rat.

The Rat raised the pot by a further £12 making it £20 for Little Johnny, the fourth player in the game. He folded.

"What's that – another £12 to me, right?" said Jo, tossing in a tenner and two pound notes. Larry looked at his hole cards then gazed at the Rat's pair of tens with an ace, and Jo's pair of kings with a four. Larry's own cards were the seven, eight, and queen of spades. With the ten of spades already in the hole, he was confident of making a flush. And with two cards to come, even a running flush was possible.

"I'll call the twelve nicker and raise it another score." Jo and the Rat each threw in the raise. The Rat was dealing.

"A seven to the pair of kings, a six to the tens, and a four of hearts to the flush – pair of kings to bet or check, Jo."

"Check."

"Forty pounds," said Larry.

The Rat started fidgeting and counted out his money.

"I've only got twenty-eight quid left."

"That's twelve on the side then –"

"Hang on! I haven't said I'm in yet for fucksake!"

"Okay keep ya shirt on," said Bob, "I was only –"

"I know, I know – just hang on a minute will ya – I'm tryin' t' think."

The Rat was getting edgy. He'd been playing for the best part of the night and Lady Luck wasn't shining on him.

The Rat's luck came mainly between the sheets.

"Okay – twenty-eight all in," he finally decided.

"Forty to you then Jo, if you're in," said Bob.

Jo studied the cards. Larry, he figured, probably had a flush, or at least four to it. The Rat more than likely had just two pairs, but Jo's own two pairs were higher. He tossed in the forty. Bob scooped up £24 and formed a second pot. The Rat dealt the last card face down. Jo didn't make his hand and checked. Larry didn't make his either but decided to go for a bluff.

"I'll bet fifty," he said.

Jo checked his money and found that he was down to £38. If he called and lost he would be broke. He pondered for a few minutes then threw his cards onto the table.

"I'm out," he said, and kicked the chair from under him to stretch his legs.

Larry pulled in the £74 side pot and waited for the Rat to declare his hand.

"A fullhouse!" he suddenly cried out. "About fuckin' time I pulled a card – a fullhouse jacks." Larry threw his cards on the table and said, "Yeah wins."

The Rat began to gather in the pot.

"You always was a lucky bastard," said Little Johnny, "if you fell into a bucket of shit you'd come out smellin' sweet."

"Oh yeah – how come I'm losin' three hundred then?" replied the Rat. "This is the first touch I've had for a month." The Rat allowed himself a wry smile at his own exaggeration.

Jo was getting fed up and decided to call it a day. He'd been losing steadily all night and he knew that if he carried on playing he would end up skint. Just as he was about to leave two men came into the room that he'd never seen before. They were looking for a game of cards.

"What kind of game you boys looking for?" asked Jo.

"Poker," said the taller of the two, "I hear all you play up here is seven card stud."

"Yeah that's right," said Jo. "How much dough you wanna lose then?"

"Who said anything about losing?" Jo looked at the scruffy, greasy-looking body that had spoken and took an instant dislike to him. It was then that he decided to carry on playing. Who knows, he thought, fresh blood might mean a change of luck. There were now six players sitting round the table.

With only £38 left to play with, Jo had to take care in the first few hands that he was in. He felt that he'd been reckless in his play for most of the night and he was determined to shake himself up.

"Bob, throw us a new deck will ya," said Little Johnny, "and chuck these poxy things down the karzi." He tossed the old deck to Bob-the-pot and began to shuffle up the new cards.

With new blood in the school the game seemed to take on fresh impetus. After an hour or so, Jo had escaped from the perilous position of £38 and he now had in front of him more than £200. Larry was still way out in front but Little Johnny was in serious trouble with only a few pounds left to play with. The Rat had about a hundred – which he counted continuously – and the tall feller, Chris, was down about eighty. Jo figured Greaseball was ahead by at least a couple of hundred.

Larry started to deal a fresh hand. By the fifth card there were four players left in the pot – Larry, Jo, Chris, and Greaseball. Larry spun the cards round the table.

"Six to the pair of tens; a queen to the fives; a seven to the possible flush and a fat jack to me – tens to bet or check." The tall feller threw in two fivers.

"Pair of tens bets a tenner," he quipped.

Jo followed suit.

Greaseball, with his king, nine, and seven of diamonds showing, raised the bet to thirty.

Larry played along.

Chris and Jo each put in another twenty.

The pot was looking good.

Larry dealt the sixth card.

"A six to the pair of tens – two pair on the table; a queen to the fives – another two pair; a three to the possible, and a seven for me – two pair to bet or check."

Jo didn't need to look at his hole cards again, he already knew he had a fullhouse queens.

"How much can I bet?" Bob-the-pot had a quick count up.

"You can bet seventy-five, Jo."

"Seventy-five it is then."

Greaseball, with four diamonds showing on the table, also tossed in £75.

Larry folded.

So did Chris.

"Just you and me then pal," said Greaseball.

"Yeah," said Jo, cringing at the word 'pal'.

"Up to you then pal."

Jo cringed again. He then looked at Greaseball's king, nine, seven, and three of diamonds – a possible running flush that would leave Jo's fullhouse standing if he had it made, but Jo couldn't believe he was sitting on three inside cards to a running flush and made his bet accordingly.

"One hundred pounds," he said, placing five crisp twenties on the green baize. Greaseball became a little hesitant, flicking his three hole-cards. He picked up his money and had a quick roll-call, then started flicking his cards again.

Everyone was quiet, waiting for the call, or even a possible raise.

A minute went by.

Another minute passed and still nothing was happening.

Before another one had the chance, Little Johnny quipped, "Is everybody dead then?"

"Shut up midget!" sneered Greaseball. "I'm tryin' to think."

Little Johnny was quick to reply. "Bet that comes hard for ya dunnit!"

"Hey, hey – let's play cards here," said Bob, "it's up to you mate to call, raise, or fold."

"Yeah," said Jo, "are you betting or what?"

"Is there a fuckin' time limit on this game then?"

"Just cut out the verbal and get on with makin' up ya mind will ya," said Jo, becoming irritated.

"I think you're just tryin' to –"

"Listen, I ain't tryin' to do anything – just make the bet or pack," said Jo, evenly. Greaseball pondered for another half a minute then counted out a hundred pounds. He stared at Jo hard before throwing the money in the pot.

"Call," he said.

"Fullhouse queens," declared Jo, spreading his cards.

"I fuckin' knew it!" said Greaseball, angrily.

Little Johnny started laughing. "Only a mug would call a bet like that –"

"Listen you fuckin' midget –"

"Oi – you fuckin' listen, greaseball –" started Jo.

"What!? Are you talkin' t' me!?"

Jo quickly scooped up all the notes and pushed them deep into his trouser pockets. "Yes, you arsehole, I'm talkin' to you – don't call my mate a fuckin' midget!"

"What are you then – his fuckin' mother!?" Greaseball went to make his move on Jo but Jo was too quick for him. As Greaseball took a swing, Jo ducked then steamed into him with such speed and ferocity that it was all over in seconds. Blood was spurting from Greaseball's split lip and an inch-long gash had appeared over his left eye. Jo wouldn't have been surprised if he'd cracked one or two of his ribs as well.

Greaseball was in a bad way. Blood was pumping from his wounds and he was in need of immediate medical treatment. Suddenly, Billy Seymour, the owner of the club, came charging into the room. "What the fuck is going on up here? I thought someone was coming through the ceiling –" He looked at Greaseball. "I think he'd better get to the hospital. He looks like he needs some stitches – what happened here anyway?"

"The mug went to give Jo some, but got some from Jo instead," said Little Johnny.

Jo looked concerned. He already had two convictions for assault on his sheet, one of them for grievous bodily harm. He hoped this creep wasn't going to cause him any problems.

"I hope your mate ain't gonna give me any headaches over this," he said to Chris. "By that I mean I hope I'm not gonna be hearin' from old bill." Chris assured Jo that the police wouldn't become involved but said his mate had two brothers that might want to do something about it. Jo wasn't worried by any brothers, he would take care of them as well if they came for him.

Billy sorted out the first aid kit and wrapped a bandage round Greaseball's head. "That should hold the flow for now – better get him to the hospital straightaway."

The two men headed for the stairs but Greaseball couldn't resist a last stab at Jo. "This ain't the last you've heard of this you bastard – I've got a tasty brother that'll sort you out."

'Bring 'im down," laughed Jo, 'bring ya whole fuckin' family down here if ya like and if ya mummy wants to know who damaged her little baby tell her it was me, Jo Waterloo!"

Jo headed for home. It was only a fifteen minute walk from the Half-Moon club and just a stones throw from the wharf where the timber boats came in.

Jo wasn't a serious thief. For him to commit a break-in things would have to be tough. He was a stevedore, but there hadn't been a cargo on the wharf for nearly a fortnight and even down on the dock, grain boats and fruit boats had stopped coming in. Something to do with unions and closed shops had seen them diverted to other ports, and work was short. Only a stroke of luck had led Jo to the £300 he had acquired the evening before and he would make sure his mate was well rewarded for the information.

It was early November and as Jo turned into the wharf road the chill wind took his breath. He hunched his shoulders and pushed his hands deep into his trouser pockets. As he hastened his gait, he began to think about Greaseball, and a feeling of remorse came over him. Why didn't I just grab him and shake him up a little, he thought, why did I have to go so far…?

Jo arrived home shortly after six o'clock. He shared a two-bedroom flat with his mate, Danny, who often worked with Jo on the wharf. If work was short like it was at the moment, the two of them would go out in Danny's old pick-up truck, totting for scrap metal or anything else that might be laying about.

Danny was still in bed when Jo got home but was soon up and about when he heard Jo making himself a pot of tea. Danny could drink tea 'till it came out of his ears if he had the chance. The only thing he liked better was a pint of ice cold beer.

Danny was nearly digging his eyes out when he hit the bright light of the kitchen. "Alright Jo – how did you get on last night – did you do it?" he asked, his fingers still digging the dust from his eyes.

"Sure did Dan – went like a dream."

"You got in alright then?"

"Yeah, no problem – the skylight was so rotten it came away in my hands – well, almost – plus I won a few quid up the Moon as well –"

"What's all that claret on ya shirt?"

"What? Oh – I had to smack some arsehole for takin' the piss out of Little Johnny," said Jo, unbuttoning his shirt.

"What did he end up like?"

"Er – I think I done a little bit of damage to 'im, Dan."

"Yeah?"

"Yeah – fuckin' mug."

"What happened then?"

"Well, he started callin' Little Johnny a midget –" Danny started laughing.

"Yeah, I know," said Jo, laughing himself. "But I didn't smack 'im 'cos of that – the cheeky bastard started askin' if I was his fuckin' mother!"

"Yeah?"

"Yeah – then he tried to stick one on me so I steamed into 'im. Billy came up and wrapped a bandage round 'im and sent 'im up the hospital for some stitches."

Danny took over making the tea while Jo soaked the shirt in the sink in case the blood stained it permanently.

"So," said Danny, "I take it you won't be goin' out earning today then?"

Jo smiled and dried his hands before taking the wad from his pocket. "You don't have to either old son – here, take this," he said, handing Danny three tenners.

"Hey, Jo – I can't –"

"Don't be daft – just stick it in ya bin. You do the same for me don't ya?"

"Well, yeah – cheers Jo. I didn't fancy goin' out – there's just nothing about anymore." He kissed the money and stuck in in his hip pocket. "Guess we'll be having a nice little drink later then," he said. Jo looked at his mate and smiled.

"Sure will Danny, sure will."

*

Jo woke up with a jump. Someone was hammering on the door and he knew it was the police. What to do, he thought, answer it or stay in bed? The pounding on the door wasn't about to go away but Jo decided he wasn't going to answer it either. Danny was out somewhere and Jo didn't fancy being taken to the nick without anyone knowing he was there. If he needed a brief, someone had to know that he'd been arrested.

Jo left his bed and dressed quickly and quietly. What was it they wanted him for, he wondered, the greaseball, or the break-in? Jo decided it had to be the former. He couldn't believe that anyone knew about the coup on the docks, it was impossible – wasn't it? Jo couldn't really make up his mind.

The pounding stopped.

Jo stood by the bedroom door, not moving, listening for any foot movement that might betray their presence. After a few minutes he moved quietly against the wall, listening intently for any sound. He heard nothing.

Five minutes went by.

Still nothing.

Jo went into the living room and rolled himself a cigarette, lit it, and inhaled deeply. Jesus, he thought, what the fuck do I do now? It **must** have been old bill – couldn't be anyone else, not pounding the door like that.

Jo decided to ring the Half Moon. He dialled the number. A moment later the connection was made. "Is that you Bill?"

"No, this is Mick – is that you Jo?"

"Yeah –"

"The pigs have been lookin' for you –"

"Fucksake! Was it about the row?"

"Yeah – they reckon you done him real bad, Jo."

"Jesus, it wasn't **that** bad – when did they come up?"

"About twenty minutes ago. They questioned Billy then had a good nose round."

"What did Billy say?"

"He said he didn't know anything about it – all he said was he wrapped some bandage round him."

"Yeah?"

"Yeah – they was only here a few minutes, then they fucked off."

"Were they uniformed plod or C.I.D.?"

"Uniformed plod – two of 'em."

"Yeah? Listen Mick, is Danny about?"

"Yeah, he's on the table – want me to give him a shout?"

"Yeah – cheers Mick.'

"Catch ya later – Danny!" A few moments later, Danny had hold of the phone. "Jo?"

"Danny listen, old bill's after me so I'm going to see Freddie and ask him if he can put me up for a few days – might give me a chance to sort things out. Does anyone know the geezer I smacked?"

"No, nobody knows 'im."

"Fuckit – listen, I'm gonna go and see Freddie then – if you hear anything let me know."

"Yeah right –"

"See you later then, Dan."

"Yeah right – see ya later."

Jo rolled himself another cigarette. He was trying to cut it down, but for now all he wanted was some smoke in his lungs and the hit of the nicotine.

He packed a few essentials into a holdall and placed it by the front door. He would go and see his long-time friend, Freddie, and lie low for a few days. With some luck, he might be able to find Greaseball and smooth things out.

First though, he had to phone his girlfriend, Christine. They had been seeing each other for nearly five years, since they were kids at school, and soon he was going to ask for her hand. He wasn't looking forward to telling her that he was going on the missing list for a few days. He dialled the number of the shop where she worked, and waited.

"Oh, hello – can I speak to Christine please?"

"Christine? I'm sorry but she isn't here at the moment. Can I ask who's calling?"

"Er, yes – can you tell her Jo called, and can you tell her I'll give her a ring later this evening –"

"She should be back in a little while."

"Er – I'll try and ring later then if I can – if not can you tell her I'll call her later."

"Yes okay – I'll see that she gets the message."

"Thanks a lot – bye." Jo cradled the phone.

Because his car was in the garage having a new clutch fitted, Jo would have to catch a taxi to Freddie's house. He grabbed the holdall and tentatively opened the front door. He peered up and down the road, and, when he didn't see any strange bodies sitting in any strange cars, he took the chance and headed for the rank. Once or twice his heart skipped a beat when he saw old bill look-a-likes, but he soon made it to the queue of taxis and was safely on his way to Freddie's.

Freddie lived in Portchester, a small town just outside of Portsmouth, and Jo felt a little easier as the cab went over Ports Bridge. As they rounded the harbour road, Jo looked out of the window and saw that the tide was out, and the boats, left high and dry on the mud, looked odd leaning at all different angles. An old World War II submarine was also stuck fast in the mud and as Jo gazed at the rotting hulk, he wondered about the men who had once manned it. Lost in a haze of thought, he closed his eyes and imagined life aboard a wartime sub….

"Hey buddy – where abouts do you want?" Jo came too with a start. "What? Oh – drop me at the roundabout – just here on the left will do." Jo paid off the cabbie and walked the last hundred yards to Freddie's house. He rang the bell and waited. After an eternity, a voice shouted out.

"Who is it?"

"It's me – Jo."

"Hang on –" After three or four bolts and chains were slipped, Freddie opened the door.

"Jo! How are ya? Come in, come in –" Jo stepped into the hall. "– what brings you up here then? I haven't seen you for a while."

"I'm in a spot of trouble, Fred – plod's after me and I need to get out of the way for a couple of days."

'Yeah sure, Jo, no problem – come in here, take a pew." Freddie led Jo into a tastefully furnished sitting room.

"Want a cuppa or something?"

"Yeah – I'll have a coffee if you've got it."

"Yeah, got tins of the stuff. I think we've had the same one for about five years." Jo laughed at Freddie's exaggeration. "So, what's happened then, Jo?" asked Freddie.

Jo gave Freddie a detailed account of the night before and when he'd finished, Freddie was quick to assure Jo that he could stay for as long as he liked. As old friends they could talk to each other easily and Jo felt at home straightaway.

A little later, Freddie asked Jo if he wanted a joint.

"A joint?"

"Yeah – you know what a joint is don't ya?"

"Yeah, I think so – it's that funny stuff the hippies all smoke ain't it?"

"Yeah," said Freddie, "it'll take ya mind off things, make ya relax."

"Well, I don't know –"

"It won't hurt you, Jo – it's not an opiate or anything."

"It won't turn me into a junkie will it?"

"No, of course it won't – I smoke it all the time."

"Well, I might try a little bit –"

"Yeah that's more like it, Jo – be a little adventurous."

Jo watched Freddie as he made the joint. First of all he split a cigarette and emptied the tobacco onto the table. He then took three rizla papers and joined them together. After sprinkling the tobacco along the length of them, he took a small polythene bag from the his pocket and removed the contents. He then took a flame to the black substance, and sprinkled it on top of the tobacco.

"What is that stuff, Fred?"

"Cannabis resin."

Jo nodded to himself as he watched Freddie continue rolling the joint. After inserting a rolled-up piece of rizla packet in one end, Freddie lit it and inhaled deeply. A moment later he handed the joint to Jo.

"Take a long draw on it and keep it down," he said, smiling to himself. Jo sucked hard on the joint, then blew out the smoke.

"No – keep it down 'till you can't hold it anymore." Jo took another long draw and held it for as long as he could before exhaling. "What's it supposed to do then, Fred?"

"You'll find out don't worry," said Freddie, smiling.

Jo took another pull on the joint.

A couple of minutes went by.

"My head feels a bit light."

"Yeah that's alright – that's what it's supposed to do."

"But it ain't doin' anything."

"I know, they all say that – you'll be alright in a minute."

Jo sat on the settee, staring at the television that was showing an old black and white comedy starring Alistair Sim. Jo started laughing.

"What ya laughing at, Jo?"

"Nothing – I'm just looking at Alistair Sim," said Jo, more seriously. Freddie looked at the T.V. then looked at Jo out of the corner of his eye, catching him as he burst out laughing again.

"What ya laughin' at now?" he said, laughing himself.

"Alistair Sim – look at his face, them eyes – he could put you in a trance with them couldn't he, like giant gobstoppers – d'you remember that geezer in The Apple Tree who had a face like a rubber mask –" Jo was in fits of laughter "– and those slits at the side of his mouth like he was permanently smiling –" Jo was laughing so much he could hardly talk and Freddie was laughing too, remembering the strange looking feller Jo was talking about. "– and what about Workman who tried to stop brain – I mean –" Jo was out of control and talking at a hundred miles an hour, reliving some of the laughs he and Freddie had shared in the past. After a few minutes, he finally came down.

"Blimey, Fred – this is good stuff innit, how come we've never had it before?"

"I've only had it myself since Trina moved in. She brought it back from Spain with her."

"Who's Trina?"

"She's the bird I'm livin' with – she's a coach driver."

"A coach driver! Fuckin' hell, Fred – I bet she got some muscle ain't she – Mick McManus ain't she –" Jo collapsed on the settee, laughing, holding his belly as the strain made it ache. The backache he often suffered from was brought on too, and he pushed his hand into the top of his buttock muscle to ease it.

Freddie and Jo continued smoking well into late afternoon. Jo felt good. He couldn't remember feeling better. As they reminisced, the nagging thoughts Jo held a few hours ago had dissipated, and instead of worrying about Greaseball and the possible consequences, he was enjoying the moment.

"You want a drink, Jo – I got some cans in the fridge?"

"Yeah, could do, Fred – my mouth's so dry I can hardly talk. You ain't got any biscuits or Kit-Kats have you? I suddenly feel like something sweet."

"You've probably got the munchies."

"The munchies?" said Jo, slightly perplexed.

"Yeah, a cravin' for chocolate or sweets – you sometimes get it on this gear. I eat everything if I get 'em," he laughed, rubbing his rotund belly.

"Looks like you're having a baby, Fred."

"It ain't this stuff," he said, holding a joint, "it's Carlsberg Special Brews that's given me this. I get five or six down my neck every day –"

"Fucksake Fred – no wonder you've a gut on ya."

"I know, but, well – fuck it, I need a drink, stuck up here every day on my own."

"Yeah, I don't blame ya – where's this can then?"

Freddie nipped to the kitchen and returned with two Special

Brews and a plate of assorted biscuits. In between sips, Jo munched his way through a dozen ginger-nuts and four or five custard creams. "Jesus! I've never eaten so many biscuits in all my life! You don't eat like that all the time on that stuff do ya?"

"No," said Freddie, "it's only cos you've been smokin'. After you get used to it the cravin' goes off."

"Thank fuck for that – if I ate like that every time I had a joint I'd end up like one of those little Michelin men."

"I already look like one," said Freddie, laughing.

"You need exercise – what d'you do all day stuck up here?"

"Nothin' – just get up, get stoned, and get pissed!"

"What d'you do for dosh then?"

"Trina looks after me. She goes out drivin' the coach an' I take care of the gaff."

"What time will she be home?"

"Not 'till tomorrow. She's in Spain again."

"Ain't raining in Spain Fred, is it?"

"Only on the plain I expect," he said, laughing.

Jo was bushed and stretched out on the settee, resting his head on the soft arm. Freddie knew how Jo would be feeling and left him to his own thoughts. Soon, Jo began to go into a mind-drift – a sensation of perpetual thought that seared into his brain like a graphic motion picture. *Old bill came creeping into his head...they were after him...Greaseball had died from his injuries and they were seeking him out...hunting him for murder...The Old Bailey...guilty as charged...you will be taken from here to a lawful place of execution...the gallows...death by hanging...they will come for you at seven minutes before eight...two warders will come to bind the hands...and the Governor will be there and the priest will be hovering in the doorway with his bible open...gone is the traditional walk because the deathcell is just through the door that has now been opened and an eight step walk is a date with the hangman...the noose around the neck that says you have four seconds left to live before the jerk comes that takes off your head...*

Jo came too with a fright. "Jesus! I've just had a fuckin' nightmare."

"I know, I was watchin' ya face," said Freddie, "I knew you was going into one."

"What d'you mean, 'into one'?"

"When you smoke you sometimes go into a sort of trance – was it a violent one?"

"They were going to hang me!"

Freddie laughed. "Don't worry, Jo – it's only 'cos plod's after you and you've got problems. It's like an emotional get-out for ya cannister. I get 'em all the time – good ain't they!"

"Well, it was different that's for sure! But I don't want another one, I prefer my head exactly where it is – right on these shoulders!"

The two of them began to wind down. They both stretched out on the settee and put their feet on the coffee table.

'What ya gonna do about this slag that's nicked ya then?"

"I dunno, Fred – I was gonna try and sort it out but nobody knows 'im. If I knew who he was I might have got 'im to drop the charge. He might take a bribe or something – that's assuming he **has** made a charge –"

"If old bill's after ya he's definitely made a charge, you know what they're like."

"Yeah." He knew what they were like alright. He remembered the last time he was in trouble. He'd been in the Rose of England public house with a few of the boys, having a quiet drink, enjoying the odd dance with the local girls. A more than usual number of sailors were in, and one of them, a Petty-Officer, was taking exception to Jo for dancing with a particular girl. He began to taunt Jo, and because the sailor was with half the ships crew, he felt confident enough to shout across the bar that he wanted Jo out in the street – 'to teach him some correctional naval discipline' – to which all the sailors laughed and whistled. Although Jo was game and had plenty of heart, this man looked as though he would tear Jo apart, but, more to save face than bravado, Jo obliged the sailor and went out into the street with him. After a few minutes Jo returned to the bar with blood on his fists. The big sailor was laying flat-out in the gutter, a mass of cuts and bruises covered his face. Jo had really pasted the mother-fucker. At 2:00am the police came to his flat and arrested him for causing grievous bodily harm. While they were there, one of the detectives investigating picked up Jo's shoes and noticed the congealed blood, thick up under the arch. Jo remembered his words. "Look, I know what happened tonight, but if you make it easy for us we can forget about the shoes. If the court sees these you'll be in big trouble." Jo reluctantly agreed to the deal but was still convicted and now carried on his sheet a section 20 G.B.H. – Yeah, he thought, I know what they're like alright.

"Do you –" Jo looked across to Freddie but his eyes were closed.

It was getting on for 6 o'clock and Jo decided to ring Christine. Although they hadn't planned on seeing each other this evening, he wanted to let her know where he was in case she phoned the flat. There again, he thought, he might leave it 'till tomorrow and pop into the shop where she worked. Or should he phone her now...? Jo seemed to be having trouble making up his mind but didn't think for a minute that the cannabis resin he'd been smoking had anything to do with his indecision. Finally, he decided to leave the phone call and meet her, as arranged, the following day.

Christine worked in the record department of an electrical retail store. She was the manageress now, but when they first met she was a part-timer working Saturdays only. Jo had often seen her in the shop and, after one or two encouraging smiles, he asked her if she fancied going out on a date with him. She enjoyed the date and they had been together ever since. Marriage was never mentioned during the first few years of courtship, but the chemistry between them always told Jo that one day she would be his bride.

A little later, an unexpected knock on the door brought the two of them up with a start. Jo was the first to react.

"Who the fuck's that?"

"Dunno –"

"You expectin' anyone – could be old bill."

"Nah – they wouldn't know I'm livin' 'ere."

The door was knocked again. Freddie and Jo looked at each other. "Persistant ain't they – you gonna answer it?"

"Let's see who it is first." Freddie nipped up the stairs and peered out through the bathroom window. He saw a man, wearing a hat and carrying a briefcase, waiting patiently for the door to open. Freddie returned to the living room.

"Relax, Jo – looks like some sort of salesman."

'Thank fuck for that," he said, breathing easier.

The door was knocked a third time.

"Fucksake – is he gonna take a nobody's in or what!" said Freddie. Jo started laughing, relieved of the momentary tension. "Anyway, now that I ain't about to be nicked, are you comin' out for a drink?"

"Well, I was stayin' in. I'm a bit short –"

"Don't worry abut dough. I've got a few quid if you fancy goin' out. Danny and Blondie'll be out I expect."

"Well, you'll have to lend me a couple –"

Jo took some cash from his pocket. "Here, take this – call it a bit of rent if ya like," he said, handing Freddie £20.

"Cheers Jo. I'll give it back to ya later."

"I don't want it back, Fred. Call it a bit of grub money or something, okay. Now, have you got a bathroom I can use?"

"Yeah – up on the right. I'll skin up a couple of joints while you're gettin' ready."

"Yeah, good thinkin' Fred," said Jo, wondering to himself whether he should have anymore. "What's it like with a drink then?"

"Nice – makes ya laugh even more!"

"Oh, good – I just hope they don't try an' take my head off again,' he said, closing the bathroom door.

At 7:45 Freddie and Jo were suited and booted and on their way to Pompey. As they sat in the back of the taxi Jo's nagging worries began to creep back into his head. If he were charged with assault, and it looked likely that he would be, the charge would almost certainly be one of grievous bodily harm. With two convictions already, Jo gave a custodial sentence a passing thought, and shuddered.

"Where we goin' then?" said Freddie.

"We'll meet Danny an' Blondie in the Kingstone first then do a crawl down to the Albany I expect. I just hope old bill aren't looking for me."

"Don't go worryin' about plod, Jo. The day shift that's been looking for you will be all tucked up in doors by now. Here, take a couple of pulls on this and forget 'em." Jo took the joint and pulled hard on it, taking the acrid smoke deep into his lungs. After smoking for most of the afternoon, the effect was immediate. By the time they arrived at the Kingstone Tavern, the both of them were well and truly stoned.

Jo paid the driver and marched into the pub.

"Hey Danny! Blondie! How are ya boys – what ya drinking? Gov'nor, when you've got a minute, a couple of pints here. Freddie what's yours, a Carlsberg?" Jo spotted one of the pensioners who did a few odd jobs down on the wharf. "Hey Wally – you want a drink? Gov'nor, get old Wally a drink right away will ya – make it lively though – old Wally don't look like he's got long left – no only jokin' Wal – another twenty years left in you yet!" Jo was talking fast and nonstop as the cannabis seared through him, and he was flying high. Blondie looked at Jo in amazement. "You're buzzin' a bit aren't ya – you been on the piss all day or something?"

"Or something's about right, Blond – Freddie gave me some of that funny stuff the hippies smoke – it's magic, makes ya feel real good – I reckon I could take on the whole fleet. Gov'nor, when you're ready –"

Jo was really high now and Danny and Blondie were bemused by his erratic behaviour. Freddie was just looking on, laughing, enjoying Jo's relatively new experience.

"What is that stuff he's had, Fred?" whispered Danny.

"Cannabis – Trina brought it back from Spain with her. You fancy a few pulls later?"

"Yeah, why not – I've never seen anything like it!" he laughed.

"I know, good innit – look at 'im now!"

Jo was racing now; he'd already supped his first pint and he was now playing the pin-ball machine. The large, shiny, ball-bearing was being flipped around at a great pace as Jo's reflexes kept him one step ahead. The replays began to click up like the sound of a short crack from a gun and the noise of it excited him, and he played the machine until his fingers ached.

After two or three pints, the boys left the Tavern and headed for the city-centre. "Shall we nip in Snowy's first?"

"Yeah, could do – Gloria might be showin' all her tits."

"How many tits she got then?" asked Jo.

"Fourteen," laughed Freddie, "fourteen tits and three arrises." All the boys started laughing.

"If she had fourteen tits she'd have to have some on her back wouldn't she –"

"Yeah, and an arris under each armpit –"

"Cor, talk about smelly armpits –" The boys were in high spirits as they headed for The White Swan, and Freddie lit the joint he had rolled earlier. They all had a few tokes on it before they entered the pub.

"He's ex-plod in here isn't he?" said Danny.

"Yeah, I think he is," said Freddie, "Don't say anything about the gear."

Blondie, Danny, and Jo all said 'no' at the same time then burst out laughing.

Exactly fifteen minutes after Danny ordered the first four pints, three uniformed old bill entered the pub.

Jo was in the toilet when he heard Freddie's warning shout but was too late to escape through the side door. As he was escorted from the pub he felt calm, almost sad, as if betrayed. He looked across to the landlord. "You will pay dearly for that phone call, mister."

*

The police van pulled into the courtyard of the Central Police station and Jo was taken in through the back door to the cells. "Step in there. Someone will come and deal with you in a few minutes," said one of the police officers.

Jo walked into the cell and the door was pulled shut. He had been in a police cell before and he knew that soon they would be back to take him to the charge-room and process him before returning him to the cells. He quickly counted out his money then shoved £400 into his underpants, some at the front, some at the back. If they found he had more than £500 in his possession, they would question him relentlessly. A moment after he'd zipped his fly, the door was opened. "Come with me, Sullivan." Jo followed the uniformed plod to the charge-room. A sergeant was standing at his desk and he cast Jo a furtive glance.

"Is your full name Joseph Sullivan?" he asked, sourly.

"No it isn't – it's Jo Sullivan with just a J and an O. Am I being charged with anything?"

"Yes –"

"Will I get bail?"

"No –"

"Oh, why's that then?"

"Because I said so that's why. Now, any middle name?"

Jo remained silent.

The sergeant, a burly six-footer, asked the question again. "I said, have you got a middle name?"

"I've already answered that question once – or can't you remember that far back, sergeant?" said Jo, evenly.

"Don't you be bloody flippant with me sonny! When I ask a question you will answer it, got it! Now, have you got a middle name?"

Jo remained silent.

The sergeant was becoming visibly annoyed and looked across to the constable standing next to Jo. "I think we have a smart-alec on our hands, wouldn't you say officer Penge?"

"I would say so, sarge," he agreed.

The sergeant began tapping his pen on the desk, and glared at Jo. "Now you listen to me, Jo Sullivan – with a J and an O – I'm going to ask you one more time – have you got a middle name?"

"I've already answered that question mister and I don't repeat myself more than twice to any fucker, let alone uniformed plod –" The blow that struck Jo was quick and unexpected. The sergeant had hit Jo full in the face and blood began to trickle from his nose. Jo didn't retaliate. He was still riding high on the mixture of cannabis and alcohol and he seemed to be enjoying the confrontation with the sergeant. But Jo had unwittingly embarked on a game he couldn't possibly win. In the mood he was in though, the final outcome was unimportant, it was now that was important, it was now that Jo was going to stand his ground and not be intimidated by the authority standing in front of him. As far as Jo was concerned the sergeant had relinquished any respect his uniform might have earned when he struck out in a moment of lost control.

"I didn't make you lose your temper did I? You didn't lose control there for a minute did you, sarge? –" The sergeant interrupted Jo's rhetoric by slamming his fist down on the desk. "Listen, Sullivan – we can either do this the hard way or the easy way, and it seems to me you want it the hard way. I'm going to try just once more to get this paperwork completed."

"All you will get out of me is my name, my age, and my address – anything else is none of your business."

'We'll see about that – age?"

"Nineteen."

"Date of birth?"

"18:10:44."

"Address?"

"21 Rudmore Wharf Road, Stamshaw."

"Place-of-employment?"

"I told you – it's none of your business."

"Place of employment!?"

"I'm not tellin' ya."

The sergeant slammed down his pen and came round the desk, standing close-up to Jo. "I'm warning you, Sullivan – I haven't got all night to fuck about with you – if we don't get this paperwork done I'll have you in the cells and give you a bloody good hiding – do I make myself clear!?" Jo suddenly realised he was on a hiding to nothing. He half-laughed. "Why didn't you say it was that important?" Jo consoled himself with the thought that if he had a row with the mother, he might find the money.

The sergeant returned to his desk. "Now – place of employment?" he said, smugly.

"Un-em-ploy-ed," replied Jo, stretched the word out as long as he could. The sergeant looked up at Jo and shook his head muttering to himself.

"Right – empty your pockets."

Jo started emptying his pockets while the sergeant listed them on the property sheet, calling out the items as he went. "One bunch of keys on ring. One comb. One nail file – what's this for?"

"It's a nail file ain't it – what d'you think it's for?"

Jesus, thought Jo, the man's not only an arsehole but a complete idiot as well. He smiled to himself.

"Something funny, Sullivan?"

"No – just thinking."

The sergeant curled his lip then carried on with the list.

"Matches. Cigarette papers. Tobacco. One handkerchief."

Jo took the money from his pocket and placed it on the desk. The sergeant looked at it, then looked at Jo. "Well what have we got here – rather a lot of money for someone who is un-em-ploy-ed isn't it?" he allowed himself a wry smile. "Where did you get it?" He counted it out. "One hundred and twelve pounds seven shillings and fourpence – a tidy sum. Where did you get it?"

"I won it."

"Oh, you won it – you're sure you didn't steal it?"

"I told you I won it – an' you ain't got no reason to think otherwise. Check with Greaseball if ya like – I done him with a fullhouse just before the row."

"Who's Greaseball?"

"He's the toe-rag that's laid charges against me." The sergeant didn't pursue it further and Jo breathed a silent relief.

"Anything else in your pockets?"

"No," said Jo. The sergeant gave officer Penge a nod and he searched Jo with a brief rub-down. "He's clear, sarge."

"Right, get his finger-prints done while I finish this paperwork."

"Is it okay if I have a fag?" asked Jo. The sergeant looked up from his desk and stared at Jo. "Yes, you can have a cigarette, Sullivan. I think you're going to need one after I've read you the charge."

"What is the charge?"

"Grievous bodily harm."

"Oh, Jesus – why G.B.H.?" said Jo, anxiously realising the gravity of the situation.

"Because the man you attacked was severely beaten, Sullivan. He needed five stitches to an eye wound, and two on the inside of his mouth, not to mention a cracked rib."

"But why G.B.H.?" pleaded Jo. "I was attacked first."

"I know what happened, Sullivan, that's why the charge is a section 20 and not a section 18."

"What's a section 18?"

"A section 18 is grievous bodily harm with **intent** to cause grievous bodily harm. Section 20 is just grievous bodily harm."

"Oh, **just** grievous bodily harm…" The words seemed to act on Jo like an antedote to the high he was on, pulling him down into a mood of despair. Prison cells began to dance about in his head…

Jo sat on the edge of the bed and rolled himself a cigarette, feeling slightly pleased that he'd managed to keep his smoking requisites, when ordinarily they would be kept outside of the cell and he would have to ask for one each time he had the urge. The bed he was sitting on was a solid concrete box, covered by a thin plastic mattress. The only moveable objects in the cell were three dirty blankets and a flimsy pillow. An open toilet bowl, stained and unclean, was fixed at the far end of the cell, and Jo made a mental note that if the need arose, he would shit in the corner rather than sit on the filthy pan.

Jo heard himself saying grievous bodily harm and began to think about the inevitable court appearance. With two convictions already, he wondered briefly if he would end up in prison, or worse still, borstal training. No, they wouldn't send him to jail, not for a fist-fight, not for defending himself – would they? Jo began to think that they **might** send him down, and he cursed himself for punching the greaseball so hard and savagely.

After a while, Jo took the blankets and made up the bed. The paper-thin pillow was stained with the grease and sweat of countless heads so he pulled the bottom blanket up over it, then layed down and stretched out. He thought of Christine. She hated him getting into trouble. The last time he was hauled before the magistrates made her sick with worry and he dreaded her finding out about this latest episode. If possible, he would avoid telling her.

Soon, Jo was taken back to the charge-room and formally charged with causing one Robert Miles Jacobs grievous bodily harm and would be appearing in front of the magistrates at 10:00am the following morning.

After being charged Jo was led back to the cells. He rolled a cigarette and stretched out on the hard bed, and closed his eyes. Thoughts of impending doom began swirling round in his mind as he thought of prison, and Christine. He tried shaking the thoughts away so that he could sleep but when an hour of tossing and turning stretched to three, he knew sleep was going to elude him.

Jo rose from the bed. He rolled another cigarette then pressed the bell that would bring someone to his cell. A few minutes later, the duty-officer opened the small flap in the door. "Yes, Sullivan?"

"I'm thirsty – can you get me some water?"

"You'll have to wait," he said curtly. He slammed the flap and walked away.

Jo waited a few minutes, then pressed the bell again.

He laid his ear against the door, waiting for footsteps.

He heard nothing.

He waited another minute then pressed the bell again, keeping his finger hard on the button. The ringing echoed deafeningly throughout the cell block. Jo suddenly heard footsteps hastening towards his cell but kept his finger hard on the bell-button until the flap was opened. The duty-officer peered into the cell. "What the hell you playing at, Sullivan!?" he shouted.

"I told you I want some water –"

"And I told you to wait – if you carry on like this you'll be in trouble. Sergeant Rolf won't stand any messin' about from youngsters –"

"I ain't a fuckin' youngster – and if I don't get any water I'll ring this bell all fuckin' night!"

Jo heard a pair of footsteps coming down the corridor. It was the sergeant.

"Open this door," he said to the duty-officer. The door was opened and Rolf burst into the cell. He grabbed Jo by the shirt. "Listen to me you little bastard – if you press that bell again without good cause, I'll give you a bloody good hiding –"

"Let go of me will ya – you got no right t' manhandle me –"

"I'm warning you Sullivan – I've dealt with smart arses like you before and I'm telling you –"

"And I'm telling you t'let go of me will ya –"

Rolf brought his hand up and slapped Jo hard on the side of the head, and shook him violently.

Jo retaliated.

He spat in the sergeant's face then brought his fist up and punched him as hard as he could on the jaw. He used his other hand to push up under the sergeant's chin to free himself, then hit him again – hard. Rolf was taken totally by surprise and reeled back against the cell wall. The duty-officer came quickly to the sergeant's assistance and, between them, they went for Jo. Rolf tried to grab Jo but Jo was too quick for him, and he side-stepped as Rolf came forward. The duty officer dived for Jo's legs, catching him just below the knees, bringing him down. Once on the floor Jo was in trouble. He tried in vain to strike out but the sergeant was too powerful, reigning blows down on Jo until his face was running with blood. Officer Penge urged the sergeant to stop the assault. "Sarge! That's enough!" he shouted, grabbing his arm. Rolf stood up and cast an eye over Jo. "That's what happens to smart arses in this station, Sullivan. Anymore from you and I'll be back."

The two officers left the cell, slamming the door behind them.

Jo got to his knees and felt with his hand the blood that was coming from his nose and mouth. He lifted his shirt to soothe his wounds as he made his way to the door where the bell was, and in an act of anger and defiance, pressed the button hard.

A solitary pair of footsteps came down the corridor and Jo stepped away from the door. The flap opened. It was Penge.

"You don't give up do you, Sullivan?"

"No I fuckin' don't – I'm still thirsty and I still want some water!"

"I'll get you your drink, Sullivan, if only to save you from Sergeant Rolf."

Two minutes later, Jo was holding a pint of cool, clear, water.

An hour after Jo's beating, Sergeant Rolf came to the cell and opened the door. "Come with me, Sullivan," he ordered. Jo followed him along the corridor and into the charge-room. "Stand there in front of the desk," said Rolf. Jo looked at him with fresh contempt as he rolled himself a cigarette.

"Who said you could smoke? You ask me if you want to smoke in this house, sonny."

"Why do I have to ask you – you God or something?"

"In here, yes, and in here you ask!" Jo went to put the tobacco back in his pocket rather than seek Rolf's permission to smoke, but it was snatched from his hand by the sergeant.

"Who said you could have it in your possession anyway?"

"Nobody – I just took it. You gonna slap me about for that are ya – you pig!" said Jo with renewed anger.

"You're asking for it, Sullivan, believe me you're asking for it." The sergeant continued sorking on some paperwork for a few minutes, then began reading out a fresh charge. The words seemed to drift over Jo's head for a moment, until he heard "– that you, Jo Sullivan, did assault a police officer in the execution of his duty –"

"You bastard –"

"– and that you did cause the said police officer actual bodily harm."

"What about me – what about you assaulting me!?" shouted Jo, touching his face. "I'm the injured party not you!" Jo couldn't believe that he was facing an additional charge of assault, until he realised why – Sergeant Rolf was covering his arse in case Jo brought charges against him. Jo tried protesting. "Listen, I'm not charging you, so why are you charging me? And you started it didn't ya – and why the fuck is the charge actual bodily harm – you ain't cut?"

"Watch your mouth, Sullivan." Rolf leaned forward, pointing to a small nick in the side of his face. "This is what makes the charge actual bodily harm, Sullivan."

"Oh, does it – so this lot you gave me is G.B.H. then," said Jo, forming his fists into tight balls.

"Don't even think about it, Sullivan," said Penge.

"Think about what?"

"You know what I'm on about. You're in enough trouble as it is without adding to it."

Sergeant Rolf looked at Jo, then the duty-officer, puzzled, waiting for an explanation for the last remarks. When none was offered he let it pass.

"Take him back to the cells."

"Can I have a cigarette now or what?" asked Jo. The sergeant retrieved the tobacco from the drawer and handed it to Jo. "Make it a good one, Sullivan. We don't want to be running after you all night."

Jo took his smoking requisites and started to walk away. "Come back here, Sullivan," said Rolf.

"Oh, come on – at least let me keep my tobacco. I'm allowed to at your discretion, ain't I?"

Rolf stared at Jo for a moment. "Alright, Sullivan, you can keep your smokes, but if you give us any more problems, just one, and you won't get another smoke all night. And don't go setting the cell on fire will you? We don't want to add an arson charge to the sheet do we?" The sergeant showed out a hint of humour and, unwittingly, Jo gave him a half-smile as he was led back to the cells.

Alone in the cell, Jo tossed and turned for most of the night and it was late into the early hours of the morning before he finally succumbed to sleep. He was still asleep when the door was opened at 8:00 for breakfast.

"Wake up, Sullivan – oh dear, what happened to you then? You look as if you've been hit by a train.'

"Ask that pig of a sergeant of yours – Rolf," said Jo, putting his feet to the floor.

"Here, take this –" said the duty-officer, handing Jo a tray of food, "– then we'll see about getting you cleaned up. What happened anyway?"

The current duty-officer was a lot friendlier than the night-shift officer and Jo didn't mind giving him a brief account.

"Well, I don't think you're too bad. It's mainly dried blood by the look of it – anyway, you have your breakfast now, then we'll sort you out with a wash n' brush-up before going upstairs, okay?"

"Yeah, thanks," said Jo.

The duty-officer left Jo to eat his breakfast, pulling the door too, leaving it slightly ajar. Jo balanced the tray on his lap and tucked into the food with ravenous appetite.

After the meal, he rolled himself a smoke and took sips from the steaming pint of tea as he contemplated the walk upstairs to the magistrates. He knew the case, or cases he thought now, would not be dealt with there and then, but he wondered whether or not he would be granted bail. Considering he was now facing two assault charges, they might hold him in custody until a date was set, and he shuddered at the thought.

Jo finished his tea and cigarette then moved to the door and peered out, looking up and down the corridor. He noticed a card pinned to a board and read to himself – Sullivan, M.C.10:100am. He took a step further into the corridor and saw two other cards pinned to boards. Only three of us going up, he thought, might put them in a good mood.

The duty-officer unlocked the top door and came into the cell-block.

"Alright, Sullivan – breakfast okay?"

"Yeah, wasn't too bad – what there was of it."

"I know, they don't give much away do they? Anyway, if you'd like to come in here you can clean yourself up a bit. There's soap and towels there, and some toothpowder in the box – I'll get you a toothbrush – and there's a comb on the top there," he said, pointing to a cabinet. "Try and be as quick as you can because I've got others to sort out as well."

"Yeah, thanks – how many of us going up then?"

"Four altogether – three of you here and an old woman. Shouldn't take too long once you're upstairs – I'll get that toothbrush for you."

"Yeah, thanks again," said Jo, appreciating his congenial attitude.

Jo stepped into the small washroom and began to clean himself up. There was dried blood over most of his face but when he washed it off he didn't look too bad. He was hoping to look battered and bruised so that the magistrates might feel more sympathetic towards him, but when he studied his face in the mirror, all he had in the way of injuries was a small cut under his eye and some minor bruising. He guessed most of the blood must have come from his nose.

At 9:45 Jo and two other men were taken along a twisting corridor to a holding cell beneath the court-house. An old woman was already there sitting on a wooden bench and Jo guessed her age was about ninety-plus. She was toothless and her appearance gave the impression that she was the co-star of a Punch'n'Judy show. Jo smiled to himself as he thought of it. With her looks and her long grey hair she was the oldest, meanest looking woman Jo had ever seen.

As the minutes ticked by Jo began to feel nervous. He took out his tobacco and quickly rolled a cigarette, lit it, and sucked the smoke deep down. Almost immediately, the butterflies settled. He took another pull – suddenly a voice screeched out, "Put that bloody cigarette out!"

"Who the fuck are you talkin' to?" said Jo.

"You laddie, put –"

"Well don't – you gross, overweight piece of shit! I need a fag, alright – if you don't like it charge me with something if you can but in the meantime – piss off and leave me alone!" Jo carried on smoking. The fat police officer muttered and mumbled but left Jo to finish his cigarette. After suffering defeat at the hands of Rolf, Jo felt good for the minor victory. From now on, he thought, if they talk to me like shit, they will get the same treatment back.

Whether it was to ease the tension, or plain curiosity, one of the men spoke to the old woman. "What you up for then, luv?"

"Mind your own fuckin' business!" she shrieked out. She scowled at him, then spat on the floor. The man looked at Jo. "Good job I didn't ask her for a ride." Jo smiled and shook his head in disbelief at the old woman. He too, wondered why a frail old lady was appearing in court after spending the night in police custody. He was to find out later that she'd cut a sailor with a Stanley knife so badly, he needed more than thirty stitches to his arms and face.

Suddenly, Jo heard his name called. As he was beckoned up the stairs, those butterflies took flight again. By the time he stood in the dock his heart was racing. He faced the magistrates and waited for the clerk to question him.

"Is your full name Jo Sullivan?"

"Yes."

"And is your date of birth 18:10:44?"

"Yes."

"And do you live at 21 Rudmore Wharf Road, Portsmouth?"

"Yes."

The clerk turned to the bench and spoke to the magistrates for a few moments, then turned back to Jo and read out the charges; he then said, "Mr. Sullivan, you may, if you wish, have these charges dealt with here, summarily, by the justices, or you may elect to go for trial by jury at the Quarter Sessions. If you decide to go for trial, a date will be set and you will be told to attend that court. However, if you decide to have the charges heard here, summarily, by the justices, the justices may, if the charges are proved, decide, if they think it appropriate, to send you to the Quarter Sessions for sentence. Do you understand?" Jo felt the urge to say no so the clerk would have to recite his oratory all over again, but he resisted the temptation.

"Yes, I understand."

"Do you wish the charges to be heard summarily, or do you elect to go for trial by jury?"

"Here, er, summarily – but I want the case adjourned so I can get a solicitor to represent me."

The clerk turned to the bench and whispered a few words, then turned back to face Jo. "Listen to the chairman of the justices."

The chairman, an ageing man with pure white hair, had a long handlebar moustache and Jo noticed the habit he had of wiping his finger along the length of it. Jo didn't like the look of him. He began to speak.

"Sullivan, we have decided to adjourn this hearing to enable you to consult with a solicitor, and you will be well advised to do so owing to the severity of the charges. In the meantime you will be remanded to re-appear in this court in six days time, that is, Friday the 11th of November. Are there any objections for bail?"

"No sir, no objections," said the clerk. Jo breathed a heavy sigh of relief. After hearing the chairman say that he would be remanded, Jo visualised himself incarcerated in the remand wing of the local prison, Winchester.

The chairman continued. "You will be remanded in your own recognisance in the sum of £25 to appear in this court on the 11th of November."

Jo had to wait for the paperwork to be completed for his bail, but was released within the hour.

*

It was a little after 11:45 when Jo walked briskly from the Central Police Station and headed for the city centre. The sun was trying to break through the scattered clouds, and the cool, fresh air gave Jo a lift after the stale atmosphere of the holding cells.

As he passed the Guildhall Square, he looked up at the two hand-carved stone soldiers that always seemed to Jo like they were guarding the war memorial behind them. They were in the battle position, fully equipped and crouched low, as if waiting for imagined marauders. They looked good and the sight of them always made Jo think of the men who fought at the front line in the two Great Wars.

Just past the railway station was The Albany, the public house that he and the boys were heading for before Jo's arrest. He poked his head round the door to see if anyone was about this early in the day. Apart from a few sailors and a couple of street girls, the place was deserted.

Jo carried on towards the main shopping precinct. He intended to get himself a decent meal in the cafe at the back of the market square, but on arrival, he found the place was jam-packed and decided to head for home.

From the town centre to where Jo lived in Rudmore was a twenty minute walk and he arrived just after twelve. Danny was still in bed. "Danny! Get up you lazy toe-rag." Jo went to the kitchen and put the kettle on and Danny soon joined him waiting for his first cup of tea of the day. He looked at Jo. "What happened to you then?" Jo told Danny in detail everything that had happened at the Central, cursing sergeant Rolf as he went.

"If I ever get the chance to do that mother – God help him. He took a right liberty – just 'cos I was takin' the piss out of 'im," said Jo, suddenly laughing.

"So you got two assaults to go up on then? I think you might be gettin' some Jo."

"You think so? I was attacked first don't forget."

"Yeah, I know – but they ain't gonna believe you are they? I think you're bang in trouble, mate."

"Um, you could be right – maybe I ought to fuck off for a while. Or what if I try an' see this Jacobs geezer, see if he'll take a few quid to drop the charge."

"Worth a try I s'pose – but it ain't him you gotta worry about, it's plod."

"Yeah, you're probably right but one charge is better than two. Maybe we should get the boys and find out where he hangs out."

"Yeah, why not – and if we don't get any joy out of 'im we'll crack a few heads for our trouble," laughed Danny. Jo looked at his mate and nodded. "Now you're talkin', Dan."

Danny was an inch or so taller than Jo's five eight, broad in the shoulder, he could take 'em out almost as easily as Jo. With Freddie and Blondie on the firm, the four of them together made a formidable team.

"When d'you think we should go huntin' then?" said Danny.

"I dunno – I'll have to find him first. All I want now is a nice soak in the bath. Oh, about Snowy – I hope you gave that slag plenty of stick afterwards –"

"Yeah, we did – Blondie threw a full pint over 'im and Freddie sprayed the whole pub with soda-water – it was really funny, Jo – Snowy was fuckin' drenched. He started to phone plod so we fucked off a bit lively!"

"Good – I'm gonna do that bastard. It's his fault I was nicked."

"Better leave him for a while, Jo. When they nicked you they made it clear they would have us if anything happened to 'im."

"Yeah, don't worry, I'll leave 'im for a while – then I'll chop a couple of his fingers off so's he can't make any more phone calls!" he laughed as he disappeared into the bathroom, and Danny wasn't sure if he was serious or not.

"Are you goin' out tonight?" shouted Danny.

"No – I'm seeing Christine." I need some soothing, Jo thought to himself.

*

Jo arrived at the shop just as Christine was about to leave. "Oh, there you are," she smiled. "I thought you were going to be late for me."

'How could I be late for you, babe – come here," he said, taking her in his arms and kissing her lightly. When they broke away, she suddenly noticed the bruising on his face.

"What have you done to your face – and there's a cut under your eye – oh, Jo."

"Hey, it's nothing, a little misunderstanding that's all. Come on, give me your arm."

They walked the short distance to Christine's house stopping occasionally to window shop, choosing furniture and curtains that they might have when they were married. Jo liked the look on her face when she saw something she especially liked and he made mental notes that one day he would buy her everything she wanted.

Christine lived in a three-bedroom flat, just a short distance from the town centre, with her parents and older sister, Jane. Jo liked Christine's family. He was always welcomed whenever he called, and if things were tough, her mother would be the first to ask if he wanted a meal or maybe a few pounds to tie him over until more work came in.

Jo followed Christine into the hall and took her coat as it slipped from her shoulders, then spun her round gently and embraced her. She was beautiful, he thought, and her long dark hair and her clear blue eyes gave him a tingle as he held her to him.

Bill, her father, came into the hall. "Hello, you two. I've made some tea – you're a bit late tonight aren't you?"

"She's been draggin' me all over the place, Bill – window shopping, you know what they're like."

"Yeah, I know what you mean, Jo. When the three of 'em get

together is the worst. If I have to take 'em shopping I get dragged into every shop in town I think," he said, laughing.

"Must be murder bein' the only male in the house. Where's this cuppa then?" They all went into the kitchen and while Christine prepared herself a light meal, Bill and Jo discussed unions and closed shops, much to the annoyance of Christine, who thought they were the most boring subjects in the world. Although he would never dream of saying it, Jo thought so too.

"No boats in yet Jo?"

"No, not yet. I spoke to one of the stewards the other day and he said it might be another couple of weeks before anything's sorted out."

"Bloody unions, I sometimes wonder if they're worth the subscriptions we have to pay 'em. Bill worked in the local dockyard but was soon to be made redundant, and he blamed a lot of the cause on the unions for trying to get too much for their members. Jo readily agreed that they did go over the top sometimes in their efforts to improve conditions, and if things were improved, men usually lost jobs somewhere along the line.

"Hey, you two, stop being boring," said Christine, sitting down at the table with two boiled eggs and a round of toast.

"Where are we going tonight then?" she said.

"I don't know – a drink, pictures, whatever you like. Don't forget my car's not ready yet so we can't go far."

"What do you want to do?"

"I don't mind – whatever you like."

"I'll get ready first then we'll decide –"

"Yes, okay."

Christine finished her meal then left the kitchen to get changed, while her father and Jo carried on talking.

A little later, Christine's mother and sister came in, laden down with shopping bags and parcels, talking furiously together about the bargains to be had at the autumn sales. Half an hour later they were still discussing the good buys they'd made, and Jo was becoming impatient.

"Come on, Chris – aren't you ready yet? Hello you two – I see you've had a good day then. Is there anything left down there?" he laughed.

"Only the rubbish – we've got all the good stuff," said Jane, raising her eyebrows. "And, we are all going to the Sunday market tomorrow. Do you want to come, Jo?"

"Er, I'll pass on that one, Jane – I'd end up carryin' all the bags!"

"You're about right there, Jo," said Bill.

"Yeah, anyway Chris, you nearly ready?"

"Yes, I'm just finishing my hair. Where we going then?"

"I don't know – you fancy the pictures?"

"If you like," she said with a smile.

At 7:45 Jo and Christine left for the local cinema. Jo bought the sweets and the popcorn, and two Kia-Oras, and they settled down in their seats. But Jo was restless and he soon regretted the decision he'd made. He was thinking about Greaseball and what he could do to stop the charge from going ahead. He would have to find out where he lived and appease his frustration one way or another.

Christine could tell that Jo wasn't enjoying the film and within the hour, between them, they decided to leave. They would go home and listen to some of the records of Christine's vast collection. Being the manageress of the record department, she had the pick of the crop at much reduced prices. They didn't go out too often, preferring instead to stay in and listen to such greats as Buddy Holly and Billy Fury, and in particular one of Jo's current favourites, Just Loving You by Anita Harris.

It was getting late and Jo had to go. It was after midnight and Christine wanted to be up early in the morning to go to the Sunday market. Before he went Jo gave Christine £200 to look after for him. "I might creep up the club later and I don't want to lose it," he said. "Put in in the bottom drawer if you like." He smiled at her, then kissed her.

"I'll see you tomorrow."

"Yes – goodnight, Jo." And they kissed again.

Christine watched Jo from her bedroom window until he disappeared into the night.

*

Jo walked down Lake Road and into Fratton Road, north towards Kingston Crescent and the Half Moon snooker club. It was well after midnight but there were still a few late revellers about, some singing and shouting but most of them hurrying to get home out of the cold air.

It was a fifteen minute walk to the Half Moon and when Jo got there the place was packed. The three snooker tables were all occupied and plenty of punters were on the sidelines waiting for a game or taking side-bets on the action. Jo walked across to the sandwich bar and ordered a coffee. Billy was behind the counter and when the order came up Jo paid him with a ten pound note. "Keep the change, Bill," he said with a cheeky wink. Billy acknowledged the repayment and gave Jo a nod. "I'll treat ya to the coffee," he said.

Jo finished his drink and made his way up the twisting staircase to the poker room. The room was full of men, some younger than Jo, but most of them much older. The two tables were fully occupied and Jo didn't fancy his chances of getting a game for some time.

Larry was sitting in his usual lucky chair and The Rat was playing on the other table. Jo told both of them about his impending court appearance and said he wanted them to turn up in court on Friday as witnesses. They both assured Jo that they would be there by ten o'clock sharp. Jo also told The Rat to make sure Little Johnny was there as well.

After giving further reminders to his potential witnesses Jo decided not to hang about waiting for a game, and left the club for home.

Jo was about halfway from the wharf road when he suddenly took a left turn and walked past The White Swan. It was a little way from the main road, quiet, almost obscure under the secondary street lighting. With the maze of alleyways and flats just a sprint away, Jo decided to do the pub some damage. If it wasn't for that son of a bitch he thought, I wouldn't have got a bashing and I wouldn't be facing two assault charges. He wanted to burn the place to the ground but for now, if he could find the right tools, caving his windows in would do nicely.

Just down the road, about fifty yards from the pub, was some derelict ground and Jo soon found a length of cast-iron drainpipe, enough to take out the three main windows if the wooden struts holding them gave way as well. He weighed the pipe in his hands, tossing it up and down, feeling the weight of it. It was a little heavy, but Jo was used to heavy work and he was fit and strong. He smiled to himself as he tossed the pipe in the air. Yes! He suddenly thought about fingerprints and took off his shoes and socks, then slipped his shoes back on, making sure they were tied tight. He pulled the socks over his hands and rubbed the pipe up and down a few times, just to be sure that no fingerprints would be left behind that could convict him.

Jo scanned the street then walked back towards The Swan. He stood three or four feet back from the windows and raised the pipe over his head, then threw it with all his strength. The pipe crashed through all three windows taking the struts holding them clean away.

The noise was deafening. But even before the pipe had come to rest, Jo was up on his toes and heading for the Half-Moon. It was closer than home plus he could count on numerous witnesses to confirm that he had been in the club for the past couple of hours.

It took Jo just a few minutes to get to the Moon, and he composed himself, catching his breath, before he went in. Billy was still serving behind the bar. "Bill, if anyone asks, I've been here for the past two hours, okay." Billy nodded and Jo went to the toilet to put his socks back on.

Less than half an hour later, Danny phoned the club to warn Jo that old bill had paid the flat a visit. Just as Jo replaced the receiver, two uniforms entered the premises. They saw Jo behind the counter and began to question him.

"I've been here for the past two hours – ask anybody." The police checked privately with Billy then left, but not before giving Jo a warning shot.

*

The new few days proved uneventful. Jo picked up his car from the garage and paid Freddie a visit to let him know what happened after his arrest. Freddie was out of gear so they couldn't have a smoke but he promised to keep some back for the weekend if Jo had his liberty, and if Trina brought some back with her.

On the Tuesday Jo kept an appointment with his solicitor who told him in no uncertain terms to expect a possible custodial sentence. The courts, he said, looked unkindly on assaults, and especially so when it involved a police officer in his own station. After consultation with his brief, Jo thought more and more about skipping bail. Only the thought of leaving Christine held him in check.

In the meantime, Jo tried in vain to find Greaseball. He asked everyone he knew to spread the word but it seemed nobody knew him. With Jo's court appearance fast approaching, it looked as if the elusive Robert Miles Jacobs was not going to be found.

When Jo did finally confess to Christine she was heartbroken and he couldn't think of anything to say to console her. He refrained from telling her that he might go down, but he guessed her fear that he might, and he felt great sadness to see her so hurt. In his dreams, Jo could hear Rolf pleading and screaming as Jo dissected him limb from limb...

A couple of days before Jo was to appear in court, he took Christine to their favourite restaurant, just a few miles outside Portsmouth. They pushed aside all thoughts of Jo's troubles and they were enjoying their time together. They both tucked into juicy fillet steaks and sipped cool wine as piped music played softly in the background. With perfect timing, about halfway through the meal, Jo took from his pocket a small, velvet covered box, and as he opened it and handed it to her, he said, "Christine, come spring, will you marry me?"

She smiled, the sparkle in her eyes outshining the sparkle of the stones on the ring and as they came together across the table she whispered to him, "Yes, Jo."

*

Jo was sitting on a bench outside of the number one court and halfway through his fourth cigarette when he heard the usher call his name. "Jo Sullivan. Case of Jo Sullivan."

Jo's heartbeat quickened as he entered the courtroom. He was led to the dock by two police officers and told to remain standing while the charges were read out by the clerk of the court. When asked for his plea, Jo said in a clear, confident voice, "Not Guilty.' He didn't feel confident though, not now. Both Larry and The Rat had failed to show and Jo cursed them for treating his request so lightly. Had he known they weren't going to attend he would have spoken to them a little more sternly. And where was Little Johnny? If it wasn't for him I wouldn't even be in this mess, he thought.

As well as cursing Larry and The Rat, Jo also cursed himself for not heeding his solicitor's advice to bring all potential witnesses to his office for a quick briefing before the hearing started.

The prosecution outlined their first case against Jo, then called Greaseball to the witness box. After taking the oath, the prosecutor began his questioning. "Is your full name Robert Miles Jacobs?"

"Yes."

"And do you live at 128A Allaway Avenue, Paulsgrove?"

"Yes." Jo etched the address in his mind.

"Please tell the court in your own words the events that took place on the evening of the fourth of November."

"Well, we was playin' cards and he –"

"You mean Sullivan?"

"Yeah. He was gettin' annoyed because I was thinkin' whether to call or not –"

"Call?"

"Yeah, we was playin' poker and I had a flush. He bet a hundred pounds and I wasn't sure what to do – but he kept tryin' to hurry me up. Anyway, I called him and he beat me with a fullhouse, and I swore – not at him, I just swore at gettin' beat that's all and he started hitting me." Jo's eyes burned into Greaseball as he spewed out his rhetoric of lies. If looks could kill a man, Jacobs would have died where he stood. The prosecutor continued. "So, you didn't do anything or say anything that might have provoked an attack on you?"

"No – I was just sitting there."

"And you can't think of any reason why Sullivan should suddenly assault you?"

"No."

"Thankyou, Mr. Jacobs. Please remain where you are."

Mr. Harrison, Jo's solicitor, took hold of some papers and began to cross-examine Greaseball. "Now, Mr. Jacobs, are you asking this court to believe that Mr. Sullivan attacked you, as you say, without any provocation? That he just rose from his seat and reigned blows down on you for no reason at all?"

"Yeah – well I expect he thought I was swearin' at him when I swore –"

"Who **were** you swearing at, Mr. Jacobs?"

"Like I said – when I got beat I just swore that's all."

"What did you say?"

"Er, I just said fuck it, or fucking hell – something like that."

"Were you angry at being beaten by Mr. Sullivan?"

"Well, I didn't like being beat but it didn't bother me that much."

"Why did you swear then?"

"I just swore that's all."

"Why did you call Mr. Marsden a midget?"

"Er, I was just joking –"

"You weren't annoyed at Mr. Marsden for any reason?"

"No."

"You're sure?"

"Yes –"

"Why did you call him a midget?" Greaseball started shifting from one leg to the other, and became hesitant.

"I – I don't know – I just said be quiet, midget or something like that –"

"I suggest, Mr. Jacobs, that you were angry at Mr. Marsden because he implied that you were a mug at the game of poker, and he laughed at you for calling the bet, isn't that so, Mr. Jacobs?"

"No –"

"And when Mr. Sullivan called you a greaseball you became aggressive, is that not true, Mr. Jacobs?"

"No."

"**Did** Mr. Sullivan call you greaseball?"

"Er, I think so –"

"Did he call you greaseball or didn't he?"

"Yes."

"Did you like Mr. Sullivan calling you greaseball?"

"Well, I –"

"Did you like being called greaseball or not, Mr. Jacobs?"

"No, I suppose not – but I wasn't that bothered –"

"Why did you ask Mr. Sullivan if he was Mr. Marsden's mother?"

"What?"

"When you called Mr. Marsden a midget, I believe Mr. Sullivan said, and I quote, 'oi, greaseball, don't call my mate a midget,' is that not so, Mr. Jacobs?"

"Er, yes –"

"And when Mr. Sullivan tried to defend Mr. Marsden, you asked him if he was his fucking mother, is **that** no so?"

"No –"

"And you were angry at him –"

"No –"

"And because you were angry you went to strike Mr. Sullivan didn't you?"

"No, it was him –"

'You were going to strike Mr. Sullivan because he called you greaseball –"

"No –"

"You didn't like Sullivan did you?"

"No – I – "

"Thankyou Mr. Jacobs. No more questions your worships."

Greaseball had his hands clenched hard on the rail of the witness box. He'd been flustered by Harrisons bombardment of questions and Jo was pleased with his brief's professional attack. The magistrates must have guessed that Jacobs was lying through his teeth, surely, thought Jo.

The usher was calling for the prosecutor's second witness, but nobody came forward in answer to his call. He called out his name again. "James Edwards. Will a Mr. James Edwards come forward please." Jo was baffled by the name, James. At the Half Moon he said his name was Chris, but the main thing though, whatever his name was, he wasn't answering and that meant he wasn't about to testify against Jo. After a short delay, the prosecution had no choice but to carry on with the case. Now it was an even battle. Jo versus Greaseball. His word against Jo's.

After the prosecutor read out the doctor's report, detailing Jacob's injuries, Jo was called to the witness box and sworn in. His solicitor had given him confidence and he felt good as he stood rigid in the box waiting for his questions. "Mr. Sullivan, in your own time please, tell the court what led you to being brought before the justices."

"Well, as already said, we were playing cards. There were only four of us to start with, then Jacobs and his friend came in. They said they were looking for a game. Everything was going fine until the big pot –"

"Can you explain that please?"

"Yes. Most of the pots are fairly small, but because everyone suddenly had a good hand the pot was a couple of hundred pounds or more. Anyway, Greaseball, sorry, Jacobs and me were the only two left in the game and he was thinking whether or not to call. There was no pressure on him at all, nobody was trying to hurry him up. After a couple of minutes, though, Little Johnny – that's Mr. Marsden, suddenly asked if everyone was dead. He's always cracking jokes and no offence was meant but Jacobs started insulting him, calling him a midget. When I interjected he became abusive to me as well. I could tell that he was getting angry at being called greaseball, and I knew he was about to attack me. I hit him first – strictly in self-defence though. My only regret is that I hit him too hard, I guess –"

"Thankyou, Mr. Sullivan. So you say that after all the swearing and insults, you were absolutely positive that Mr. Jacobs was about to assault you, and you only struck out in self-defence?"

"Yes sir, that's exactly right."

"Thankyou. Please remain in the witness box." Jo's brief sat down and the prosecutor stood up to begin his cross-examination. "Mr. Sullivan, would you say you were a violent man?"

"No."

"But you attacked Mr. Jacobs with such ferocity that he needed five stitches to an eye wound and two stitches to the inside of his mouth. Wouldn't that suggest to you that a violent man had inflicted those injuries?"

"I disagree."

"You say Mr. Jacobs was about to assault you – why didn't you just stop him with a protective stance?"

"I'm not sure I know what you mean –"

"I mean, Mr. Sullivan, that instead of beating Mr. Jacobs so severely that he needed seven stitches to his wounds, why didn't you just stop him from hitting you by parrying his would-be-blows?"

"You're not serious are you – I would have been injured myself if I had to fight like that."

"Why did you call Mr. Jacobs a greaseball? Was it to provoke him?"

"No – I only called him a greaseball after he called my mate a midget. It was your man that was doing the provoking."

"You were provoked into attacking Mr. Jacobs then?"

"No sir. I've told the court how it happened. He was really mad at himself for calling the bet and got even madder when I called him greaseball. He was about to attack me and I defended myself and there is nothing you can say that's going to alter it."

The prosecutor shuffled through some papers and then turned to the bench. "I have no more questions for Mr. Sullivan your worships."

Jo was told by the clerk to return to the dock.

After closing arguments from both sides, the magistrates adjourned to their chambers to consider their verdict. The way Mr. Harrison had pieced together the facts in his summing up, Jo was quietly confident of acquittal.

Fifteen minutes later the magistrates were back in their seats. The chairman began to speak. "Jo Sullivan, we have considered this case very carefully, and we were inclined to believe that under the circumstances, you probably would not have attacked Mr. Jacobs for no apparent reason, as he has suggested. We feel that there must have been some provocation and indeed, Mr. Jacobs may well have been intent on an assault on you. However, even if that were the case, we feel strongly that, owing to the severity of the injuries sustained by Mr. Jacobs, you went further than was reasonable in defending yourself, and therefore we find the case against your proved."

Jo's heart sank as he absorbed the chairman's final words.

The chairman looked up from the bench and started talking again. "In so far as the other case against you, you may, if you wish, have the case dealt with today, in front of this bench, or you can ask for an adjournment and let it be heard in front of a different bench at a later date. In any event, you may wish to discuss the alternatives with your solicitor in which case this court will be adjourned for fifteen minutes."

Jo was called by Mr. Harrison to sit with him in the well of the court. "Well, Jo, what do you want to do, go ahead now or put it back to a later date?"

"What do you think is best?"

"Well, if I were you, I might be inclined to have the case heard now. That way, if the case **is** proved, you'll have more chance of a lesser sentence having them coupled together. I feel I must also advise you that if you were to change your plea to one of guilty, the bench may look on the decision favourably, and quite honestly Jo, after being convicted on the G.B.H. charge, your chances of acquittal against the police are pretty remote as you probably realise yourself."

"Yeah, you're right – I've got no chance against them. What do you think I'll get if I go for it now?"

"I really don't know. The way the chairman spoke, well, I got the impression he thought Jacobs was the instigator, but with an additional charge against a police officer, I really couldn't say what the outcome will be –"

"Sod it! Let's get it over and done with now."

"You're sure about it?"

"Yes, I'll have it done today – I might just get lucky."

"Well, let's hope so. I'll try my best for you."

"Yeah, thanks Mr. Harrison. Listen, if I go down, will you make a phone call for me?"

"Yes of course. Whatever the outcome I'll see you afterwards."

Jo returned to the dock. A few minutes later the justices resumed their places at the bench. Jo's solicitor stood up and addressed the chairman. "Sir, in view of the fact that Mr. Sullivan has been found guilty on the first charge, he feels that it would be in his best interest, and that of the courts, to change his plea on the second charge from not guilty to one of guilty."

"Yes, thankyou Mr. Harrison."

After the clerk of the court finished reading out the facts on the second charge, the magistrates decided, after agreement from both sides, that a full hearing was not necessary in view of the fact that Jo had changed his plea to guilty.

Initially, Jo was relieved that he wouldn't have to listen to Rolf's undoubted catalogue of lies, but after listening to the statement read out by the clerk, Jo began to wish that he hadn't changed his plea. The way it came across, he almost convinced himself that he was going away forever. In mitigation, Harrison tried to show that it was Jo who came out worse after the confrontation with sergeant Rolf, but it looked quite obvious to Jo, and probably everyone else, that the magistrates were not impressed.

The chairman asked the clerk if there was anything known. "Yes sir. Mr. Sullivan has two previous convictions. In this court, on the 12th of July, 1962, he was convicted of grievous bodily harm and fined £25 with costs of £3. Also in this court, on the 14th of February, 1962, he was convicted of common assault and fined £10 with costs of £3. He was also ordered to pay compensation of £8."

"Thankyou, Mr. Simmons," said the chairman.

The magistrates began conferring with each other, whispering together, deciding Jo's fate.

Jo stood rigid, almost cataleptic, as he waited for sentence.

"We have come to the conclusion that your past record and indeed your record here today, shows you to be a young man who will strike out regardless of the possible consequences of such actions. Although we feel that you may have had reasonable cause to defend yourself in the case of Jacobs, we feel that an assault on a police officer cannot pass by without a deterrent sentence. Therefore, in an effort to curb your violent tendencies, we have decided to send you to a detention centre for a period of six months."

Jo was devastated. As he was led to the cells he caught sight of Rolf and shouted out at him. "You bastard! You fuckin' pig! I'll have you –" Jo was quickly ushered down the steps by two police officers and taken to a holding cell, still cursing and swearing at the injustice. After a chat with his solicitor and a promise from him that he would pass on a message to Christine, he gradually lost his anger. It was going to take him a lot longer though, to lose the bitter taste of a sentence of detention.

Jo sat in the cell wondering what it would be like in a detention centre. He'd thought about the possibility of imprisonment, or even a spell of Borstal training, but detention had never entered his head. He thought that was for young 'uns only.

Before he had a chance to brood on his predicament, Jo was taken from the cell, handcuffed and whisked away in a police car. Within an hour of being convicted and sentenced Jo was on his way to Haslar Detention Centre, Gosport, just fifteen miles from Portsmouth. If they could have flown across the harbour, Haslar would be just two miles from the wharf where Jo lived.

The forty minute journey was uneventful. They took the same harbour road that Jo had taken the week before when he'd visited Freddie, and he saw the same boats stuck fast in the same mud, as if time had stood still, almost.

Jo was feeling slightly apprehensive and rolled himself another cigarette.

"Better make that a quick one, Sullivan – you won't be doing any smoking in there."

"Ain't you allowed to smoke in detention then?"

"Not likely – they'll have your guts for garters if they catch you smoking."

"Fucksake!" cursed Jo, now bitterly regretting his change of plea.

I should have gone for trial, he thought, cursing himself again.

Before he had a chance to finish his cigarette, the police car pulled up outside of the gates and Jo stubbed it out before a screw had the pleasure of telling him to do so.

The two uniformed plod took Jo, still handcuffed, to the reception area. After being signed over, and after the removal of the cuffs, Jo began his detention proper.

"Right! Stand in front of the desk and empty your pockets!"

Jo cleared his pockets while the screw listed the contents and put them in a plastic bag. Jo left the money until last and wondered if he would say anything about the amount.

"Where did you get this little lot then? Steal it did you? Rob some little old lady did you?" he said, taunting Jo.

"No, I won it –"

"I won it, sir! In here you call every officer, sir! – Do you understand!?"

"Yes – sir," said Jo, reeling from the sound of the screw's voice.

"Right. Over here – strip off and put all your grubby clothes in that box. Then get in that bath and wash your filthy body!"

As he began to strip, for some reason, Jo started smiling.

"Is something funny, Sullivan?" shouted the screw.

"No, I –"

"No sir!"

"No, sir," said Jo, trying to keep a straight face.

"You won't have anything to smile about in here, Sullivan. By the time we've finished with you you'll wish you'd never robbed any old ladies!"

"I never ro –"

"Shut up! Don't talk back to me unless I ask you to! Understand!"

"Yeah – I think I'm gettin' the message – sir."

The screw looked at Jo for a few moments, as if assessing him, but didn't comment further.

"After you've stripped, you've got three minutes to wash your filthy body!"

Jo finished undressing and began to run the water. When three inches covered the bottom of the bath, the screw told Jo to step in.

Two minutes later he was ordered to get out and given a towel to dry himself.

Jo was soon kitted out. He was given three sets of clothing, one for work, one for after work, and one for inspections and parades. After a P.T. kit and other minor items were handed to him, he was taken across to the main building where ninety-three other teenagers of varying ages were housed – and he went across at the double. Everywhere any inmate went in Haslar was at the double. Anyone caught walking, except in certain circumstances, were placed on report and hauled in front of the Governor for punishment.

Once in the main block, Jo found himself running down a long corridor, and with all the kit he was carrying, it was hard going. There were three dormitories leading off the main corridor, and at the entrance to each dorm were four cells where inmates were housed on their induction.

Jo was ordered to halt outside of 'A' dorm and told to mark time. When the screw caught up, he unlocked one of the cells and told Jo to step inside.

"I'll send an inmate down to show you how to stow away your gear and make up a bed-pack. The sooner you learn the sooner you'll be in the dorm with some company – you get the picture, Sullivan?"

"Yes sir," said Jo, sussing the system. If you called 'em 'sir' they weren't too bad – if you didn't, they shouted at the top of their voices. Jo quickly came to the conclusion that he could put up with calling a soppy screw 'sir' if it was going to give him an easier life – yes-sir-ree!

A few minutes later, a young 'un of fourteen or fifteen entered Jo's cell. "Hi, I've come to show you the ropes, okay."

"Yeah, sure – thanks. What's it like in this place – they like to shout a bit don't they?"

"Yeah, they do to start with but after a day or two, if they see that you do as they say and call 'em sir, they'll leave you alone and start on someone else. If you don't call 'em sir they make it really tough for ya."

"Yeah? What do they do then?" asked Jo, seeking confirmation of his good judgement.

"Well, for a start they keep you in solitary, then they give you plenty of hassle while you're down there – you ain't not callin' 'em sir, are ya?"

"No, I can handle the sir bit for a while – what do they call you then?"

"My name's Robert, really, but everyone calls me Pepi. What do they call you?"

"Jo."

"Right o' Jo," he said with a cheeky grin. "How long did you get?"

"Six months."

"Six! You'll be one of the elite then."

"Elite? What ya talkin' about?"

"Most of the kids are doin' three. There's only about twelve, I think, doin' a six. They always seem to get the best jobs – 'cos they're doin' longer I s'pose. What did you get the six for?"

"A G.B.H. and an A.B.H. on an old bill."

"Wow man! Better watch out for the London mob – they think they run the place and if they think you're tough they might try it on with ya."

"Don't worry, Pep, I ain't gonna play tough. I just want to get this over and done with without any agg from anyone. Do me a favour will ya – don't tell anyone what I'm in for."

"Wouldn't do any good, Jo – the whole place will know why you're here 'cos the kids in reception read all the files and everyone knows everything."

"Well, it doesn't really matter – so long as nobody bothers me I won't bother them. How long –"

Pepi suddenly heard keys coming.

"– And then you take this blanket and fold it –"

"You all right in there, Smith?"

"Yessir – just showing the new boy the bed-pack, sir."

"Well get a move on. It'll be dinner time in fifteen minutes and I want this room ship-shape before then."

The screw carried on down the corridor and Pepi continued to show Jo how his room should look, and where all his kit should be placed. With all the information young Pepi passed on to Jo, he felt as if he'd been in detention for ever instead of just an hour or so.

At twelve o'clock sharp all the inmates finished work and returned to the dormitories to get changed for dinner. The sound of their boots against the marble floor was deafening. As the inmates passed Jo to get to their respective dorms, they eyed him up and down, appraising him, making up their minds about him. One of them stopped.

"Hello Jo, you just got here?"

"Hey Ray, how ya doin' – I didn't know you were in here."

"Yeah, been here a month. How long ya got, six ain't it?"

"Yeah, how did you know – I've only been here five minutes?"

"I heard someone from Pompey's just got a six so it must be you, right?"

"Fucksake – don't take long in here does it?"

"Nah – the whole place will know by tea-time. Anyway, I gotta go, they only give ya a few minutes to get changed, I'll catch ya later, Jo."

"Yeah, see ya later." Jo was pleased to see a friendly face. Ray's old man ran a fruit and veg stall in the market, and Ray worked with him sometimes. Although Jo didn't know Ray too well, he knew him well enough to know that he could more than handle himself when it came to a row. If there was any trouble about, Ray would make a useful ally, and Jo had a nasty feeling that, sooner or later, trouble was coming. In these sort of places there was always trouble lurking somewhere, and because Jo was in for assault it was inevitable that someone, sometime, would try their luck.

Jo stood in the door-jam wondering what to do. Pepi had gone to get changed for dinner and Jo was left standing by the door feeling stupid and uncertain. Soon after all the boys had disappeared into the dormitories though, a screw came along and gave Jo back his purpose by telling him to move out with the rest of 'A' dorm when the bell sounded for dinner. His place in the dining hall would be at table 28.

Jo felt better. Not knowing what to do was alien to him, so when the bell did go, Jo joined the rest of the inmates with confidence and headed for the dining hall.

The thirty tables in the hall were arranged in strategic manner so that the screws could keep an eye on all of their charges at the same time. There was a strictly enforced policy of silence at meal times which meant – NO TALKING. The signs around the hall said it clearly enough.

Jo picked up a metal tray from the pile and joined the queue. He could feel he was under scrutiny. A hundred pairs of eyes were making their appraisal, wondering what this new boy was like – and how tough he was. Jo wasn't bothered though, it was obvious, he thought, that they would want to know who the body was that had punched the head of a police sergeant.

Jo collected his food and sat down at table 28. There were three other inmates sitting with him, two were about Jo's age and the other a lot younger. As soon as Jo was seated the young 'un was on him, questioning him. "You from Pompey?"

Jo looked at him and nodded gently.

"You're doin' a six ain't ya?"

Jo nodded again.

"You done a copper didn't ya?"

Jo gave him another nod, and noticed, with amusement, that he only spoke when he was about to take a mouthful of food.

The young 'un was persistant. "G.B.H. or A.B.H.?"

Jo mouthed a fork full of mashed potato and quickly cast his eyes round the hall. 'You tryin' to get me nicked, sunshine?"

The young 'un looked away and carried on eating his meal.

The other two sitting with Jo were eyeing him up. In between a mouthful, one of them spoke. "You in for G.B.H. or A.B.H.?"

Jo scanned the hall and mouthed a carrot. "Both."

"Real tough cookie then –"

"Are you talking, Allen?" shouted a screw.

"No sir," spluttered Allen.

"You are lying, Allen, and you are on report!"

Allen gave Jo an eye to eye and took a chance with another sentence. "I'm in 'A' dorm and I'll see you later about payin' my fine, swede."

Jo gave him a short glance and carried on with his meal. Fucksake! he thought, barely two hours in and it's started already. Jo figured he would have to sort this one out as soon as possible. If he left himself open to intimidation, he would be taking stick until he was forced to prove himself one way or the other. Jo decided the inmate, Allen, would he his first step up the ladder of Haslar's hierarchy. He wanted to take him out now but resisted the temptation, after all, he thought, it wouldn't be right without giving him fair warning.

Jo looked up from his plate and caught Allen giving him a severe eye. Jo took a mouthful of potato. "Listen, Allen, do yourself a real favour and leave me right out, okay? If you mess with me you'll have a mean row on ya hands – and if you call me swede again, I'll break ya fuckin' jaw!"

Jo leaned back in his chair in case of any immediate action from Allen, and stared into his eyes. Allen ducked his head and carried on eating. After the warning, Jo knew enough to know that he wouldn't be getting any trouble from Allen, unless it came from behind or if he had one or two backing him. If it was a straight one to one, Jo would tear him apart.

The time allowed for dinner was forty minutes and by 12:45 Jo was back in his cell. Apart from the 'A' dorm cleaner, Pepi, all the rest of the inmates had returned to work.

At two o'clock Jo was ordered to change into his best set of clothes and taken across to the administration block for an interview with the Governor, as all inmates were on their arrival at Haslar.

Jo was led into an office.

"Stand in front of the desk and give your full name to the Governor and stand to attention at all times!" shouted a screw.

"Jo Sullivan, sir."

The Governor, a man in his forties, was studying Jo's file. "I see from your record, Sullivan, that you are a young man hell-bent on a career of violent encounters, not only with authority, but with anyone who offends you." The Governor looked up at Jo. "Well, what have you got to say about that, Sullivan?"

"I only fight in self-defence, sir."

"Self-defence? It states here that you attacked a police officer while in the execution of his duty – and in his own station, I see."

"The officer –"

"Quiet Sullivan!" said the screw.

The Governor continued. "You have been sent here by the court in the hope that your violent nature might be curbed. We will do our best to see that it is. We will not tolerate violence of any kind here, Sullivan, and any incidents in this detention centre will be dealt with both swiftly and severely. Do I make myself clear, Sullivan?"

"Yessir."

"Now, as you are serving a six month sentence you will be eligible to four weeks remission. Your provisional date for release is April nine next year. I say provisionally because any loss of remission will set your release date further back. The rules are straightforward – you obey them, and you obey them to the letter. If we feel that you are deliberately abusing the chance the court has given you or if you make mutiny, or if you incite any inmate to riot or be responsible for any other social disorder, we may if we think it appropriate, send you back to the court for re-sentence. In our experience that usually means Borstal training or a prison sentence, one considerably longer than the six months you are currently serving. Do you understand all that, Sullivan?"

"Yessir."

"Good. The initial report I have here indicates that you are prepared to enter into the spirit of Haslar. Would that be correct, Sullivan?"

"Yessir."

The Governor looked at the screw. "Thankyou, Mr. Hines, that will be all."

Jo was taken back to 'A' dorm and set the menial task of scrubbing the floor of his cell. When that was done he had to polish it until, Hines said, he could see his face in it. Jo washed and polished the floor three times before Hines was satisfied. It didn't look any different from when Jo first started and he guessed the repeat orders to do it again and again were only meant to test his tolerance and resolve.

After emptying the water and cleaning out the bucket, Jo was called into the 'A' dorm office and given a book of rules and regulations, plus a roster of the routine he would follow from now on. He was also given pen and paper for letter writing. Each inmate was allowed to write one letter per week and it was to be written in the dining hall on Sunday afternoons.

"Right, Sullivan, take the booklet and roster and study them so that you know what you're doing at all times. You may sit on the chair in your cell but you may **not** sit on the bed – and change out of those overalls so that you're ready for tea."

Jo was sitting in the chair browsing over the roster when Pepi looked in through the flap in the door. "Hey Jo," he whispered, "I hear you had words with one of the London mob. They was all talkin' about it in the dorm – the kid Evans said you were gonna break Allen's jaw – wow man – you didn't waste any time did ya?"

Jo left the chair and moved across to the door. "I only told him to leave me out or else – what's bein' said then?"

"Nothin' much – they're just talkin' about it that's all. I gotta go now – I might see ya on association if they let you out. Bein' new, they might keep you in – depends what screw's on. Anyway, I'll see ya later."

"Yeah, see ya, Pep." Jo sat back in the chair and thought about Pepi's words. Allen had probably lost some face and he might have to try and get it back. Jo would make sure that he stayed on red alert whenever he was out of his cell.

Tea-time came and went without any further incident and so did the rest of the weekend because Jo was kept locked in his cell, except for mealtimes, until Monday morning when he was moved into the dorm.

The only thing that caused Jo any heartache, was the thought of Christine. He wrote to her an endearing letter regretting deeply the hurt she must be suffering. He explained to her how it all happened and hoped that she would understand and be waiting for him on his release. He enclosed a visiting order with the letter, although it would remain invalid until Jo had served twenty eight days.

After Jo was moved into the dorm, he was taken across to the recovery shop for work. The tasks were menial. Work in the recovery shop was the salvage of nuts, bolts, springs, valves, copper-wire – everything that could be undone or taken from the various electrical appliances that were scattered around the workshop. The dismantling of televisions and radios was the main source of employment in the recovery shop.

At nine-thirty Jo entered the gymnasium for his first bout of circuit training. Already laid out on a dozen coconut mats was the apparatus to be used. Jo changed into his gym kit and waited for further instructions from the physical training instructor. "Right, Sullivan," he began, "have you ever done any circuit training before?"

"No sir."

"Right, let me explain it all to you. As a new boy you'll be on the green circuit. There are three coloured circuits, green for beginners, then blue, then red. They are all the same circuits except that you do more repetitions of each exercise as you improve. You will complete three circuits and you will be timed after you've finished them. You will be expected to improve your times each time you come to the gym. All clear so far?"

"Yessir."

"Good. Come with me and I'll show you the various exercises you've got to do. Don't try and rush them. If you do them correctly, and with the right application, you'll find the circuit gets easier as you go along."

The P.T.I. took Jo round the circuit, showing him each exercise in turn. There were bench-presses, sit-ups, press-ups, exercises with medicine-balls, two or three weightlifting exercises, squats – twelve in all, that ensured every muscle of the body was used.

Jo completed his first circuit in thirty-two minutes.

The P.T.I. entered Jo's time in his record book and told him to take a shower. After all the inmates had completed their circuits and showered, they were taken back to the recovery shop for the last hour before dinner.

After they had eaten, the inmates were given thirty minutes of drill on the parade ground each day before returning to their various places of work. During the afternoon they were given another bout of circuit training or, twice a week, taken to the running track. As with the circuit, each run was recorded and had to be improved upon each time a run was made.

Jo's first mile took nine minutes, much to the disgust of the instructor.

It was then back to work for an hour before tea. After the meal, and when all the dormitories and toilets and shower areas had been thoroughly washed, scrubbed, disinfected, polished and cleaned, the inmates were finally allowed to relax on association.

The regulators saw association as a social and behavioural training exercise, designed to help inmates adapt and integrate in harmony with other inmates.

The boys of Haslar saw it differently. To them it was the time to duck and dive, to seek out contraband like home-made booze or cigarettes, and, rarely, cannabis resin.

It was also the time when the Haslar hierarchy was sorted out.

On association there were a multitude of activities for the boys to indulge in – snooker, darts, crib, table tennis, television, various arts and crafts, model making, even needlework and embroidery if any inmate fancied taking the chance. The association area was made up of one large room that housed the snooker table and the tennis-table, with other, smaller tables, for crib or chess. Leading from the main room were smaller rooms where the T.V.'s were, and the darts.

On his first association Jo felt like a fish on dry land. With so many activities to choose from he wasn't sure what to do, finally settling at one of the small tables where chess sets had been set out.

Within a few minutes Pepi had joined him. Although two or three years younger than Jo, Pepi seemed to belie his age with his maturity and Jo was quite happy to have him in his company. He was also full of information. Jo learned from him which screw to avoid, where the hooch was, if there was any about, who had the smokes and who was who in Haslar generally. He also pointed out the members of the so-called London mob. There were six altogether – two of them in 'A' dorm. Pepi said Allen was one of the bullies of Haslar, often getting some of the young 'uns to polish his boots or press his trousers.

"Do you play chess, Pep?"

"Yeah – you wanna game then?"

"Make ya first move, son."

Pepi moved a white pawn to queen four. Before long the two of them were involved in an enthralling game of chess. Pepi was an attacking player and Jo had to keep his wits about him to stay on equal terms. After a dozen or so moves, Jo was a bishop and one pawn down and in a bad position.

"I hope you fight better than you play chess," quipped Pepi.

Jo laughed. "Why, you wanna try me, little 'un?"

"Nah – I'll just whip ya at this game –"

"You ain't won yet, 'erbert – just 'cos I'm a bishop down –"

"– And the pawn, Jo, don't forget the pawn."

Jo laughed again at his cheeky manner.

Suddenly, someone kicked the leg of the table, scattering the pieces across the table – but it was an accident. One of the young 'uns had run across the room to retrieve a ping-pong ball and charged into the table. Pepi gave him a sharp reprimand as Jo reset the pieces. A short time later Jo resigned after making a severe tactical error.

"You wanna try an' get even, Jo?" said a triumphant Pepi.

"Yeah, why not – set 'em up while I have a piss. Where's the karzi?" Pepi pointed out where the toilets were and watched Jo as he left the room.

Jo was standing at the urinal, just about to zip his fly, when they came in. It was Allen and two of his cronies.

If anything was going to come out of Jo's threat on Allen, Jo knew it would happen while he was away from the main room, and even as he made his way to the toilet, that all-knowing feeling in his stomach had begun.

While playing chess, Jo was taking stock of the inmates. The vast majority were younger than Jo, free and easy, enjoying the limited time they had on association to forget Haslar's rigorous schedule, and they gave Jo no cause for concern. The half-dozen that were glued to the snooker table were in a different category. They were the ones who lived on reputation, relished the knowing that they were the untouchables, the 'daddies', and anyone seen as a threat to their standing would have to be taken out and put in place.

With his threat on Allen, Jo had unwittingly become a legitimate target for them, a challenge for them to put down.

That all-knowing feeling that Jo had when he left the hall was the surge of adrenalin, the chemical agent that warns the body and mind of imminent danger.

But for Jo, it wasn't quite imminent yet.

As he walked to the toilet, he had a few minutes to absorb the adrenalin into his bloodstream. With a few deep breaths, the initial surge had slowed to a gentle trickle until he was fully prepared for any assault on his being. At the first sign of threat Jo would instinctively attack. That first threat came when Allen and his cronies approached Jo in the toilet.

As soon as they were in range, and without a word being spoken, Jo gave Allen a devastating right upper-cut, sending him reeling backwards. He gave the second a body-blow, catching him just above the stomach line, taking his wind. As he bent forward holding the pain, Jo smashed him hard on the side of the face, sending him crashing to the floor. He grabbed the third by his shirt and pulled him onto a head-butt, splitting his eye. Howling, he held up his hands high for protection but Jo had already changed tactics, giving him a left and a right to the ribs. Jo then steamed into Allen again, punching him with two hard blows to his face. He grabbed Allen and pulled him close. "I told you not to mess with me! This is just a warning – if anyone else comes for me I'll put 'em in the intensive care unit!" Jo shook him hard. "**D'you understand you mother!?**"

"Yeah, yeah –" Jo let go of Allen and turned to his mates.

"Have you two mothers got the message!?" They both nodded, nursing their wounds, and Jo knew they wouldn't be back.

"Get ya'selves sorted before goin' back out – and Allen, if you grass on me you'll be the sorriest man in the world."

Jo checked himself in the mirror and straightened up before returning to the main hall. When he passed the snooker table a fresh surge of adrenalin rushed through him. He stopped, then spoke sharply. "There's three of your mob on the floor in the karzi – if anyone else tries me I'll cripple 'em for life!"

Jo made his way across the room and resumed his place at the chess-table. Pepi saw the tell-tale signs on Jo's fist. "What happened,

Jo? You been gone for ages!"

"Nothing much, Pep – just had to sort Allen and his two mates out that's all."

"Did ya do 'em?" he asked with incredulous enthusiasm.

Jo laughed. "Well, I did give 'em a couple of slaps. They followed me to the karzi –"

"Yeah? What did they say?"

"Nothing – I didn't give 'em a chance," smiled Jo.

"Wow man! They'll be after you now won't they?"

"I don't think so, 'erbert – I don't fuck about ya know! Anyway, let's forget about 'em – my turn to be white, yes?"

"Make your move, daddy."

Jo won the second game of chess and the score was now one each. The third game was interrupted by the call to return to the dormitories for evening lock-up and lights out.

Jo's swift dispatch of three members of the so-called London mob catapulted him from obscurity to the pinnacle of Haslar's hierarchy. In that one, brief, violent encounter, Jo had assured his standing among the inmates – and that's how he wanted it. He knew Allen would have to try and save face after it became public knowledge that he'd been threatened with a broken jaw, and he knew Allen wouldn't be capable on his own.

On his way across the hall, Jo had psyched himself up for a major confrontation, and secretly hoped that at least three **would** come for him. He also knew that as soon as they entered the toilet he was going to attack them – before they had a chance to talk or intimidate him in any way.

Cunning too, was also part of Jo's make-up. When three men go after the one, they don't expect the one to start first, and that's what Jo had relied on. He knew too, irrespective of the outcome, that he would become someone to be avoided, and that above all was his main intention.

The authority of Haslar though, saw it differently. As the news of the assaults spread among the inmates, so did it also come to the attention of the screws, and at 10:30 next morning, Jo was hauled in front of the Governor.

"Stand in front of the desk and give your full name to the Governor and remain standing to attention at all times," spewed out the screw, as if someone had just re-plugged him in.

"Jo Sullivan, sir."

The Governor continued studying the report in front of him then finally looked up at Jo. "Sullivan, I have in my hands a report that suggests that you are responsible for the assault of three inmates. Is this true?"

"No sir."

The Governor was taken by surprise. "No? You say that you weren't responsible for an assault on inmates Allen, Jones, and Collins, during association last evening."

"No sir," repeated Jo, feeling safe in his denial with the knowledge that he'd been assured no report of the incident had been made by the three inmates.

The Governor was unconvinced.

"Well, Sullivan, you may deny the allegation but I know by this report, that indeed you were responsible, and only the fact that the three inmates concerned have refused to confirm our beliefs, have you been saved from the probability of being returned to court for re-sentence. However, you will not escape punishment because of lack of confirmation."

"You can't punish –"

"Quiet Sullivan!" shouted the screw.

The Governor continued. "Sullivan, although I cannot punish you for the assaults, I can remove you from the main population if I consider you to be a disruptive, which I so do. Therefore, until further notice, you will be taken to the segregation unit and given, shall we say, more personal guidance to your training whilst you are here. Thankyou, Mr. Hines, that will be all."

"Right, Sullivan, about turn, quick march!"

Jo was taken immediately to the segregation unit where the regime was a gruelling, relentless, non-stop assault on the body with no time for relaxation or thought.

Everything Jo did in the unit was physical. They put him to task at weight-training, circuit-training, continuous running and marching until every muscle in his body ached, and then, when he thought he would be rested, they continued the pressure with more exercises. While waiting for meals, he was told to mark-time or go to the floor and perform countless press-ups.

There was no respite to the rigorous schedule except for meal-times or when he was in the shower. Three or four times a day he was ordered to change into full military dress, complete with knapsack laden with weights, then made to run the small circuit of the segregation unit. When he took a final shower at the end of the day and given his bed, sleep came within minutes.

Every morning at six o'clock sharp, Jo was rousted from his bed and ordered to clean and scrub his cell from top to bottom. When the screws were satisfied that the cell was spotless, he was made to clean the rest of the unit. Before breakfast came, he was taken to the small yard and given a thirty minute bout of physical exercises. After a twenty minute break for his meal, the assault on his body continued, and, with the memory of the recovery shop still fresh in his mind, he relished it! Instead of languishing in the shop, unscrewing nuts and bolts and pulling out wire, Jo felt like a gladiator being trained for the arena.

As the days went by the tasks seemed to come easier. Before entering detention, Jo was already accustomed to heavy labour and now, with relentless application, he was rapidly increasing his stamina. With his cessation of smoking, Jo became fitter and stronger than he'd ever felt before. Because of the non-stop routine he had no time to think, and because he didn't think or dwell on his position, the days went fast – and so did the weeks.

Every morning at ten o'clock, the Governor paid a visit to the unit to check on Jo's obedience and resolve. Every day too, he was given a medical by the visiting doctor as required by statutory Home Office regulations.

At the end of each day, alone in his cell, Jo examined his body in every detail and he could see that his frame had tightened, that his arms and legs were just that much bigger as the muscle pushed against the skin.

The only time Jo saw another inmate was in the church every

Sunday morning when he exercised his right to attend. After the brief respite, he was returned to the unit to continue the gruelling routine.

One Wednesday afternoon, nearly four weeks into his sentence, Jo was told to change into his best outfit. Apart from when he attended church, Jo had never been told to do this before and a twinge of anxiety came over him as he was taken across to the administration block.

When he was shown into the small room his anxiety quickly dissipated when he saw Christine sitting at a table.

She smiled when she saw him. "Hello, Jo –"

"Hello babe – I didn't expect to see you yet." He held her close then kissed her gently before letting her go.

"I thought I had to be here over a month –"

"I know," she beamed, "but I phoned them and they said I could come today."

"I'm glad – I really miss you."

"I know – I miss you too. Are they looking after you for me? Your cheeks are all rosy," she laughed.

"Are they," said Jo, rubbing his face. "Must be all that good food they're giving me. How did you get here?"

"My dad brought me over. He's been laid off so he's got some free time at the moment. What's it like in here then?"

"Well, I can handle it. They really keep you at it – feel them muscles," said Jo, flexing his arm. She gripped the top of his arm. "Mm, hunky," she purred.

Jo looked at her for a moment, taking in her beauty.

"Chris, I'm really sorry about this. I –"

She touched his hand. "It's alright, Jo, you don't have to say anything now. I know it wasn't your fault, it's just in your nature. Perhaps I'll have to keep you with me all the time," she said softly.

"Yes I'd like that – just you and me."

The two of them continued talking for nearly an hour before the screw watching over them called time on the visit. Jo couldn't believe it had gone so quickly and began to protest.

"But she hasn't been here five minutes – can't we have a bit longer? It's only three o'clock yet."

"Sorry, Sullivan – you've had longer than allowed already."

Jo looked at Christine with open hands. "Sorry, babe, but you gotta go."

"Yes, but I'll see you again soon."

They kissed briefly and she was gone.

After she had left the room Jo felt sad and an empty feeling came into his stomach, a feeling he had never experienced before.

Jo was taken back to the segregation unit. With Christine dancing in his mind his emotions were in turmoil and in frustration he worked even harder at everything they gave him. His body didn't ache so much and when he didn't fall asleep immediately after lights out he felt robbed.

As they continued with the rigorous training, Jo began to lose the fear they first installed in him, and he began smiling at them, trying to antagonize them. When they caught him smiling they made him work all the harder and the harder he worked out the better he liked it.

He had made up his mind that he could do the entire sentence in the unit if it had to be – but it wasn't to be. After nearly six weeks in the seg, and just a few days before Christmas, the Governor returned Jo to 'A' dorm and the normal routine of Haslar.

Pepi, whom Jo had befriended briefly, was still the dormitory cleaner and he greeted Jo like a long lost brother.

"Hey Jo! Wow man, how are ya? How'd they treat ya down there?" Pepi could hardly get his words out quick enough and Jo had to ease him up. "Pep, easy will ya – gimme a chance to get my breath back," he smiled.

"Yeah, sorry Jo – I just didn't expect to see you again.'

"No, I didn't expect to see you either. How long you got left anyway?"

"Nearly three weeks – nineteen days to be exact."

"Yeah? I wish that was me," he said, looking round the dorm.

"Yours'll come soon enough, Jo – it don't take long in this place. Better get this lot away, yeah – it'll be tea time soon." Pepi helped Jo stow away his gear and sort out the bed-pack.

A short time later the dorm was full of inmates changing out of their work-clothes into their second-best for tea.

Out of the three inmates that Jo had battered, only one remained – Allen. The other two had been discharged during Jo's isolation. Allen spoke to Jo as he passed him by.

"No hard feelin's mate, yeah?"

"No hard feelin's Allen. You done okay by not grassin' on me – it wasn't your fault they put me down there."

Allen breathed easier.

After his integration back into normal routine, life became mundane for Jo. Christmas came and went with hardly a ripple to the usual schedule, and after the two day break Jo found himself back in the recovery shop dismantling radios and T.V.'s. Life was so boring, he wished he was back in the segregation unit, pumping iron, increasing his strength and stamina.

But Jo's life was to change for the better though, because two weeks later, after completing a red circuit in near record time, he was offered the job of gym orderly.

The job meant that Jo would be responsible for keeping the gym clean and the shower and changing areas clean, and for setting out the gym for circuit training. It meant that he would spend the whole day, apart from mealtimes, in the gymnasium.

He became exempt from all drill practice and parades and all his energy was cycled into the running of the gym. He cleared away the apparatus each day then cleaned the gym from top to bottom. When he'd finished all the cleaning, he re-set the mats and the equipment in readiness for the following day's training sessions. Any spare time he had was used to improve his already impressive times on the red circuit. Other times were used at trying to master the techniques of the parallel bars. When he could walk the length of them on his hands, Jo knew he had mastered them.

The only time Jo relaxed the self-imposed assault on himself was on association when he played chess with Pepi. During the three weeks leading up to Pepi's discharge, they played thirty seven games. Pepi winning nineteen, Jo thirteen and five drawn. Pep was a good player for one so young and Jo learned a few new tactics from him. When he was finally released Jo was sorry to see him go and hoped his own time would come soon.

It did come soon, just as Pepi had promised it would. Before long, Jo could see the end of it looming just round the corner. During the time leading up to his discharge Jo came within forty-three seconds of equalling the record set for the red circuit. What was it the Governor had said when he first arrived, thought Jo, – a career hellbent on violent encounters – well, if that was true, then Haslar was the perfect training centre.

For the last week of his sentence, Jo asked the P.T.I. if he could transfer to the garden party, to add a little colour to his face and breathe fresh clean air after tasting the continuous odour of sweating bodies. He readily agreed.

While pottering about in the garden shed, Jo had time for reflection.

Although, initially, he felt anger and frustration at having his freedom taken from him, he held no lasting thoughts of retribution against those who took it, and with his frame now honed to perfection, he was quite satisfied with the swap – after all, he thought, what was five lost months in exchange for a perfect body.

*

Jo was finally discharged on a cold Tuesday morning in early April. The sky was dark and rain poured down as he stepped out through the half-gate. A chill wind added to the gloomy day.

But the wind and rain didn't bother Jo because a few yards away was Danny, sitting in his old Ford pick-up. Jo's face lit up when he saw him. "Hey, Danny boy!"

"Jo!" Danny leaned across the opened the passenger door and Jo jumped in out of the weather. "Well, how was it then? You're looking pretty good, man –"

"Yeah, I feel pretty good too – get ya mits round them!" said Jo, flexing his arm.

"Fuck me – put on some muscle ain't ya."

"Yeah – like a gladiator school in there. All they do all day is train you up!"

"Yeah? Wouldn't mind some of that meself." laughed Danny.

"It wasn't **that** good, Dan. Anyway, get me away from here, James – oh, hang on a minute –" Jo got out of the truck and looked up and down the road. There was a lone screw making his way towards them, about fifty yards away. Jo nipped smartly across to the gates, unzipped his fly, and urinated, guiding the spray as high up as he could before returning to the truck. "That's better – now, are you gonna get me away from here before I'm arrested or what!" They both laughed as Danny slammed his foot down, leaving twelve feet of blue smoke hanging in the air. As they passed the screw, Jo gave him a mock salute with one hand and a middle finger with the other.

While they drove to Portsmouth, Jo gave Danny a running commentary of his time inside, reliving every event. By the time they reached the flat, Danny probably knew as much about detention as Jo did.

Later, when he saw Freddie and Blondie he told the stories again, and then again, until the novelty of his release dissipated and Haslar paled in his memory.

Jo and Christine continued their courtship, deciding between them to hold the marriage over to the following year, giving them ample time to save for a deposit on a house maybe, and save too, for any lean times that may lay ahead.

In his absence, the troubles on the wharf had finally been settled and now all the workforce were employed on a union ticket. Jo quickly secured one, partly because of his past association with the wharf but mainly because of his friendship with one of the stewards of the union.

With them both now working, Christine and Jo were managing to save a fair amount each month, and with the occasional boost Jo gave their bottom drawer when he had a touch at the Half-Moon, they were ahead of their intended monthly target. They saw each other most evenings but only ventured out occasionally, preferring instead to stay in and listen to Christine's ever increasing collection of records.

Jo still went out with the boys at weekends though, but since his release from Haslar, had managed to stay clear of any major trouble. He'd been involved in one or two minor skirmishes, but nothing serious and nothing that bought him to the attention of plod – and that's how Jo wanted to keep it. If he was convicted again on an assault charge, it wouldn't be a few months of detention, it would be prison. The thought of a lengthy prison sentence kept Jo well in check – until that was, one cold January night nearly ten months after his release from Haslar.

It started off just like any other Friday night with Jo, Danny, and Blondie all enjoying a drink in a pub called The Tramways. Freddie had planned to join them after they hit the Borough Arms. Around eight o'clock, just as they were about to leave, an old friend of Danny's came in and joined them at the bar.

"Hello, Dan – long time no see."

"Oh, 'allo Bob, how ya doin'?"

"Yeah, not too bad – you fancy a drink?"

"Er, well –" Danny turned to Jo and Blondie. "Shall we have another one here – this is an old mate, Bob."

"Yeah, if ya like – I'll have a bottle of brown," said Jo.

"And I'll have a pint," said Blondie, knocking back the last dregs in his glass.

Bob was a seaman in the merchant navy, home on leave after a three month stint aboard a cargo ship. He was free and easy in manner and soon began telling stories about life at sea, much to the amusement of the boys.

After a few more pints, Jo decided it was time for pastures new and knocked back the last inch of beer in his glass. Bob said he had his car outside and offered to drive them if they fancied it. They all agreed and after leaving the pub, they all piled into his nice, new, Austin Cambridge.

As they went to pull away, a car came up behind them, tooting madly at the way Bob had pulled out prematurely from the kerb. Bob braked hard but as the car passed them, Bob's new Cambridge suffered the loss of its offside mirror.

Instead of stopping to exchange details, the car sped off, its four occupants jeering and shouting as it went. Bob was enraged after realising the damage to his mirror and set off after them in hot pursuit.

With speeds reaching seventy miles an hour, Jo began to feel uneasy and urged Bob to call off the chase. When he didn't respond, Jo began to get angry.

Eventually, they caught up with the car, a Ford Consul, when it suddenly stopped on an isolated stretch of road just short of the seafront. Bob jumped out of his car and made his way towards the Consul, parked about ten yards in front. As he approached, three young men got out and moved towards him.

"Looks like he's got trouble, Jo" said Danny.

"Fuck 'im – he nearly got us killed getting to 'em – now let's see what he can do."

"I'll have to help him," said Danny, opening the car door.

By the time Danny made the ten yards, his mate was taking a beating from two of the men – and Danny looked like he was going to be next. Blondie left the car and went to join the affray.

It was a mistake.

Blondie had been drinking heavily, much more than Danny and Jo, and was knocked almost unconscious without throwing a single punch. Danny was still okay and well holding his own until, suddenly, all three of them turned on him.

By the time Jo reached him, he'd already taken more than a few blows. When he saw Danny go down, Jo steamed into the three men with manic rage and, armed with a short club, he soon had two of them cowering in defeat. Suddenly, Jo was punched hard on the side of the face by the fourth occupant of the car who had crept up on Jo's blind side. He tried giving Jo another, but Jo saw it coming and ducked low, giving him a huge left hook as he came up. Then two of the thugs began to run. Jo saw them and gave chase, finally cornering them when they ran into a blind alley. It was too narrow for them to double back past Jo, and he battered them both until they were laying flat out on the cold paving-slabs.

Jo returned to the car and jumped in the back seat. He saw the other two, who had started the affray, slumped up against their car nursing their wounds. After Jo's initial assault on them, Danny, and Blondie when he'd recovered, had finished them off. Danny, Blondie, and Bob got back in the car.

"Get this fuckin' heap movin'!" shouted Jo. Bob fumbled with the ignition but soon had the Cambridge speeding away from the carnage.

"You fuckin' mother! Why didn't you leave it like I said!?" screamed Jo. "If I'm nicked over this I'll be away forever!"

"Why should you be nicked – they started it didn' they?" said Bob. "Besides, they deserved it for takin' off my fuckin' wing-mirror –"

"Stop the motor – stop the fuckin' motor!" shouted Jo.

Bob slammed on the brakes and the car screeched to a halt. Jo leapt out and wrenched open the driver's door, pulling Bob out of his seat. "Listen you fuckin' half-wit, I done those two in the alley real bad – when I say if I'm nicked I'm in trouble I mean it! It's a certainty they'll need hospital treatment. Now, if anyone's got your number and you're pulled in, you better pray that I'm not implicated. If I am, I promise you I'll take out both your eyes. Now, get back in the car and drive towards Landport lively!"

While Bob drove them back towards the city-centre, Jo had already decided what he was going to do. When they reached the top of Lake Road, Jo told Bob to pull over.

"Right, now listen – I'm gonna fuck off. If you're pulled by old bill over this, you didn't see me after we left The Tramways, okay. I hope you ain't but I can't afford to take any chances – is that alright with you Dan, Blond?"

"No problem, Jo."

"No me," said Blondie.

"Better make sure your mate really understands, Danny. I don't want to end up doin' bird because some mug who couldn't even have a row chased after four geezers. I'll see you back at the flat later. See ya later Blond."

Jo left the car and made his way to Christine's, just a few hundred yards from where he was. With a bit of luck, she would be his alibi if things turned out for the worse.

Jo soon made the short distance to Christine's and rang the bell. Christine opened the door. "Jo! What are you doing here? I didn't expect to see you tonight."

"No, well – I just didn't fancy seeing the boys that's all," he said as calmly as he could. Jo poked his head round the door of the living room and said hello to Christine's mum and dad – and noted the time. It was nine-twenty.

After spending a few minutes in the bathroom checking himself over, he joined Christine in the bedroom and stayed with her until after midnight.

Jo arrived back at the flat about twelve-thirty. Danny was cooking himself a light meal.

"Alright, Jo?"

"Yeah, I'm okay – what about you – you look a bit sore round the chops. Let's have a look at you." Jo held Danny to the light and examined his face. He had a few bruises and a nasty little cut under his eye, but was otherwise okay. Jo checked his own face in the mirror – nothing. One of them had managed to give Jo a punch but it wasn't hard enough to cause his skin to bruise and there was no visible signs that he'd been in a fight. Surprisingly, even his fists were relatively free of any tell-tale signs. Even so, Jo decided to high-tail to Freddie's – just in case. He dialled his number and waited.

"Hello, Freddie?"

"Yeah – is that you, Jo?"

"Yeah – you fancy some company?"

"Yeah sure – you in trouble again?"

"Well, I could be, Fred – I just don't wanna hang around and find out that's all."

"You'd better come up then."

"Yeah, cheers mate – I'll see you in a little while."

Jo cradled the phone and began to pack his holdall. He turned to Danny. "You think anything is gonna come out of this, Dan? I really pasted those mothers in the alley – there was claret all over the place. Jesus, I can't believe what I've done. You reckon your mate will be sound if plod gets involved?"

"Yeah, I think so. I told him good that if he grasses he'll be a dead man. I reckon he got the message."

"I hope to God you're right – but I'm fuckin' off just in case. If anything **does** come of it, I'm off for good." Jo pulled a couple of tenners from his pocket. "Here's some rent money just in case I ain't back for a while. I'll give you a ring tomorrow."

"Yeah, right – listen, I'm really sorry about tonight, but I had to try an' help him out, Jo –"

"Yeah I know, it wasn't your fault – I just wish I'd have got to 'em sooner. You was doin' okay 'till they all started on you," laughed Jo. He slapped his mate on the back. "Anyway I'm off. I ain't takin' no chances hanging about down here."

"Right – catch ya later."

"See ya later, Dan." Jo picked up the holdall and left the flat.

As he went over Ports Bridge Jo noticed that the tide was out again and he began to wonder if someone had blocked up the harbour – or whether it was a bad omen.

After arriving at Freddie's house, Jo began to relax a little. Trina was home from a recent trip abroad and the two of them were out of their minds on dope. Within fifteen minutes, Jo too was out of it. Soon, Trina went to bed, leaving Jo free to tell Freddie his latest problem. Halfway through the story, Freddie suddenly burst out laughing. "Fuckin' hell, Jo – you don't mess about do ya? You bash fuck out of a couple of geezers then chase after two more and bash fuck out of them as well!" Freddie was in fits of laughter and talking non-stop. Jo had never seen him so wrecked. Freddie was laughing so much, Jo couldn't help but laugh himself.

"No wonder they call you Jo Waterloo – marching into battle –"

"– It ain't funny, Fred," said Jo, almost pissing himself trying not to laugh.

"I know," said Freddie, nearly doubled-up, "but I was just thinkin' about you with a sword in ya hand in charge of all them Romans – Tribune Marcellus Sullivan ain't ya, head of the Royal Pretoria Guard and champion of the arena, holder of the Mexican Cross –"

"The Mexican Cross? I thought we were in Rome. You've gone completely off your trolley, Fred." But Jo was in fits of laughter as well, imagining himself at the head of an army. "Yeah, but not a Roman army – I wanna be with Spartacus and his little mob –"

"Yeah, you'd be alright with him – gladiator wasn't he?" said Freddie, still in fits.

"Yeah, but I don't want to end up like him though – fuck being crucified!" The thought of crucifixion brought Jo down to earth for a moment, because if plod found out about his latest performance, they **would** crucify him.

"Anyway, I'm off to bed," said Freddie with a glint in his eye. "Trina might be waitin' for me. See ya in the mornin'."

"Yeah, see ya later Freddie-boy."

Jo stretched out on the settee and gradually slipped into a drug-induced sleep. Subconsciously, he began to torture himself...*numbers kept ringing up on a cash register, but instead of pound signs they were abbreviated year signs...5yrs...10yrs... 15yrs...then they changed into little boxes, little rooms, minute prison cells with just enough room for a body to lay down in...a coffin...lots of coffins, rows and rows of them all painted with a bright red cross and every time the cash register was pressed a coffin sprang up and on the coffin was a picture of himself, blood running from his eyes and his ears...*

Suddenly, Jo found himself surrounded by several police officers. They had crashed in through the front door and were now arresting him for grievous bodily harm.

"How the fuck did you know I was here?" said Jo.

"Never mind that now, Sullivan – you're under arrest."

Freddie came charging down the stairs as Jo was being escorted from the house. "What's going on?" he protested. The police officers ignored Freddie and led Jo away. "See you later, Freddie," he shouted.

Everything seemed to be happening in slow motion. When he got outside, Jo saw a police van and heard the sound of paws scratching on metal. Dogs? Just as he was about to be placed in a police car, Jo saw his chance. The plod escorting him had relaxed the grip on his arm, and Jo made a run for it.

Dressed in shirt-sleeve order and running like a bat out of hell, Jo soon found himself on the marshland separating the sea from the harbour road.

Portchester was only a small town and Freddie's house was on the outskirts, only a short distance from where buildings ceased to exist.

He wished he could have gone in the opposite direction where forests and farmyards would have given him more cover.

Jo kept running.

Scattered along the harbour road, just above the high water mark, were various sheds and small buildings, used by fishermen to stow their tackle. A few hundred yards further along was a huge scrap-yard and Jo decided to seek refuge in among the rotting hulls.

He could hear voices getting closer, blue flashing lights were everywhere. He then heard barking dogs. They were closing in on him. If he could just make it to the scrap-yard, he would be in with a chance.

Underfoot, the ground was becoming softer as he edged nearer the water-line, distancing himself from the harbour road. With the small bushes and the couch-grass and with the undulating contours of the beach, Jo still had cover and knew he couldn't be seen from the road. They could probably hear him though as his footsteps squelched on the soft mud.

The scrap-yard was just ahead, and soon, Jo found himself standing on the wrong side of a wire fence. He quickly scaled it and landed on the firmer ground of the scrap-yard.

All round him were the skeletons of boats, countless numbers of them, rotting, waiting their turn to be devoured by the breaker's torch, or until time and the elements eroded them.

As Jo lost himself in the maze of the yard, he heard dogs barking at the perimeter fence. They had found his entry point. While furthering himself from the fence, nipping in between the alleys of boats, he saw two police cars pull up to the closed gates. Soon they would be in the scrap-yard, and with the dogs to aid them, they would soon hunt him down.

As he edged further in, Jo suddenly came across an old-fashioned pike – a long handled pole with a barbed metal point – and decided to keep it for protection against the dogs in case they attacked him.

Jo moved closer to the water-line. Some of the boats were moored further out on the mud-flats and he wondered if he could try and secure his escape across the mud and swim the harbour to safety – but that was impossible – the cold water would kill him within minutes.

Jo then came across the remains of the World War II submarine that he'd seen so often from the harbour road, and decided to board her. Just as he was about to, a German Shepherd came charging towards him, teeth bared. Jo turned as the dog was about to pounce, and thrusted the pike deep into its chest, killing it instantly. A second dog came for Jo almost as quickly and unexpectedly as the first and was disposed of in the same swift manner. Now, with the dogs out of the way, the police would be blind and Jo started to look for a way to escape.

He was at the far end of the scrap-yard now, a fence hemming him in extended way out past the high-tide mark. Jo didn't want to risk the fence because of the noise. Just to the left of the fence, at its furthest point, were two cabin cruisers, moored together with anchor ropes trailing down to the mud. Jo guessed the distance between the boats and the end of the fence at five or six yards, and he wondered if he could board one of them without detection.

To help in his plan, Jo quickly scanned the yard until he found two planks of wood. He would use them to lay on the mud if it became too soft to walk on. He moved steadily along the side of the rusting sub. Its huge hull was leaning over and Jo prayed that it wouldn't suddenly lean any more and crush him. He passed under the stern, grasping the propeller to steady himself against the clinging mud. The short planks he was carrying were hampering his passage but he eventually made the fence and edged his way along to the end of it.

By the time he had reached the end of the fence, the mud had claimed both of his shoes.

He looked across to the cabin cruisers. The distance between them and the fence was more than he thought. Instead of the few yards that he'd first guessed, it was more like fifteen or twenty and he was beginning to feel apprehensive at the thought of crossing the mud.

He looked out across the flats and caught the sheen of the water as it gradually began to fill the harbour. Another hour and the tide would be in.

Jo looked behind him. He could still see the flashing arcs of light as the police continued their search. But they couldn't see him, twenty or thirty yards out on the mud-flats, partly hidden by the last concrete post holding the fence. As he stood in the mud he began to sink and had to keep shifting his legs every few moments to stop himself becoming trapped.

Jo was unsure what to do. The small cruisers looked inviting but the distance in between was giving him second thoughts. The alternative behind him though, was even worse, and with the thought of languishing in a prison cell, he laid the first plank down on the mud.

Jo crouched to his knees and moved along the plank, then placed the second plank out in front. He then pulled the first plank free of the mud and repeated the process.

About half-way across it started to get harder. When he placed the short plank out in front and crawled onto it, the one behind was becoming harder to pull free from the clinging mud.

Jo looked up to see how much further he had to go – about ten feet, he guessed. He looked out across the harbour. The water was coming in fast. He edged his way a little closer to the cruisers, his heart pounding. Suddenly, while trying to release one of the planks, he slipped into the mud. A massive surge of adrenalin swept through his body as the mud oozed past his knees. As he struggled to free himself the mud liquified and he sank further in.

Jo began to panic. Soon, the mud was oozing past his stomach – then his chest. When it started creeping past his neck, Jo screamed out. "No! Oh no! No!"

"Jo! Jo! You're okay – you're having a dream," said Freddie, shaking Jo by the shoulder.

"That was too much – fuckin' good stuff for nightmares innit, that gear."

Freddie laughed. "They weren't gonna take ya head off again were they?"

"No, not this time, Fred – this one was a little slower."

Jo reached for one of Freddie's cigarettes, lit it, and inhaled deeply.

"I thought you packed up smokin' fags?"

"I think I've just started again – anyway, what you doin' up, I thought you'd gone t' bed?"

"I wanted something to eat, then I heard you moanin' n' groanin' so I thought I'd come in and save ya. You fancy another joint?"

"Fucksake Fred – I'm still stoned now."

"Well I'm goin' back t' bed then – see ya in the mornin'."

Jo finished his cigarette, then he too went to bed.

After a restless night, Jo got up around noon. The first thing he did was to phone Danny. When he didn't get a reply, Jo began to feel uneasy but tried not to show it when he joined Freddie in the kitchen.

"Alright Jo – you want somethin' to eat. I'm doin' some eggs n' bacon if you want it?"

"Yeah I wouldn't mind some, Fred – I'm bloody starvin'."

"Yeah, it's the gear that does that – you want some toast?"

"Sounds good to me."

Jo made himself comfortable and scanned the morning paper while Freddie prepared breakfast. After they had eaten, Freddie began to skin up a joint.

"Jesus Fred, you don't waste any time do ya?"

"If you're gonna fly you may as well start early that's what I always say," he laughed. Jo smiled and watched him put the joint together. A few minutes later they began to get stoned.

Half-way through the joint the phone rang. It was Danny and he wanted to speak to Jo urgently. He grabbed the receiver. "Hello, Dan? What's wrong?"

"Jo, I – well, it's bad news I think – they know we done those geezers – well, I think they do –"

"What's happened then?"

"Well, I nipped round to see Bob but he wasn't in so I nipped in the Moon. About twenty minutes later Blondie's missus phoned – he's been arrested."

"Who, Blondie?"

"Yeah –"

"Oh no, they're probably after us as well then. Where are you now?"

"I'm out Southsea – what we gonna do, Jo?"

"Fuck knows. If I'm nicked over this I've had it – I might shoot off somewhere – you fancy coming with me?"

"Yeah why not – it don't smell too good round here does it – where would we go then?"

"I've got an idea where – I'll have to make a phone call first and get back to ya. What's the number where you are?"

Danny gave Jo the number and they both hung up. Jo sank down in a chair and held his head, trying to think what to do. If he stayed, sooner or later he would be arrested, and if he skipped town – then what? And Christine, what about Christine…?

Jo finally came to a decision and asked Freddie if he could use the phone for an outside call. He dialled the operator. "Oh, yes – could you connect me to an outside number please – yes, it's Sevenoaks 49382. Yes, Sevenoaks, Kent. Thanks." Jo waited a few moments for the connection.

"Oh, hello? Mum? It's me, Jo – how are ya then?"

"Jo! How are you – why haven't you called me lately?"

"Well, you know what it's like, ma – I kept meaning to."

"Yes, I know. How are you anyway – looking after yourself?"

"Yeah, I'm okay ma – listen, I was wondering if I could come up for a few days – me and Danny?"

"Yes of course you can, you know you don't have to ask. Are you in trouble again, son?"

Jo detected concern in her voice. "No – I'm not in any trouble, ma – I fancied getting away for a while, that's all. Is that okay with you?"

"When shall I expect you then?"

"I thought I would come up today if that's alright?"

"Yes of course it is – you be careful driving up –"

"Yes I will – listen, I gotta go now, I'll see you in a few hours okay – 'bye then."

"Yes, 'bye son."

Jo cradled the phone. "That's it then, Fred."

"Are you off then?"

"Yeah, I'm not hanging around here waitin' to be nicked."

"No I don't blame ya. I'd be on my toes as well if I was you. D'you want to take some gear with ya – if you get captured and can't have a smoke you can eat it and get the same effect – you want some?"

"Yeah okay – can I use the phone again? I'll have to ring Danny and see if he wants to come with me."

"Yeah help y'self – you don't have to ask." Jo dialled the Southsea number. "Hello, Dan – it's me. Listen, I've just phoned my mother and she said we could go up there. She's got a couple of spare rooms we can use – you fancy it?"

"Yeah why not – where does she live?"

"Sevenoaks. It's about a two hour drive. Listen, I've got to go to the flat an' pick up my gear – you want me to pick you up there or where you are now?"

"I'll meet you at the flat."

"Alright, I'll see you there in about an hour, okay? Oh, and Dan – make sure there's no old bill about. See ya in a minute."

"Yeah."

After Jo had gathered up his gear he turned to Freddie.

"Well Fred, what can I say – I don't know when I'll be back –"

"Here, don't forget this," Freddie handed Jo a chunk of cannabis. "You might need that."

"Yeah thanks Fred. Right, I'll be off then – take care of ya'self."

"Yeah, see ya later soldier."

Jo picked up the holdall and left the house.

As he headed for Pompey, the huge scrap-yard that had featured in his nightmare loomed towards him. He looked out across the harbour and noticed that the tide was in for a change, and he took the sight of the water breaking high on the beach as a good omen.

While he was driving, Jo began to think of his mother and his family. His parents had divorced when he was fourteen years old. His father still lived in Portsmouth, and Jo saw him now and again, but his mother had moved to Sevenoaks, setting up in business running a small cafe. She had married again and Jo's stepfather, Henry, helped with the running of the cafe. Jo hadn't seen much of Henry and he didn't know him all that well, but if his mother was happy with him then that was okay with Jo.

Jo's mother was a fine cook, and with her years of experience had turned a once quiet cafe into a thriving little business. Above the cafe were two furnished rooms and a bathroom, now unused, and Jo was hoping he and Danny could stay there for a while. His mother and Henry, and his younger sister, Pauline, now lived in a three-bedroomed flat, just a few minutes away from the cafe. Jo also had an older sister, Irene, and she lived in Sevenoaks too, with her husband John.

Charlie, Jo's older and only brother, usually lived with the family in the flat but at the moment he was working in Birmingham on long contract for a shop-fitting company. Since his parents divorce, Jo had seen his brother once.

When Jo pulled into the wharf road Danny's pick-up was parked outside of the flat. After nipping into the corner shop for tobacco, Jo joined him inside and began packing his gear. Danny had already packed his two cases.

Just as he was about to clear the bathroom, Jo's heartbeat raced into overdrive when four burly police officers came crashing through the front door of the flat. Within fifteen minutes Jo found himself in an interview room at the Central Police Station. Before long, two men came into the room.

"Right Sullivan – I'm Detective Sergeant Willis and this is Detective Constable Walker. You know why you are here of course."

"No – no I don't."

"We think you do. Where were you around nine o'clock last night?"

"Why do you want to know?"

"Just tell us where you were," said Walker. Jo guessed he was the heavy. "Why should I? I haven't done anything."

"So you've got nothing to worry about – now where were you?"

Jo didn't like the look of Walker. He was a big man with ruddy cheeks. His nose had small purple veins running all over it, and the way his neck bulged out over the collar of his shirt made Jo feel sick. Because of his size and appearance he looked intimidating, but Jo had already made up his mind that all this mother was going to get out of him was frustration.

"Am I being charged with anything?"

"Depends what you tell us, Jo," said Willis, using the softly, softly, approach. If you weren't involved then you won't be charged with anything."

"Involved in what?"

"Don't try an' be smart, Sullivan," sneered Walker.

"I'm not trying to be smart – I just wanna know why I'm here that's all."

"Were you out Southsea sea-front about nine o'clock last night? You mate Blondie said you were."

"No, and no he didn't."

"Where were you then?" asked Walker.

"I ain't tellin' ya – in fact I ain't answering any questions –"

"Why you cheeky –"

"– until I've had a word with my solicitor," finished Jo, evenly.

"So you want a brief then, Jo – must have something to hide I'd say."

"I've got nothing to hide – I just ain't answering any questions that's all. That's my right isn't it?"

"Yes, but –"

"But nothing. If I'm not required to answer, that's it, I ain't answering."

"You know we won't be able to give you bail if you don't co-operate with us?"

"I guessed as much."

"We'll leave you to think about it for a few minutes."

The two men left the room. Jo started to roll a cigarette then suddenly remembered the cannabis that Freddie had given him, and hastily tucked it into his Y-fronts. Jo had forgotten all about it. He began to feel better knowing he could be stoned the whole weekend if they kept him in. With dope in his possession, the police had lost the remote chance they had that he would weaken and make a voluntary statement.

Jo began to wonder why detectives were investigating the case, and why he wasn't already being charged. He started to think that maybe they weren't too sure about his involvement. He couldn't tell them he was at Christine's because he didn't get there until nine-twenty, and he needed her to say he was there by nine o'clock latest. If he left it for a while it would be easier to convince her that he **was** there by nine. Either way, he wasn't going to say one word that might harm the slim chance he had of getting out of any charges they might bring. If it meant being held at the Central for a day or two, he could handle that, and with cannabis to take his mind…

A few minutes later Willis and Walker were back.

"Well Jo," said Willis, "are you going to make life easier for yourself and tell us what happened last night? It would go a lot better for you if we could say you were helpful to us – and we might be able to release you. What do you say, Jo."

"Well, after careful consideration, and because of your refusal to tell me what all this is about, I have come to the conclusion it would be in my best interest to remain silent in case I incriminate myself in matters not relevant to your present enquiries – how's that?"

Walker started clapping his hands in a low, deliberate manner. "How long did that take to put together smart boy?"

"No time at all, plod – came right off the top of my head."

"What did you call me?" Walker moved towards Jo and Jo quickly stood up, causing the chair to topple over. Willis intervened. "Take it easy, Jo. Nothing's going to happen to you here."

"Tell him to keep away from me." Willis nodded to Walker and he resumed his position leaning up against the wall.

Jo picked up the chair and sat down as Willis tried again to get him to talk. "Jo, we know what happened last night, and we know it wasn't your fault. We think it was probably self-defence so if you give us your side of the story, charges might not be laid and we could probably let you out in a couple of hours. Come on Jo, give us your version so we can help you."

Jo wasn't fooled. "I've got nothing to say – I don't even know why I'm here."

"It looks like we'll have to keep you here until we get this sorted out – could be quite a while if you can't help us. You can write a statement yourself if that would help."

Jo remained tenacious. "I'm sorry, but I've got nothing to say until I've had a word with my brief. Are you going to ring him for me?"

"We'll see," said Willis. A moment later, the two detectives left the room again.

After they had gone, Jo began to think about his position. He soon came to the conclusion that, although they probably guessed his involvement, they didn't have an airtight case and they needed his own statement to cement their suspicions.

After leaving Jo to stew for thirty minutes, Willis and Walker returned to the room. Willis opened the dialogue.

"Right Jo, this is the position. Last evening four men were assaulted and we have reason to believe that you may have been involved along with Michael Clark, Daniel Fowler, and Robert Jones. They have now been charged. What we would like to do now is put you on an identification parade. Are you prepared to do this?"

"Yeah I don't mind," said Jo. He caught the short glance the two detectives gave each other as they left the room yet again.

Jo began to wonder about the I.D. parade. Blondie and Danny, and Bob, couldn't have said anything or he would have been charged long before now. Jo guessed all they had was the chance that he'd be identified on a line-up. After another thirty minute wait in the interview room, Jo was taken to the charge room. Willis was flicking through some papers. "Well Jo, because of certain problems we can't go ahead with the I.D. parade at this time. What we would like you to do is report back here at two-thirty tomorrow afternoon. You will be released on police bail until then. If you fail to show a warrant will be issued for your arrest and you would probably be kept in custody. You understand Jo?"

"Yeah sure," he said, trying to hide his delight.

"Right, you will have to sign some paperwork and then you can go – but Jo, don't think this is the end of it. We think you were involved and if you're picked out on the line you will be charged." Jo was kept another twenty minutes then released on police bail.

Jo couldn't believe his luck as he skipped out of the door and down the steps of the Central Police Station. It was half-past-six when he found himself on the street again. He decided to head straight for the flat and see Danny. Blondie and Danny had been released on bail and Jo was anxious to find out what had been said. He jumped in a taxi at the rank and was home within a few minutes. Danny was in the kitchen making some tea. "Alright Jo – have they charged you?"

"No, not yet – I'm out on police bail. I've got to report back tomorrow and go on a line-up. You've been charged ain't ya?"

"Yeah – two counts of G.B.H. and one A.B.H."

"Jesus – how did they know you an' Blondie were there?"

"They arrested Blondie 'cos one of the geezers knew 'im."

"Yeah?"

"Yeah, and we think they got Bob 'cos someone got his number plate."

"How come they charged you then?"

"Well, I told them more or less what happened – except tellin' 'em about you – I thought it was about the only chance I had with Blondie and Bob being nicked. If I tried to deny it we'd have no chance of a defence – this way, at least we can say they were the ones that started it, and they were, and if we can prove it, well, it won't look so bad if we're done will it? I told 'em Blondie was more or less knocked out straightaway and I was just helpin' Bob 'cos he was bein' done. But they was more interested in who done the two in the alley. I said I was by the car and didn't know anything about it, so did Blondie and Bob."

"They probably think that was me – hey, I'm sorry you've been nicked Dan, but thanks for keeping me out of it. Where's Blondie now?"

"Home I s'pose. I said I'd meet him in the Kingstone later."

"Yeah? I'll probably see you in there then – first, I've got to see Christine and **remind** her that I was round by nine o'clock. When you gotta go up?"

"Wednesday ten o'clock."

"It won't be dealt with then though will it?"

"Dunno."

"I doubt it – you better sort ya'self out a brief. Give Harrison a ring on Monday. Oh, if I ain't out of the Central by tea-time can you give him a ring for me – they might try 'an keep me in if I don't say anything."

"Good job you didn't say anything – you'd have dropped ya'self right in it if you had 'cos we all said you left us at the Tramways."

"Yeah, nice one Dan." Jo grabbed Danny by the neck and gave him a shake.

After a wash and shave, Jo donned a fresh set of clothes and left the flat for Christine's. He hadn't planned on seeing her tonight but he needed to in order to secure his alibi.

He arrived at half-past seven and rang the bell. Bill answered the door. "Oh, hello Jo – come in. Christine's not here at the moment though – was she expecting you?"

"Er, no – I just wanted to ask her something that's all. Where is she then?"

"I'm not sure Jo. Jackie came round for her about seven and they both went out."

"Okay Bill, I'll see her tomorrow – er, Bill, you wouldn't remember what time I got round here last night would you? I know it was before nine but I'm trying to think exactly what time it was."

"Er, I'm not really sure Jo, I know it was about nine but I couldn't say for sure. Why do you want to know?"

"Well, the thing is Bill, two or three of my mates got into a fight last night and because I sometimes knock around with them the police think I might have been mixed up in it. I told them I was round my girlfriends house but I don't think they believed me."

"I see, well, I know you were here about nine – if they question you again and they still don't believe you were here, tell them to come and see me."

"Thanks Bill. If they do come round, don't tell 'em you've spoken to me about it or they might think I've put you up to it – you know what they're like."

"No, don't worry – I won't say anything."

"Thanks again Bill – oh, 'an please don't say anything to Christine will you – she'll only start worrying."

"No, I won't say anything."

"Thanks – I'll see you tomorrow then."

"Yeah – I'll see you later Jo."

Jo left the flat and headed for the Kingstone Tavern. Before he went much further though, he stopped at a phone box and called his mother, explaining why he wouldn't be visiting after all, and promising he would ring her more often in the future.

Later, in the Kingstone Tavern, Jo met up with Danny and Blondie. Between them, they discussed ceaselessly the events of the past twenty four hours. With Danny's and Blondie's relatively minor convictions, even if they were found guilty, they all agreed that the sentence wouldn't be too severe, a heavy fine coming out favourite.

The following day, at two o'clock sharp, Jo presented himself at the desk of the Central and asked for sergeant Willis. After a short wait he was taken to an interview room. More than half-an-hour later, and after he'd smoked his way through four cigarettes, Willis came in.

"Well Jo," he said, "it seems once again we are unable to proceed with the line-up. We're going to release you again on police bail to reappear here at two o'clock Tuesday afternoon."

"What's the problem then," asked Jo.

"Regretfully, the witness can't make it today. He's assured us he'll be here Tuesday."

After signing a new bail sheet Jo was released. While leaving the station, he began to ponder…

…regretfully, the witness can't make it today…

…the witness can't make it…

…the witness…singular…one witness…our single witness can't make it…

When Jo reported to the station on Tuesday, inexplicably, and without being lined-up on an I.D. parade, he was formally charged with two counts of grievous bodily harm and one count of actual bodily harm.

"What the fuck happened to the I.D. parade then?" he said to Willis.

"We think we have enough evidence without it."

"What evidence? You haven't got any fuckin' evidence and you're not putting me on a line in case I ain't picked out!" screamed Jo.

"It's not like that –"

"Put me on a line then!" insisted Jo.

Willis was getting impatient. "We can't do that at this time – and besides, if you weren't identified the charge would still hold because of other evidence which I am not prepared to discuss. If you weren't mixed up in this you'll get your chance in court. That's all I've got to say on the matter. Now, I'm sticking my neck out and releasing you on police bail to appear in court tomorrow morning. I could hold you, Jo – and if anyone else were in charge they would probably keep you in custody."

"How come you ain't then?"

"Let's just say it's your lucky day shall we."

"Very funny," said Jo, pursing his lips. Jo refrained from giving the detective any abuse in case he suddenly changed his mind on the bail and kept him in custody. Twenty minutes later Jo was released.

Back at the flat, the first thing he did was to book an appointment with his brief. After securing a nine o'clock slot with Mr. Harrison, Jo decided to roll himself a joint in an effort to rid his mind of the worry. He joined three rizlas together, just like he'd seen Freddie do, and spread some tobacco along them. After burning the cannabis, he sprinkled it along the tobacco and rolled it up. With a roach in one end, it was now ready for lighting. Jo looked at it for a few minutes, wondering whether or not to smoke it. If I get **too** stoned, he thought, I might not be able to think straight. With that thought in mind, Jo struck a match and put it to the joint.

Within minutes, Jo began to feel better as the chemical mingled into his brain. Now, instead of the reality of facing a prison sentence, Jo was on the periphery of another world...*here there wasn't any trouble...no pigs to slap you about...no greaseballs to leap at you...no tell-tale tits...cry-babies aren't allowed...*

– please sir, he hit me –

*– oh **did** he –*

– yes –

– I will arrest him –

– does it matter what I done first –

– no of course not –

– will he go to jail –

– yes –

– why –

– because of all those little scratches on your face –

*– oh, it doesn't seem fair somehow – considering we were kicking seven bales of shit out of his mates – oh well, it doesn't really matter I suppose, because where I am now – where the hell **am** I now? Oh yes – just drifting over the Central in a Harrier jet, missiles primed, homing in for the kill…yeah…or better still, let's take this path and glide over a cool mountain where all the land is virgin, sweet and crisp…where the entrance card is a four leaf clover – yes sir – the year 1840…it's the raw west…up against The Rockies and The Rio Grande, carving out a homestead…hey Gringo – why you wearing thee watch when you can't even fuckin' read…?*

Jo suddenly realised he was laughing to himself and he tried lifting his head from the soft arm of the settee, but couldn't because it felt too heavy. He laid it back down then closed his eyes again, his mind drifting…taking him…*back among the concrete and the dark rooms – escaping now, on a dream-wave that's gliding through…taking him, lifting him away from the dark and the gloom up into the high cirrocumulus…flying…a hundred miles an hour, following the contours of the land – about an inch above it…across the oceans and the open fields, standing on the edge of the world…hey honey, come with me – climb up on my back and we will go together – but hold on tight though, I don't want to lose you, not now…*

Jo heard a ringing in his ears. The sound was alien to his present wavelength and he tried to shake away the hideous sound, until he realised it wasn't coming from his head. He looked up and zoomed in on the phone, then moved slowly towards it.

"Hello?"

"Hello, Jo – it's me, Chris –"

"Hi babe –"

"Are you coming round only it's nearly half-past seven?"

"Half seven! Jesus, I must have fallen asleep – give me a chance to have a quick wash an' I'll be straight round."

"Tch, trust you – I'll see you in a minute then."

"Yeah, I won't be long." They broke the connection and Jo went to the bathroom to freshen up, wondering where all the hours had gone.

He arrived at Christine's about ten-to-eight and stayed with her until after midnight. She never guessed that he was still half-stoned.

At 9:00am the following morning, Jo met with Harrison and discussed the case in detail. After giving him a full account, and with Christine's father willing to testify supporting Jo's alibi, Harrison was confident that Jo should not have been charged and advised him to elect for trial by jury. There was only one problem – the three others on the indictment would automatically go to trial along with him. Harrison said he would talk to them later and convince them that a trial by jury was the best course to take. When he did speak to them, they readily agreed to take his advice.

At 10:15 Jo, Danny, Blondie and Bob, were all standing in the dock of the magistrates court. Jo was relieved to see that the chairman was not the same one that had sent him to Haslar nearly a year before. If it came to a fight to secure bail, it would be better to be unknown to the bench.

After the charges were read out and a choice of venue offered them, they were all released on bail in their own recognisance in the sum of one hundred pounds. Jo, in particular, was more than happy with the ease of securing bail. With his previous form, and with the current charges he was on, a visit to Winchester would not have come as a surprise. When the bail sheets were signed they were told to attend the Quarter Sessions for trial in six weeks time, then released. After leaving the court-house, the four of them still couldn't work out why Jo had suddenly been charged.

In the weeks leading up to the trial, Jo carried on life as usual. Work was still plentiful on the wharf and he and Christine continued to save on a regular basis. Although arrangements were being made for their forth-coming marriage, Jo still hadn't plucked up the courage to tell Christine about his impending trial. He finally confessed to her just a couple of weeks before he was due in court. She was devastated. She couldn't believe that Jo had withheld such a serious matter. After many tears, Jo gradually convinced her that he wasn't mixed up with the assaults and had been charged only because of his association with the boys.

Jo mentioned the possibility perhaps, of the two of them leaving

Portsmouth after they were married, and start afresh somewhere else. The idea appealed to Christine, and they began to plan ahead with the idea in mind.

Before long the trial date had come, and Jo, along with the three others, surrendered themselves to the court. The trial began at ten-thirty and after the jury were sworn in and the charges read out, the prosecution outlined their case. "Members of the jury, the case before you is a simple and straightforward account of various assaults that we the prosecution – say culminated into assaults of a grievous nature. Let me lead you into the facts – facts, I might add, that will hardly be disputed by the defence. The four accused were in a car, an Austin Cambridge, which pulled away from the kerb into the path of a Ford Consul. The driver of the Consul was forced to swerve in order to prevent a collision and in doing so, caused damage to the off-side wing-mirror of the Cambridge. The Consul failed to stop. That in itself, is an offence but it is not the matter of this court. The accused then sped after the Consul until they caught up with it when it pulled over to the side of the road. The occupants of the Cambridge, the accused, then left their car and approached the occupants of the Consul when they then, systematically and without quarter, assaulted them, causing varying degrees of bodily harm. Those then, are the facts. And these –" he continued, as he took hold of a package, "are the photographs of the said assaults."

The Q.C. handed the usher a set of photographs and he in turn handed them to the foreman of the jury. The judge was given a set and so were the defendants.

As soon as Jo saw the photographs he knew Danny and Blondie were on their way to a prison sentence. Bob was going too but Jo didn't care about him, he was just a ship passing in the night and if he was left rotting somewhere for a thousand years that would be okay with Jo. But for his friends he cared, and by admitting that they were involved were almost certain to be found guilty, irrespective of whether they started the fight or not – and a plea of self-defence would be no defence either because of the severity of the injuries.

Jo was the only one of them in with a realistic chance of acquittal, and a pang of guilt came over him as he thought of it. He considered his chances as he cast his eyes over the photographs. He could hardly recognise the faces, hidden almost, in among the multiple cuts and bruises, and he whispered a prayer to his unknown guardian angel.

Jo passed the photographs along and took a quick look at the judge. He was an awesome figure and Jo looked away quickly before he was caught staring at him.

The prosecuting counsel continued. "I would now like to call the first witness for the crown." The usher called for Michael John Wicks. After Wicks had been sworn in, the Q.C. began to question him.

"Is your full name Michael John Wicks?"

"Yes."

"And were you the driver of a Ford Consul bearing the registration mark DDP 519, on the 9th of January this year?"

"Yes."

"Please tell the jury what happened on that evening."

"Well, we was drivin' along and suddenly a car pulled out in front of us. I had to swerve round it and broke his mirror when I passed –"

"Why didn't you stop?"

"Er, well I didn't know I'd done it 'till he told me – then he hit me."

"Until **who** told you, and subsequently hit your, Mr. Wicks?"

"Er, that one – the one on the end."

"Please let it show that the witness has identified Robert Jones. Now Mr. Wicks, please tell the court what happened after you stopped the car."

"Well, I got out of the car and he – Jones, and another one –"

"Can you identify the other man please?"

"Er, yes – the one next to Jones."

"Please let it show that the accused, Clark, has been identified by Mr. Wicks. Please continue."

"Well, er, he said something like – you've broken my fuckin' wing-mirror – then he started punching me."

"Yes, please carry on."

"Then my mates got out of the car and they were beaten up as well."

"Who beat them up?"

"Er, Jones and Clark – and the other two I'spose. I'm not really sure who was hitting who."

"But you **are** sure that you were first attacked by Jones and Clark?"

"Yes."

"Thankyou Mr. Wicks. Please remain where you are."

Jo's counsel was the first of the defence counsels to question Wicks.

"Mr. Wicks, you say Jones and Clark attacked you but isn't it true that Mr. Jones approached your car on his own first, and that you and two of your friends got out of the Consul and confronted him?"

"No."

"Who do you say actually assaulted you?"

"Jones."

"But you said a moment ago it was Jones **and** Clark."

"Well, I know it was Jones – and Clark was with him."

"But as far as you know it was only Jones who hit you?"

"Er, yeah – I know he hit me first."

"What happened after you were hit – were you knocked down?"

"Yes, I was knocked down –"

"By the side of the car?"

"Yes, er, yes –"

"So you couldn't say what was going on after you were knocked down?"

"Er, no but –"

"Thankyou Mr. Wicks. No more questions."

Danny, Blondie and Bob had the one counsel, contrary to advice, and Jo could see already how difficult it was going to be for him to defend each of them individually. He began his cross-examination.

"Mr. Wicks, why did you stop where you did?"

"Er, well, they kept following us and we wondered why so we stopped."

"Did you suspect there might be trouble?"

"Er, no –"

"I suggest that you did, Mr. Wicks, and I suggest that the reason you stopped where you did was because it was an isolated spot and you and your friends were making ready for confrontation – isn't that so Mr. Wicks?"

"No."

"And in fact three of you alighted from the car."

"No – it was just me at first –"

"And the three of you together began to assault Mr. Jones."

"No."

"I have no more questions for this witness m'lud."

The prosecution called their next witness, and the next until all four of them gave their own different versions of the assaults – and each one in turn contradicted the other. As Jo listened to the evidence he became aware that only one of them had positively identified him. Jo's Q.C. had carefully, and with subtlety, isolated him from the other defendants and he was feeling more confident with every passing minute.

When the prosecution called the name of an independent witness, Jo's confidence waned a little. Jo looked round the courtroom to see who the witness was and caught the stare of Walker and Willis. Walker was wearing a cynical grin and Jo felt a twinge of apprehension as the mystery witness swore the oath. The prosecutor began his questions.

"Mr. Hillier, what is your occupation?"

"I'm a taxi driver."

"And were you on duty on the evening of the 9th of January this year?"

"Yes."

"And did you have reason to stop in Queens Terrace on that evening?"

"Yes."

"Please tell the jury what you saw."

"Er, yes. I had to pick up a fare, and as I stopped I saw two men walking away from a Ford Consul and get in a Cambridge."

Jo began to fear the worst as he listened to his evidence.

"What else did you see – were there any other men there?"

"Yes. I saw two men by the Consul. One of them was on the floor and the other was standing holding his face."

"When you saw the two men get into the Cambridge, was there anyone else in the car?"

"Yes – I saw someone in the driver's seat."

"Was there anyone else in the car apart from the driver?"

"Er, I'm not sure if there was then, but when they drove away I think there was four of them in the car."

"Thankyou Mr. Hillier. Please remain in the witness box."

Jo's Q.C. rose to his feet.

"Mr. Hillier, when you saw the two men get into the Cambridge, where did they position themselves?"

"One got in the front beside the driver and the other one got in the back."

"So both the nearside doors were opened were they?"

"Er, yes."

"Mr. Hillier, you said you didn't see anyone else in the car at that time apart from the driver – so if I said in fact there were only three men in the car after the two you saw get in – you could accept that could you?"

"Er, I could at that time, yes –"

"Did you see another man get into the car as it drove away, Mr. Hillier?"

"Er, no –"

"Thankyou – you may step down Mr. Hillier."

Jo breathed a little easier after the uncertainty of the taxi driver's evidence. Jo didn't remember seeing any taxis about on the night in question and he wondered if Hillier was a put-up by Willis and Walker. Jo turned to the two C.I.D. men, and reciprocated the cynical grin given to him earlier, making sure none of the jury saw him do it.

When the taxi driver was not wanted for further questions, the case for the prosecution was concluded. After the demolition of Hillier by Jo's defence counsel, Jo was gaining confidence of acquittal. With only one positive I.D. against him, and a cast iron alibi from Christine's father to come, Jo figured the jury would he hard pressed to find him guilty.

The defence opened their case by calling Jo to the stand. He took long deep breaths to calm himself, and after swearing the oath, he was ready to defend his life. Jo's counsel, Mr. Oliver Hamilton-Jones, began his brief questioning.

"Mr. Sullivan, please tell the jury where you were at 9 o'clock on Friday the 9th of January?"

"At my girlfriends house."

"Were you at any time in Queens Terrace on that evening?"

"No sir, I wasn't."

"Did you see Clark, Jones, and Fowler on that evening?"

"Yes – I saw them earlier in The Tramways public house. About twenty-to-nine I left them and went to see my girl."

"Thankyou Mr. Sullivan. Please remain in the witness box." Hamilton-Jones resumed his seat and the prosecutor began his cross-examination.

"Mr. Sullivan, when the Consul collided with the Cambridge, how long was it before the Cambridge sped off in pursuit?"

"I don't know. When I left the pub, I went off in the opposite direction to them. I never saw anything and I never heard anything."

"I see. So if one of the witnesses, under oath, swears that you were one of his assailants, he would be mistaken?"

"Yes sir, he certainly would," said Jo, evenly.

"I see – yes, thankyou Mr. Sullivan. No more questions."

Jo returned to the dock. Christine's father was then called to the stand and sworn in. Hamilton-Jones opened the dialogue. "Mr. Lovell, can you please tell the court if you saw Mr. Sullivan at your home on Friday the 9th of January?"

"Yes I did, yes."

"Do you know what time he arrived?"

"Er, not precisely – but it was before nine o'clock."

"You are absolutely sure it was before nine o'clock?"

"Yes I'm sure."

"Thankyou Mr. Lovell. Please remain where you are."

The prosecutor rose to his feet. "Mr. Lovell, how are you so sure it was before nine o'clock?"

"Well, we always have a cup of tea about nine and when I went to the kitchen to make it, Jo was in the kitchen with Christine. When I took the missus her cup the news had just started so he must have been in the house before nine."

"You're sure it wasn't the ten o'clock news you were about to watch?"

"It was the nine o'clock news on B.B.C. – we always watch the news on B.B.C."

"Yes, thankyou Mr. Lovell. You may stand down."

Bill left the witness box and lipped to Jo that he would see him later.

As far as Jo was concerned the trial was over – but for Danny and Blondie, and Bob, the ordeal was far from over, and as each of them were called to the stand, Jo felt for them as they struggled to justify the injuries caused under the guise of self-defence. With the prosecutor making reference to the photographs at every opportunity, they were in a hopeless position.

After closing speeches by counsel, the judge began his summing up. Jo couldn't make up his mind whether the judge was on his side or not. When it came to the witness who had positively identified Jo as his assailant, the judged seemed to overestimate his importance, but merely left it to the jury to make up their own minds when assessing Bill's evidence. When the judge finished, the jury were retired to consider their verdicts.

The four defendants were given permission to leave the dock and Jo slipped out of the court with Danny and Blondie for a needed cigarette.

"It don't look too good does it, Jo?" said Danny.

"No mate, it don't –"

"I reckon you might get off though," he said "and if you hadn't battered those two so bad we might have had a chance too –"

"What?" said Jo, catching the undertone in Danny's voice. "I only done 'em 'cos they were kicking fuck out of you, old son – don't hold that against me."

"Yeah – it ain't Jo's fault. If anything it's that fuckin' mate of yours fault. If he'd stopped like Jo told 'im, none of this would have happened," said Blondie.

"Yeah you're right. I'm sorry Jo, I didn't mean –"

"Forget it, Dan. Let's hope you don't go down that's all."

As he thought of the photographs though, he couldn't believe that his mates would escape without a custodial sentence. And if he himself were convicted, well, Jo tried not to think about it.

After the longest two hours in the world, Jo and the boys were recalled to the dock as the jury filed back into the courtroom. The usher asked the foreman if he and the jury had reached a unanimous decision on all of the charges.

"Yes," he replied.

"How do you find Robert Jones, on the first count of causing actual bodily harm, guilty or not guilty?"

"Guilty."

"How do you find Michael Clark, on the first count of causing actual bodily harm, guilty or not guilty?"

"Guilty."

"How do you find Jo Sullivan, on the first count of causing actual bodily harm, guilty or not guilty?"

"Not guilty." Jo nearly collapsed with relief – but quickly realised the more serious charges were yet to come.

Danny was found guilty on the first count.

The usher continued. "How do you find Robert Jones, on the second count of causing grievous bodily harm, guilty or not guilty?"

"Guilty."

"How do you find Michael Clark, on the second count of causing grievous bodily harm, guilty or not guilty?"

"Guilty."

Jo held his breath, his heart racing.

"How do you find Jo Sullivan, on the second count of causing grievous bodily harm, guilty or not guilty?"

"Not guilty." Jo closed his eyes and gave thanks to his guardian angel.

"How do you find Daniel Fowler, on the second charge of causing grievous bodily harm, guilty or not guilty?"

"Guilty."

Danny, Blondie and Bob, were also found guilty on the third count of grievous bodily harm. Jo was acquitted. When he heard the judge tell him he was free to leave the court, he almost stumbled over Blondie's feet in his haste to leave the dock. "Good luck boys," he whispered, then made his way to the back of the court.

After mitigation from the defence counsel, and after Danny's and Blondie's previous convictions were read out, the judge was ready to deliver sentence.

"I am inclined to believe the incident could, and indeed would have been avoided if the driver of the Ford had been honest enough to stop after damaging the wing-mirror of the Austin Cambridge, for I feel that he must have known that he'd caused some damage. I also feel certain that confrontation was the plan when the Ford stopped in Queens Terrace. However, the atrocious injuries sustained on them and inflicted by the three of you, were far beyond the bounds which would be reasonable in the circumstances and I hereby sentence you accordingly. Robert Jones, you will go to prison for six months. Michael Clark, you will go to prison for twelve months, and you Daniel Fowler, will also go to prison for twelve months."

Jo was sitting at the back of the court when he heard the sentences handed down, and he was devastated. He was hoping and praying that they would walk out with him.

Jo left the courtroom and was making his way to the exit of the building when he was approached by detective Walker.

"I suppose you think you're clever, Sullivan – but I know the truth," he said.

"Oh yeah," said Jo, feeling agitated by his intrusion.

"Yes Sullivan – shall I tell you your part in it?"

"I wasn't there – remember?"

"But you were, Sullivan. Jones was the first out of the car – then assaulted. Then Fowler went to help him, then Clark, and then you went charging in didn't you? And when the two of them ran off you chased after them and cornered them in the alley didn't you –?"

"I don't know what you're talkin' about –"

"Oh yes you do, Sullivan – and I'm not going to forget it. The first chance I get I'm going to have you and put you away."

"What the fuck you on about – you got something personal against me – 'cos I called ya plod is it, 'cos that's all you are – a plod wearin' a ten-pound suit from Burtons."

"The first chance I get, Sullivan – remember that."

"Yeah – well I gotta do something first, plod."

Walker suddenly produced a cynical grimace. "Have you?" he whispered.

Jo was left wondering how in damnation Walker knew what he knew – and about the hidden threat of a fit-up…

After Jo left the court-building he took a slow walk home to his flat, thinking constantly about the threat made on him by Walker. The more he thought about him the more he became convinced that a move away from Portsmouth would be his only chance of staying out of prison. He and Christine had already discussed the possibility of a move, and she had shown more than a little interest in the idea. With the date of their marriage fast approaching, and with the threat from Walker, the idea would have to be discussed again – and with more urgency.

Jo arrived back at the flat about four thirty, and had an hour to kill before meeting Christine from work. The flat was quiet and depressing without Danny around and Jo considered who, out of his friends, might want to share the flat with him, but dismissed the idea as soon as he thought of it. If he was moving, it didn't really matter.

Jo had a bite to eat, washed and shaved, and changed into a fresh set of clothes before setting off to meet Christine from the shop. He arrived in his car a few minutes before it was time to close and when Christine saw him pull up, a huge smile crossed her face. Jo gave her a thumbs-up. Soon, she was sitting beside him and they were on their way home to her flat.

"Well, what happened then – is it all over?" she asked.

"Yes babe – not guilty of any of the charges your honour."

"Oh Jo, thank goodness for that. I think I would have died if you were sent away again."

"I think I would have too – Danny and Blondie both got a year in prison. If I'd been done they'd have thrown away the keys. I, er, had a detective threaten me afterwards."

"Threaten you – why?"

"Well, he thinks I was involved and he said he was going to get me one way or the other –"

"Oh Jo, what are you going to do? You will have to report him won't you?"

"That wouldn't do any good babe, they'd just laugh at me. Anyway, he wouldn't admit it would he?"

"Who is this – detective?"

"One of the ones that arrested me. For some reason he really don't like me – I think it's 'cos I called him plod. Anyway, I've been thinking – you know we talked about moving, well, maybe we ought to. What do you think?"

"Yes, I think it might be best –"

"My mum's got a little flat over the top of the cafe we could use. We could live there until we find a place of our own – what do you think then?"

"Yes, I think we will – you will only be in more trouble if we stay here. What will you do about a job though?"

"Well, what I thought – is I'll move up there first, get the place all sorted out, paint it, and decorate it, and make it all nice n'cosy – then get a job. It shouldn't be hard gettin' a job, not up there."

"You won't know what wallpaper I like –"

Jo started laughing. "Trust a woman to come out with something like that – pick some out and I'll take it with me."

Jo parked the car and the two of them climbed the few steps to the flat. Christine's parents were both in the kitchen.

"Okay Jo – how did it go? I couldn't stay because I had to pick up the missus – did you get off?"

"Yeah – not guilty of anything!"

"Thank God for that," said Christine's mother. "They should never have said it was you in the first place. Come and sit here and have a nice cup of tea, Jo."

Nobody guessed how guilty he felt as he took the seat.

After the excitement of Jo's acquittal had been talked out, Christine and Jo decided to tell her parents about their intended move to Sevenoaks. They already knew Christine had been thinking about a move after they were married, and weren't unprepared for the news. After learning of the threat to Jo by detective Walker, they were inclined to agree that a move was a sensible idea.

The wedding was only seven weeks away and for the rest of the evening Christine and Jo were engrossed in discussion about how they wanted it to go and who would be there. Jo was thankful that most of the arrangements were being sorted out by Christine's parents. Jo's mother had sent a cheque to cover some of the expenses, and everything was well in hand for the wedding to take place on the 26th of May.

During the following weeks Jo worked out his notice on the wharf and made arrangements for his move to Sevenoaks. He informed the landlord of his intended move and, between them, agreed that the deposit held would serve as rent until Jo gave up the flat.

He had been in touch with Danny's parents and took all his belongings to their house, along with his old Ford pick-up.

Jo called on Freddie a few times and Freddie agreed to be Jo's best man at the wedding. He also agreed that Jo could stay at Trina's house the night before the big day.

Soon, Jo was all set to leave. On the Sunday evening he took Christine out for a farewell meal and on Monday morning, just four weeks before the wedding, Jo left Portsmouth with a clean slate to begin a new life in Sevenoaks.

*

The next few weeks proved difficult for Jo. After the novelty of re-uniting with his family had worn off, Jo found himself lonely and homesick and he yearned for the company of Christine.

In the first week Jo painted and decorated the entire flat. He also built a partition at the top of the stairs giving the flat more privacy as well as preventing cooking smells from permeating through the rooms. Jo was pleased with the work he had done on the flat but decided to delay any further improvements until Christine was with him.

After finishing work on the flat, Jo began to hunt for a job. He quickly became disillusioned though, when his relentless efforts proved negative. There were jobs around but so far, none of them held any appeal.

Jo picked up the daily paper and turned to the racing pages. There was a bookmakers office just a few doors along from the cafe and Jo looked in most afternoons, more to pass the time really, than his desire to back the horses. The owner of the shop had a meal in his mother's cafe most days, and Jo had spoken to him a few times. After more disappointment in failing to find work, Jo was down-in-the-mouth when he entered the shop.

The bookmaker, Bert, was a big man with a full belly and he always seemed to have a smile on his face, and Jo guessed it was all the money he was taking that kept it there. When Jo walked in, Bert was chalking up the odds on the board as they were being called out over the tannoy system.

"Hello Jo – hey, cheer up, it can't be that bad can it?" he said.

"Oh, hello Bert – no I'm alright – just can't find a job that's all."

"Can't find a job eh," said the bookie, casting an eye over Jo.

"No. They keep saying I'm too young or haven't got any experience."

"Keep trying Jo, something will come along." Bert finished chalking the odds and returned to the other side of the counter. Jo picked out a couple of horses and placed his bet. After listening to them get beaten, he left the betting-office and joined his mother in the cafe.

"Hello son, no luck yet?" she asked.

"Nah – can't get a look in anywhere. I thought it would be a piece of cake up here."

"Never mind Jo, you'll find something soon."

She was right.

The following day, Jo was sitting at one of the tables when Bert came in and joined him with a cup of tea.

"Hello Jo," he said, "I've been thinking about you. How would you like to work for me in the betting-shop?"

Jo's mouth was agape with surprise. "The betting-shop – you mean work in the betting-shop?"

"Yes Jo – I mean a job in the shop if you want it. I'm prepared to give you a trial run and if you prove to be made of the right material, I might be able to make it a permanent position – what do you say?"

Jo could hardly contain his excitement at the prospect of working in a betting-shop and Bert could see he was almost lost for words. "Well, thanks Bert, I er, well, I didn't expect anything like this – when do you want me to start?"

"How about in the morning?"

"Yes that's fine – thanks a lot –"

"Don't thank me, Jo – just be in the shop at nine o'clock and we'll go all through it. You might not fancy the job after I've told you all about it."

"Oh, I will Bert, I will –"

"Right then, I'll see you in the morning." Bert left the cafe and Jo rushed into the kitchen to tell his mother the good news. "Guess what – Bert just offered me a job in his shop!"

Henry slapped Jo on the back. "Well done, Jo – your mother said you would soon get something."

"What d'you think then, ma – you reckon I'll make a good bookmaker?"

"Yes, I expect you'll do alright," she smiled.

"Do alright? I'll be the business," he said, trying to stretch his sixty-eight inches to seventy.

After phoning Christine and passing on the good news to her, Jo relaxed on the settee, relieved at last that he'd managed to secure a job. He never dreamed he would ever be working in an office and the thought of it gave his ego a hefty boost.

For the rest of the day Jo was on a high and he constantly thought of the betting-office and what the job would be like, ceaselessly scanning the racing pages of the newspaper, as if they were going to give up the information he wanted.

Jo was up early in the morning, and took extra care in his presentation. He donned his second-best suit and spent fifteen minutes deciding which tie would go best with his blue striped shirt. At five-to-nine he came down from the flat and sought appraisal from his mother. "Well, how do I look for my first day in the office?" he beamed.

"Oh, very smart Jo, very smart," she said. Henry and his young sister, Pauline, both agreed with her.

"Right – I'll be off then, mustn't be late must we!" he laughed.

Jo walked into the betting-shop at precisely nine o'clock, and wondered briefly how anyone could start work so late in the day. Bert was behind the counter making a pot of tea and he told Jo to slip the lock on the door. "We don't usually open until ten. I've asked you in early so I can explain everything to you. I must say, you're looking very dapper, Jo."

"Yes, er, I thought I'd wear a suit –"

"Yes Jo, very good – I like to see a smart young man. Now, come round here and I'll give you a rundown on what you'll be doing. First of all, what are you like at writing and, which might be more important, what is your arithmetic like?"

"Well, my writing is okay I think, and yes, my arithmetic is pretty good – or at least it was when I was at school."

"Good. Now, what I'm going to do is start you off as a board-man, that is you have to write out all the names of the horses on the board, with the time of the race, and which meeting it is. Then, when the odds come over the blower you write the price against the horse. We've got a lovely big board so it makes the job nice n' easy. We'll also see if you have the potential to be a counter-clerk and, if you have the ability, we'll see if we can make a settler out of you – and a settler is the important one, because he's the one who works out how much money I have to pay out to the punters, okay?"

"Yes, er, do I call you Mr. –"

"No no – just call me Bert. We don't stand on formality here, Jo. Just be yourself. Now, your other duties will be to display all the newspapers round the office – the more the merrier so that the punters get really confused, and to keep the shop tidy in general. Oh, and always make sure there are plenty of pencils and betting-slips available. Now, I don't know if you're aware of it, but I own several shops and if you have the ability and inclination, well, who knows where you might end up."

Jo never gave a thought to the possibility that Bert might own more than one shop, and he was impressed. "Thanks Bert, I really appreciate the chance you're giving me."

"Think nothing of it. Now, you'll want some wages I expect? I can –"

"Oh Bert, I think I'd better tell you before I start – I'm getting married in a couple of weeks – Saturday the 26th."

"Don't worry about the Saturday, I'll get someone in to cover for you. Now, wages. I can start you on £25 for a five day week, and as you progress I'll review the situation, is that okay, Jo?"

"Yes, that'll be fine." Although the money was a little less than he was accustomed to, Jo was more than happy with the package presented to him, and he was keen to start work.

And so began Jo's initiation in the world of the bookmaker. Although an integral part of the running of a betting-shop, the boardman's role was fairly simple and straightforward and Jo soon became adept in his duties. Bert was impressed with the way Jo displayed the runners and the way he wrote out the odds against them.

Within a week Jo was already studying a book specially designed for counter-clerks and settlers, and because he showed outstanding potential, Bert promised to send Jo on a course for settlers at the London School of Turf Accountancy at the soonest opportunity. In addition, Bert gave Jo a couple of days off to prepare for the wedding.

Jo was feeling on top of the world with the way things were going and he was glad he and Christine had decided to move away from the war-zone of Portsmouth. It was almost with reluctance that Jo left Sevenoaks on the Friday afternoon and headed back to his hometown in preparation for his union with Christine the following day.

As Jo made his way to Pompey he thought about the impending wedding. His parents and sisters, his brother Charlie, his brother-in-law and nephews, would all make the journey down late Saturday morning. Jo's mother had already posted a notice declaring that the cafe would be closed at eleven o'clock sharp. With all the friends and relatives invited from both families the guest list had exceeded the original estimate, and now more than fifty people were expected at the reception which was to be held in the Blue Lounge of the Royal Hotel. The ceremony itself was to take place at three o'clock in the magnificent church of St. Mary's.

As Jo neared Portsmouth, he veered from the main road and headed for Portchester for his prearranged meeting with Freddie. With two of his best friends sitting it out in a prison cell, Freddie and Jo had decided on a quiet night in instead of the usual rave of a stag night.

Before long, Jo was at Freddie's making a phone call to Christine letting her know that he'd arrived safely and would be at the church well ahead of her.

"So, what's it like up there then?" asked Freddie.

"Yeah, it's alright Fred. You won't believe it but I've got myself a job in a betting-office!"

"A bettin'-office? You? You'll be robbin' 'em of all the money won't ya?"

"Nah, course I won't – the owner's gonna train me up to be a settler so it could end up a fair ol' job. I ain't gonna risk losin' it for the sake of a few quid – well, not to start with," he smiled.

"Yeah, that's more like it!" laughed Freddie.

"Have you got any of that gear?"

"What gear – oh you mean dope? No, I ain't had none for a week. I'm gaspin' for a bit –"

"Good job I brought a bit with me then innit?"

"You've got some? Cor, I've been gaspin' for a week for a joint – where did you get hold of some then?"

"It's the bit you gave me that time." Jo took the cannabis from his pocket and tossed it over to Freddie who immediately unwrapped it, sniffed it, and fingered it like he'd never seen a piece before. "Ain't you had none of this since I gave it to ya?"

"Nah – well, I did have one – but I thought I'd save it for emergencies. Good job I did ay?"

"Yeah not 'alf – I'd better skin up one straightaway, make sure it's still alright."

"Yeah I s'pose you'd better Fred," said Jo, smiling. He sat and watched Freddie as he rolled the joint with meticulous precision. After lighting it, Freddie drew the smoke deep down before letting it go. He took a couple more pulls then passed it to Jo. "Ta. You heard from Danny and Blondie yet then?"

"Yeah, I've had a letter from Blondie – 'e don't stop moanin' in it. I'll go an' get it in a minute. You'll laugh when you read about 'im having a shit."

"Where's Trina then?"

"Still abroad somewhere – gettin' me some gear I 'ope!"

A few minutes later Freddie went to the kitchen and fetched a couple of cans and the letter from Blondie. The two of them stretched out on the settee while Freddie read out a few extracts. "Here, listen to this bit – 'I've settled in alright but only after throwing out an old tramp they put me in with. I said to the screw, who's that, and he said, that's your cell-mate and I said he ain't staying in here with me because I can smell him from here, but the screw said he was and slammed the door. When they opened us up for tea I got all his gear and slung it all up the landing, then kicked him out. Ha Ha. I tell you Fred, he was about a hundred years old and stank worserer than a polecat. I got nicked but now I'm on my own. Ha Ha. I've had lots of rucks with the laundry cons because they keep giving me shirts with all the buttons missing and the jeans that come halfway up my legs. I told them if they were taking the piss there would be trouble and they soon sorted me out okay. (Good job they did I'da killed 'em) ha ha. And the food is shit. We had a kinda stew the other day and the dumplins' were like pieces of congealed cardboard, but apart from that everything is okay. ha ha –' Can you imagine him in there, Jo – I bet he's causin' havoc," said Freddie, laughing.

"Yeah, I can imagine those jeans as well can't you." Freddie and Jo couldn't stop laughing. "Here, listen to this bit – 'I went for a shit the other day and me cheeks were all squashed up 'cos the pans are so small, and when you sit on them there's only a little bit of door and they can see your legs from the knees down and your head from the waist up. It really pisses me off –!"

Jo laughed even more imagining poor Blondie's plight.

"Listen – 'really pisses me off and the karzi paper is that horrible slippery stuff. IZAL it's called innit, and you need about a hundred sheets of it to wipe your arse cos it's so shiny and slippery. What I do now is crap in the cell and lob it out the window ha ha –' "

"Cor, you imagine one of Blondie's hitting you on the side of ya cannister!" said Jo.

"Ugh yeah – bein' in the nick an' someone throws a pile of shit at ya – be too much wouldn't it? I'd be checkin' every window just in case. Imagine it all stuck on ya neck, and then you've got to get it all off," laughed Freddie.

"Yeah – be all in ya fingers –"

"And then you're called for a visit –"

"Yeah – and the screw won't let you wash it off –"

"And you have to wipe it all over him instead –"

"And end up in solitary for about a year –"

"Yeah – and all because Blondie threw a shit-parcel out of the window," said Freddie finally, holding his stomach.

"Listen to this bit, Jo – 'I was in bed the other night and I felt an itch on my leg but I didn't take any notice and then I woke up and started scratching both legs. Anyway I woke up in the morning and there was two dead cockroaches all squashed up on my back and two live ones were running about in the bed when I pulled the covers back and I nearly shit myself. I am now having a lot of trouble getting to sleep' – How would you like them in ya bed then Jo?"

"Ugh – poor Blondie," said Jo, trying not to laugh. "I'll have to send him a few lines."

"Yeah, he says in the letter to make sure to write to him. I'll give you his number before you go back."

Freddie and Jo continued laughing and joking, sipping cans of lager and smoking joints until late into the night. As they smoked more cannabis the quieter they became until, subdued, they lost each other as they drifted away in their own thoughts.

Jo remembered the last two occasions when he'd smoked with

Freddie, but with no problems to haunt him his thoughts were now lighter and more pleasant...*the hang-man was running away but laden down with a heavy rope, he was not making headway...several skeletons – all wearing a purple sash, were chasing him, trying to catch him, wanting to devour him...then he was gone...following behind came rides on the waves across blue-green waters...Christine was there, dressed in pure white...he in clear blue, tip-toeing hand in hand on the crest waiting for the albatross and a trip through the woolly clouds...come on honey, up this staircase we'll go, until we reach the castle where the battlements are shining and the portcullis is drawn...*

The following day, under the full majesty of the peals of the church bells, Christine and Jo were married.

PART TWO

Soon after they were married, Jo's younger sister had fallen pregnant and Christine took her place in the cafe for a while until she too, became pregnant. After giving birth to their younger son, Jason, Christine gave up working for a wage and concentrated her time on raising the boy and taking care of the home. A year later Christine gave birth to their second son, and they named him Steven.

In the meantime Jo's mother and his brother, Charlie, had pooled their resources and formed a partnership together after purchasing the freehold of a hamburger bar. After the partnership was formed Christine and Jo moved out of the two rooms of his mother's flat, into a spacious two-bedroomed council house.

Jo still worked in a betting-office. Within a month of starting work, Bert sent Jo on a course for settlers at the London School of Turf Accountancy. After completing the ten-week course, Bert's faith was rewarded when Jo showed him a certificate, stamped – With Distinction.

Jo took to bookmaking like a duck to water and within six months he was the manager of one of Bert's smaller offices. Apart from a part-time counter clerk, Jo more or less ran the shop single-handed and was paid good wages and given tax-free bonuses when the shop did well. Bert soon became impressed when the profit margins of the shop increased after Jo took over and he questioned him about it.

Jo had dug out the previous six months figures, and in particular the records showing the amount of money given away to companies like William Hill and Ladbroke in the way of hedging – money laid off by a smaller bookmaker to reduce their liability if a particular horse or dog was overbacked. Jo pointed out many instances where the previous manager had hedged money unnecessarily. He had studied well and he knew when a race was over-round or over-broke, that is, if a race – whatever the result – would win or lose money for the bookmaker. By keeping a strict book, Jo was able to reduce the hedging to a minimum, thus increasing the profits of the shop. Jo advised Bert that if all his shops were to hedge their bets to one main office within his own small group, and not to the likes of William Hill, he would save many thousands of pounds over the course of a year.

Bert was so impressed with Jo's ability and understanding, that he soon set him up in an office within the flagship of his own small empire, giving him all the authority he needed to ensure all the hedging of bets would be carried out from one office. If there was any money to be laid off to the big boys, it would be done only after Jo had made his own book from Bert's eight shops.

About four years after the successful co-ordination of the offices, Bert dropped a bombshell by telling all his staff that he was selling out to a company called Park Lane Racing Ltd. He assured everyone that their jobs were safe but Jo knew the job wouldn't be the same once Bert sold his interest and a large company took over.

Within a month of Bert's declaration, Park Lane were in possession of Bert's shops and in the shake-up, Jo was back running one of the smaller branches of the group. All hedging in future would now be carried out from their own head office in London.

Jo missed Bert. He was a likeable man and Jo owed much to him for giving him his chance when he first moved to Sevenoaks. Jo missed the money as well. In Bert's employ, Jo was on good money – a lot of it tax-free – but since the takeover his wages were greatly reduced.

After several months, Jo became disgruntled with his new employer. Whereas Bert and his managers would often encourage the punters to bet on certain horses by offering them better prices than those shown on the board, or by offering them some races tax-free, Park Lane ran their offices strictly by the book. The vast amount of paperwork they wanted completed, also added to Jo's gradual discontentment.

Disillusioned because of reduced wages and status, and because of the ever increasing workload, Jo began to plan with meticulous deviousness, a way to syphon some of their profits into his own pocket. But it was far from easy.

Park Lane had installed photographic machines in every office and all betting-slips had to be passed through the machine before the start of each race. Every day too, a blank sheet of paper was photographed which then showed the time it had been inserted. It was then checked against the talking clock, TIM, after dialling the appropriate number. Because of their accuracy, the internal security staff were rarely called out to alter the clocks on the machines – and it was that precise accuracy that helped Jo skim hundreds and hundreds of pounds from the coffers of Park Lane Racing Ltd.

Several managers, and other staff, had been caught stealing in the first few months after the takeover, and all were subsequently and successfully prosecuted and dismissed from the company – all, that is, except Jo.

Other managers had tried, in vain, to fiddle the photo machines, either by trying to stop the clock by disconnecting them from the mains, or by using powerful magnets, or simply by putting fraudulent bets through the machine hoping nobody would notice or blaming any discrepancy on human error.

Jo tried a different tactic. After failing in his own efforts to bypass the machine, or slow down the clock, Jo suddenly discovered a way to beat the system.

The clock in the machine changed, naturally, with every minute of time that passed, and as a horse race took longer than a minute to run, it was impossible to place a bet after the result was known because the clock would show that the bet was placed late.

The greyhounds were different though. Jo realised that certain sprint races took only about thirty seconds to run, and the result was often announced within forty, to forty-five seconds after the start of the race. If a bet was already made out, with only the trap number of the winner to be added, one would have ample time to add the winning number and pass the slip through the machine before the clock ticked over to the next minute.

Because the clock on the machines didn't register the seconds, Jo had found an infallible way to beat the security of Park Lane Racing – and for added protection, he made sure each winning bet was written out by someone other than himself.

After discovering the loophole in their security, Jo took extreme care in selecting a regular punter to help him in the planned coup. When he thought he had the right man, Jo offered him the chance to make extra cash by joining him in the fraud. Jo's co-conspirator was unemployed and Jo told him to always be in the shop when greyhound racing was scheduled to be broadcast over the tannoy.

Jo wasn't greedy. Because of his astuteness and cunning, he managed to carry on the scam for nearly two years before investigators began to wonder why the shop, under Jo's managership, was making less percentage profits than other shops with similar turnovers.

With increasing awareness he began to suspect that he was under scrutiny from the undercover staff of Park Lane Racing, and ceased making fraudulent bets when he suspected one of them was in the shop posing as a regular punter.

About ten days after he was questioned by the security staff, two detectives from the fraud squad interviewed him about certain bets. Jo knew they were in no position to prove dishonesty was afoot, but nonetheless handed in his notice before the company had the chance to dismiss him on some other pretence. Park Lane Racing accepted his resignation and after nearly seven years working for a bookmaker, Jo was out of a job.

After leaving Park Lane Racing Jo tried to secure another post in bookmaking, but when three weeks of hunting turned into three months, he gave up looking and drifted in and out of dead-end jobs until he found one driving heavy lorries. The wages were just barely acceptable, and Jo would have kept the job but the long hours behind the wheel brought on his recurring back pains and he was forced to hand in his notice.

Jo had always been plagued by pains in his back, ever since his early days on the wharf, and over the years they were getting worse. At one time they got so bad that Jo had to visit his doctor who promptly sent him to the hospital for examination. After X-rays were taken, the orthopaedic surgeon told Jo there was nothing he could do except advise him to exercise certain muscles and sleep on a firm bed.

Luckily for Jo, he had a sister called Irene…

Christine and Jo didn't go out very often after they were married but sometimes they would visit Jo's sister Irene, and her husband John. On one such visit, when she saw Jo was in pain, she began a series of healing sessions.

Unknown to Jo at the time, his sister had the gift of spiritual healing, and through other, more experienced healers, she was being taught how to use these and other spiritual powers. Jo didn't know anything about the teachings of spiritualism but after many visits to his sister's home, and with her explanations, he gradually became aware of the meaning of life.

Jo had always been intrigued by man's religious beliefs but he could never quite bring himself to believe in the Christian church as they portrayed it. Something was missing. The Bible, and the teachers who used the Bible, never brought out in Jo the certain something within him that he knew should be there.

Jo guessed there must be **something** in man's belief – it wasn't feasible somehow, that more than half of the worlds population could believe in something that was completely and utterly non-existent. Every country in the world had a religious following of one kind or another, and as Jo listened to his sister's explanation to life's ultimate mystery, he became aware that the pains in his back were completely gone – and because of it, held her almost in awe…

*

Although Jo had a job now, it wasn't as a settler sitting in a cosy office, he was now a labourer with a road gang. Instead of using his brains settling bets, Jo found himself using brawn digging up roads and laying tarmac. But the money was good, and he could live with the idea of having a pick 'n' shovel in his hands instead of pen and paper.

The only thing he came to regret about working on the road gang, was the company he began to run with.

Jo had been away for a week with Christine and the two boys, soaking up the sun at a holiday park in Cornwall, and tomorrow he was due back at work. Jo hated Mondays. They were always a pain after the weekends and tomorrow would be particularly grim after a week of relaxation.

As it turned out, Monday wasn't as bad as he'd feared it would be. He only worked for half a day because of an accident that had seen two men severely burned when a lorry reversed, knocking over a pot of near boiling tarmac.

Tuesday wasn't too bad either because the gang was short of two men and only half a load was delivered for the rest of the gang to spread. By the time the weekend had come round Jo was back into full swing, and was looking forward to a drink with a couple of pals from the gang.

Before he started working with the road gang Jo hardly ventured from the house, apart from when he visited his sister or his mother. When he became friendly with Ron and George, two of his work-mates from the gang, and they invited him to join them for a drink at weekends, he was more than glad of the chance to socialise with them.

Jo didn't know it at the time, but Ron had gained more than a reputation for being a hard man and a few months earlier became involved in a long-standing feud. His brother-in-law was severely beaten by a couple of young thugs and Ron sorted them out good and proper. In a tit-for-tat reprisal, Ron was attacked and beaten by three men. He then recruited a couple of pals and retaliated by crashing into a pub called The White Hart, causing havoc and injury with pick-axe handles and short clubs.

Ron was playing pool while George was giving Jo the story, and Jo was feeling slightly ill at ease at the thought of getting mixed up in a major feud.

"How long's this been going on?" he asked.

"About two or three months – Ron and a couple of his mates paid a visit to the Hart a few weeks ago an' done two of 'em there an' then in the boozer."

"Yeah? Do much damage to 'em?"

"Yeah I think so – I wasn't there but they reckon there was blood an' snot all over the place."

"Is it all over now or what?" asked Jo, wishing suddenly that he was back in-doors with Christine watching television.

"It should be – unless they're fuckin' silly. Ron can be real mean if he wants to be."

"Glad to hear it," said Jo, laughing. "You want another drink?"

"Yeah cheers Jo – I'll have a lager."

Jo went to the bar and ordered a round of drinks. He called across to Ron. "You want a drink?"

"No, not now – I've got to nip an' see someone in a minute, unless you wanna put one in for me," he grinned. Jo paid for the three drinks and took his own, and George's over to the table. "Where's Ron goin'?"

"Dunno – he ain't said nothin' to me."

Soon, Ron finished playing pool and joined them at the table.

"Where you goin' then?" asked George.

"I've got to go an' see Liddy – Alf's givin' me a lift over there so you can take my car if ya like an' I'll see you in the Nelson – about half-nine." Ron threw his keys to George and left the pub. About an hour later, George and Jo also left the pub.

Jo was sitting in the passenger seat of Ron's old Vauxhall waiting for George to get the engine started, when he noticed a pick-axe handle wedged in between the seats. He took it in his hands. "Fucksake – is this what he uses?"

"Yeah, if he has to – you wanna look in the glove-box!"

Jo laid the pickaxe handle on his lap and pressed the button that released the flap. Inside the compartment was an array of weapons, including long-bladed knives. "Jesus! There's enough blades here to equip a butchers –" Before Jo had time to finish the sentence the windscreen was caved in by someone wielding a base-ball bat and Jo nearly jumped out of his skin hearing the sound of the sudden impact of wood hitting glass.

Within a second of the windscreen going, both doors of the car were wrenched open and George and Jo were under attack from four men armed with clubs.

Jo heard George scream out in pain as he was struck on the legs and shoulder and dragged from the car. While George was being dragged out Jo was clubbed on the legs as he tried to edge further into the car, and he raised them up to avoid more blows. One of the men bent over and tried to grab Jo and pull him out but Jo saw his chance and kicked him full in the face, sending him sprawling onto the tarmac.

Jo grabbed one of the long-bladed knives and the pick-handle and quickly got out of the car. As he did, he was clubbed hard on the side of the head. He fell to this knees but, instinctively, lunged out with the knife and sank the blade deep into the leg of his assailant before he had the chance to club Jo again.

The thug screamed out in pain and bent forward to grasp his wounded leg. Quickly, Jo rose to his feet and smashed the pick-handle across his jaw as hard as he could. The young thug dropped the base-ball bat and howled in agony as he sank to the ground. On hearing his screams, one of his cronies began to make his way round the car.

The one that Jo had kicked in the face was now standing but he seemed wary of further confrontation and he backed away as Jo went forward, raging, almost foaming at the mouth as he screamed obscenities at him.

The older of the four men, the one that had been attacking George, was undeterred as he came round the front of the car. He was holding a club in each hand, but hesitated when he saw blood on the blade of the knife that Jo was holding out in front of him.

Jo edged nearer towards him. The mother that Jo had stabbed in the leg was still on the floor nursing his wounds and Jo kicked him hard in the ribs, causing him to roll over in more pain. Jo then saw the base-ball bat that he'd been carrying was still on the ground, and with calculated risk, Jo threw the pick-handle **he** was carrying, straight into the face of the approaching thug, catching him full in the mouth. As he hollered out, Jo quickly scooped up the loose bat and steamed into him, clubbing him viciously on the head and shoulders. As he cowered to protect himself, Jo smashed the bat against his legs until he fell screaming to the floor.

After seeing Jo's rage, the other men moved away out of his range, giving him a chance to make his way round the car to see how George was doing. He was half up against the car, blood seeping from his wounds. Jo went to help him up – suddenly, George screamed out a warning, and as Jo spun round – with the knife still in his hand – he felt the blade sink deep into the chest of his would be attacker.

The man dropped the club he was brandishing and sank to his knees, clutching his chest. Jo trembled for a second, looking at him in bewilderment as he saw the colour drain from his face, and Jo knew he was beginning to die…

Jo grabbed hold of George and the two of them hastened away from the carnage. After they had travelled a hundred yards or so, Jo heard the ominous sound of sirens in the distance. "We've gotta get out of here – any suggestions George?"

"Yeah, a mate of mine lives just up the road a bit –"

"Let's get there sharpish then."

George was in a bad way. His nose was broken and his lips were smashed, and he had several other cuts and bruises. Jo's own injuries weren't nearly so bad with only a small cut on the side of his head and some minor bruising on his legs. While his physical injuries were only superficial, the trauma that was beginning in his head was more serious. His thoughts were racing so fast he could hardly believe what had happened – one minute he was sitting peacefully in the front seat of a car and the next he was killing a man…

Is he dead…? No, he can't be, please don't let him be…he probably went that colour when he saw the size of the blade – fuck me, anyone would, seeing ten inches of cold steel plunging into your chest…but he might not be dead though, the blade might have by-passed the major organs, missed all the main arteries…please, please, dear Jesus, he mustn't die, please don't let him die – what if he does die though? God, what's happening to me – I must be tripping, someone's put a tab in my drink, given me a Mickey Finn...

After finding refuge in George's mate's house, Jo began to wonder more about the man he'd accidentally stabbed. When he saw him sink to his knees he **knew** he was dying and now he was living his worst nightmare. He turned to George. "See this knife, George – I want you to stab me with it. If that scroat dies and I haven't got any wounds –"

"Oh, Jo no, I can't –"

"What d'you mean you can't – you've got to!"

"No Jo, I couldn't do it –"

"Listen, just stab me in the shoulder, in – out. It won't be a problem – then I can go straight to the hospital. I've got to have some stab wounds –"

"I know – but I just can't do it, I –"

"What about your mate?"

George's mate, Billy, nearly freaked out at the suggestion and Jo turned back to George. "Listen George, I've been done three or four times already for grievous assaults and if I'm done again without a clear chance of self-defence, I'll end up bein' done for murder or something – you've got to give me some or I'm fucked!"

"But it **was** self defence – with all them geezers tooled up like they were it's gotta be self defence."

Jo knew he was right but he wanted a nice little stab wound, thankyou very much, just to be sure, to be a hundred per cent certain that they couldn't argue when it came to the plea. Jo considered stabbing himself but it wasn't so easy and if it turned out wrong they might suspect that it was self-inflicted and he would end up worse off if it came to trial.

"George! Take this knife and –"

"I can't. I'm sorry Jo but I can't."

Jo was beginning to get angry at his stubborn refusal. "What the fuck is your problem!? All I want is a little stab wound in the fuckin' shoulder – I don't want you to kill me!"

When George didn't reply Jo sank down in a chair and held his head in disbelief. "I can't believe this is happening to me, I just can't believe it…" he whispered.

Jo didn't know what to do. He couldn't come to terms with the idea that he might have killed someone. He began to think about the possibilities. He knew he wasn't very well known but he also knew the police would have his identity in no time at all, and he seriously considered giving himself up.

He looked up at George and was about to ask him – no, plead with him, when he noticed his friend, Billy, was rolling an extra long cigarette. "Is that a joint?" he asked.

"Yeah – you want a pull on it?"

"Yeah, I wouldn't mind – you got any for sale?"

"Yeah, how much d'you want?"

"I dunno – how much is it?"

"I can do you a quarter for a tenner," he said, passing Jo the joint. Jo pulled hard on it, taking the smoke deep down. After tasting the cannabis, he went to his pocket and dug out two fivers. "Give me a quarter then."

Billy handed over a neatly wrapped chunk of gear, and Jo tucked it into his Y-fronts for safe keeping.

Jo hadn't smoked any dope since Christmas, some eight months ago, when he last saw Freddie and he was already feeling its effect. Before he got too wrecked he decided to ring Christine but discovered that Billy wasn't connected. The nearest phone was a few hundred yards down the road but Jo didn't fancy the walk at the moment, preferring instead to smoke more gear in the hope that his mind wouldn't keep recalling a shiny blade sinking in and out of a man's chest.

Before long though, Jo plucked up the courage and made the walk to the call box. He dialled the number, taking deep breaths to calm himself. Christine answered the phone.

"Hi Chris, it's me – listen, I..er..well, there's a game of cards goin' at George's and I thought I might play for a while."

"How long will you be?"

"I don't know – er, I won't be long –"

"Alright – don't be too late though will you."

"No, I'll try not to be – but if I am don't go worryin' will ya –"

"Jo –"

"Yeah?"

"– Is everything alright? You sound as if something is wrong."

"What d'you mean – nothing's wrong, I just –"

"Jo there is, what is it? I can tell by your voice that something's wrong –"

"Oh Chris – I don't know what to say, I –"

"What's happened? Have you been in a fight or something?"

"Er..well..yes – but it wasn't my fault, I was just sitting in a car –"

"Don't tell me now Jo, just come home –"

"I can't, not just yet – I think I'm in trouble, babe – I don't know what to do –"

"Oh Jo –"

"Chris, I'm so sorry – I'll give you a ring later okay, when I know what's happened."

"Oh Jo, please – why can't you come home now?"

"I just can't, not yet, not 'till I know what's happened?"

"Jo –"

"I'll call you as soon as I can – gotta go now –"

"Jo please –"

Jo cradled the phone and left the call box, trying in vain to stem the flow of tears that were running down his face.

He didn't go back to Billy's house, instead he found himself heading towards the police station. The more he thought about it the more he was convinced that it was the best course to take.

Sooner or later they would track him down and it would look better for him walking in through the front door rather than being arrested and handcuffed and taken in through the back. As he neared the police station he began to hesitate, not knowing whether to go in and surrender or go home and try to forget it all happened, praying for some miracle that would tell him it was all a game, that the Gods were playing with him, testing him for some reason…

Yeah…let it be a game – I don't mind playing for a while if I can go home afterwards, if I can go home to Christine…Is he dead – or have the surgeons got to him…please, let them get to him, stitch him right

– 122 –

back together again...yeah, I'll be alright...just don't die man, don't you fuckin' die you son of a bitch...what was I supposed to do – let him cave in my skull so a newspaper can blazen across a front page...MANS HEAD CAVED IN...A twenty-eight year old father of two was brutally beaten to death late Friday night after coming under attack from four young thugs armed with baseball bats...yeah, all nice an' dramatic...well fuck you man, it's survival of the fittest...one witness described the attack as unprovoked...a police spokesman...the police..?

The cannabis was beginning to play tricks with his mind because when he saw the blue sign, he hesitated again. Walking into a police station was alien to Jo and just as he was about to enter, he suddenly changed his mind and walked away.

If he did give himself up and the mother **was** dead, he could be remanded in custody for up to a year before going for trial, and Christine would be left struggling on social security payments. Before he could even consider giving himself up Jo decided he would have to acquire some money, enough to make things a little easier for her if it did turn out for the worse.

First though, he needed some money now to make good his escape. He stopped at a phone-box and dialled a number. After a moment or two, his brother answered. "Hello?"

"Hello, Charlie – it's me, Jo –"

"Oh, 'allo Jo –"

"Listen Charlie, I'm in real trouble – I've got to get away for a while –"

"What's 'appened then –" said Charlie.

"Well, I was sittin' in a motor an' suddenly these geezers started smashin' it to bits – well, cut a long story short I stabbed one of 'em – I think he might be dead –"

"Dead!"

"It was an accident, Charlie – I sort of spun round and I had a knife in my hand – I've got to go on my toes an' try an' get some money together – can you lend me a few quid? I'll give it you back as soon as –"

"Yeah sure – come round the flat now."

"Cheers Charlie – I'll see you in a minute." Jo left the booth and made his way towards Charlie's flat, keeping well away from the main roads.

Ten minutes later he was ringing the door bell. Charlie opened the door and led Jo into the small flat. "Sounds like you're in a spot of trouble – how the fuck did it happen?"

"Charlie, you won't believe it – I was sittin' in a motor with my mate an' suddenly four geezers I've never seen in my life started cavin' in the windscreen an' attackin' us with base-ball bats – 'ere, have a look at this lot –" Jo pulled up his trousers and showed Charlie the bruises. He then told the rest of the story. "You reckon he might be dead, Cha?"

"Phew – it don't sound too good does it – what you gonna do now?"

"I was thinkin' of shootin' off somewhere, try an' get hold of a few quid just in case. I don't wanna end up doin' bundles of bird an' leavin' Christine scratchin' on social. I need a few quid to get away though – if you can?"

"Course I can." Charlie went to a drawer and pulled out some notes. "Is fifty enough?" he asked, handing Jo five tenners. "Yeah – thanks Charlie, you've saved my life. Can you do me another favour – phone Christine tomorrow and let her know that I'm alright, and tell her I'll phone as soon as I can."

"Alright –"

"An' I'll give you a ring tomorrow an' you can tell me if you hear anything, yeah?"

"Yeah – make it about eleven."

"Right, I'm gonna shoot off then – I'll see ya later, an' thanks again for the dosh."

"That's alright – just don't do nothing silly."

Jo left the flat and walked quickly towards the station, deciding in his haste to catch a train to London. It was getting on for eleven o'clock and the last train didn't leave until twenty past, giving him ample time to grab a coffee from the van parked on the corner.

Soon, the train was moving and Jo was on it, wondering how far he was going to get with his hairbrained idea. The odds were stacked against him but after considering all the options, Jo guessed he had nothing to lose.

A few minutes after the train pulled out of Sevenoaks station, Jo nipped to the toilet and skinned up a small joint and smoked it before returning to his seat. Staring aimlessly into the passing blackness, seeing nothing but his own reflection, his mind began to run, began tormenting..

..Are you dead you mother? Are you alive you son of a bitch?..dead or alive...wanted, ten thousand dollars reward, dead or alive...we are not in America, Mr. Sullivan, here you must allow yourself to be bludgeoned into the dust...dust to dust...ashes to ashes...from the earth you came, here now do you return...don't die man...don't be dead you mother..

The train pulled into Charing Cross just after midnight. When Jo left the station he turned into Villiers Street and walked aimlessly down towards the river. Soon, he found himself sitting on an iron bench in Victoria Gardens where the night air felt fresh and sweet.

After a few minutes, he retrieved the lump of gear from his pocket and rolled a small joint. When it was lit, he sucked hard and took the smoke deep down before letting it go. Before long, the dope began to slow down the thoughts that were raging through his mind. All he could think about at the moment was Christine, and how much she would be worrying. It was bad enough for Jo, but at least he knew what the nightmare was all about whereas she would be going half-crazy with worry, probably made worse when Jo put the phone down on her.

A little later, Jo skinned up another small joint. As he sat on the bench smoking, trying to kill his mind, he noticed one or two men had looked at him as they passed, showing more than casual interest. Jo checked himself over, making sure there was no blood on his clothes, and as he did, he suddenly realised they were probably homos sussing him out. The thought of them thinking that he might be queer made Jo feel slightly uneasy, but with more deliberate thought, he began to ponder the possibility of going home with one of them and robbing them.

As he sat there, he thought about the possibility – what if they sussed what he was up to? What if they put up a fight? While he was thinking, a man walked by – one that had passed by a little earlier, and as Jo looked at him, he hesitated, then sat beside Jo on the bench.

"Hello," he said.

"Hi," said Jo, his heart thumping.

"Are you waiting for anyone?" said the man.

"Er..no..I'm just sitting here," said Jo, nervously, wondering what the hell he was doing.

"Are you, er, looking for anything?"

"I don't know –"

"I've got a place a few minutes from here – I've got a car."

Jo hesitated for a moment – then went for it. "Okay."

They left the park and walked along the Embankment. As they walked, Jo's mind was in turmoil, trying to think what he was going to do when they got to his house, wondering if he had any money. When they stopped and he slipped a key into the lock of a two year old Rover, Jo was encouraged.

As soon as they set off, Jo wanted to know where they were going and whether or not he lived on his own, but felt too nervous to open his mouth.

"My name's Michael by the way – what's yours?"

"Er, John –"

"Well, John, relax – you seem a little tense."

"Er, well, I do feel a little nervous," said Jo, hoping and praying that Michael wasn't going to get carried away and start groping him in the car.

They drove for about ten minutes or so before pulling into a side turning off Faringdon Street. Soon, they were entering his house. "Do you live on your own?" asked Jo, as evenly as he could.

"Yes – makes life a little easier don't you think?"

"Yes," agreed Jo, casting an eye round the elegant house.

"What do you do?" asked Jo, innocently.

"Anything you like, darling –"

"No – I mean what do you do for a living?" said Jo, almost too hastily.

"Oh, stupid of me – I run a little bar in Holborn – what do you do?"

"I..er..well, I work for a bookmaker," said Jo, cursing himself profusely for not being quick enough to think of something else. "Have you got a bathroom I can use?"

"Yes, just down the hall – second door on the left."

Jo gave Michael his best smile and went in, locking the door behind him. His pulse was racing as he looked around the room. On the back of the door was a dressing gown and Jo quickly removed the cord from the loops. After finding a razor, he cut the cord in two and tucked the pieces into his waistband. When Jo came out of the bathroom, Michael was waiting for him. "Come, let's go upstairs," he said.

Jo followed him up the stairs. Before reaching the top, he took out one of the lengths of cord and wrapped it round his fingers until it was a manageable size then suddenly, pounced on Michael and pulled the cord round his neck.

"Don't struggle!" screamed Jo, forcing him to the floor.

"All I'm after is money! If you give me any problems you'll be sorry – I'm going to tie your hands, alright!"

"Yes..yes.."

Jo pulled out the second length of cord and tied his hands behind his back. He then removed the cord from Michael's neck and tied his ankles. Now that he was firmly secure, Jo breathed a little easier. He never dreamed it would be so easy. "Have you got any money – if you tell me where it is I won't cause any damage," said Jo, sounding as mean as he could.

"There's money in the drawer..in the bedroom..just take it and go, please.."

"Keep your head down on the floor – don't look at me!"

Jo took out his handkerchief and started opening the drawers. When he pulled out the bottom one he found a cash box. He quickly opened it and took out the piles of notes.

Jo was getting excited. He then systematically searched the rest of the bedroom for jewellery and anything else that might be of value. There were several gold chains and bracelets in a small drawer of the dressing table. When he searched the wardrobe, Jo could hardly believe his luck when he came across a cache of gold and silver coins. After finding the coins, he went into the adjoining bedroom.

"Who's room is this?" he shouted out.

"My wife's –"

"I thought you said you lived on your own?" said Jo, suddenly fearing being disturbed by a live-in boyfriend.

"We're separated – she stays sometimes when she's in town," stammered Michael.

Jo pulled a pillowslip from the bed and began to empty the contents of a jewellery box into it. When he searched the drawers he found another pile of notes. After checking the bedroom thoroughly, Jo returned to the main bedroom and scooped all the coins and jewellery into the pillowslip. He was nearly ready to go. "How much cash was in the box?" he asked, excitedly.

"About..five or six hundred –"

"Jesus – where's you car keys?"

"In my pocket..in my jacket –"

Jo found his jacket and took out the keys. "Has your car got any alarms on it?"

"No –"

"You're sure – if any go off I'll be back –"

"There's no alarms –"

"Right, I'm going to gag you –"

"No, please! I get asthma – I won't be able to –"

"Alright, alright, take it easy – I won't gag you. How do I know you won't shout out?"

"I won't – I promise –"

"Right, I'm going – I..er..I'm sorry about this –"

"Just go, please.."

Jo descended the stairs and made his way to the front door and was just about to leave when he noticed five silver tea-pots in a cabinet in the hall. He opened it and took one out, instantly recognising the Georgian hallmark. He quickly searched round the house until he found a small suitcase, then emptied the contents of the cabinet and gently placed them in it. After stuffing in a towel to stop them clanking against each other, Jo snapped the suitcase shut and left the house.

A few minutes later he was sitting behind the wheel of the Rover and heading for Blackfriars Bridge. Ten minutes after leaving the house, Jo parked the car in a quiet street and took a taxi to Waterloo Station.

It was getting on for 3:00am when he entered the station and he was hoping to find somewhere open where he could grab a coffee and a bite to eat, but all the food shops and snack bars were closed and he had to settle for a can of coke and a chocolate bar from a vending machine.

Considering the time, there were still quite a few people milling around and Jo had trouble finding a quiet spot. He eventually found one in the carriage of a train and as he stretched out on the seat, he contemplated his next move. As he was sitting in the taxi being taken to the station, he had already decided to head for Portsmouth and seek out Freddie who would know someone that would take the loot off his hands, and maybe find him a safe haven.

Jo also thought about Christine. She would be frantic with worry by now so he suddenly decided to call her. He left the compartment and looked for a phone-box. After dialling the number, Christine was quick to answer.

"Hello, Chris –"

"Jo! Where are you – I'm out of my mind with worry –"

"I know – I'm really sorry, babe –"

"Where are you?"

"I'm in London –"

"London? Oh, Jo – what's going on – what's happened?"

"Well, me an' George were attacked by four men –"

"Why?"

"I don't know – I think they got me mixed up with someone else – they just started goin' crazy –"

"But why did they start on you?"

"That's what I'm sayin' – they just went mad, smashing the car up, then they started hittin' us with pickaxe handles. I've got bruises all up my legs and on my head."

"Are you hurt?" she asked.

"No, I'm not hurt – but I think one or two of them are, that's why I didn't want to come home – not until I find out exactly what's happened to 'em."

"What d'you mean – how badly were they hurt?"

"I don't know for sure but, well, I think one of 'em was really hurt –"

"When are you coming home then?"

"I don't know – as soon as I've found out what's happened to 'im – listen babe, I'm nearly out of change – if anyone comes round to see you tell 'em you don't know where I am okay? Don't tell anyone I'm in London – I've gotta go now 'cos the pips are gonna go – I'll give you a ring later."

"Jo –"

"I'll ring –" The phone went dead. Before leaving the booth, Jo wiped away the tears that had run down his cheeks.

A couple of hours later, Jo boarded the first train out of Waterloo that was heading for Pompey. He immediately nipped to the toilet and rolled a joint. There weren't many people taking the first train out, but he didn't want to risk being pounced on by some undercover man and be caught with a suitcase full of stolen goodies.

After covering the wooden rim of the pan with toilet tissue, Jo sat down and put a match to the joint, forever trying to rid his mind of the nightmare he was in. All he could see in his distraught state was a man sinking to his knees clutching his chest. Jo began to wonder – if he **was** dead – whether or not he knew he was dying, and he tried to swap places with how he could have felt…

…he was about to club me on the top of the head with a base-ball bat but suddenly had a ten inch steel blade sticking in his chest…he would have seen it go in and pulled out…then what? Would he fear that he was dying? Would he even know – or would he just go numb with shock and sink into unconsciousness? Yeah, he would know alright, his instincts would tell him that his life was slipping

away...and he didn't scream out...why didn't he scream out? Because dying men don't make a noise do they, they just sink into a calm and die...think positive son, don't keep thinking that he's dead, think he's alive...think that they got to him in time you stupid prick...you heard the sirens going – it was probably an ambulance racing in to save him...yeah, they got to him alright, everything's going to be sweet – they might not even find out it was me...course they will, they'll soon find out it was you...so what if they do, it was self-defence wasn't it? Surely they wouldn't do me for killing him would they? I should have taken George to the hospital...taken pictures of all his cuts and bruises...yeah, that's it, get some pictures baby, get them all blown up to poster-size so they can see every detail...although we feel you may have had some justification in defending yourself, we have come to the conclusion that you went too far...you went too far...but it was an accident you mother, can't you see – I just spun round and the blade went in him...he impaled himself on the blade...suicide, almost...only an idiot with a death wish would attack someone holding a giant butcher's knife for fucksake...George, why couldn't you give me a couple of nice little stab wounds man, all my troubles would be over if you had...just a stab wound or two...Jesus, please...don't let them do this to me...twenty five years behind bars...

Just before seven o'clock, the train pulled into Portsmouth and Southsea station and Jo was glad to be moving.

Freddie had split with Trina more than three years ago, and he was now back in his home plot in Landport, less than a ten minute walk from where Jo was now at the station.

After finding a phone and dialling Freddie's number, Jo was pleasantly surprised when he answered straightaway.

"Hello?"

"Freddie – it's me, Jo."

"Jo? Oh, 'allo Jo – what you up to – it's only seven in the mornin'?"

"I know – I didn't expect you to be up – how come you are?"

"I've had a line of whizz –"

"Whizz?"

"Yeah, keeps ya awake that's all – where are ya?"

"I'm at the station – listen Fred, I've got some tom an' some antique silver – will your Jimmy take it you reckon, I need some ready-cash quick?"

"Yeah, Jimmy'll take it – you comin' round then?"

"Yeah, I'll be round in a minute."

"Alright – I'll put the kettle on."

Jo hung up and made the short walk to Freddie's house, tucked in just behind the main shopping centre. Soon, he was sitting in the kitchen, sipping hot coffee and emptying the contents of the suitcase onto a table.

"Looks like you've had a touch, Jo – where d'ya get it all?"

"Fred, you won't believe what I'm gonna tell ya – I'm in real bad trouble, mate – I think I've killed someone."

"Killed someone! You're jokin' –"

"I ain't Fred – I don't know for sure but…well, I'm pretty sure – that's why I've fucked off –"

"What happened then?"

Jo detailed the whole story to Freddie.

"So where did all this lot come from?" he asked.

"Oh – this ain't nothing to do with the row – this lot's another story, Fred – you'll laugh when you hear this – I went home with a poof and robbed him," said Jo, laughing.

"Went home with a poof – how come?" asked Freddie.

"Well, after I fucked off I ended up in a park in London. This geezer started chattin' me up an' I went back to his house with him an' tied 'im up and robbed 'im!"

Freddie laughed. "Didn't try an' touch you up did he?"

"Fucksake Fred – I thought he was going to though – when we were in the motor I thought any second he's gonna grab my nuts!"

"Good job he didn't want it –"

"It fuckin' was – I'da slung 'im in the river and fucked off with his car – how much you reckon this'll come to then, Fred?"

"Dunno – there's a few bobs worth there. Those tea-pots must be worth a grand on their own I should think – we'll nip an' see Jimmy later."

"I'll need somewhere to stay as well, Fred – any ideas?"

"Stay 'ere can't ya?"

"Better not, mate – if that scroat snuffs it, plod will be lookin' for me everywhere, especially down here."

"Yeah, you're probably right – Gimpy'll have a room I expect – we'll go an' see 'im after we've been to Jimmy's."

"Good man. So, what ya doin' these days then? said Jo, giving Freddie a slap on the back.

"Not a lot, Jo – knock out a bit a' gear here an' there."

"Earn a few quid?"

"Mustn't grumble I s'pose," he said, with a pursed smile.

"What's this whizz stuff you've had then?"

"Speed – amphetamine sulphate – ain't you ever had any?"

"I ain't, no – what does it do?"

"Just keeps ya goin' that's all – makes ya feel active an' lively and if you have a smoke with it, it spaces you out – you want some?"

"Yeah, why not – I need to be on the alert."

Freddie nipped into the garden and returned with a small bag of white powder. He opened it up and sprinkled some of the contents onto a rizla and folded it up, then handed it to Jo. "Swallow this with some coffee 'cos it's really bitter if any gets out." Jo took the rizla and swallowed it with a gulp of coffee. "How long does it take to work?"

"You'll be flyin' in half-an-hour I expect," he said, a huge grin spreading across his face. "And if you wanna sleep tonight you better take some chloral with ya –"

"Fucksake Fred – I'll be a junkie in a minute."

"No you won't," he said.

About forty minutes later, Jo began to creep into a state of well-being as the sulphate dissolved into his bloodstream. He wasn't thinking so much and what thoughts he did have were lighter and more positive.

Within two hours, the sulphate had really taken hold and Jo was pacing up and down, anxious to get moving.

"Are you gonna phone Jimmy then, Fred – he should be up an'

about by now shouldn't he?"

"Yeah, I'll give him a ring."

Ten minutes later they were sitting in Freddie's old Ford and heading for Portsea, an old district of Portsmouth. Soon, they were in Jimmy's house and once again Jo found himself emptying the contents of the suitcase onto a table.

Besides the five teapots, four of which were Georgian, were sixteen Krugerrands, twenty sovereigns – all of them Victorian, more than twenty silver coins, several gold chains and bracelets and five diamond rings.

After careful perusal, Jimmy offered Jo a price. "I'll give you two grand for the lot," he said.

Jo was hoping for more but decided not to haggle. "You got the cash now?"

"Yeah – how warm is this lot?" he asked, still eyeing the rings, a ten-X wedged in his right eye socket.

"It was lifted at two o'clock this morning – out of town."

"Good. I'll get the dough for you." Jimmy left the room and returned a moment later with two bundles of twenty-pound notes. After stuffing the money into his jacket pocket, Freddie and Jo left the house and made their way to Gimpy's place, situated on the other side of town in Eastney.

On the way, Jo dashed into a post-office and bought a large registered envelope, slipped in the two thousand, scribbled a quick note to Charlie, addressed it, and handed it back to the counter assistant. Tucking the receipt in his back pocket, Jo returned to the car. With more than eight hundred pounds still in his possession, he quickly counted out three hundred and handed it to Freddie. "A little drink for ya old son."

"Well..er..that's very decent of you old chap," he smiled, "may you live long and prosper, and may your children –"

"Alright Fred," said Jo, laughing, "there's only three hundred there, not the whole two grand!"

They both laughed as Freddie edged his way through the morning traffic.

Before long they were sitting in one of Gimpy's converted bedsits. Jo had known Gimpy for many years but hadn't seen him for quite a while. He quickly explained his predicament to Gimpy and he in turn was quick to assure Jo complete privacy, offering him a room at the back of the house. After giving Gimpy two weeks rent money Jo was given a key, enabling him to come and go as he pleased.

Freddie and Gimpy began smoking a joint but Jo was feeling too lively to sit around the house, and if he was to stay in hiding he needed some clothes and other essentials. He left the house and made his way to the nearest parade of shops, a five minute walk from Gimpy's house.

On the way back he called into a newsagents and bought an ample supply of tobacco and a daily paper. After letting himself in, he joined Freddie and Gimpy on the settee and began to scan the paper, hoping and praying that he didn't come across any stories about a man dying from stab wounds.

Then he saw it…

MAN STABBED TO DEATH IN GANG FEUD

A twenty-four year old father of two was brutally stabbed to death last night outside of a pub in Sevenoaks, Kent. A police spokesman said the man, who has not been named, was the victim of a gang feud that had been raging for more than three months. The man, an unemployed fitter, was rushed to hospital but was found dead on arrival. One eye-witness said his killer was armed with a 12" long carving knife. Police are looking for a man 5'8" to 5'10" tall, late twenties or early thirties, stocky build with fair hair.

Jo read the story again, then again before passing the paper across to Freddie. He laid his head on the back of the settee as he tried to take in the reality that he'd killed a man. Before reading the story there was still hope, a gossamer chance that the surgeons might have got to him, but now, all that was gone. In place of the thin ray of hope that Jo had been clinging to, came the thick arm of the police who would be hunting him relentlessly until they had him in the dock facing a murder charge.

Although the stabbing was an accident Jo knew the police, when they finally caught him, would charge him with the ultimate crime and it would fall on Jo to prove it was otherwise.

Jo cursed when he thought of George. If he had stabbed Jo once or twice like he wanted him to, he could have gone to the hospital for immediate treatment, then used their records to back his claim of self-defence. Without any serious injuries to show them, Jo knew he was doomed from the start and the only thing a jury were going to be asked was whether or not his death was intentional.

Freddie handed the paper back to Jo, and looked at him with concern. "What ya gonna do now?" he said.

"I don't know, Fred, I honestly don't know – all I was doin' was sittin' in a car minding my own business," said Jo, leaving the sentence hanging.

"Jo, if it happened like you said, mate, you should be alright. It was an accident –"

"I know, Fred, but they don't take any notice do they? You gotta be fuckin' dyin' before they take a plea of self-defence – I've been through it all before, remember?"

Jo was becoming distraught. He knew how the system worked and he knew when it came to a trial, the picture of how it happened would not come out – it never did. If the jury could see that picture, he would be okay but in the cold black and white of a courtroom, well, Jo tried not to think about it.

"Anyway, I'll worry about my destiny later – let's have a smoke?" He pulled out a small piece of gear and joined together three rizlas. "You say you're knockin' out some gear, Fred?"

"Yeah, d'you want some?"

"Yeah, you better get me a lump – and make it a big lump!"

"We'll have to go back to my place for it."

"It might be safer for you if I stayed here – I've got enough for now – maybe you can bring it out later for me."

"Yeah, no problem," said Freddie, nodding.

Jo turned to Gimpy. "Listen, I expect you've sussed Gimp, that

I'm in plenty a' trouble – you still don't mind me stayin' do ya?"

"No, stay as long as ya like – what happened then, Jo?"

"Well, cuttin' it short – I was attacked by two or three geezers with bats and ended up killin' one of 'em."

"Fuckin' hell – does old bill know it's you?"

"I dunno yet – I just fucked off a bit lively. I'm gonna give the missus a ring later an' see if anyone's been round."

"Well, as I've said, you can stay here as long as ya like."

"Yeah thanks, Gimp – I appreciate that," said Jo, finally putting a match to the joint he'd rolled.

"Listen Fred, I've just been thinking – there's a fag shop on that parade and there's an empty shop next to it. I was thinking of tryin' to screw it – must be a few bob's worth of snout in there – what d'you think Fred, do you know anyone who'll take 'em?"

"Yeah, no problem gettin' rid of snout."

"Jo, don't mind me buttin' in, but if you're after a good few quid, why don't you try a chemist shop?" said Gimpy.

"A chemist? Wouldn't be much in there would there?"

"Cor, you're fuckin' jokin' – you grab all the goodies from the D.D.A. an' you'll make a fortune!"

"Yeah? Tell me more, Gimp – what's a D.D.A. by the way?"

"It's the cabinet where they have to keep all the dangerous drugs. D.D.A. stands for the Dangerous Drugs Act, and they have to keep 'em all locked in a cabinet which makes it very handy for anyone who wants to nick all the drugs that's worth money."

"Yeah? What sort of dough ya talkin' about?"

"Well, could be anything – three, four, five grand – depends what quantities they're holding. They all have to keep the same stuff an' if they're holdin' a lot of stock you could clean up – more than you'd get in a tobacconist's."

"Yeah?"

"Yeah – and it'll be a lot easier than carryin' a million boxes of snout around."

Jo laughed briefly at Gimpy's exaggeration, but saw his point. "Yeah, you're right there – how would I know what to take though?"

"You take everything in the cabinet – just scoop the lot into a bag.

It's all worth money."

"Yeah? And d'you know anyone who'd take it all – for cash?"

"I do, yeah – he'll take everything you get."

"And he'd give me cash straightaway?"

"Yeah, definately."

"Umm, I'll have to think about this – it sounds a lot easier than fags."

"It is Jo, believe me –"

"Have you ever done one then, Gimp?"

"One or two," he smiled.

"What about the one on the parade – you done that one?"

"No – I used to do 'em out in the country."

"Well, I think I'll have another stroll down the road and have a look at it – you say just scoop all the contents into a bag an' that's it –"

"Yeah – as I say, if he's holdin' plenty of stock – Diamorphine, Durophet, Diconal, Palfiam, Seconal, Duromorph, Methadone –"

"Fucksake Gimp – you know all the names don't ya?"

"Forgotten most of 'em – anyway, go and have a good look and if you fancy it I can give you a nice big holdall and a jemmy for gettin' the cabinet open – just ram it in between the doors an' it'll spring open – and the D.D.A. will be the one with a little keyhole in it – some of the others will just be sliding cabinets, and it'll be in the back of the shop in the actual pharmacy."

"Right 'o Gimp, thanks – I'll creep down an' have a look at it – what you doin' Fred, stayin' here or –"

"I might as well shoot off an' get that gear for ya. You want some more fast-stuff as well don't ya?"

"Yeah –"

"And some chloral?"

Jo lowered his head in mock embarrassment, "Yes please, Fred."

"You need any gear, Gimp?"

"No I'm alright, Fred – I get mine from the doctor," he laughed.

A few minutes later Freddie was speeding off in his car and Jo was walking back to the parade of shops, taking note of any alleys and possible escape routes as he went. The parade consisted of half a dozen shops, and opposite them was a huge cemetry. As he neared the parade he noticed a narrow access road, obviously used for deliveries and for the collection of refuse. He was glad to see there was access from both directions.

Jo strolled past the front entrances of the shops, noting the position of the chemist. A tobacconist was on the corner, then came an empty shop, then the chemist. Next to his target was an estate agent's office, and next to that was a fruit 'n' veg shop.

After taking note of the shops he carried on walking then crossed the road and walked back again, looking up at the second level of the building. The fruit 'n' veg had living accommodation over the top, but as far as Jo could tell, the rest of the block was office accommodation, used by Hill Parker & Co. Solicitors.

Jo carried on walking. A little further on he crossed the road again and strolled back slowly towards the shops. When he got to the empty one, he feigned interest by studying the 'to let' sign. He went up close to the door and peered in. There were several tables and chairs scattered round, and after seeing an old counter that had been half demolished, Jo guessed the previous owner had used the premises as a cafe, endorsed when he saw the remains of an old menu in among the debris.

A minute later he was staring into the window of the chemist shop, then he went inside. There were two or three customers waiting to be served, giving Jo ample time to look round the shop. He craned his neck trying to look over the top of all the cosmetics piled high on the counter, and then he saw it. The cabinet was on the back wall, a notice pinned to it proclaiming the Dangerous Drugs Act.

As he neared the counter, Jo moved across and perused the sunglasses, looking into the pharmacy to see if there was access to the back. He didn't see any. Then, when he took a few steps nearer to the counter, he saw a passage leading from the pharmacy that must have led to the back of the shop. Jo felt better when he saw it.

After buying a tube of throat lozenges, he left the shop and made his way round to the back. There was a six foot fence running the entire length of the access road. Opposite, running parallel to the fence, was a huge brick building giving ample cover if Jo had to scale the wooden fence to gain entry through the back of the shop.

While he walked casually along the access road, he noticed the windows of the tobacconist were heavily barred, as were the chemist's windows. The disused cafe though, looked accessible and Jo wondered if he could break in and tunnel his way through the wall to the pharmacy. He guessed the wall would be a nine-incher, or maybe a double nine-incher with a cavity in between the two shops.

After a further trip round the block, casually looking at the chemist's windows and door, and the offices above, Jo headed back to his bed-sit, thinking all the while how he could gain entry to the chemist and relieve them of all those nasty drugs.

Jo hadn't attempted a break-in since he was a teenager, and he was having doubts as to whether he could pull it off. In ordinary circumstances he would have dropped the idea quicker than a hot potato but with the thought of Christine struggling on social security, Jo considered the possibility more deeply.

When he got back to the bedsit, he let himself in and went straight to his room to think. After putting together a three-skinner, he stretched out on the bed and tried to come to a decision. The thought of a possible three or four thousand pounds sitting in a flimsy wooden cabinet urged him to consider every possible way that he might gain entry to the shop.

Born under the sign of the scales, Jo was the epitome of the astrologist's dream when it came to indecision, swaying to and fro, this way and that, battling ceaselessly within himself until he'd played out all the scenarios. When he did finally settle on a solution, he usually followed it through and now, with the decision made, he was going to have the contents of the D.D.A., and he was going to have them tonight.

Jo rose from the bed and went to see Gimpy. He knocked on his door. "Gimp – it's me, Jo," he said quietly. Gimpy opened the door and invited him in. "Alright, Jo – did you have a look at it?"

"Yeah – I'm gonna do it tonight. Can you give your mate a ring an' let 'im know there might be something about? And can you let me have the jemmy an' the holdall?"

"Yeah no problem – I'll get 'em for ya now." He left the room and returned a moment later with the bag and the jemmy. After wiping them down, he handed them to Jo. "Thanks Gimp, I'll give ya a drink if I get lucky."

"You don't have to do that, Jo –"

"Well, I will anyway – listen, if I do pull this off, will your mate come round here or –"

"Yeah, he'll come round here. He likes gettin' his hands on a D.D.A. – he'll be round ten minutes after I ring 'im I should think. When ya gonna do it?"

"About eleven – just before the pubs shut."

Gimpy didn't ask how Jo was going to break into the shop and Jo was glad he didn't. If he heard Jo's bizarre plan, he probably would have tried to talk him out of it.

Just after seven, Freddie returned as promised, bringing with him the goodies that Jo had asked for. "There's an ounce of gear in there," he said, handing Jo a package, "and some whizz as well."

"Thanks Fred – did you get the chloral?"

"Yeah, I've got it here," he said, pulling out a small container from his pocket. "There's thirty mil there – half of it should get you t'sleep – or take the lot if you want to make double sure."

"Right o' Fred – I'll go an' tuck this lot away somewhere."

Jo left Freddie and Gimpy and went to his room. He put the chloral in a drawer and opened the package, taking out the sulphate. He sprinkled some onto a rizla and swallowed it before putting the rest in the drawer. With the plan he had in mind, Jo needed to be on full alert.

He stuffed the ounce of resin into his Y-fronts, just in case of arrest.

After spending most of the evening smoking joints and sipping cans of lager, Freddie and Gimpy were out of it.

Jo had given the cans a miss and spent most of the time thinking out his plan.

At ten forty-five he was ready to go. "Right boys, I'm off to do a little burglarin' – I'll see you in a minute."

Jo left the two of them sitting on the settee and went to his room to collect the jemmy and the holdall. After rolling himself a cigarette, he took a couple of long pulls on it and left the house.

When he got to the newsagents, he stepped into the phone box that was on the corner and dialled 999. Almost at once a voice asked, "Hello, which service please?"

"Oh, put me through to the police!" said Jo. A moment later the connection was made. "Police emergency –"

"Oh yes, there's a major disturbance going on at the Red Lion, Milton. There's more than a dozen men fighting in the car-park and some of them are armed! Can you send some men at once – I think one of them has been stabbed!"

"Can I have your name please, sir?"

"No, I'm sorry – I'm with a lady I shouldn't be with, please hurry!"

Jo slammed the receiver down and made the few yards to the chemist shop. There were one or two people around but none of them were close enough to the shop to cause him any concern – and with old bill winging their way to the disturbance at the Red Lion, Jo was confident that he would get the two or three minutes he needed.

He took the jemmy from the holdall and looked at the shopfront for a moment and then, with all the strength he could muster, Jo kicked in the door of the chemist. The alarm was triggered in an instant and the glass shattered as the door shuddered against the doorstop.

Undeterred by the deafening noise, Jo ran into the shop and made his way to the pharmacy. With one yank from the jemmy the cabinet flew open. He quickly scooped the contents into the holdall, holding it high so that none of the glass containers smashed against each other. When he'd cleared the cabinet, he zipped the bag and ran towards the door and out into the street, his heart racing.

There were several people in the vacinity of the shop, all of them curious about the sound of the alarm-bells, but none of them pursued Jo as he ran off into the night.

He took the road that ran parallel to his bed-sit and only after he was certain that he wasn't being followed, did he double back and let himself in. He was still breathing heavily when Freddie and Gimpy came into the hall.

"What happened, Jo – did it come on top?" asked Gimpy.

"No, it went like a dream –"

"Did you do it then?" asked Freddie.

"Yeah, course I did –"

"What that quick – you've only been gone ten minutes!"

"I know Fred, that was the plan – I just crashed in through the front door –"

"You're joking!" said Gimpy in amazement.

"No – I just done the front door – ran in – done the cabinet – and away. I made a 999 call first tellin' old bill there's a major disturbance at the Red Lion –"

"You didn't –" said Freddie, smiling.

"Yeah, I did Fred – I said there's a big fight goin' on in the car park and can you please send some men at once!"

By the time Jo finished telling the story, all three of them were laughing.

"Fuckin' 'ell Jo, that's brilliant!" said Gimpy.

"Yeah, fuckin' magic," agreed Freddie, nodding his head, imagining Jo in full flight taking on the D.D.A., "especially gettin' a few old bill to charge off in the wrong direction!"

"Yeah," laughed Jo, "I liked that bit myself. Anyway, let's see if it's all been worth it shall we – you're the expert, Gimp – I'll leave it to you to surprise me. I need a joint."

Jo sat down at the table and put together three rizlas, watching Gimpy's face as he emptied the contents of the bag.

"If you come across any Fylon, Gimp, let me know will ya?" said Freddie.

"What are they then, Fred?" asked Jo.

"Slimmin' tablets – same as whizz but ten times better."

"Yeah? I'll have a few of those myself then."

Within a few minutes Gimpy had emptied the bag and piled all the jars and boxes and packets onto the table. Jo had never seen so many pills and capsules, all of them coded with numbers and letters, or by colour. Among the array of hypnotics, barbituates, anxiolytics, antipsychotics, stimulants and analgesics, were dozens of morphine ampules, worth seven or eight pounds each by the time they reached the street. Also in the cabinet were two jars of dia-morphine – pure heroin.

When Gimpy came across a box of Fylon, he passed it over to Freddie. "Here you are Fred – there's enough there to make you disappear altogether!" he said laughing.

"Thanks Gimp – is it okay for me to have some 'a these Jo?"

"Yeah sure, take what you want – save some for me though."

"There's another couple of boxes of 'em 'ere if you want 'em Jo," said Gimpy.

"Yeah – sling 'em over," said Jo.

Without counting every pill, and only guessing the amount of powder contained in the jars, Gimpy estimated Jo might get around three thousand, possibly more.

"Well done, Gimp – is there anything you want out of this?"

"Er, I wouldn't mind a few Durophet –"

"You better take 'em then – before your mate gets round."

"Yeah, I'll give 'im a ring now – how many can I have?"

"Take what you want – you got what you want, Fred?"

"Yeah, these'll do me," he said, clutching a box of Fylon.

About ten minutes after Gimpy made the call, his mate was sitting at the table sorting his way through the multitude of drugs, aided and abetted by a set of scales and a copy of MIMS, the doctors bible.

An hour later he offered Jo a price. "I can give you thirty-three hundred for the lot – cash," he said. Jo nodded approval. "Sounds good to me. You interested in any more if I get hold of any?"

"Yeah, sure – I'll take these all day long – Gimpy knows that don't ya Gimp?"

"I should do – you had enough of 'em off me!" he said.

Soon, the dealer was gone and Jo was relaxing on the settee, a three-skinner burning slowly between his fingers. He was feeling good. He couldn't believe how easy it had been to rob the chemist and he wondered how many more he could plunder before he was apprehended. Another four or five would see his total haul creep to around twenty thousand pounds and Christine…

…Christine…oh Jesus, what have I done to you, why is this

happening to us…we were so happy together…me and you and two
fine sons but now they are hunting for me, trying to take me from
you, but I won't let them baby, they're not going to have me, no sir,
not until I've robbed every chemist in the land…

Jo suddenly rose to his feet. "I must make a phone call."

Jo left the house and walked in the opposite direction to the chemist until he came across a phone-box. He could have used the phone in Gimpy's house, but phoning Christine was too emotional for him to make with two of his friends sitting so close by. He slipped a few coins in the slot and dialled his home number. Christine soon answered.

"Hello?"

"Hi Chrissy, it's me –"

"Oh Jo, I've been waiting for you to call –"

"I know, I'm sorry babe – it's the first chance I've had really – has anyone been round looking for me?"

"No, nobody's been round – why don't you come home Jo, this is really worrying the life out of me – and the boys want to know what's happening as well. Please Jo, come home."

"Listen, what I'm gonna do is this – on Monday, after you've sorted out the 'erberts, I want you to catch a train to London and I'll meet you there and we can have a talk, and if things are still the same maybe I'll come back with you and see what happens okay?"

"But why can't you come home tomorrow?" she pleaded.

"Well, I don't want to risk being arrested at home – if they are going to arrest me that is – they don't even know it's me yet. I'll give you a ring tomorrow okay? Christine?"

Jo could hear her sobbing on the other end of the line, and he too began to feel his own tears building.

"Chrissy, please don't cry – I feel so bad about this, but..there was nothing I could do, babe..I was just protecting myself – you've got to believe that Chrissy –"

"I do Jo, I do – it's just that I want you home with me. I'm so worried about you – you might even get into more trouble if you're hiding from the police – have you got any money?"

"Yes, I'm okay for cash – Freddie gave me a few bob and he's putting me up for a couple of days. Listen, I'll give you a ring tomorrow to tell you what train to catch okay?"

"Yes alright –"

"I'll make it a bit earlier if you like – have a chat with the boys – don't go worryin' okay – I'll see ya later."

"Yes –"

"Still love me?"

"You know I do – that's why I worry about you –"

"I know – I gotta go now – I'll ring you tomorrow. I love you – bye babe –"

"Bye –" Jo broke the connection and left the phone-box.

The sound of Christine sobbing had reduced Jo to tears. Every time he called her, he felt the hurt she was suffering and because he loved her so much, it hurt him beyond imagination.

Jo tried to shake Christine from his mind as he made the short walk back to his bed-sit. He began to think of the money he had acquired so far. With the two thousand that he'd already sent to Charlie, and the near four thousand that he had in his pockets, he felt a little better. Six thousand pounds was going to make life a lot easier for Christine if he was going down, and he wasn't about to retire from the burglary business yet, no sir, not until he had twenty or thirty thousand – or fifty or sixty would be even better.

Jo didn't get up the next day until late in the afternoon and the first thing he did was take a long, cool shower. After donning a fresh set of clothes, he left the house in search of another chemist.

The first one he came across had a sturdy metal door, and with two keyholes in it, Jo doubted it would give way as easy as the one he'd crashed the night before.

The second shop he looked at showed more promise. It had an old wooden door and was located in an ideal position, just off the main road. The only trouble was, he couldn't see right into the shop and he didn't know where the D.D.A. was. If he crashed the door and spent more than two or three minutes inside, his chances of escape would be greatly reduced. With his freedom at stake, Jo decided to wait until he could enter the shop as a customer and look at it more closely.

While making his way to Freddie's house, Jo saw another shop with a similar, old fashioned wooden door. He made a note to visit that one as a customer as well.

Before calling on Freddie, Jo made a phone call to Christine and arranged to meet her in London the following day, telling her to catch the ten-sixteen from Sevenoaks. He would meet her at eleven o'clock at Charing Cross.

Jo spent the rest of the day with Freddie, smoking dope and sipping cans of lager, reminiscing old times until they were both too exhausted to talk further. Just after midnight, he summoned a taxi to take him back to his desolate room.

The next morning, at nine o'clock sharp, Jo walked into the main post-office and posted three thousands pounds to his brother. He then dashed across to the railway station and caught the nine-fifteen to Waterloo.

To keep himself calm, and at the same time ensuring that he stayed on full alert, Jo had taken three Fylon tablets. Freddie had told him that they weren't as heavy as sulphate and the comedown didn't leave the body so drained.

While sitting in the first-class compartment, idly staring out through the window at the passing countryside, Jo wondered what he was going to say to Christine. He knew it would be an emotional meeting but he hoped she wasn't going to make it difficult for him.

At ten forty-five the train pulled into Waterloo. He alighted from the train and hurried across the station and down the steps to Waterloo East for the connection to Charing Cross. Within a few minutes he was on another train. Jo wouldn't have been surprised if Christine was on it as well considering all trains from Sevenoaks stopped at Waterloo East – and it was nearly eleven o'clock. With that thought in mind Jo had boarded the first carriage so that when it pulled into the platform he would be at the barrier waiting.

Although he never really thought himself as being on the run, he was still fearful that the police might have followed Christine and his heart was beating just that much faster as he scanned the crowd that were making their way down the platform towards the barrier.

Then he saw her. He also saw his sister, Irene.

After taking in the surprise of seeing his sister, Jo craned his neck, looking over the crowds for any old bill that might be following them. When he didn't see any he relaxed a little, but nevertheless, moved right away from the barrier so that Christine and his sister couldn't see him. When he was sure as he could be that they didn't have a tail, Jo moved towards them.

Christine was the first to see him, and smiled. When they came together Jo held her tight for a few moments before letting her go. "Are you okay – I've missed you so much," he said, embracing her again.

"I've missed you too," she said.

"I see you've brought re-enforcements then – how are ya sis?" said Jo, moving across to kiss her on the cheek.

"Yes, I'm fine Jo – I hope you don't mind me being here but, well, I think Christine needs a little support at this time."

"No, that's okay sis – I think I'm glad to see you now that you **are** here. You wouldn't believe how worried I am – you haven't got any inside information have you?" he half-laughed.

"Afraid not, Jo – but I might have some sound advice for you –"

"Yes, I thought you might – let's go and grab a hot drink."

Jo led the two ladies into the station restaurant and ordered three coffees. After finding a quiet table, they sat themselves down and began to discuss Jo's monumental problem. "Listen," said Jo, "I know you want me to go back with you but I want you to know what happened first. It's important to me that you know it was an accident Chris – you know I couldn't just stab a man –"

"I know you couldn't," she said, taking his hand. "I believe you when you say it was an accident, but we've got to sort out what to do now –"

"I know – but I can't just hand myself in can I? They might not even know it's me yet –"

Christine looked at Irene and then back to Jo. "They know it was you, Jo. Three detectives came to the house last night," she whispered. Jo pursed his lips and cursed his luck. "Ah well, it was on the cards I suppose. What did they say?"

"They wanted to know where you were, and when was the last time I saw you. When I said you weren't at home they asked if they could check, then left."

"So, what do I dow now?"

"Well Jo," began Irene, "I think you should seriously consider giving yourself up – go to the police station and tell them what happened. It would look better if you gave yourself up wouldn't it?"

"It would yes, but I can't do it yet. I don't think I could handle suddenly being locked up."

"But Jo, you can't hide forever," said Christine, "sooner or later they will find you."

"I know they will, babe – listen, I **will** give myself up, but not just yet – I need a bit of time to get use to the idea of walking into a police station, okay?"

"But Jo –"

"Christine, you've got to bear with me on this. I can't go back with you now and walk into a police station – I'd end up a nervous wreck. Just give me a week, then I'll give myself up, I promise – what do you think sis, a week isn't goin' to make any difference is it, not to them?"

"Well, maybe a few days won't make a lot of difference, but you must give yourself up Jo, for your own good."

"I will – I just need to get use to the idea that's all."

While looking at Christine, Jo suddenly realised how she must be feeling. Usually, she was brimming with radiance and was full of life, but here, sitting at the table, she was listless and her face showed signs of restless nights.

All at once it came home to him.

He hadn't really accepted that he was responsible for a man's death, nor had he accepted the possibility of long-term imprisonment, but Christine had – and she was suffering the reality of it.

"Chris, I.." Irene saw the moment and left the table.

"I'll get some more coffees," she said.

Jo took hold of Christine's hand and began to give back to her the emotion she had lost, the emotion she needed most – hope.

"Chrissy, in a few days I'm going to give myself up, but because a man was killed they might keep me in custody. When I go for trial though, I'll have a good chance of acquittal. Did the police tell you we were attacked by four men armed with clubs?"

"No, they didn't say anything about it – just that they were looking for you."

"Well apparently, there was some kind of feud going on – that I didn't know anything about. Anyway, I was attacked because I was sitting in this geezer's car who was involved in the feud – there must have been plenty of witnesses who can say we were attacked so I'll be able to prove it was self-defence okay? I just don't want you worryin' too much."

"But I can't help it – the police said you were in serious trouble."

"Yeah well, they would say that wouldn't they – so that you would try and make me give myself up – it's an old trick of theirs."

"I still can't help worrying though – what if they don't believe it was an accident?"

"Don't go thinking like that okay?" he said, running a curved finger down her face. "You gotta think that they **will** believe me, alright – positive thinking – isn't that right sis?"

"What's that?" said Irene, returning to the table.

"I was just telling Christine to only think positive."

"Yes, that's right. Negative thoughts are not to be encouraged." Irene passed fresh coffee round the table. "I was thinking," she said, "you could always come and stay with us until you decide what to do."

"Er, I don't think that would be a good idea really – the police could easily check whether I've got any brothers or sisters. No, what I'll do, is go back to Pompey for the rest of the week – get myself use to the idea, then give myself up. I just don't want you worryin' that's all," he said to Christine, "if I know you are okay it makes it easier to handle – and I was thinking, you can tell the boys that I'm working away – tell them I'm on long contract or something. How are they anyway – I really miss 'em?"

"They're okay – they miss you though."

"Where are they now?"

"Jenny is looking after them –"

"I was thinkin' of gettin' 'em a present or something. What d'you think they'd like?"

"Jo, you don't have to do that – I don't suppose you've got much money anyway, have you?"

"No, I'm alright for money – Freddie is doin' okay at the moment and he gave me a few bob to help out."

Christine smiled. "I like Freddie – how is he these days?"

Jo laughed. "Well apart from his depression, his hernia and his insomnia, I think he's alright. Anyway, what shall I get the 'erberts?"

"Jo, I don't think you need to –"

"I know – but I might not see 'em for a while…" Jo had to stop thinking about them, and he opened his eyes wide to stop the tears from forming.

It was only now, looking at Christine and thinking of his sons, did he fully realise that he might be losing his family. He wished he could lift Christine high in the air and tell her that it was all a dream, a horrible nightmare designed to test their love, but was all over now, and he could return home with her.

Before his emotions could get the better of him, he suggested they leave the restaurant and take a stroll down the road before they saw his distress.

Soon, they were crossing St. Giles Circus and heading along the Tottenham Court Road, looking in toy shops and bookshops trying to find suitable presents for the boys. When Jo didn't find anything he liked, he decided to give them a tenner each instead. Knowing the 'erberts like he did, he guessed they would prefer the cash anyway.

Because Christine had to be back for the boys, and Irene had to be back to prepare her family's evening meal, the two of them had decided to catch the two-twenty from Charing Cross.

During the brief three hours they were together, Christine and Jo talked constantly, covering all the problems she was likely to face. He told her to phone the social security office and get them to send the appropriate forms so that she could claim benefit. He told her to return the forms by post rather than have to suffer the indignity of everyone listening if she had to explain her predicament in person.

He also told her that Charlie was going to help with a little financial support.

Also discussed was the probability that they would have to move again. Once it became public knowledge that Jo had killed someone, he would be a marked man. He wasn't particularly worried that he couldn't handle the situation, but if suddenly attacked, any man was vulnerable and with the dead man no doubt having many friends and relatives, Sevenoaks would not be a safe place to live.

He didn't explain it to Christine like that though, he told her it was for her peace of mind and for the sake of the boys.

Because of the Fylon, Jo's mind was racing and he could hardly believe the time had gone so quickly. Before he knew it, they were on the two-twenty pulling out of Charing Cross and Jo was saying his goodbyes before the train reached Waterloo East. It was only a three or four minute journey.

"You take care now, okay – I'll give you a ring every day. Bye sis, thanks for coming up with Christine – take care."

"Yes, you take care too, and remember – just a few days now, you've got to consider Christine above all else – remember too, to keep your head when you think there is nothing to lose and ride above any thoughts that will harm your progress – you must be strong and not be drawn in to shadows where false dreams lie, and where lesser men dwell. Remember too not to panic with emotions that aren't meant to be. It is a journey you are on, a journey of life – God bless you, Jo."

While she was speaking, Jo was almost transfixed by her words, and his sister saw it. "Oh, I'm sorry – I didn't mean to go off –"

"That's okay," said Jo, "I like to hear your words when you talk like that. I'm not sure I know what they mean but, well, they sound sort of strange, as if there's a message hidden among them –"

"There is, Jo – you've just got to work it out somehow."

The train pulled into the station and shuddered to a halt. "Right, I'll see you girls later then," he said kissing them both. "And I'll ring you tomorrow," he said to Christine, kissing her again before alighting from the train. "Give my love to the 'erberts."

"I will – take care Jo, and please don't leave it too long."

"I won't, I promise – bye, bye sis –"

Almost as soon as Jo slammed the door the train started to move. He waved and said a final goodbye and stood watching the train until it disappeared from his view. When it was gone he stayed on the platform, imagining the train speeding its way back to Sevenoaks. He imagined the driver, gripping the controls and increasing the speed until the train was going too fast for the curve…

Before he imagined anything more, he shook himself out of it and walked towards the exit.

When he was safely on his way back to Portsmouth, he nipped to the toilet and rolled a couple of single skinners. After smoking one of them, he returned to his seat and let his mind drift on the mixture of amphetamine and cannabis. It was a relatively new experience for Jo, and the combination of the two drugs allowed him to explore some of the paths that lay ahead. The disturbing thing was, all the paths ended with a brick wall topped with razor wire and tall turrets. Before he got to those walls though, there were adventures to be had and he enjoyed the moment as he let his mind run.

Before long, Jo was back in Pompey and casting his eyes over the two chemist shops that he'd found the previous day. They were ideal and with similar layouts in each shop to the one he had already broken into, he didn't visualise any problems.

Later in the afternoon he bought a pair of thin leather gloves and a woollen ski-hat that he could pull down over his ears when he entered the shops. To aid his disguise further he bought a pair of thick rimmed glasses with clear lenses. After careful thought, he also bought a rubber truncheon so that he would be on equal terms if he came up against confrontation with plod.

At ten-thirty Jo was preparing for break-in number two.

He was casually dressed and the blue and white ski-hat didn't look out of place as he walked past the shop. The Street was deserted and the subdued light gave him a little cover. When the moment was right, Jo kicked in the door with a thundering crash, setting the bells ringing. He ran to the back of the shop. Within thirty seconds he had the cabinet open and was scooping the contents into the holdall. Less than two minutes later he was on his way out of the shop, the prize firmly in his hand.

When he left the shop, a man, aged about forty, began to chase him, urging him to stop. Another man, a lot younger, had come out of his house, wondering about the sound of the alarms.

The man chasing Jo urged the younger man to phone the police and Jo saw him disappear into the house.

Jo carried on running and with his escape route already planned he would soon be lost in the sprawling housing estate of Somerstown.

After he had been running for a minute or so, he stopped when he still heard the footsteps of his pursuer close on his heels. "Don't follow me any further or I'll hurt you!" he shouted out. The man stopped running, but edged towards Jo with slow deliberate steps and Jo cursed when he realised he wasn't taking heed of his warning. Jo knew he could take the man out there and then if he wanted to, but his main priority was to distance himself from the shop before the area was surrounded by old bill. With them already having a witness that could point them in the right direction, it would soon become imperative that he shook off the man following him.

A minute later Jo was clearing a low fence and darting through a narrow arch that led to a play area. There were rows of small sheds and numerous trees and bushes in between the block of flats, giving him plenty of cover from the road.

As he moved deeper into the maze of flats, he could still hear the heavy footsteps of someone chasing him. Suddenly Jo stopped, placing the holdall down beside him. A few seconds later the man came into view. He slowed when he saw Jo had stopped to confront him. He was breathing hard and Jo guessed another few minutes would have seen him tailed off.

Jo looked at him closely. He was obviously fit and with a height advantage, Jo wondered briefly if he was going to give him a hard time. "What the fuck is your problem mister!?" he shouted.

"You've just burgled a shop and I'm going to arrest you – I am an off-duty police officer!" he said.

"Oh –" uttered Jo, taken completely by surprise. He didn't look like old bill and for a second Jo was unsure what to do. Plod saw Jo's indecision and moved in for the arrest.

Jo remained placid, waiting for him to come into range and when he did, he kicked him hard in between the legs. Seeing him crumple to the ground, Jo stood over him for a moment, making sure that he wasn't about to do any more running. When Jo remembered the time he himself was kicked in the groin, he knew plod wasn't going to move for a while.

The agonising pain would have seered through his body and would now be creeping into his lower stomach, causing cramp-like aching nausea. If Jo had caught him full, he would be vomiting in a few minutes. When Jo saw his screwed up face, he felt fleeting sympathy for him before grabbing the bag and running off through the maze of the estate.

An hour later, after skirting all the main roads, and darting into alley-ways or behind bushes whenever he saw an approaching car, Jo was back in the safety of his room.

He was still hyped up. To calm himself, he rolled a joint and made a mug of coffee before stretching out on the bed. A little while later he went to Gimpy's room, and told him he had another parcel of drugs. Gimpy soon phoned the dealer.

Within the hour, Jo was in possession of a further three and a half thousand pounds.

Late the next day, Jo posted a third registered letter to his brother. By the same time tomorrow, Charlie would be holding eight and a half thousand pounds for Christine's welfare. As he left the post office he held the receipt in his hand and searched his pockets for the other two, wondering what to do with them. If he was arrested and they found the receipts, they would probably swoop on his brother and confiscate the money. He nipped back into the post office and bought a stamped envelope and posted them to Charlie, telling him to destroy them on receipt of the registered mail. Jo knew the chances of registered letters going missing were fairly remote, but possible, and he didn't want to risk not being able to claim in the event that one of them did go missing.

With his mind at peace, Jo skipped out of the post office and made his way along Commercial Road towards Freddie's house. On the way, he decided to pop into a branch of John Temple and rig himself out with a set of new clothes.

It was a mistake.

After making the purchases he went to leave the shop but was obstructed by a huge man, over six feet tall and weighing more than fifteen stones. Jo tried to side-step his great bulk but the man closed off the small gap. "D'you fuckin' mind – I'm tryin' to get through!" he screamed.

"Don't I know you?" said the man, preventing Jo from leaving the small confines of the shop. Jo looked up at him and studied him more closely. He seemed familiar. Then suddenly, he realised who it was – Walker, the detective who had threatened him several years before.

Jo tried to push his way past but Walker was too big to move so easily. "I do know you. It's Sullivan isn't it?"

"Just let me pass will ya?" said Jo, realising the danger he was in.

"You aren't going anywhere Sullivan – I believe the Sevenoaks police want a word with you."

Jo's heart-beat went into overdrive. He dropped the bags he was carrying and threw two quick punches into Walker's stomach, hoping to wind him but Walker absorbed the blows and grabbed Jo by the coat, trying to force him to the ground. While grappling with Jo, Walker suddenly shouted to the staff in the shop. "I'm a police officer – phone the police immediately!"

Jo began to panic. He kicked Walker several times, trying to find his groin, and punched him until he wriggled free of his grip. When he tried to force his way past, Walker caught him with a blow to the side of his face, knocking him back. When he realised he wasn't going to get past the huge bulk of Walker's frame, Jo looked for a different way out. "Is there a back way outta here!?" he shouted. Nobody answered. He ran further into the shop, searching frantically for an escape route. With the police being alerted to a major disturbance in the main shopping precinct, it would only be a matter of minutes before the shop was surrounded.

After failing to find an alternative exit, Jo turned on Walker again and tried to fight his way past him. Jo rushed at him and dived for his legs, catching him just below the knees, bringing him crashing to the floor. Jo sprung to his feet and made a dash for the door but Walker caught his leg and Jo went down. As Walker tried to drag Jo towards him, Jo used his free leg and kicked Walker full in the face, splitting his lip. Walker howled out and relaxed his grip, enabling Jo to scramble to his feet. Walker got to his feet as well but his huge size slowed him up and Jo was already at the door, trying to pull it open – but it wouldn't budge. One of the staff had locked it. Jo spun round and grabbed a small show-case from the counter and hurled it at the door, shattering the panel of glass but before he could get through, Walker had come up behind him, blood seeping from the wound on his lip. Jo feigned, dodging to the right and caught Walker with a huge left hook, followed with a kick to his groin, missing by an inch, catching his hanging gut instead. It shook Walker slightly and Jo tried for the hole in the door – and made it through before Walker could grab him.

Just as Jo thought he was home free, three uniformed plod came running into the doorway of the shop. Jo charged towards them, punching and kicking as he tried to battle his way through. But it was no use. The restrictive space gave him no chance to get past and when Walker came up behind him, punching him hard between the ribs, Jo fell to his knees and was overpowered. Within minutes he was handcuffed and bundled unceremoniously into the back of a police van and taken to the Central Police Station.

The van screeched to a halt in the courtyard of the Central and Jo was hauled out and dragged, almost, in through the back door to the cell block.

Walker was following close behind, trying to kick Jo's feet from under him until he was led into a cell. After the handcuffs were removed, the police officers left the cell and slammed the door.

Jo rubbed his wrists and took count of his bruised body. He had lacerations on his head and face and his arms and legs were suffering from the result of being clubbed with a truncheon.

Jo could hardly believe what had happened. The odds of bumping into Walker must have been astronomical and Jo cursed and cursed as he thought of it.

A short time later the cell was unlocked and Jo was taken to the chargeroom and processed. A sergeant stood behind the desk and he ordered Jo to empty his pockets, noting each item on the property sheet. When he counted out the money, he gave a low whistle. "Five hundred and twenty pounds. That's a lot of cash – where did you get it?"

"That, is none of your business," scowled Jo.

"Isn't it? Oh – perhaps the C.I.D. might think it's their business – they want to talk to you."

"They will get the same answer," said Jo evenly.

After signing the property sheet Jo was led into a small interview room, closely followed by two detectives. One of them was Walker. He was carrying a cut lip and several bruises and Jo couldn't resist taking a stab at him. "Been in the wars have ya?"

"Don't get funny with me, Sullivan – I'll knock you all over this room!"

"Oh yeah – like you did in the shop – you slob!" Walker went for Jo but Jo pushed the table in front of him to block his path. Before the situation got out of control the second detective quickly intervened. "Okay! Let's take it easy shall we!" Walker held fast. "Just watch your mouth Sullivan, you're not on the street now –"

"Yeah, just don't try an' take liberties, alright –"

"Sullivan – sit down will you. I'm inspector Morrison. We'd like to ask you a few questions. First, where did you go when you left Sevenoaks Friday night?"

"How come I haven't been cautioned then?" said Jo, easing himself into a chair.

"The caution is only a technicality. Sullivan, but, if that's what you want I hereby formally caution you – you do not have to say anything but anything you do say will be taken down and may be given in evidence. Okay now?"

"Yes," replied Jo, "because now it's official that I don't have to answer any of your questions."

"We still want to know where you were," said Morrison.

"You can want all you like – I'm not answering one single question so you might as well just put me back in a cell until they come for me."

"Until who comes for you?"

Jo shook his head and looked at Morrison. "Do me a favour will ya – don't insult my intelligence. Godzilla there, told me the Sevenoaks police wanted a word with me, so I imagine they will be on their way to get me, wouldn't you?"

"That's as maybe, but as far as we're concerned we want to know what you've been up to and where you got hold of more than five hundred pounds."

"And I told you that I'm not telling you – that's clear enough isn't it – that's my right isn't it?" insisted Jo.

Morrison was getting annoyed. "Yes, but it won't do you position any good by refusing to co-operate with **us** – we're nothing to do with the Sevenoaks police. What we want to do is clear up a few loose ends that's all."

"I've got nothing to tell you," said Jo, folding his arms.

"There's been a number of burglaries and robberies since Friday, Sullivan, and if you don't tell us what you've been up to – we might have to stick you up for a few of 'em," said Walker.

"Don't threaten me you arsehole! I told you I ain't talkin' to ya, so just put me back in a cell," said Jo, getting up from the chair.

"Sit down Sullivan!" shouted Walker.

Jo suddenly went into brain overload, grabbed the flimsy chair and smashed it against the wall. "Now I can't sit down can I?" he said defiantly.

Morrison glared at Jo for a moment then gathered up the papers in front of him. "We'll talk to you again later."

"Don't waste your time, plod – all you'll get out of me is aggravation!"

After Morrison and Walker left the room, the duty-officer came in and took Jo to a cell. Some time later he was fed and given a pint mug of tea and a long awaited cigarette. When he knew he wouldn't be disturbed he searched his Y-fronts for the cannabis and broke a small piece off, then slipped it into his mouth and sucked it until it dissolved.

A few hours later, when the Kent police came to escort him back to Sevenoaks, he was so out of it he hardly knew what day it was and as he sat in the back of the car, handcuffed and flanked by two old bill, he couldnt' even remember whether or not Morrison had tried to question him again.

After the lengthy drive, Jo was feeling numb as he was led into the police station. As expected, he was taken to an interview room where two detectives were waiting to question him.

"Right, take a seat Sullivan. I'm Chief Inspector Wilson and this is Sergeant Reed. You know why you are here of course – what we would like –"

"Before you go any further, can I make a phone call to my wife?"

"Not at the moment, Sullivan – maybe we might be able to later – after all the paperwork is out of the way –"

"But she will be expecting my call –"

"We can't do anything about that now – as I said, maybe later."

Jo was persistant. "Why can't I make the call now? It'll only take a minute or two –"

Chief Inspector Wilson was equally persistant. "I'm sorry, no phone call. Now, we believe you may have been involved in a serious incident on Friday night last – what we would like you to do is tell us your story, starting with what you did, say, from Friday tea-time onwards." Wilson leaned back in his chair, waiting for Jo to give him the information he wanted. He was to be disappointed. "Yeah well, maybe later," said Jo, looking Wilson straight in the eye.

"What d'you mean, maybe later? We need to hear your side of the story so that we can determine if there are grounds to charge you or not."

"As I just said, maybe later – the same as you said to me when I asked for a phone call, remember?"

"Sullivan, if we've got to sit here all night we will."

"You'll be wasting your time – if you think for a minute I'm gonna sit here answering questions while my missus is sittin' at home worryin' herself to death you got another think coming – and another thing, if you think I'm gonna sit here all night, you've got **another** think coming."

"Sullivan, let's get one thing clear from the start. You are facing a possible murder charge, and if we don't get the right answers from you, you **will** be charged with murder."

But Jo already knew they were going to charge him with murder. If they knew it was him that had done the stabbing a murder charge would follow automatically and it would fall on him to try and prove it was otherwise when we went for trial. Even if they believed he was attacked he would still go ahead with the ultimate charge, because, Jo knew, they had no alternative.

"We both know what's going to happen so why don't you just get on with it – I'm tired and I want to get my head down," said Jo, flippantly.

Wilson could hardly believe his ears. "Are you serious Sullivan, or are you playing games?"

"What ya talkin' about?"

"I'm talking about your callous attitude! A man has been stabbed to death and all you want to do is get your head down!"

"What about you – I asked if I could phone my wife so that she wouldn't be tearing her hair out but you didnt' even let a thought **begin** let alone **give** her a thought, and you've got the front to call **me** callous – you don't even know what the word means."

Wilson listened for a second, and Jo saw it.

"Yeah – now why don't you two just go away and do what you gotta do."

Wilson pursed his lips and looked at Jo hard before rising from the chair. "I'll talk to you again," he said.

A few minutes later Jo was taken to a cell and he was relieved to be on his own at last. He stretched out on the thin plastic mattress and pondered his position. A murder conviction carried an automatic life sentence which could mean anything from ten to twenty years behind bars. The thought of spending so many years in a cell like the one he was in now filled him with apprehension and forboding.

As he lay on the bed, his mind was plagued with thoughts of doom and despair and he prayed for sleep, prayed for some miracle that would take him home to Christine and his two sons until finally, his mind could take no more and he lapsed into oblivion.

The next morning, looking haggard and drawn and without any further attempts from Wilson to question him, Jo was formally charged with the murder of David Johnathon Morgan.

* *

Deep under the Crown Court building was a holding cell more than fifty feet long, used for housing prisoners during breaks in their trial or while they were waiting to be taken to prison after sentence. A narrow wooden bench ran down one side and at the far end of the cell was a single urinal, stained and unclean.

Graffiti was everywhere. The walls, the wooden bench, even the low arched ceiling carried messages and obscenities of every description. About half-way along the cell in a space between 'eighteen months' and 'death to all pigs' Jo etched his own personal legend –

J.S. – Nine Years Imprisonment

A FEW YEARS LATER

Jo had been in prison for a long time and as he gazed out through the barred window and across the prison yard he stared at the perimeter wall, dreaming of life on the other side of it.

Officially, he had twelve months left to serve but with a parole hearing coming up, he was optimistic about his chances of early release – and if he failed with his parole application, there was always the possibility of getting some of the remission back that he'd lost in the earlier years of his sentence.

Jo had been through hard times in prison. The severity of the sentence had hung heavy with him and he felt anger and outrage knowing he was going to serve so many years for something he considered was a lawful killing.

In Canterbury he languished for more than a year before going to trial and after sentence, he spent more than twenty months in the grim, hell-hole that was Wandsworth, nine of them in solitary. After Wandsworth he was shipped to the notorious top-security prison, Parkhurst, where an air of tension hung over every landing and stabbings and grievous assaults were a common occurrence.

After spending nearly four years in Parkhurst, Jo was finally sent here, to Maidstone, to finish his sentence.

Time was easy in Maidstone. In place of the ever-present threat of riot and rebellion that was synonymous with Parkhurst, here in Maidstone life was relatively quiet and peaceful, mainly because of the many drugs that were widely available throughout the prison.

Jo was feeling good. Most of the cons were employed in the various workshops of the prison, but Jo had applied for one of the cleaning jobs on the wing soon after his arrival, and he'd struck lucky in getting one, probably because he was assigned light duties by the doctor.

The advantage of being a wing cleaner meant that when the job was done, he was free to roam the wing as he pleased, or venture out onto the playing fields for a couple of hours in the mornings and afternoons. The only thing that marred Jo's complete well being were the persistent pains in his back that had returned to haunt him, but with the tablet he'd just taken, even they would soon be gone.

It was early July and Jo started the day just like he did every other day – he washed and shaved – he had his breakfast – he did his chores – he had his dinner – and then, at half-past-two in the afternoon, he took an unscheduled bath…

As he soaked in the bath, with the July sun beating in through an open window, and with a joint burning slowly between his fingers, Jo began to mind-drift. The Lebanese Gold he'd managed to secure was a rare capture indeed and the more smoke he inhaled, the more he drifted.

The line of amphetamine sulphate that he had taken earlier was also beginning to take effect.

Jo hadn't felt so good in a long time and as his mind opened up, the grim reality of prison left him and he slipped gently out of the open window. As he drifted, in his drug-induced stupor, he suddenly found himself skipping along the perimeter wall with perfect balance, and if he wanted to – if he really felt like it – he could do a few handstands and somersaults…

…ha…in a minute a screw is going to see me and he will think I'm trying to escape…and then there will be several screws, all straining their straggly necks looking up at me wondering how I can hop over the razor wire, and they will be confused…soon they will try and get me down from the high wall…the fire-brigade will come and the police will be there, but just as they're about to prod me from the wall with their long poles – a second before they fire the tranquillising darts – I'll nip across the yard on a cushion of air and land high on the roof…yes!…then, when their minds are overwhelmed in awe, I'll fly down among them and as they rush in to overpower me – with their hypos held high – I'll kill a dozen of 'em – or better still, I'll fuck their heads right up by shrinking them 'till they're all three feet tall…ha!…or maybe I'll make all their arms and legs disappear, so that when I give 'em all a couple of slaps they'll be wobbling about like so many toy weebles…yes sir, come on mother – take a stab at me and I'll send you straight to the promised land, wow!…and when I've had enough of that I'll climb high and cruise away on the first white cloud I can find…yeah…laid back on a cloud smokin' a pipe full of weed, watching the world…

While Jo was lost in his dreams, soaking in the cool water, he suddenly noticed his hands were covered in thick, black lines and they baffled him, setting him to wonder how they got there. They weren't there when he had lunch. Nothing on the wing had been painted – he hadn't **been** anywhere.

He grabbed hold of a bar of soap and rubbed his hands together, trying to rid them of the mysterious black lines. When they didn't disappear straight away he rubbed them more profusely and when they still didn't vanish, he hunted for a scrubbing brush and ran the stiff bristles across his palms and knuckles until he drew blood.

As he watched the droplets hit the water, he racked his mind trying to think where the lines could have come from. After failing to solve the mystery, his thoughts turned to Howard Hughes and the obsession he had with clean hands. As he thought of him, Jo began to imagine great wealth. Bubbling up from his mind came a vision of factories and production lines, airlines and printing presses – and while lost in deep thought, he suddenly, mysteriously, lifted his feet from the water – and stared at them in disbelief.

Howard Hughes, one of the worlds richest ever men, was believed to be obsessed with cleanliness but on his death it was reported in several newspapers and magazines, that his feet were encrusted with stale, rotting skin, and his toe-nails were long, yellowing, curling hooks more than two inches in length.

When Jo saw his own feet were unclean he began, unwittingly, to compare himself with Howard Hughes and in so doing – entered the world of delusion.

But to Jo it wasn't delusion, to him it was real. A deliberate wave of thought that was being fed to him by some mystical force, urging him on, showing him the right path to riches and then, like an erupting volcano, came the words…

…a book!…write a book!…yes of course, a book…why didn't I think of it before…I'll tell the whole fuckin' wide world about the injustices …about the needles and the strip-cells…the beatings…the kickings and the tears – but whoa, slow down there baby, we don't want it all doom and gloom do we, no sir, leave a little space for some fun…oh yes, we will have some fun don't worry about that, lots of games maybe, and a riddle here an' there just to keep everyone on their toes, yes sir, I can't wait to get going and it'll be easy – just write about a thousand pages a day and then print 'em all up on my own printing press, and sell 'em…ha…you send me a clean, crisp, five pound note and I'll send you a copy of my mind all printed out nice 'n neat and when I've made two or three million I'll start giving it away 'cos who needs all that much money baby, not me, no sir…

And so, with those thoughts streaming out of his mind, Jo became engulfed in total delusion, a delusion of grandeur so intense that he believed everything he was thinking was going to happen. It was impossible for it not to be so.

Jo's euphoria was never ending. The more of the Gold he smoked the further he delved into his mind, as if seeking out the source of his dream and he thought of his sister, Irene.

She was a spiritualist and he and Christine often visited her home, listening to her explanations to the meaning of life.

Spiritualists believe in reincarnation and the immortality of the soul, and it is the evolution of the soul that forms the basis of their beliefs. They believe the lessons that stem from our lives on earth reflect on the progress of our souls. His sister had told Jo that there **is** life after we die because the soul is immortal, but because the soul has a will of it's own, sometimes the material desires of life on earth sees it making errors and instead of gliding through the tunnel of judgement on a wing towards the light, the tunnel becomes cloudy and dark as the misjudged errors try to drag the soul down into the lower planes of the astral world instead of rising up the ladder of perfection.

Irene had warned Jo, on a visit, under conditions of near-seance, that **his** soul was in danger. Because of his life-style and his taking of a life, **his** soul was on the bottom rung of that glorious ladder, the very bottom rung, the very last chance before his soul would be lost forever among all the other lost souls that were left wandering on the lower planes.

As all those thoughts flashed through his mind, Jo thought of the last few years and how he'd stayed clear of trouble with a conscious effort, ever fearful of slipping from that bottom rung.

Jo was still on that bottom rung now, clinging to it with all his might, afraid that one day he might slip – just a slip, and he might not make it through the tunnel.

That fear he carried with him was what some men might call the fear of God…

More than five hours later, long after he'd left the bathroom and returned to his cell, Jo was still hovering in the wonderful and glorious world of delusion, that magical place where he could peep into the parallel plane where his guardian angel was forever striving to keep him from slipping into oblivion. Jo saw all this, and more, and he took the delusion as a reality, a token of reward for all his suffering and sorrows, and he knew it all to be true.

At 2:00am, just as Jo was about to begin his masterpiece, and while he was still under the magical influence of delusion, a word came along his band of thought that was alien to the wavelength he was on. The word didn't register at first and he wouldn't have known it had passed but for the slight blip to the flow – there it was again…

…*price*…

Deep, deep in the matrix of his mind it was there…

…*price*…

faint and distant. Jo didn't like this word, it was interfering with his train of thought – then it seemed to get nearer…

…*price*…

then it was clearer…

…***price***…

and then came another word…

…*paid*…

Jo was beginning to feel uneasy and he tried to block out these two imposters, but the more he tried to shake them from his mind the clearer they became…

…*paid…price*…

until he couldn't shake them because now they were all that he could think of…

…*price…paid*…

and then, with trepidation and fear, the two words came together in a sentence…

…*paid…price…a price to be paid!*

The sentence sent a surge of adrenalin rushing through him…

…*a price to be paid*…

– then –

...sister...price to be paid...dead...sister...

and in a micro-second the sentence was formed in his head and Jo screamed out, "No! No! No! No! Oh no, please!..."

...YES!...

...no please!...

...your sister is dead...the price to be paid is your sister...

Jo grabbed a pillow and held it to his face, screaming and pleading and praying to it not to be true – but he knew it **was** true, because in the same dramatic way he believed the delusions in his ecstasy, did he now believe them in his fear.

The delusion had turned full circle and now, instead of the high reached at the height of his drug-induced euphoria, Jo was reeling in mental agony on the side-effects of the same drugs.

After fifteen minutes of praying and pleading, Jo heard this thinking say...

...no, it's not your sister...

but before he had a chance to savour his relief, he heard...

...it's your son...

Jo went into sheer panic and he screamed out in anguish at the thought of losing one of his sons. "Leave me! Leave me! Please, not my son!"

Then the words changed again.

When he heard Christine was the price, Jo collapsed into the corner of the cell, crying and babbling and gibbering like a man wavering on the brink of insanity.

When the sun hit his window in the morning, Jo was laying on the bed, still fully dressed, holding a pen and an A4 exercise book.

The page in front of him was blank. He had been waiting for the dawn to break, waiting for a new day to begin before attempting the impossible.

During the night, after he'd become more rational, but while still under the influence of delusion, Jo had made a covenant, a secret pact with those all knowing entities which exist somewhere far beyond man's imagination and with the covenant made, he wondered if he could write a book.

Jo didn't have a clue how to write a book. He could see the picture in his head of how he would like it to be but when it came to writing it down on paper, his mind went blank – even thinking where to start was becoming a major hurdle. He wondered if he should start where it all began, here, in this cell, just a short time ago.

He thought he was going crazy. If he did write a book, a loved one might perish, but then, with his beliefs to sustain him, Jo finally came to the conclusion that his destiny had already been mapped out and the killing of a man all those years before might be the price – but if it wasn't, and it was his karma to suffer more, then that is the lesson learned that might see his soul progress towards the next step of the ladder – and with those thin straws to cling to, he put pen to paper…

A Book — I must write a book.

But how the fuck do you write a book?
I s'pose I should go to the library
and get some books about how to
write books.

COMEDY   WIZARDS
HORROR
THRILLER   T.V.

A thirty-five year old hunch-back was
arrested early yesterday morning and
charged with being drunk and disorderly.
The hunch-back, who has not been
named, told the Justices that it might
have appeared to the officers that he
was acting in a disorderly fashion
but in fact it was his hump which
was shivering with cold that was
giving them the impression.
The hunch-back was found guilty
and was duly hanged on the 8th July
1784 at Newgate Prison.
Afterwords, everybody said it was a liberty.

Chapter One

Page 1.

This is the story of a
man who thought he could
write a book. He had
some kind of vision

25,000 copies

10,000 COPIES.

TITLE
A PAINFUL TIME
By Jo Sullivan

THE NINE Year NIGHTMARE
By Jo Sullivan,

Once upon a time

July 7 -

A ~~PSYCHIATRISTS~~ MY PSYCHIATRISTS DREAM

So!. You are going to write a book!
What's it going to be called —THE
I'm coming to take you away
book!. You can't even think of
the first line of the first
sentence — you're so out of
your head you can't even think
man!.

ONE MILLION YEARS B.C.

I need stake money baby, 'cos I'm
gonna tell everyone how it is —
how it was Yessir I'm gonna blow
the lid right off wowee! I can't
wait to get going man, I'm gonna
write about a million miles a minute
until my arm falls off and then I'm
gonna print it on my own printin' press.
After I've got it all printed and packaged
I'm gonna advertise — mail order
maybe — and after I've made a
cont'...

–173–

a million or two, I'm gonna
start giving it all away – who
wants the first thousand?

Death in a Closed Room
                Chapter One

a strib cell they called it.
an eight by eight room
with concrete walls and a
high ceiling. Part of the
ceiling seemed to be
missing...

RE-EDUCATION NEEDED

Education I was robbed of!
an imaginary company
            Kegs   you've got
                         a screw's about.

A Case History

By DBDummit

Into a bucket of shit went
the turds of Tommy Smith — long,
dark and fat they were, and
they smelled... 1/10

Come On Man

A man who treats his horse
badly in this country was a
fool. The strawberry roan 1/10

If only we were magicians; we
could slip through the key-holes
with a blade held high — but not
the blue-coats. We're not Indians
are we, hunting soldier blue,
no sir, we've got some white
witch doctors instead to play
with... 3/10

boas 150-1

What's happening man – I thought this was going to be easy, but I can't even think of the first sentence, I can't even think...think! Get some words out of that head, baby, let 'em run right onto the paper...

Right – once upon a time there was a wise old man – no, you lunatic, there wasn't a wise old man, there was a stupid prick who knew he was going out of his mind...

It all started a few days ago. I was having a hot bath, enjoying the comfort of the hot water – no, you ain't gonna make it baby, you just ain't gonna make it son...

He was just fourteen when his mother told him the bad news...

When his mother told him she was going away, he felt numb and wondered what his father had done to cause such...

Once upon a time there were three fat cats all sitting on top of a television set. One of them had one eye, one of them had three eyes, and one of them didn't have any eyes at all...

It all happened so quickly – one minute he was having a bath and the next minute he was going insane...backwards and forwards, to and fro, in a minute the words will flow...help wanted – lunatic requires professional help...Irene...yes, a letter to Irene....Dear Irene, I am gradually going out of my mind and I wondered if you could help me...?

Soon it would be time for breakfast and Jo fancied a pull on a small joint before facing the multitude of faces that would be lined up at the hot-plate, and he rolled one up.

Jo had been lucky in one respect since his imprisonment, he nearly always had a supply of cannabis resin. Freddie, Jo's long-time friend, visited him frequently and he always brought with him a parcel of gear, including a large chunk of hash. Sometimes in the parcel was a bag of sulphate and quite often a quantity of painkillers too.

Jo's brother, Charlie, also visited him often and he too always brought Jo a fair-size lump of resin to help kill the long days. Because Jo had a good, steady supply, he had enough to sell some off so that he could buy extra tobacco and other essentials from the prison canteen.

Although Jo was on a breeze with the amount of gear he had, it also had it's dangers. The burglars – the screws that suddenly pounced and searched – were more than aware of Jo's involvement with drugs on the wing, because other, low-life cons, informed on him by putting notes in the letter box for the screws to find. They did that, sometimes because of jealousy, but more often than not it was done because they owed money and if Jo was caught selling gear he would be shipped to a different prison, thus saving them the debt if he were gone.

Jo had been in prison too long to be caught napping though, for whenever he was in his cell, especially at mealtimes and evening lock-up, he always wedged the door with a PP9 battery. Soon after he'd arrived he cut a hole in the lino covering the floor and scraped away some of the concrete. When he slipped the battery into the hole, it was impossible for the screws to open his door until it was removed.

At all other times, except when he had a small piece out for immediate use, all Jo's gear was kept safely between the cheeks of his arse – after first being wrapped in soft toilet tissue – and he was always amazed how much he could put there without it falling out.

After smoking the joint, and after hearing the bell-call for breakfast, Jo left his cell and made his way to the dining-hall. Although the cons were allowed to sit at the tables to eat their meals, most of them – including Jo, chose to return to their cells – not because they preferred their own company but because the time allowed was hardly enough to chew through some of the tough meat, let alone finish the whole meal.

While collecting his grub, Jo saw his mate. "Hey Pat, where ya been – I thought you'd be up for a quick smoke?"

"I was goin' to, but the S.O. kept me in the office for an hour rabbitin' on about my chances of parole – I couldn't get away from 'im," he grimaced.

"Yeah? You goin' out on the field later?"

"Yeah – looks like it's gonna be nice an' sunny again."

"Yeah – come up an' we'll have a puff before we go out."

"Yeah alright – I'll catch ya later."

Jo gave Pat a nod and left the dining-room. Jo had met Pat in the prison hospital, Canterbury. Jo was in the hospital because all remand prisoners facing a murder charge were taken to the hospital and kept under observation for the first three weeks in case they tried to injure themselves, or worse, succumbed to the temptation of suicide. Pat was there because he had a broken leg. He soon told Jo that he was attempting to rob a supermarket at gunpoint but it had all gone wrong. The police had been tipped off and they were laying in wait. They let him enter the store to carry out the robbery and were waiting to pounce when he came out. But the trap went wrong and Pat was on the verge of escaping before a police car knocked him in the air, breaking a leg. He was now on remand awaiting trial, expecting anything from eight to twelve years in the can.

He got nine.

Jo liked Pat. He was easy going and took a few years inside as an occupational hazard. He'd carried out many robberies and he lived the high life on the proceeds and he didn't consider a few years in prison too high a price to pay for his life-style.

When Jo told his story, Pat was more than sure that he wouldn't be convicted of murder and might even beat the manslaughter alternative. With Jo being convicted by a 10-2 majority of manslaughter, he was nearly right on both counts.

After finishing his meal, Jo resumed his position on the bed. With pen and paper in his hands, he began to think…

Come on man, stop all this fucking about – you aren't gonna get anywhere like this. You gotta lay back and think, think how you can put a story together…yeah, you can do it son, just get it all sorted out in your head and then transfer it to a white, crispy, A4 pad…you can do it baby, you can do it…

Jo laid down his pen and rose from the bed, rubbing his lower back hard to ease the nagging pain. He felt for his cache of drugs and plucked a painkiller from the package. He cursed when he saw he was down to his last three pills. He began to curse the doctors too, for not prescribing a stronger painkiller. As he pressed his hand hard into his buttock muscle, he thought of all the mistreatment he'd received at the hands of the so-called doctors.

Because a number of cons were always trying to wriggle out of work-detail, when Jo first reported sick the doctor was viewing him as a probable malingerer and virtually dismissed Jo's complaint by prescribing him asprin water.

Jo had always suffered from pains in his back, probably brought on by years of lifting heavy grain sacks and cement bags, but usually they weren't too bad – and when he was visiting his sister and she laid her hands on him, they left him altogether.

Just after his conviction though, they returned with a vengeance. Freddie was keeping him supplied with tablets, DF118, or sometimes, Temgesic, but when Jo was in real pain his limited supply often ran short and he was forced to visit the prison doctor.

Jo remembered the day well. The morning after being prescribed asprin water, Jo reported sick – and this time he wasn't about to let the doctor dismiss his claim so lightly.

Yes, Jo remembered alright and as he pulled on the joint, his mind went back…

…He was sitting on a wooden bench, waiting impatiently for a medical screw to call him into the doctor's office. Jo had already explained his problem to the doctor the day before, but after a cursory examination the doctor was curt and unsympathetic, prescribing only a mild analgesic. Jo himself knew what the problem was, a prolapsed disc in his vertebrae was pinching the sciatic nerve, causing severe discomfort and often agonising pain. Jo remembered a time when he was playing football with his son. He twisted his back and was hospitalised after the nerve became trapped in the disc, forcing him to spend more than twelve weeks confined to bed.

Although the pain wasn't as bad now, as he sat on the bench, they were bad enough to warrant better treatment than he'd received to date.

While Jo was sitting there waiting to be called, he pursed his lips and glared at the screw standing at the entrance to the doctor's surgery. The screw caught his stare. "What's the matter with you, Sullivan – you don't look your normal cheerful self?" he said, with cynical sarcasm.

"You wouldn't look cheerful either if you had the shit treatment I've had – you lot are all the fuckin' same – "

"Alright Sullivan, that's enough – "

"Bollocks! Fuckin' tell me it's enough – I'm telling **you**!"

The screw was a fat, ugly, pig-of-a-man and on his face was a multitude of pustules and warts – one of them extending from the corner of his left ear, down onto his bulging neck.

"One more outburst like that, Sullivan – "

"As long as **you** don't outburst is the main thing," said Jo, turning to a fellow con. "Look at the state of his moo'ee for fucksake – if that lot burst we'd **all** be in trouble. He shouldn't be allowed out in public with all those mountains of pus all over 'im."

"You're on report Sullivan – "

"Yeah? Fuckin' good job too – you infected growth."

The screw turned away.

The cons enjoyed the verbal assault but their laughter was antagonising the screws in the hospital and suddenly there were three or four of them wanting to know what the racket was all about. Jo saw the wart whispering to the other screws.

A minute or two later Jo was called into the doctor's surgery. After flitting through some papers the doctor looked up. "Well Sullivan, what can I do for you today?" he said.

"I explained it all yesterday – d'you want me to go all over it again?"

"No, that won't be necessary – it was a problem with your back I believe."

"Yes, and – "

"And I prescribed an analgesic for the pain. Did you receive the treatment?"

"Yes – but I don't think paracetamol or aspirin water is a suitable treatment," said Jo, becoming irritated by the doctor's aloof manner.

"I think I'm the best judge of that don't you?" said the doctor, looking at Jo over the top of his glasses.

"Quite frankly, no I don't. I'm in agony an' you give me asprin water that wouldn't even get rid of a headache. You don't even know why I'm in pain."

"Well it could be a number of things, Sullivan – "

"But it isn't, it's a prolapsed disc that's trapping the sciatic nerve and if you took the trouble to examine me properly instead of listening to these bags of shit telling you otherwise – "

"Watch your mouth, Sullivan," said the wart.

"You better watch **your** mouth screw – you might find it not working in a minute." Jo looked at him and sneered at him and had an almost overpowering urge to smash his face. The screw turned to the doctor. "Have you finished with Sullivan, sir?"

"Er, yes I think so – "

"Just a minute – **I**, haven't finished yet – I wanna know what you're doin' about my back – an' what painkillers you're puttin' me on?"

"All I can do is advise you to rest as much as you can and sleep on a firm bed."

"Ha! That's a laugh. Have you **seen** the beds we have to kip on? said Jo, getting angrier by the minute.

"Well, no – perhaps a bed-board might help. I'll make out an order for one and I'll also prescribe a stronger painkiller."

"What will that be?"

"I don't think you need to know the exact name – "

"Doctor – I would like to know **exactly** what I'm taking, if you don't mind – "

"Come on Sullivan – the doctor's already told you – "

"Keep your fuckin' nose out of it will ya – this is nothing to do with you. Now, doctor, if you could please tell me, what **exactly** are you prescribing me?"

"I've already told you I'm giving you a painkiller."

"And I want to know what it is – why won't you tell me?"

"I really don't think we're getting anywhere like this."

"Why won't you tell me for fucksake!?"

"Really – officer, I think that will be all – "

"Yeah, yeah, I'm going," Jo started to turn "you're only a fuckin' quack anyway."

"You're on report number two, Sullivan," said the wart.

Jo ignored him and left the room before his temper got the better of him. The wart followed him out. "I suppose you think you're clever talkin' to the doctor like that?" he said.

"Listen you scroat, all I wanted to know was what medication he was giving me – you'd want to know wouldn't ya? Why the fuck shouldn't I know – just 'cos I'm a con I'm gettin' treated like shit."

"Well, if the cap fits, Sullivan – "

Jo looked at him for a second then punched him as hard as he could, causing an inch-long gash to appear on his cheekbone. Punch number two sent him crashing to the ground. Within moments, the alarm was pressed and Jo was being overpowered by several screws. He tried to fight back but sheer weight of numbers soon saw him battered then injected with a powerful tranquilising drug before being thrown unconscious into a strip-cell.

A few hours later Jo regained consciousness. He tried lifting his head but felt that, if he did, he might not be able to breath because his throat was so dry. When he turned over and got to his hands and knees, he saw a jug of water and grabbed it and eagerly gulped half of it down.

After satiating his thirst, Jo felt the pains throbbing from his battered body. His lips had been smashed and he had a cut over his left eye. His arms and shoulders were severely bruised as were the tops of his legs. Where Jo had raised them to protect his head, they too, showed the marks of the baton.

Jo had been in many fights during his life, but he'd never felt quite so – so injured before. It was as though he'd been the subject of a carefully planned assault, causing maximum pain and discomfort with the minimum visual signs of injury. They had beaten him across the arms and shoulders with their batons, and probably a few kicks had gone in as well. They also made sure that he wouldn't be clenching his fists for a while too.

But Jo knew it was coming. As soon as he hit the screw he knew what the outcome was going to be – and it frightened him. But it wasn't the inevitable beating that frightened him – it was the hypodermic needle that they would be plunging into his body that held Jo's fear. Ever since he could remember, Jo had carried a phobia about needles and to be held down and injected was something out of his nightmares. But with sheer animal instinct, Jo fought against the onslaught from the screws until the adrenalin rushing through his body overtook any fears of needles, and he didn't even feel the point when it sank deep into his leg.

About fifteen minutes after Jo regained consciousness, the door was opened and three screws, all dressed in white coats, edged their way into the cell. One of them was holding a small measure of liquid. "Take this, Sullivan," he said.

"Keep away from me or I'll take one of ya fuckin' eyes out!"

"Steady, Sullivan – nobody's going to come near you – just take this medication."

"What is it?"

"Just something that will make you feel better – "

"Yeah, but what is it – I don't want it."

"You've got to have it. After what you've had, this'll get you back to feeling normal. It's for your own good and if you don't take it orally, well – "

Jo reluctantly took hold of the small container and looked at the pink liquid for a moment before throwing it down his neck. After seeing him swallow the medication the three screws left the cell.

Jo waited with apprehension for the drug to show some effect. He felt for his parcel, relieved to find that it was still wedged safely between his cheeks. He then fumbled in his pockets for his smokes but before he had time to put one together, he sank down on the thin mattress and closed his eyes.

After sleeping for more than five hours, Jo was surprised to find that he did feel better when he finally woke from his enforced sleep. Although his arms and shoulders were aching like hell, and his hands were throbbing with a nagging pain, his head felt clear and with a clear head, he could soon take some resin and lose himself in it's magic.

Before long he was taken from the strip-cell and marched across to the main wing of the prison. After a cursory search he was ordered into one of the bleak cells of the segregation unit. Tomorrow morning he was to face the Governor for punishment.

Jo looked round the dingy cell. In the corner was the obligatory piss-pot and along one side was a low, camp-like bed. The only furniture in the cell was a small, re-inforced cardboard table and chair. The heavily barred window was high up in the wall and even on tip-toe, Jo couldn't see out of it.

Jo hardly knew what day it was and had less idea of the time. As he sat down on the concrete floor and leaned his back against the cold wall, he began to wonder when food was coming. The day **felt** late, and he was beginning to think they had forgotten he was there. When a slop-out came and went without a meal following it, Jo got on the bell. A few minutes later a screw peered in through the flap. "What d'you want?" he sneered.

"What I want is something to eat – when's it coming round?"

The screws pursed lips suddenly turned into a cynical grimace. "Meals are all finished for the day. You'll get a mug of tea later – if we don't forget you." He slammed the flap and walked away. Jo banged the door with his knee and screamed out after him. "You better not forget me you mother! I'll bury you! I'll bite ya fuckin' nose off!" You wouldn't forget me then, he thought, not if I rip ya lips away from your mouth you wouldn't.

After his short outburst, Jo put his ear to the door, listening intently for any screws that might be lurking about. Quite often, especially after one of their own had been damaged, they would charge into a cell with a mattress held out in front of them for protection, and batter the inmate further.

Jo was on red alert waiting for it to happen, but when they didn't come, he guessed the punishment he'd already suffered might have been enough to satisfy them.

When a mug of tea was finally offered, Jo was able to relax knowing that the screws who patrolled at night didn't have keys to open the cells. After waiting a while and when he was completely sure the coast was clear, he retrieved his parcel and broke off a small piece of gear before returning it to his cheeks. After rolling a joint and lighting it, he stretched out on the bed and let the night drift.

At 7:00am sharp Jo was woken by the sound of the door crashing up against the metal frame of the bed. Within moments he was up and dressed and screaming abuse at the screw. "Did you have to open the door like that you fuckin' pig!"

"Slop out, Sullivan," he said, ignoring Jo's remarks. Jo looked at him hard before grabbing his piss-pot. "You open my door like that again an' you'll get this lot over ya every time you do it," he said, making his way to the recess. "You're nicked, Sullivan – "

"Oh no – " said Jo, feigning a statue-like pose, " – I'm not nicked am I? Oh dear Jesus please help me I'm nicked."

"Get cha' breakfast, Sullivan – "

"Yeah yeah – gimme a chance t' slop out will ya – unless **you** want this lot," he said, taking hold of the lid. The screw turned his face. "Just get a move on," he muttered.

Jo emptied his pot and rinsed it under the tap before giving himself a quick rinse. A few minutes later he was back in his cell eating breakfast, cursing profusely every time the hot tea touched the cuts on the inside of his mouth.

After eating, Jo rolled himself a cigarette and noticed he was running low. He had more in his cell on the main wing but he wasn't banking on having any by the time his personal belongings were delivered to the block.

At ten o'clock Jo was unlocked and taken to the Governor's adjudication cell. "Stand in front of the desk and give your full name and number to the Governor," bellowed out one of the screws. Jo smiled to himself as Haslar came flooding into his mind and he couldn't resist an inside joke. "Have I got to remain standing to attention at all times as – "

"Give your name and number to the Governor!"

"Sullivan, 530 – "

"Your full name and – "

"Alright Mr. Wates, thankyou," said the Governor.

"Sir!"

"If you could now read the charges Mr. Corbin."

"Sir. At approximately ten-twenty yesterday morning, Sullivan assaulted one of the members of the hospital prison staff, causing a laceration to his cheek. He also assaulted two other officers which resulted in minor bruising. There are four further charges of threatening and abusive language to an officer, sir."

"Thankyou Mr. Corbin. Now, Sullivan, I see from the charge sheets you have declined to put forward a defence. Have you anything to say now?"

"No point is there – you ain't gonna believe anything I say."

"I see. Well, as far as the assaults are concerned, they will be dealt with by the board of visitors. As for the other charges, threatening and abusive language to an officer, you will forfeit twenty eight days remission – seven days on each charge. I am also making an order that you be segregated from the main population until the assault charges are heard."

"So, I'm gettin' solitary before being heard then?"

"No Sullivan, there is no order for cellular confinement. I'm putting you on G.O.A.D. – Good Order and Discipline."

"Same thing innit?"

"I think you will find it is not quite the same thing. That will be all Mr. Corbin, thankyou."

"Sir. Right Sullivan – "

Jo was soon returned to his cell, relieved that he was on G.O.A.D. instead of cellular confinement. On C.C. they would have confiscated all his personal possessions and taken his bed out for the day, only returning it at night for him to sleep on. Although he was confined to the cell until the hearing in front of the visiting magistrates, at least on G.O.A.D. he would be a little more comfortable than he would on the punishment of C.C.

Later in the morning his belongings were brought down to the unit and he was surprised to find everything was intact, including his tobacco.

The only thing he was concerned about now was his supply of dope. He hadn't had a visit for nearly three weeks and his stash was running low. Jo guessed he had enough left, if he was prudent, to last him three or four days and if he abstained from smoking during the day he would be alright for nearly a week. Not smoking during the day though, was alien to Jo and already he was gasping for the hit of the resin.

When, eventually, he heard the sound of the hot-plate coming to life, he was more than pleased with himself for holding out.

Soon the door opened.

"Slop out, Sullivan," said a morose screw.

Jo emptied his pot, relieved himself, washed his hands, refilled the water-jug and collected his meal before hearing the door being shut by a screw.

He was out of his cell for nearly eight minutes.

After eating, and when he was sure all the screws had left the unit for their own food, Jo decided to build himself a dream-machine. He laid out the materials and checked that everything was present. After being satisfied that he wouldn't have to move again he took a three-inch long piece of silver foil and wrapped it round a pencil. He slid the cylinder from the pencil and folded one of the ends over until it was airtight, then made nine needle-holes in it, just short of the fold.

He now held a pipe. After sprinkling on the fuel, a dream-machine was made and all that was needed to get it going was a naked flame.

The resin was harsh in it's raw form and Jo had to take care that he didn't cough the smoke straight out. He struck a match and touched it against the hash, inhaling slowly. After repeating the process once more, he was just out-of-it enough to take the edge off…

The days were long in the segregation unit. They were long enough on the wing but at least on the wing there was company sometimes, and there was time out of the cell, time to go hunting.

Jo quickly settled into a routine. After breakfast he rested a while before undertaking a series of vigorous exercises. Initially, he still ached from the beating handed to him by the screws but now, with a gruelling routine of sit-ups and press-ups, squats and running on the spot, those aches made way for the different aches of stretched tendons and overworked muscles.

After an hour of working out, he rested briefly before continuing until the second slop-out of the day.

At ten o'clock the Governor paid his daily visit to the unit, followed closely by the statutory visit from the doctor.

With an hours exercise in the yard a short time later, the mornings were more or less taken care of.

After dinner, and with the help of two or three pipes, the afternoons and evenings were also taken care of.

It was only a few days later when he finally ran out of gear did the days begin to drag. With a hit or two from the resin he could lose the hours, but now, in reality, Jo had to use his mind and serve prison-time proper.

The mornings weren't too bad, especially as he was out of his cell for an hour, walking in the fresh air of the yard.

It was the afternoons and early evenings that saw the clock moving backwards almost, but even then, if he could lose himself in a crack in the ceiling, or watch a spider spinning it's web, sometimes the hours still disappeared somehow.

When he'd re-read his magazines for the tenth time he would slide the bed across and stand at the window feeding pigeons. After years of being thrown scraps from cons, some of them were tame enough to take food from the hand. When the food was gone, or when they'd had enough, he sometimes went fly-hunting. There were always one or two flies buzzing about and after rolling up an old magazine, he hunted them down – imagining they were flying doctors.

He soon became head-honcho. He noticed that during the day they kept in flight, hardly ever landing, making them hard to swat. Late in the afternoons though, they landed more frequently and Jo lost many hours splatting them against the flaking walls.

But usually, after he'd finished his gruelling routine of exercises and done with feeding pigeons and killing-flies, all there was to do was lay on the bed and think. Without dope to chase away the reality, all Jo's thoughts turned to his wife and sons and when he thought of them he knew he was serving real, hard-time, imprisonment.

On his eighth day in the seg, and three days after he'd run out of gear, Jo was called out for a visit. He hastily made himself presentable and was escorted to the visiting room.

After a quick search of the many tables that were placed strategically round the room, Jo spotted his brother sipping a hot drink and quickly joined him.

"Charlie! Nice to see ya – how ya doin'!?" he said, taking his hand and grabbing the back of his neck.

"Hello Jo – yeah, I'm doin' okay – you?" he asked, resuming his seat.

"Yeah, I'm alright – they got me in the seg at the moment."

"Why?"

"I had to smack a couple of screws – they were really takin' the piss – the fuckin' doctor wouldn't give me any painkillers an' a couple of screws were givin' me some stick so I had to knock one of 'em out," laughed Jo, embroidering the story.

"Tch…fuckin' ell Jo – "

"I know – but I couldn't help it. My back was really givin' me some gip – "

"How much remission ya lost?"

"Twenty-eight days – plus I've got some more to go up on."

"Fuck me, Jo – you're never gonna get out the way you're going."

"I know – I'll have to start tryin' to hold my temper down – but if I stay outta trouble for nine months they start givin' it to ya back – "

"Do they?"

"Yeah apparently – if you don't get nicked for nine months you can apply to the Governor for time back."

"Be a miracle if you stayed outta trouble that long."

"No, I'll be alright. Anyway, what's happening outside? Mum okay? Business makin' a few quid?"

"Yeah, everything's going alright – Christine and the boys popped in the other day – I told her I was coming to see you and she sends her love – "

"Good – "

"And I gave her some money – "

"How much d'you give her?"

"Fifty quid – "

"Yeah? What did she say?"

"I just said it was from the family to get a few things for the 'erberts."

"Still got plenty left have we?" smiled Jo.

"Yeah, I've got it in a special account – "

"Did you…er…manage to…?"

"Yeah – I've got it in my hand now – an ounce."

"Yeah? Is there any screws behind me lookin' at us?"

"No – you want it now –?"

"Hang on – " Jo's eyes were everywhere, watching every screw in sight. When the moment was right he nodded. "Still clear behind?"

"Yeah – "

"Hold on – I'm…just…wait…ing…now!" Charlie opened his hand and Jo took the resin and quickly wedged it between his cheeks, via a purpose-made hole in his jeans. After all this time, Charlie and Jo were quite adept at making the switch and it only took a few seconds. For additional security, before he left the room he eased the resin into his anal tract in case he was singled out for a strip search.

After securing the parcel, Charlie and Jo always breathed a little easier. Wandsworth was saturated with young, egoistic screws who were always on the look-out for a capture. Jo had witnessed more than once, one or more of them pouncing on a con and his visitor and taking the gear. Jo had briefed Charlie, and Freddie, that if ever a screw tried to tackle **him**, they were to remain seated and he himself would take care of the situation, even if it meant knocking 'em all out one by one.

Soon the half-hour visit was called to a halt by a surly screw. Jo voiced his usual protest at the brevity of the visit, sometimes gaining an extra ten minutes but usually, like today, the screw repeating that the visit was over.

"Well – don't look like we're gonna get more time – I'll see you in about a month," said Charlie, kicking away the chair from under him.

"Yeah – thanks for coming Charlie-boy – I'll see ya soon. Give my love to mum – "

"I will – take care Jo."

Back in his cell, Jo pulled the bed in front of the door and sat down at the other end of it with his feet against the wall, and eased out the resin. After washing the cling-film, he unwrapped the package and peeled a small piece away from the ounce before replacing it between his cheeks.

He then retrieved the pipe that he'd hidden and sprinkled some of the dark brown cannabis over the holes. Within a few minutes, Jo was on his way to abracadabraland…

A few days later Jo found himself in front of the board of visitors. As expected, he was found guilty of the assaults and given ninety days loss of remission on each of the three counts. He was also given fifty-six days cellular confinement with the loss of all privileges, such as they were. The only real difference Jo could envisage was the loss of his bed during the day. That difference though, was to cause him even more problems.

He was still suffering from pains in his back and if they took his bed it would be detrimental to his health.

The first day of his C.C., as opposed to the G.O.A.D. he was already on, Jo offered little protest and allowed them to take his bed but when the doctor made his statutory visit to the seg, Jo was ready for him.

A screw opened the door and the doctor peered in. "Everything alright Sullivan?" he said, in his usual aloof manner.

"As a matter of fact no, it isn't."

"Oh – what's the problem?"

"Well, you remember of course me complaining about pains in my back – "

"Yes – "

"And you remember me telling you that a Consultant Orthopaedic Surgeon confirmed I had a prolapsed disc that was aggravating the sciatic nerve – "

"Yes, yes – " he uttered.

"Well, I seem to remember you agreeing with him that I should rest my back as much as possible – "

"Yes that's right, rest is about the only cure – "

"So you still hold by that do you?"

"Yes of course – what is the point of – "

"The point is they've taken my bed and I'm having to sit in this," said Jo, grabbing the small, cardboard chair.

"Would you say this helps my back or further aggravates it?"

"Er…It would be better if you didn't sit in it all day but quite frankly I think I'm missing the point. What is it you're trying to say?"

Jo took a deep breath and tried to remain calm. "The point is doctor, they've taken my bed and now I can't rest my back like you've advised that I should. I'd like you to make out the appropriate order for me to get it back."

"He can't have his bed, sir – he's on punishment." said a screw.

"Oi! Keep ya nose out will ya – this is a matter for the doctor, not some bag of shit wearin' a uniform. Now, doctor, will you do that? You **are** the doctor – "

"Er…I'm not sure I can interfere – "

"You are **not** interferring. You're the doctor and if you say I need a bed to rest on – that's it – I need a bed – unless you want me to lay on the concrete floor all day?"

"I'm not sure I'm in a position to give you your bed if you are on punishment – I'll have to check with the Governor first."

"You don't have to check with him – you're the bloody doctor for fucksake – "

"I'll still have to discuss it with the Governor – "

"There's no gettin' through to you is there – and while we're at it – how come you ain't put me on remedials – "

"I'll see to it that you get remedial treatment – "

"And what happened to the bed-board I was supposed to get nearly two weeks ago?"

"Er…I did make out an order as far as I remember – "

"Yeah, sure you did – just piss off will ya!" said Jo finally, unable to contain himself any further. The screw gave Jo a cynical sneer and slammed the door.

A short time later when Jo was opened up for exercise he broke into a trot when he hit the yard, trying to rid his mind of all the frustration that was building up.

He couldn't shake the doctor from his thoughts. He knew the doctor had the authority to over-ride any order or punishment imposed by the Governor but here he was, side-stepping and unsure because he didn't want to rock the boat, making Jo angrier by the minute.

When he returned to his cell an hour later he was feeling a little calmer. While pacing the yard Jo had come to the conclusion that all his unvented frustration was causing him stress and if they were causing **him** stress, maybe he ought to cause them some. Before declaring war though, Jo decided to warn the Governor first.

Ten o'clock the following morning, the Governor paid his usual call on Jo's cell. "Morning Sullivan – everything alright?" he said.

"Er…just a minute Gov'nor – I'd like a word."

"Yes, what do you want?"

"Has the doctor spoken to you about me having my bed?"

"Yes, he did mention something to me about it, but he didn't make any order for you to retain it while you're on C.C."

"But he told me it would be better for my health if I did have it – and only after one of your men told him I was on punishment, did he start changing his mind – "

"As far as I'm concerned Sullivan, he hasn't said a bed is absolutely essential for your well being."

"But that's not what he told me – "

"Sullivan, unless the doctor tells me otherwise your bed will be removed from the cell each morning – "

"Gov'nor, I'm giving you an' your screws fair warning. If I ain't allowed to keep my bed I'm going to fight for it – I'll cause so much havoc down here you'll think it's World War three – "

"Are you making threatening – "

"Gov'nor, what I'm saying is that I'll fight for my legal rights. The doctor knows it and so do you so if there's any trouble coming it'll be down to you."

"Sullivan, let me warn you. If you continue with the attitude you seem to be adopting, I can promise you that you will be serving a far longer sentence than the one you are currently serving. Your bed **will** be removed each day unless the doctor advises me otherwise – good morning."

When the doctor made his rounds a few minutes later, Jo couldn't wait to get at him.

"Ah, doctor – and I use the word doctor in the loosest possible terms – can you tell me why you told the Governor that I didn't need my bed when you told me yesterday that I did?"

"I never actually said you **needed** it, I – "

"Yes you did!"

"No, what I said was it would be better if you had but I didn't consider it paramount – "

"You spineless piece of garbage! How can you stand there an' tell me I don't need a bed when I'm in fuckin' agony every poxy night!"

"I'm sorry, there's nothing I – "

"Well get the fuck out of my cell then you useless pile of shit!"

"You're on report Sullivan," said a screw, pulling the door shut.

"Fuck your report!" shouted Jo.

After the door was slammed, Jo went to the floor and did a few press-ups, wondering if he had gone too far in declaring war on the Governor and his army of screws. He knew he could never beat them but he could certainly cause a few injuries along the way and over here in the seg there were no hypodermic needles to slow him up.

As the day wore on Jo became stoned and mellowed out until all his anger was long gone. In the mood he was in now, he didn't fancy going to war and the more he thought about it the more he wondered how he could keep his bed without a bloody and painful battle, until he realised there was no way he was going to keep it.

With the threat already made though, Jo might have to carry it out – unless he could think of a way out without losing face.

After hours of thinking Jo came to the conclusion that there was only one way to play. If they were going to take his bed he was going to make it as unpleasant for them as possible – but not with his fists – the plan Jo had for them was far more suiting…

At half-past-six the next morning, Jo left his bed and quickly dressed. He went to his pot and examined the contents. In the pot, curled and thick and resting in among a small amount of urine, was his own excrement. He retrieved a plastic fork from behind the ventilation grill and began to stir the mixture into a pliable paste. After stripping the bed of the sheets and blankets, he covered every inch of the metal frame with the pungent mixture.

Now, if they wanted to take his bed they were more than welcome, thought Jo, smiling to himself. He sat on the floor facing the door, waiting impatiently for it to open.

When the door was finally opened, the smell nearly knocked the screw over. "Jesus – "

Jo burst out laughing. "What's the matter then – ain't you gonna come in an' take my bed? Come on, get this fuckin' stinkin' bed outta here!"

Two other screws were hovering by the door but when the smell hit them as well it was as far as they wanted to go.

"Come in gov'nor, don't be shy – it's nice an' fresh – came right out of my own aris late last night!"

Jo hadn't laughed so much for a long time and with the couple of pipes he'd had while waiting for the door to open, his fun was enhanced. The screws though, were not amused and Jo could feel their disappointment at not getting their chance to batter him. "Slop out Sullivan an' get ya breakfast!" said one of them.

"What – an' miss all the fun? Nah, I'll just sit here and watch shit moving shit – "

"You think you're a real clever bastard don't ya – but don't think we're going to sort it out – we get cons to do jobs like this."

"Yeah? Mugs you mean – no con I know would do it – "

"Get ya breakfast Sullivan – unless you want to stay in this cesspit!"

Jo got up from the floor and shuffled past the screws to the recess. After washing thoroughly he collected his breakfast. "In here Sullivan," said a screw, pointing to a different cell. Jo went in and heard the door slam behind him.

While sitting at the cardboard table eating his breakfast, he wondered if he was going to suffer any reprisals but soon came to realise that most of the screws had little or no bottle and Jo doubted if any of them wanted to risk personal injury – and like the man said, a con would have the unsavoury task of cleaning up the mess.

For his trouble, Jo lost a further fourteen days remission plus another seven for swearing at the doctor. To date, he had now lost more than three hundred days and as it began to sink in, he cursed his temper and lack of control.

After realising that he'd suffered defeat over the loss of his bed, Jo began to brood – not intentionally, it gradually seeped into him like a festering poison and it was the agonising pains in his back that was the cause. Even the resin couldn't rid his mind that he was being denied basic medical treatment. If he were on the outside, he could visit a doctor and receive immediate help but here, in the filthy, stinking, prison that was Wandsworth, he was reduced to carrying out primitive acts in order to try and secure something which the doctor had told him he needed to assist his recovery – a firm bed.

He was also being denied adequate painkillers. If he was prescribed them, the pain would go and so would the tension and the stress that went hand in hand with pain.

The more Jo thought about it the more he festered inside. He was morose and scornful, growling at every screw in sight, and soon, if nothing was done, he was going to take somebody's head off.

A few days later, while laying on the hard concrete floor, Jo thought of a way that might bring attention to his plight.

In the morning he made an application to see the Governor and at ten o'clock he was led into his office. "Yes Sullivan, I believe you made an application – "

"Yes, I want to apply for a special letter to my solicitor. I also want to apply to see the board of visitors and I also want to apply for a special visit," said Jo evenly.

"May I ask the reason for these requests?"

"Yeah, sure you can – I'm an angry man and I'm seething with frustration. I'm in severe pain and nothing is being done about it. The doctor isn't taking my problem serious and he hasn't the backbone to over-rule any order that you have made and I'm nearing the end of my tolerance. I know that if nothing is done soon I'm going to do something I might live to regret. I want to see the board of visitors and explain it to them, and I want to write to my solicitor in the form of an affidavit, declaring that if I don't receive adequate medical treatment within a certain time, I'm going to seriously injure one of your staff."

"I see – and you think that will solve your problem do you?"

"Gov'nor, if you can't see that what I'm proposing is a plea for help then you shouldn't be the Governor of a prison. I'm in agony sometimes, and I want something done about it now. I'm not making a threat, I'm just trying to warn you of my nature – you already know my record of violence and if you think you can leave me isolated and in agony you're very much mistaken. I don't want to do any more time than I have to, but I don't know what else I can do – unless you have a solution," said Jo finally, offering the Governor a get-out.

"Well, you are obviously in distress – perhaps if you saw the doctor again – "

"But he won't give me a strong painkiller. For some reason all prison doctors think all cons are after drugs. All I want is the pain to stop – I'm not even bothered about a bed anymore so long as I ain't in pain all day – that's all I want, just to get rid of this nagging, throbbing, pain that's driving me mad!"

"Alright Sullivan, leave it with me and I'll have a word with the doctor."

"Thanks – oh, and Gov'nor, if I'm a happier man I won't be growling at your men all day so think of it as doin' them a favour if it makes it easier for you to swallow."

"I'll bear that in mind, Sullivan," said the Governor.

Whether it was because the Governor could feel Jo's frustration or whether he was more concerned about his men and the possibility that one of them might be hurt, Jo was never to know, but the next day, after a lengthy examination by the doctor, Jo was prescribed painkillers DF118, in liquid form. He was also put on remedial exercises and given a hard board to place under the mattress each night.

With a measure of DF118 four times a day and with daily remedial exercises in the gym under the guidance of a P.T.I., Jo gradually lost the nagging pain until it became a bearable ache, and that he could live with.

By the time he had finished his fifty-six days of cellular confinement, Jo was feeling better than he had in a long time – but he never did get his bed back. That would have been just too much to expect of them.

"Hey Jo!" shouted Pat, pushing up against the door. "Let me in," Jo rose from his bed and moved towards the door, kicking away the PP9 battery before he could open it.

"Alright Jo – was you asleep then?"

"No, I was miles away – thinkin' about those slags in Wandsworth. What's the time?"

"It's gone ten – they'll be callin' for the field in a minute – you're goin' out aren't ya?"

"Yeah – I've already rolled a couple a' spliffs – "

"And **I've** got a flask of booze."

"Yeah? What's it like?"

"The business – I had a taster before I bought it – "

"Good – that last lot we had was shit. Who made this?"

"Joey – a tenner for half a bucket. I've got another two flasks t' come – we'll have 'em tonight shall we?"

"Yeah why not – I feel like gettin' pissed." Jo slapped Pat on the back and they both laughed.

Soon they heard the call for the field. Maidstone was an easy prison and all inmates that weren't required to work in the shops, such as cleaners and those who served on the hot plate, were allowed to roam the prison for an hour or so in the mornings and afternoons. Besides an array of activities including snooker, darts, television, a running track and gymnasium, Maidstone also had an outdoor swimming pool.

Jo grabbed a pillow and a towel, and a chess set, and they both left the cell, slamming the door behind them.

As they made their way towards the gate, the smell of human waste drifted from the recess. Jo almost retched when his nose caught the pungent fumes. "Jesus – "

"Fuckin' hell – "

They both held their breath as they hurried past the recess. All three bowls were blocked and overflowing, spewing toilet paper and excrement across the floor. By the time they reached the gate leading to the field, two plumbers were already on their way to sort out the problem. "Rather you than me gov'nor," quipped Pat as they slipped out into the fresh air. "Fuck that job ay – the whole system must be blocked."

"Yeah – how old you reckon this place is?" said Jo, eyeing the round turrets that were dotted around the prison.

"Dunno – a couple of hundred years I should think – like an old fortress innit?"

Jo looked at the old building and felt a little strange…

…this whole place is strange…circular buildings three stories high with doors leading out onto nowhere, into open space…I keep hearing water…all the bowls in the recess are overflowing, paper trailing like entrails from a corpse. It's running deep now, tracing a pattern on the tiles, surging forward towards the gate like a – hang on, hang on…I've been here before…have I? No, don't be daft – hey, can you see it…can you see those white beards dancing on the shit? Can you see it still, carving a path, getting deeper as it runs along…but here comes some pain now in a shiny white coat, skipping along my spine…slamming another piece in like a lowering drawbridge…twisting and bending using a hammer and tongs…do they know it's haunting and taunting me…?

"Jo – are you alright?" asked Pat, bringing Jo out of his thoughts.

"What? Oh yeah…yeah, I'm alright – I think – "

"Is your back givin' you stick again?"

"It is a bit – "

"A couple of cups of this'll soon sort you out," said Pat, handing Jo a mug filled with hooch. "I've been assured that this stuff will cure any ailment known to man – except this new plague maybe," he laughed.

"New plague? What new plague?" asked Jo, settling himself down in a more comfortable position.

"Didn't you listen to radio two last night – they was on about a new kind of disease that was sweeping across Africa – something to do with the immune system – they reckon it could be worse than the bubonic plague – "

"**Worse** than the bubonic plague – "

"Yeah, they had all sorts of doctors and professors on there sayin' we could all end up in the shit if they don't find a cure in time."

*...if they don't find a cure in time...a cure in time...Keep away from the time baby it's only early yet – about an hour in an' this dream is a long one so tighten the harness and batten down all the watertight doors 'cos we're heading straight into the shit...yeah, we're all going on a trip – everyone loves a trip so come on a trip with me. We'll start at the beginning when the jaw opens and closes as if on a stiff hinge and the stomach wants to leave the body. The need for a toilet becomes imperative and when **that** business has been taken care of the head takes over... Just cruising along, gently bubbling over – itching to get moving like the high cumulus racing across the sky...hey look at that sky moving baby...yes! A Saturn-five chemical warhead heading this way, straight from mumbo jumbo land carrying the plague. Do they know it's coming yet? Don't worry about any four minute warnings, just strap a supersonic missile on each leg and I'll deliver the message – silver darts from huge rubber lips, exploding into scabs and pink-milk eyes...ay-e-ya-ya...*
...Come on now and lift your head...
sit down with a joint instead
of laying there, amid the gloom...
...Yes I want to laugh and have some fun
so I'll leave it now the game has begun...
...GAME?   What   fuckin'   game?   LEAVE-MY-HEAD-ALOOOOOONE...

"Hey Jo?"

"Eh – what?"

"You alright?"

"Who me? I'm sweet – couldn't be better. I could run straight through that wall!"

Pat laughed. "Yeah? And what about the two screws standin' there?"

"Take 'em with me – miniaturise 'em and stuff one in each pocket and go straight through the wall. Screw 'em up – ha – screw 'em up – wrap 'em up in escape-proof bags – have lots of fun and games with them and do their heads – sling 'em into spider-webs and stand 'em on top of lightbulbs with their socks on – stick wasps on 'em then bring 'em back to normal size and ask them how come they've suddenly gone insane…"

Jo was talking at a hundred miles an hour.

"Fuck me Jo – this is bloody good booze innit?" said Pat laughing, stopping Jo dead.

"Yeah – " said Jo smiling dreamily. "Right out of the days of goblins and soothsayers and a mage in a grey cloak, hunting for the formula which will save the world – "

"You don't need any more of this do ya?" said Pat, looking at Jo sideways.

"Don't take any notice of me – I'm just practising out loud."

"Practising what?"

"Um…practising to think – I think…?"

"How long have you had this problem?"

"Well…doctor…it all started yesterday. I was soaking in the bath, enjoying the afternoon sun, when I suddenly had a taste of…rapture…"

"Er…could you explain that please" said Pat, playing along. "The bit about tasting rapture – what's that mean?"

"Er…no, you wouldn't understand – you'd have me taken away," laughed Jo.

"No I won't – I promise – make ya'self a little more comfortable if it'll help – "

"Pat – fuck off – "

"No, come on – lay ya head down on this soft pillow and tell the doctor all about it – "

Jo was beginning to grin "Fuck, off, – "

"And then when you've told us your problem we can give you a nice, big, injection – "

Jo shuddered.

Pat caught Jo's reaction. "No, only kidding – they only do that if you end up goin' du-lally."

"Do they?"

"Yeah – I've seen 'em get hold of someone in Wandsworth."

"Yeah – what happened?" asked Jo, with morbid interest.

"He just went off his head – screamin' he had the power in his hands an' all that – about eight screws just leapt on 'im and jabbed 'im up – they ended up takin' 'im away in a giant cricket-bag – "

Jo cringed. "Mama-mia…" he whispered, his teeth clenched.

"You don't like needles do ya Jo?" grinned Pat.

"No – I fuckin' don't!"

"What happened yesterday then?"

"I dunno – I just had an overpowering urge to start writing a book or something – really weird it was."

"Every prisoner's dream innit?"

"What is?"

"To write a book – "

"Oh, yeah – but this was different – like I was being **told** – really weird – "

"Wasn't hearing voices was ya?"

"No, nothing like that – just an urge to try an' write."

"Go an' get that old typewriter then – "

"What typewriter?" asked Jo, feeling a slight stir in his gut.

"They've got an old one over the classes – they let you have it in ya cell if you want – "

"Do they?" said Jo, trying to hide his excitement.

"Yeah – Jimmy Boyle used it when he wrote his book – "

"Alright, alright – " said Jo, playfully grabbing Pat by the neck, " – you fuckin' wait."

"What's this book gonna be about then?"

"Fuck-knows!"

"Fucknose – is he the leading character – ?"

Jo started laughing. "I'll sling you in that pool in a minute," he said.

After a smoke and another cup of booze each, Jo got hold of Pat and did sling him in.

When the call came to end activities on the field, Jo went straight to the education block to seek permission for access to the typewriter. Duly granted, he hastened to his cell – itching to get his fingers dancing across the keys.

He removed the cover and stared at it. The machine was more than twenty years old and after ten minutes of bashing about, Jo realised the only letters he was going to get out of it were capital ones. He cursed out loud "You fuckin' mother! Why, haven't, you, – got any small fuckin' letters!?"

He suddenly became conscious that he was talking to himself, and looked round the empty cell stupidly.

What the fuck is happening to you, son...they'll be taking you away soon, oh yes – they'll be walking towards you all dressed up wearing long white coats – six-inch hypos filled to the brim – No. No. Now the game has begun...
...it's time for some fun...
...yes, yes, – okay baby, let's get the engine started here, get a little juice in there son – are you on me brother? Is that you grandad...? Okay, here we go then – once upon a time there were eighty one green bottles hanging on the wall. Humpty-dumpty leaned over thinking they were the king's men...
Come on, come on...the quick brown fox jumped over the lazy dog...

Jo fed another sheet of paper into the machine and knocked out a few words.

THE QUICK BROWN FOZ
THE QUICK BROWN FOX JUMPS OVER THE LAZY DOG

JUMPED   JUMPED   OVER   THE   LAZY   DOG   AND
FETCHED   IT   HIM   SELF   HIMSELF   MYSELF   HIMSELF

...yes...the quick brown fox jumped over the lazy dog and fetched it

himself...he was in too much of a hurry to wait for the dog and besides, the dog probably wouldn't have a clue...

...the quick brown fox jumped over the lazy dog and grabbed the unsuspecting chicken by the throat – then it ripped its head off...jumped over the dog and grabbed the unsuspecting chicken by the throat, then quietly tip-toed into the forest...yes...

THE WILY FOX HAN'T EATENFOR MORE THAN A WEEK. WHEN HE SAW THE CHICKEN OF THE

WHEN HE SAW THE CHICKEN PERCHED ON
...the wily fox hadn't eaten for more than a week...when he saw the chicken pluck a juicy worm from the soft earth, he made his run...

THE WILY FOX HADN'T EATEN FOR A WEEK

THE WILY FOX HADN'T EATEN FOR OVER A WEEK, WHEN HE SAW THE CHICKEN PLUCK A WORM FROM THE SOFT EARTH HE MADE HIS RUN

DEATH IN A CLOSED ROOM
                    CHAPTER ONE
THE DOCTOR OPEND HIS EYES AND WONDERED WHY HE WASN'T AT HOM WITH HIS WIFE

THE DOCTOR WOKE UP SUDDENLY, WONDERIN WHYTHE QUICK BROWN FOX
    *"/@£ &'()
    $^{-1}$4?)('&_£* ABRACADABRA ^{1}4*?"(/@£_&

THE DOODLEMASTER
THIS IS THE STORY OF THE DOODLEMASTER GENERAL

ALL RIGHTS RESERVED BY D B DUNNIT
A DEE BEE PRODUCTION

Jo stood up and dug his hands deep into the top of his buttock muscles. His back was aching more than ever and he was out of painkillers. He stretched out on the bed and rolled himself a single-skinner, hoping the drug would take his mind away from the nagging pain. As he drew the smoke into his lungs, he began to think about doctors. Slowly he slipped into a mind-drift and Jo saw the script unfold as if on film...

A short time later, Jo began to feel uneasy again. Still dancing in his mind, torturing him, was the thought that someone he loved was about to die. Any moment he was expecting a screw to enter his cell and break the bad news.

Jo didn't realise it, but he was still hovering in and out of delusion and now, as he gazed out through the barred window of his cell – his eyes fixed on an approaching summer storm – anxiety encroached him and a slow trickle of adrenalin was creeping into his gut in the form of impending doom.

As the sky grew darker, so did his thoughts.

With the first flash of lightening came a picture of his elder son being crushed under the wheels of a giant road-roller.

When thunder followed a few minutes later he saw his younger son torn apart by a pack of wild dogs and Christine, she's on her way to the prison but, oh God...she's not going to make it – the train is going to run off the rails and plunge down into the swollen river. Jo could see her – upside down and face up in a pool of water, blood running from her eyes...

...he cried out... "Oh, dear Jesus...help me..."

Suddenly, another clap of thunder echoed over the prison and a jagged bolt of lightning illuminated the grey sky. In his state of agitation, Jo saw a thousand faceless souls crying as the torrential rain poured from the low clouds, dancing across the tarmac, it seemed, as the wind raced in behind. In between the faceless souls were the faces of his own loved ones and he cried out again...

"Oh, please – "

In desperation, he pulled the drawer from the locker and spilled the contents onto the bed. He grabbed an envelope and took out the photographs of his family, holding them close to his chest – as if his actions would protect them in some way.

He began to weep. "Please, don't let it happen…don't take them from me…oh, Christine…"

Jo was now totally engulfed in fear, terrified that his delusions were going to turn into reality.

He paced up and down the cell for a few moments then pounded the door with his fists. He shouted in anguish.

"Help…please…I…oh, dear God…"

He kicked the door and held his head, trying to blot out the dread that was racing through him.

After a while – an eternity – two screws were standing at the open door. "Are you alright, Sullivan?" asked one of them. "I…it's my wife… something's happened…where is she?" mumbled Jo, almost incoherently.

The two screws looked at each other before one of them said, "Have you taken anything, Sullivan? Have you taken any drugs?"

"It's my wife…I want to see her…what have you done with her…oh Jesus, where is she…I'm so frightened…"

"Come on now, don't worry – nothing has happened to your wife. Let's get you across to the hospital – they'll give you something to calm you down, okay?"

Tentatively, they led Jo from the cell and made their way to the hospital wing. On the way, Jo heard one of the screws talking on his hand radio, warning the staff that a short fuse was on the way. Jo heard the words but they drifted over his head, unsure of their meaning.

When they entered the hospital Jo saw several screws, all wearing short white coats, standing in a semi-circle outside of a cell. A man in a grey suit was hovering near the doorway and when he saw Jo he nodded to a senior screw.

Two screws then took Jo by the arms and gently coaxed him into the cell. "You'll be alright," one of them assured him, "just sit yourself down on the mattress."

Jo sat down, unsure what was happening.

"Lay out on the mattress, now – you'll feel better if you do – "

As Jo spread himself on the mattress, five more screws entered the cell and Jo wondered briefly why so many of them were gathering round him.

All movement seemed to be in slow motion.

Suddenly and dramatically, they seized him and turned him over onto his stomach, his face pressed into the mattress by a screw holding the back of his neck. At the same time, his arms and legs were pinned behind his back – folded and locked into each other in such a way that now, only one screw was needed to take the strain.

Jo then felt the point of a needle sink into his rump.

He struggled and tried to scream out but his face was still hard up against the mattress and he was having difficulty breathing.

As soon as the needle went in, the screw holding Jo down began to shout, "Go!…Go!…Go!…" and each screw in turn hurried from the cell. When the last of them had gone, the screw pinning Jo to the mattress released his grip and ran to the open door.

By the time Jo unfolded and got to his feet, the door was slammed shut. He screamed out in frustrated anger. "You mothers! You fuckin' mothers!"

With his fist clenched, Jo punched the heavy metal door until several bones cracked and then, as he watched his hand turn into a bloody mass, he sank to the floor and slipped into a black void.

– don't let them die…please don't let them die…I'll do the dying for them…

Several hours later when Jo opened his eyes, he knew he was dying. His throat was so dry he could hardly breath and what little air he did take in was in slow, shallow breaths.

He felt completely dehydrated.

As he lay on the concrete floor, his arms to his sides, he gradually realised that it wasn't his believed Christine that was soon to die – it was him.

"Oh no…" he gasped, "…it's me…oh, Christine…I'm not going to make it…I'm not going to make it, baby…"

A great fear began to creep into Jo, a fear he knew had haunted him all of his life – the fear of dying. Now, here it was, looming over him, about to take him on that perilous journey into the tunnel – but before it could take hold, Jo saw an apparition of his sister, her words echoing in his mind. "Don't panic, now…don't panic…"

All at once. Jo went into a calm.

As he heard his sisters words, a strange, inexplicable, band of tingling heat began to inch it's way through his body.

Jo remained motionless, not even daring to breath.

Within a few seconds his whole frame felt as if it was glowing. When the band of heat passed through his body and into his head, Jo experienced a feeling of great comfort, a feeling of peace and tranquillity – as if a heavy mantle had been lifted from him, and he wept.

While savouring the moments of blissful content, lost in his own imagination, a figure seemed to appear before him. He had a silver-grey beard and white wispy hair and he was wearing a purple cloak. In his hands was a huge book with a red cover and on the cover was the word 'IF' written in pearl. The figure smiled for a moment then whispered

…if you can keep your head when all about you are losing theirs…

before disappearing just as mysteriously as it appeared.

After the figure vanished, Jo saw a garden of flowers spring out of the floor, each one of them was a different colour.

*…this can't be a dream can it? I'm awake and my eyes are open…I can pick one if I want to pick one…if I can move across to where they are…but I don't want to move…I **can't** move…yes, yes you can – crawl if you have to, but pick a flower from that wonderful garden…the blue one standing all on it's own…yes…reach for the flower…oh, but where am I going…oh no –*

> *Stay calm little one*
> *You are with me*
> *Let your mind run*
> *I will be with you*

...yes, oh yes – you'll catch me if I fall though, won't you...?

As your Guardian, I will be with you where ever you are.
Let your mind run little one, let it run now...

                                          ...come
lay your head on the soft pillow. If you wish, refresh
yourself with milk and honey...

...yes, that sounds good. Milk and honey...but where am I...?

You are here with me...

...yes, and it is wonderful to be with you – but where are we? All I
see are specks of light...

You are in transit. I am here to help you. Your mind is reaching out
for guidance and has reached a stage where it can decide whether to
continue it's search for spiritual awareness or return to a material
world as a healer or teacher. I can tell you nothing of the astral
planes, save that your soul is a young soul, and as such, may dwell in
the empyreal tunnel. If you choose to return to a material world, I
will help you in your quest for the furtherance of your soul. As with
all progress in a material world, you will face temptation and
indecision and your path may be long. You will make the right
decision now but you will not remember.
I will mark your hands.
If your aim is pure, you will remember.

...are you God?

I am the Guardian that dwells within you.
I am a pattern for you to seek out.
Rest now, and let your mind run...

...yes-sir-ree-diddly. I like this game – Confusion I'll say it's

called...I'll be the inside-out-back-to-front-man...

...the upside-down-in-and-out-man...
...a rubber-round-the-head-man...
...an inky-doodle-dux-machine...ha...
...a Soulmaker...

...I'll go undercover – codename – Fumblemonkbox...

Ha...yes – Fumblemonkbox – it's got a kind of ring...

"Excuse me, sir – would you mind telling me your name?"
"Of course not, officer – It's Monkbox."
"Christian name, please sir?"
"Fumble."

The police officer repeated the name out loud as he wrote it down in his notebook. "Fumble Monkbox – unusual name. You wouldn't be taking the piss by any chance would you?"

"What happened to the 'sir' then – and how come I'm now suddenly taking the piss...?"

...yeah, I can see the hidden video and the compensation – maybe I ought to get it changed by deed-poll, all nice an' legal...ha... yeah...

Stirring, and staring into the space around him, all Jo could see were dots of light. He was laying on his stomach, his face hard-up against the cold floor and a light blanket covered him.

What are those lights
where am I
what is on my back
what planet am I on?

As his eyes focused, Jo saw minute beams of light coming through the tiny needle-holes of the blanket that was covering him. For a brief moment Jo wondered where the blanket had come from –

it wasn't there before…there was a garden…wasn't there…?

Jo shrugged the thought from his mind and the blanket from his back, and turned over onto his hands and knees.

As soon as he did, pain began throbbing from his damaged hand. He held it out in front of him and stared at it in disbelief. The knuckles were split and his hand had swollen to double it's normal size.

Pain ebbed from it in pulsating and relentless agony.

While looking at his hand, Jo suddenly noticed a jug of water on the floor near the door. He'd quite forgotten how parched his throat felt and how difficult he was finding it to breath. He knelt and grabbed the jug and took several long gulps of water.

Jo leaned against the wall and cast his eyes round the cell. There was no window in the cell and the only light came from a low-voltage bulb, throwing a yellowish hue over the smooth walls.

There was no bed in the cell, no chair or table – even the usual obligatory piss-pot was conspicuously absent.

Then he noticed the ceiling.

It wasn't normal.

Half of it had been carved away and re-plastered, spiralling into a tiny peep-hole. It was like a tunnel, disappearing into an inch-wide hole through which the screws and doctors could observe him.

Jo moved across to the mattress and crashed out on it, laying his injured hand across his chest. He stared into the hole in the ceiling, his mind oblivious to everything and everyone except the mysterious figure that seemed to have appeared before him.

…did he really appear or was it an apparition…an hallucination? But he looked so real – and even if he didn't appear I must have at least thought of him to be thinking of him now – carrying a large red book with the word 'IF' on the cover…
…is that a message from the other side, from my Guardian… if…if…that word keeps haunting me…Irene…if you can keep your head…when all about you…are losing theirs and blaming it on you…if you can trust yourself when all men…doubt you! Yes of course you stupid prick! It's a poem…some kind of philosophy – I

remember now at school – that streak-of-piss-of-an-English-teacher...Keats or Chaucer or someone and the poem was called 'IF'...

Yes...yes...yes...you've cracked it son – you gotta get hold of a copy of this 'IF' a bit lively 'cos there must be some real head-honcho clues in it – but, tch – they must know I hate trying to solve puzzles and riddles...

...riddles...

...lots of games and a riddle here and there...well – ha, I've just got one of 'em – it must be – couldn't be anything else, not even coincidence – not this late in the game...

The door opened quietly.

Three screws edged their way into the cell. One of them was holding a small plastic container.

Jo moved back to the far corner. "Stay away from me. I'm warning you – "

"Take it easy, Sullivan – all we want to do is take a look at your hand and give you some medication," said one of the screws. "I don't need any medication – why do you want me out cold all the time?" demanded Jo.

"This won't put you to sleep – it'll just relax you, stop you from having those terrible thoughts about your family."

Jo remembered the last time he was forced to take medication, and he remembered too, how much better he felt after taking it. He moved towards the screw and took hold of the small measure. He held it up in front of him, trying to decide if it was the same pink liquid that he'd taken before but in the subdued light he couldn't tell.

"You say I won't sleep on this?"

"Well, you might doze off later," said the screw, "but that's not what it's for."

Jo swallowed the liquid in one gulp.

"What's this stuff called?" asked Jo.

"Chloropromazine – it's a strong tranquilliser."

"Chloro...?"

" – promazine," offered the screw. "Bit of a tongue-twister, eh?"

"Yeah…chloro…promazine – what does it do?"

"Well, it acts on the limbic system – part of the cerebrum that handles emotional reactions. It should relieve all your tension and anxiety – get rid of all your nasty thoughts," smiled the affable screw.

Jo smiled in return. "Good," he said, "for a minute there I thought I was going insane – "

"Yeah, well – you should be alright now. Anyway, let's take a look at your hand – you gave that door quite a bashing." The screw took hold of Jo's hand. "Mm, that's a nasty injury – let's get you along to the surgery."

The screws led Jo from the strip-cell and took him into a small room at the far end of the passage.

"I won't have to go back in there after will I?" Jo asked.

"No – we'll sort out an ordinary cell for you for a few days then put you back on the wing."

"Thank fuck for that – that cell's brain damage," said Jo, happy to be talking.

"Yeah, pretty grim, eh," the screw replied, bathing Jo's hand.

"How long was I in there?"

"Er, about thirty-six hours I think."

"Thirty-six hours! But…I couldn't have been…I mean – have I been asleep nearly all that time?"

The screw looked at Jo in mild surprise. "No, far from it, Sullivan – you were awake most of the time."

"Was I? What was I doing – I hardly remember anything."

"I don't know. Apart from the machine-guns you were in a world of your own, I think," he smiled.

…machine-guns…?

The screw finished bathing Jo's hand then smeared antiseptic cream on the wound. After placing a small piece of lint on top of the cream, he bandaged his hand. "How's that feel now?" said the screw, pleased with his handywork.

"It still hurts like hell – but it does feel a little better."

"Good. We'll change the dressing again tomorrow, okay?"

"Yeah. Gov'nor, tell me something will you – why did they hold me down and jab me up – I wasn't giving anyone any grief?"

"It's policy. We can't afford to take the chance that someone might freak out – and you were in a pretty bad state of mind, really confused. Do you remember what you were going through?"

"I remember all of it – up until I was K.O'd – about my family mostly."

"How do you feel now?"

"Not too bad I s'pose – I think I just want to lay down."

"Yes, I expect you do – let's find a room for you."

Soon Jo was led from the small surgery and shown into a larger, more normal cell. The walls were covered in light, pastel shades and the full-sized window gave him a feeling of open space as he looked out across the hospital garden.

He stretched out on the high bed and rolled a single-skinner, thankful that his mind had rid itself of the dread that had caused him to be admitted to the hospital.

With his thoughts lighter, Jo began to question himself, and, unwittingly, he began to play a head-game that was to prove to be, later, more enlightening than anything he could ever imagine…

…Okay, so you've gone a little crazy – now let's find out why shall we?

…Yeah.

…Let's start at the beginning – you were taking a bath and smoking Lebanese Gold…the sun was beating down on your face and you felt good.

Yeah.

…You were thinking about Howard Hughes and then you started trying to get rid of those mysterious black lines.

Yeah, that's right –

– And when they wouldn't come off you hunted round the bath-house until you found a scrubbing brush, then you ran the stiff bristles across your knuckles until you drew blood.

Yes – why did I do that? And how did those lines get on my hands? And thinking about it now, I don't remember how they disappeared either. They were still there when I left the bath – wow – if they disappeared just as mysteriously as they appeared...?

> *round and round*
> *the thoughts will go*
> *when you're there*
> *I'll let you know*

Why do you keep thinking in rhyme –
you never used to –
now you are doing it all of the time –

> *A long grey beard and white whispy hair*
> *I'm sure I saw him standing there*

Yeah, head-games and mind-drifts just to keep everyone on their toes...

> *head-games are fun but hard to play*
> *follow the rules or be taken away*

Yes, maybe I'll play the first game with the doctors. They already think I'm half-crazy and if I play along with them I can be getting them at it and at the same time I can be working on early release through the pretence of mental impairment...
...yes, yes, it could work...
I can pretend to still be a little unbalanced and they might keep me in the hospital for a while and then release me into the care of the out-patients department of the local asylum...yeah...and it makes good sense as well considering I've been refused parole three times already going through normal channels. This way they're bound to release me early, maybe in a couple of months even – and what could you lose? Nothing as far as I can see. All they could do if they sussed is send you back to the main wing – yes!

Now, how do I convince them that I'm crazy…?

The following day, because he had shown signs of mental distress, the authorities had summoned a psychiatrist to the prison and Jo was taken from his cell and shown into an office.

Seated behind a large desk was a man dressed in a dark blue suit. He appeared to be in his late seventies and at first Jo thought he was looking at a Boris Karloff lookalike; then he reminded Jo of the little man carrying the large red book. The doctor had white hair and a grey-white beard and the surplus skin under his eyes looked as though it was filled with fluid. Criss-crossing his nose were tiny blood-purple veins and a row of warts seemed to come out of his left eye in the shape of a crescent moon. Jo wondered for a moment if he was looking at a hologram and absent mindedly looked over his shoulder for the apparatus that might be throwing the image.

Thinking about it, Jo began to laugh.

Interlocking his fingers and resting his hands across his chest – thumbs pointing skyward – the doctor leaned back in his chair and observed Jo who was by now wiping the tears from his eyes.

"Mr. Sullivan, please – take a seat."

"Oh, dear – sorry about that – I was just thinking how I'm gonna describe you in my book."

"I see," said the doctor, showing a slight smile in spite of closed lips. "May I ask why I am to be a subject in this…book of yours?"

"Everyone is gonna be a subject – every screw, every doctor, every mother I've ever met is gonna be in it. I'm gonna tell the whole fuckin' world how they tortured me mentally and physically and how they left me in agony for weeks at a time and if that doesn't work I'll write about the times when I smoked with Charlie Richardson and had tea with Reggie Kray, and maybe I might even tell everyone how I got hold of a picture that was painted by the Yorkshire Ripper, depicting the scourging of Christ before He made his way to the Crucifixion – and how the screws made a fortune out of him. Yeah, everyone is gonna be a subject if necessary – even if it ends up a foot thick! I've even made up a slogan already – by hook or by crook – you will read my book – ha!" blurted out Jo, ferociously attacking the nail on his little finger.

"I see…er…are you writing this book now?"

"No, I'm writing another book first then I'm gonna write about life in prison after that."

"When did you decide to write a book?"

"I didn't decide – I was told."

"Who told you?" asked the doctor, hanging on Jo's words.

"I don't know yet – "

"Was it a voice that told you to write a book?"

"Yes."

"Who's voice was it do you think?"

"I don't know yet – my guardian angel's, maybe – who knows? I'm not gonna say it's God am I?"

"Why not?"

"Because I'm not that daft that's why – "

"But you said a voice told you to write a book?"

"Yes, but I didn't say it was God did I? I don't want to end up in a lunatic asylum do I?"

"No, of course not," said the doctor, leaning his elbow on the desk, gently stroking his beard. "Tell me, did this voice also tell you your family were in danger?"

"In danger?" said Jo, screwing his face.

The doctor caught Jo's discomfort. "I say that because I see here in my notes that you were…concerned about your family, in particular, your wife – "

"Yeah, well – that's all been sorted out – she's gonna be alright," said Jo quickly, switching his teeth to his other little finger.

"Good. I expect you're glad she's going to be alright?"

"Course I am you fuckin' idiot! D'you think I enjoyed seeing her die!?"

"I'm sorry…I didn't mean to imply – "

"Forget it, forget it – " said Jo, instantly cursing himself.

"Tell me, Jo – you don't mind if I call you Jo?"

"No."

"Jo – if it's not too painful – why do you think everyone is alright now – as far as your family are concerned I mean?"

Jo continued to chew his nails to the quick.

"Well, I made a covenant – a promise that I can't tell **anyone**."

"I see, and now you believe that your family will be safe?"

"I **know** they will – if anything, it'll be me that does any dying."

"Why do you say that – did a voice say you were going to die?"

"I can't talk about that – it's sacred information."

The doctor leaned back in his chair and paused for a moment before continuing. "Tell me, Jo – do you know if anyone in your family has ever suffered mental illness, or had any kind of breakdown?"

"Not that I know of – why?"

"Well, if there was any history of mental disorder – "

"What ya tryin' to say – that I'm fuckin' silly or something?"

"No, no, – I'm just trying to eliminate the possibilities that may have brought on your…agitation – but, if you say you know nothing of any…problems, so to speak, well – it must be something else. Now, I see here in my notes that you have already been asked about drug abuse – are you sure you haven't taken anything that might have induced your present state of mind – it's quite important that you tell the truth in this matter."

"I haven't taken any drugs," lied Jo.

"I see. Well, Mr. Sullivan – Jo, I think this is about as far as we can go at the moment. I'll prescribe some medication for you which should help. Other than that, try not to think too much – read a good book or something if you can – the main point being, you've probably done too much thinking and that in turn has turned your emotions upside down – "

"Apart from that I'm okay, yeah?"

"Er, to be perfectly frank, it's not always that simple when it comes to the mind – especially if voices rear their heads, but don't worry – I'm sure it's only temporary in your case."

"Right'o doc – will I have to see you again?"

"Er, I'm not sure it will be me, but you'll certainly see someone, yes," said the doctor, somewhat hesitantly.

Alone in his office, the doctor leaned forward and pressed the rewind button of a tape-recorder, waited, then pressed the play button.

A burst of laughter, a deep, almost contagious sound, lasted fourteen seconds – Mr. Sullivan, please – take a seat – oh, dear – sorry about that – I was just thinking how I'm gonna describe you in my book – I see – and may I ask – click!

The doctor swivelled in his chair and looked out through the barred window. Thoughts in his head caused lines to appear on his brow. Jo Sullivan was jogging through his mind.

...hysterical laughter – I was just thinking how I'm gonna describe you in my book – he was laughing at me...what was so funny...it won't be funny where he's going...a voice...manic agitation...delusion...nervous debility...no drug abuse...no previous history of mental illness...a voice...his guardian angel...sacred information – he was terrified, sir – thought something was going to happen to his wife...

The doctor swang back to his desk and retrieved a form from a top drawer. Half way down the form, in a space reserved for diagnosis, he wrote –

Manic Agitation – Paranoid Delusion – Nervous Debility
Acute Schizophrenia

Recommendation – Section Two Observation

Back in his cell, Jo wondered why he hadn't carried out the plan he'd thought of the day before. He knew it would have worked – he'd dreamed out all the scenes frame by frame until he was out and walking into the arms of Christine.

Jo liked dreaming his film, his book. The more cannabis he allowed to mingle into his brain, the further the film went until, after one joint too many, the image disintegrated into a haze of empty blackness – but for now – with his first hit of the day, the film was clear.

Jo always liked starting at the beginning. Usually, every beginning was different, sometimes starting when he was a young man working his way through, sometimes when he entered prison but lately – since his release from the strip-cell – they all started with an entity in the shape of a beam of light, making it's way towards the planet.

Jo saw himself back in the strip-cell, staring into a black tunnel waiting for death to come for him. Then came his sister in the guise of an angel and she said, "Hold on now – don't panic beloved one – "

On the film, as the credits are rolling, the entity circles the planet. While orbiting the planet, a history is unfolding within the entity and on the screen, split second images give hint of the chaos: long-wigged Law Lords studying tiny black marks in between rows of letters; a child trapped in a small room, sobbing, trying to solve a Rubic cube; great forests burning; wars raging; famine and torture, suffering and frustration – a sphere trapped in a square cage.

As the entity sweeps down across the globe, it homes in on a lost soul, and enters it. The music accompanying the entry is in quadro-sonic, music that sends a band of tingling heat along the spinal column and into the brainbox.

On the film, Jo then imagined he was in control of a mystical force which was a Soulmaker – a seeker of lost souls, and a lost soul was a confused mind struggling to find it's way forward.

The Soulmaker, an imperceptible wave of thought that had evolved through it's own perception, was now homing in on Jo's confusion and was about to join with his pre-conscious but, with the thought of a saviour about to join him, Jo felt great emotion, left the film, and mind-drifted into a biblical epic where Christ was on his way to the crucifixion.

...the pain remembered in the music as He carried the cross...

...the sound of a hammer striking nails...

...Father, forgive them – for they know not what they do...

Why did you suffer the cross, Man?

Would you not die on a cross for the ones you love?

Yes, I would die for them…but I don't have to die, do I? It's not my time to die is it…?

Jo was quickly reaching the conclusion that he was going insane and decided to write a letter to his sister, Irene.

He went to a drawer and dug out a letter-sheet that had been issued to him at Parkhurst, but was as yet unused.

In replying to this letter, please write on the envelope:

Number..................................Name.......................H.M. PRISON
PARKHURST
NEWPORT I.O.W.
PO30 5NX

Dear Irene,

*I know what the game **is** – it's the 'guess who's going to die' game. Jesus – can I play such a game without knowing myself? How does it end? Do I just sit here waiting and thinking, worrying and wanting? I'm not sure I can play such a game without going crazy. My mate thinks I'm insane already.*

How do I get this letter to you without the screws taking me away to where the lunatics are held? Ah, but of course, from within my mind where all the clues that were coming through when the game was first beginning to ebb are now safely locked – but nobody else dies do they?

Please don't let anyone else die.

Perhaps he's dead already. Is that a straw to cling to, because I feel that I am clutching at straws?

I thought I was tripping last night. Keats…no…Kipling…Yes, it was he who came into my mind and floated in front of me in a whispering dream, and he was carrying a red book.

When I realised what the game was it was terrifying and I screamed out for you. Then I screamed out for everyone that I love.

Now I am smiling, thinking – no, it's impossible to sit here like this, driving myself mad, not getting anywhere.

But I don't have to play, do I?

I can escape from it, be running away can't I?

No, I can't do that because don't forget there's a body floating about out there waiting to turn into a corpse and it could be mine.

Shall I send this letter to you?

Are you confused, dear sister, because I think you are dead? Or will it be me that becomes dead, thus making this letter words from the grave...?

How long do I carry this on? Six months? A year? I need to come down – ease right off the gas – I was up there doin' around three hundred...

Not too much emotion to start, please – I keep crying. It's embarrassing – I might have to kill someone if they laugh at me so I've got to start acting normal or I'll never get out don't you see...?

Jo stared aimlessly into the blank letter-sheet, wondering how his mind had become so irrational. Is there a God...is there some mystical force out there trying to show me the way...my own Soulmaker, he thought...

Jo knew that there was.

He took hold of a pen and began to write to his sister.

In replying to this letter, please write on the envelope.

Number. **b062o** .... Name. **J. SULLIVAN** .H.M.PRISON
PARKHURST
NEWPORT I.O.W.
PO30 5NX

Hi Sis

I am gradually going out of my mind and I wondered if you could help me love Jo.

Less than twenty-four hours later Jo found himself handcuffed and shackled, sitting in the back seat of a car and heading for the psychiatric unit, Parkhurst. Before reaching Parkhurst however, Jo was to spend a night in Wandsworth.

Jo, and the three screws escorting him, left Maidstone around noon and remained virtually silent throughout the near two hours it took them to reach Wandsworth Prison. During the journey, completely monged and almost smothered by the unnatural silence, Jo slipped into a negative mind-drift, imagined death, and lived out seventeen variations of dying in a road traffic accident.

By the time they reached South-East London and the gates closed on the car after it entered Wandsworth, Jo was glad to step out of it and regain control of his own destiny.

Unchained and processed through reception, Jo was quickly taken across to the main wing and shown into cell D3-32.

As soon as the door was slammed shut an unease swept through him and he began to feel strange. His head didn't feel right but then – just as suddenly – he felt okay again.

...yeah, this'll do me for a night – all tucked-up nice n' peaceful with a lump of gear between the cheeks that could feed half the wing...ha...Wandsworth...you ain't having me this time, no sir, not with what I'm carrying...

Jo laid his bed-roll out and placed his personal belongings – all bagged up in a pillow-case – down on the low bed. Looking round the dingy cell he noticed it didn't have the usual triangled table that always sat in the corner...

...every cell in Wandsworth has a corner table with a jug and a bowl, so why hasn't this one...I won't be able to bathe...I'll be unclean...

Another twinge of unease ran through Jo.

...no, oh no – we ain't playin' any of those games, no cleanliness and Godlyness games thankyou very much and besides, I feel I have some friends here with me...

Then Jo noticed there wasn't any glass in the small panes and that a shutter-type window had been fitted on the inside of the cell that Jo could open and close as he liked. All the heavy bars were still in place and Jo couldn't see out of the window and across the yard unless he stood on the bed.

When he did look out of the window and he wasn't standing on the bed, all he could see in silhouette against the sky, was a stone cross that adorned the roof of the prison church.

As well as the triangled table, also missing from the cell was the pin-board and the plastic mat that went a little way in covering the black bitumen flooring. If Jo didn't know better, he might have thought he was in a strip-cell.

After putting together a three-skinner, Jo was soon sucking in the magic smoke that would hasten Wandsworth's disappearance into an empty mist. It happened quickly.

As the cell began dissolving, Jo's mind slipped into delusion again, waiting for the dreams and nightmares to come to life. First of all, when he looked to the corner where the triangled table should have been, he saw three figures all sitting on the floor, cross-legged and holding pens and paintbrushes…

…hey, that's Kipling…so you have come to me at last…I knew you would of course – it was obvious you had to come to me sooner or later because I reasoned it out that you are my guide, aren't you – please, are you? Are you he that will send tingles dancing through me as the ink flows out across the paper, feeding me…

…ha…and you…you are Shakespeare – I've seen your face on a banknote…and you are Titian, greatest of painters…Jesus, who can I be in among such men. I can't write or paint – I can hardly draw a simple match-stick man…dear Jesus, please let me play…I want to play so much…

Jo turned away from the images of the figures and his eyes fell upon a pile of letters that were protruding from the pillow-case that contained his personal possessions.

Most of the letters Jo received were from Freddie and nearly every one of them was written on different coloured paper than the one before. When Freddie had used up every sheet of coloured paper he could find, he went through the entire felt-tip range.

From there he went on to writing on paper where Bambi's and squirrels and other small animals surrounded the borders. Other paper had flowers on it and some were type-written, minus most of the commas and full stops.

Somewhere among the dozens of letters was one written with a yellow felt tip on orange paper and Jo smiled when he recalled it took him a day and a half to read under the 40-watt glow of a prison light.

Jo dug into the pile and pulled one out. It was typewritten, and he began to read it…

Sunday night February 19th – Time "Closein time
                                                    10-45pm

                                                    Fred.
                                                    Portsmouth.

Page One.
––––––––––––––––––––––––––––

Allo Jo,

Before i get goin on this letter i thought I'd let ya know I'm only gonna type one page. I aint had a reply from my last letter to ya.
Not even a blimp if ya please, i cant help thinking ya never received it?
If ya did receive it ya can understand why i'm only gonna do this one sheet.
As you know i wrote i mean typed a few pages and if ya didn't get it i'm sure i'm not gonna sit here typein page after page for nothin.
To think all my material goin to waste ha, ha, ha. Thats what i call unchristian, dont worry i know how the system works?
There they are – "eres one who likes typein, let him carry on typein a couple of Thousand pages then in about July we'll let this Fred know he's not allowed to corrasponed to Sullivan.

Cor don't i like that then, i better get on with the news etc or i wont have no room left will i Jo.

A bad thought just hit me as i finished that last sentence? Picturein ya censore saying to himself – go on please do get ya news typed down cos Sullivan ain't gonna get it anyway.

Right i'll start, Reggie and Gilby started a nice one on that charge Reggie was tellin us about Xmas in that pub we saw him in.

They got 4years each, if they gets done on em others they'll be doin plenty i should think.

I wouldn't like to do their remission.

Dusty got bail for a thousand quid, and he aint a bit worried or concerned cos he said they ain't got nothin on him so he should get away with it but old Dusty always says that, then before ya know it a couple of years passes then ya say i aint seen old Dusty for ages then someone looks up and says hes inside doin four years and hes done two alreaddy.

Anyway Jo how are ya gettin on? hows ya back? as ya know ive done nothin for bleedin years except been writein letters to my mates brothers uncle and uncle Tom Coberlee too. ere guess who i bumped into a couple of Saturdays ago? there i was taken shelter from the pouring rain at the bottom of New. Rd and along came bush-baby Bailey and he didn't have a hair outta place. he must get through some laquer i should think cos there was a gale force wind blowin. i told im about you and he said it was about time they caught up with him, always carryin about a motor-bike chain and a couple of daggers but ya know what Fred he said, last time he was in trouble he fucked off to kent, now this time when he gets out he'll be back ere. i couldn't stop laughing…

After reading part of the letter, seeing the pile of other letters smothered in colours and pictures and smiling animals, they gradually appeared to Jo to take on the guise of wrapping paper and he suddenly shouted out –

"I can be Father Christmas! Yes, that's me – I've always wanted to give everyone presents, give 'em lots of shelter and protection so they won't go cold and hungry…please, yes, let me be Father

Christmas…"

Jo was gradually reaching the point of no return as his thoughts took him further and further into the realms of delusion – or was it enlightenment?

…I've been here before haven't I…this is de-ja-vous ain't it…I'm gonna believe all my thoughts and all of my dreams and then the nightmares will come in the shape of death for my loved ones, and then you will go insane – no, no you won't – not now, not now that you believe, not now that you know your Angel is with you and if those demons come, send them round the world with Mary and her little lambs…ha…you're fucking crazy, man…
…Nah, I ain't crazy – I'm just getting used to the idea that I've got a guardian angel looking over me…

Later, as day changed to night, Jo was back at the window staring into the stone cross that seemed to shimmer and take on the glow of flourescent light as the moon crossed the clear sky. Transfixed by the sight of the cross and by the shadows of the razor-wire that fell upon it in the shape of the Crown of Thorns, Jo listened to thoughts that lived deep within him…

Only after the passing of more than two weeks did the pain in Jo's hand begin to subside to a more bearable ache. During those weeks he lost all desire to write because every time he dreamed a story-line, dread was just a sentence away – usually in the guise of one of his loved ones perishing in agony.

Because Jo was under total observation, and because he knew any visitors he might have would be also closely observed, Jo stopped sending out V.O.'s and was soon to be without resin. He was already without sulphate and the few painkillers he did once have were long gone.

Whenever he was given medication by a screw, he feigned swallowing and spat out the green-and-white capsules at the first opportunity. Before long, the only alien drug coursing through Jo's veins was nicotine, courtesy Her Majesty in the shape of three half-ounce packs of Old Holborn per week.

Without drugs, the days were to become long, long, days in the psychiatric unit.

Instead of writing, unable to concentrate on reading, incapable of working-out – trapped in a concrete box measuring five paces by three – all Jo could do to nullify the clock was doodle, and doodle he did.

The following pages are some of Jo's thoughts as he coped with the cold reality of isolation, and he called them –

DREAMTIMES AND DOODLES

That's better — now, I will write down all my thoughts as we go —.

*…you won't be able to do that, loony, 'cos right now we're on the trail of a doctor and if I tried to write while I was thinking I wouldn't be able to think **slow** enough – I wanna torture some of 'em, box one or two up and ship 'em out – crate a couple up in a tea-chest and ship 'em out to the smallest island in the middle of the Pacific somewhere so that by the time they get there and I let them out they will be so fucked-up they won't be able to straighten out any of their arms and their legs and their necks – ha, but I don't want to **think** about any of that…*

*No, that's right – just relax son. Take it easy on the head or you'll drive yourself mad…play some little games instead…ha, yeah we'll play games alright don't worry about that **but** why am I in this room again, a small room with a high ceiling and a watertight door…no, it's not the **same** room but it smells the same and there isn't a window or if there is it's so far up the wall I can hardly see it…it's warm in here and it's old which means cockroaches will roam when the sun begins to sink…*

But why am I in this
room again, a different
room with a high
window and a watertight
door — the doodlebug
room where the nightmares
come true and the blood
runs cold —

DAY ~~ONE~~ 6.50 PM
So they think I'm
crazy do they? I've
already told them I'm not.
Why don't they take any
notice I wonder. I don't
remember hurting anyone

So it must be something else,
but I'll track it down –
maybe I'll get a Pinkerton
man on the job, ——

(LES LEE DE GEORGIO ~~SAID YOU'LL NEVER~~
~~WEAR ONE OF US~~ BENNY $\frac{199\frac{5}{6-6-}}{}$?) A. FOF

The cowboy pulled in on the
reins

The year ~~was~~ 1543 and the
handgun ~~was the best~~

Come on baby, you can do it,
with guns ablazin' –
automatics that never need
~~relod~~ reloading.
Mission: Wipe out total
population   dream
                machine

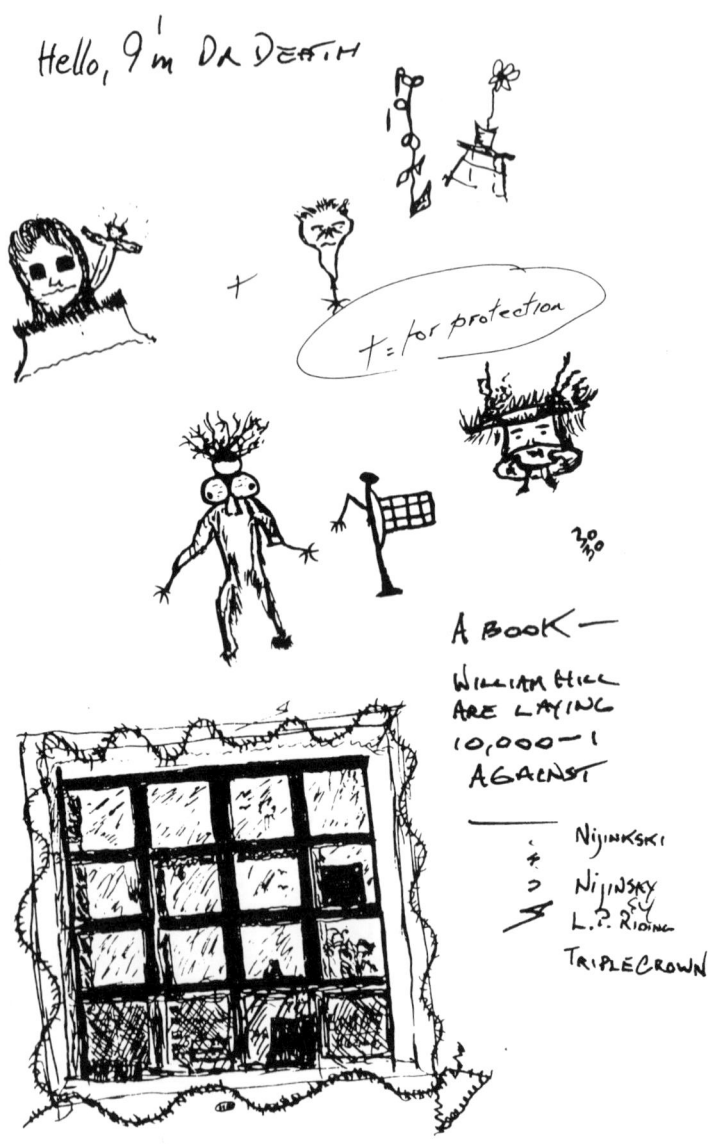

Hello, I'm Dr Death

+

t = for protection

A BOOK —

WILLIAM HILL
ARE LAYING
10,000—1
AGAINST

Nijinkski
Nijinsky
L.P. Riding

TRIPLECROWN

Bury me deep,
recluse me,
keep me away from
the sunlight

Jesus,
where are you, Man?

W
X
Y

The WXY MAN.

William Hill
are
laying 1000-1
that you don't make it
son —.

DAWN RUN 1st

25 yrs.

Hi man, who's holdin all the gear?
Fuckknows
Fucknose huh (I wonder where he is and what he looks like)

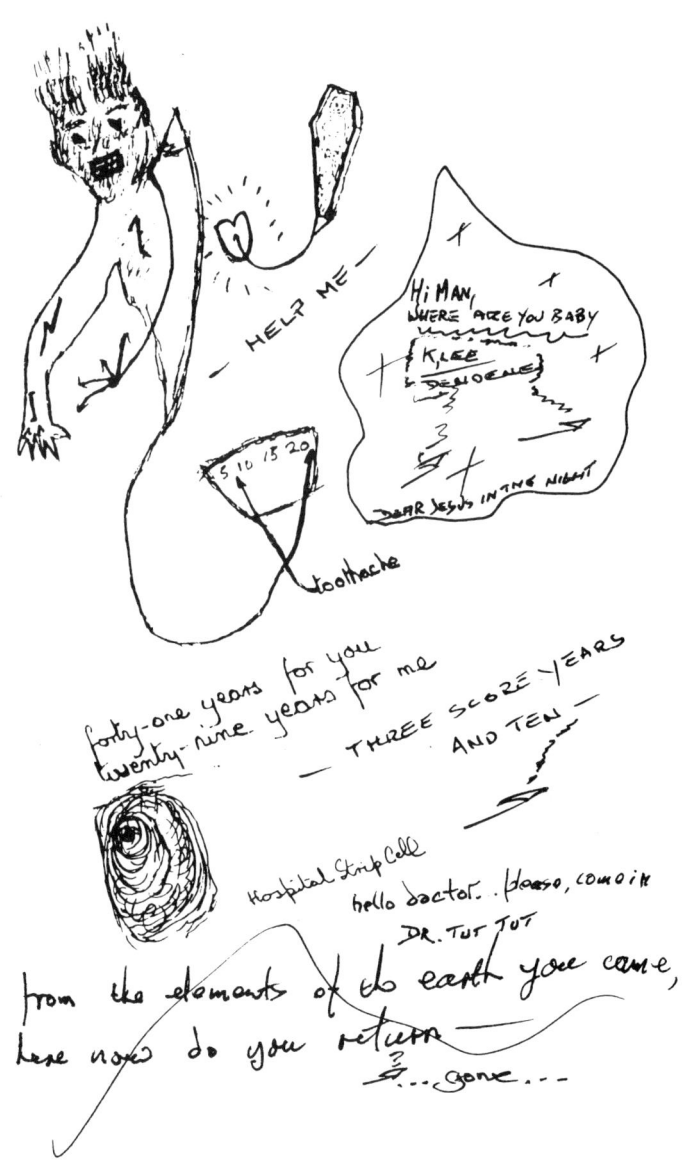

HELP – DIA-MORPHINE
URGENTLY REQUIRED
BY DYING MAN —

PLEASE REPLY

P.O. BOX NUM. 7
PARKHURST
I.O.W

The Assassins — order one.
Kill One Hundred Doctors.

No.1 DR. SHONE
No.2 DR. (?) HANDB
No.3 DR. (?) LOWH?
FOR DR. SHONE NOW?
No.4 DR BENNET
No.5 DR BARON
No.6 DR. TUTTE
No.7 DR. PRICE
No.8 DR. (?) MILTON?
No.9 DR. GOHILOW
No.10 DR
ALL TO BE
DELIVERED ALIVE
TO THE DESIGNATED
PLACE OF EXECUTION

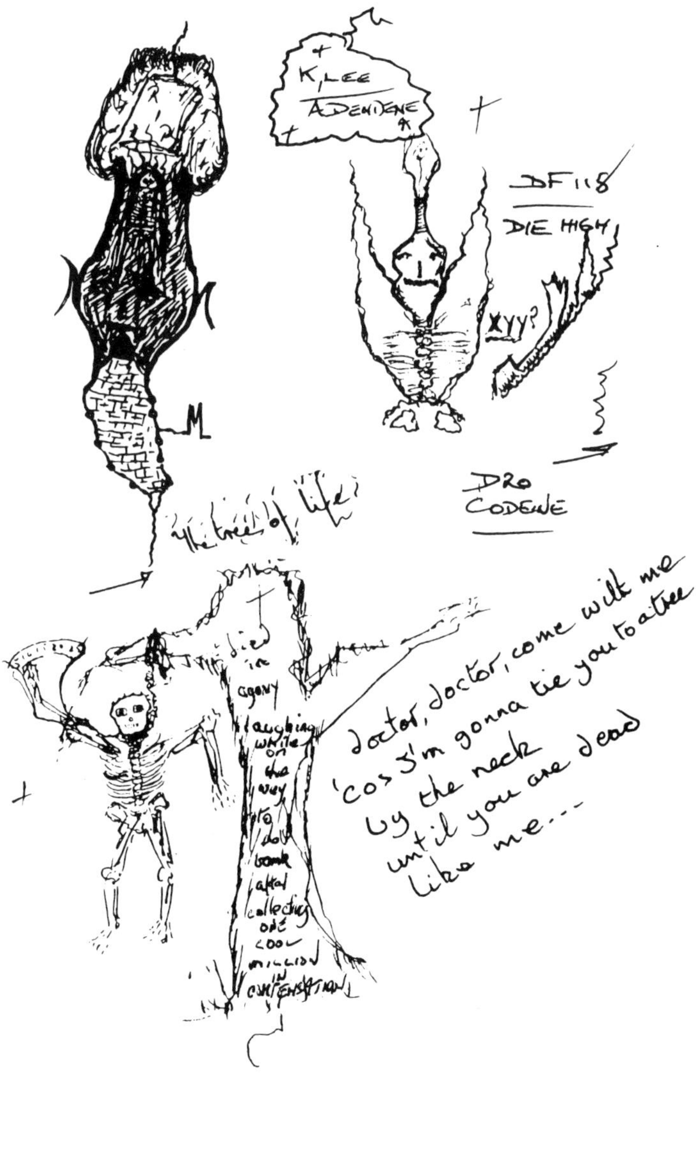
K, LEE
DF118
DIE HIGH
XYY?
the tree of life
died in agony laughing while on the way to do bank after collecting one cool million in compensation
doctor, doctor, come with me
'cos I'm gonna tie you to a tree
by the neck
until you are dead
like me...

...why don't they believe me when I tell them I'm in great pain – they would if I had them in a small room, a replica cell...

DEATH IN A CLOSED ROOM

...The doctor woke up and found himself naked in an icy-cold cell. There was no window in the cell and the only furniture was the bed he was laying on.

One end of the cell was partitioned off with a wire grill and behind it was a strange mass, light coloured and scaly, like papier-mache.

The doctor rose from the bed to take a closer look. There was a small opening at one end and he concluded that it must be a nest of some kind. He couldn't work out what sort of nest it was though, because it was huge, more then three feet across, oval-shaped and unlike anything he had seen before.

The doctor returned to the bed, pondering the nightmare he was in. The last thing he remembered was a needle stabbing into the side of his neck as he sat behind the wheel of his car. After finishing duty at the prison, the doctor was looking forward to having dinner with friends but he was now imprisoned in a cell and wondering if he was going insane.

There was no telling if it was night or day. His watch had been removed and the only light came from a single bulb hanging from the ceiling. He was pacing the cell, shivering, when suddenly the door opened. A man stood in the doorway holding some blankets. He threw them at the doctor then quickly closed the door.

"Wait!" yelled the doctor. "Please, what's happening to me?"

There was no reply.

The doctor grabbed a blanket and wrapped it round himself, then grabbed another.

Several hours passed before the door was opened again. The same man stood in the doorway and he seemed vaguely familiar to the doctor.

The man entered the cell. "You will be fed twice a day," he said, then turned to leave.

"Please wait!" cried the doctor. "What are you doing to me? Who are you – please!" But the man had already left the cell, slamming the heavy metal door behind him.

The doctor sat on the bed in despair and looked at the food on the tray that his keeper had just laid down. There was a piece of cheese, several slices of bread and a pile of red jam. He pushed the tray away, unable to eat.

As he stared around the cell, the doctor tried to remember where he had seen that face before, but he couldn't quite – yes, he thought suddenly, a prisoner somewhere…

The doctor began to tremble and grabbed another blanket, throwing it round himself.

After a while, the cell began to get warmer and he relaxed a little as his body absorbed the heat. As he warmed, he started to nibble at the food and gulped down half the water that was in the jug on the floor. After he had eaten, he stretched out on the bed and drifted into an uneasy sleep.

An hour or two later, the doctor woke abruptly at the sound of the door crashing against the bed. He raised himself up, still holding the blankets to cover his nudity. He pleaded with the man. "Please, what's going on here? Why are you keeping me prisoner?"

The man looked down at the doctor, imagining his fear. Then he spoke. "Do you remember me doctor?"

"I...I'm not sure...u...a prisoner somewhere..."

The man turned to leave.

"Please! Don't leave me here! Please – "

"Doctor, I think you'd better get something into your head and keep it there – you are never going to leave this cell alive."

"But...but you can't be serious," stammered the doctor. "What d'you mean – I'm never leaving this cell alive? What are you going to do to me? Please – I can't take any more of this."

The man leaned against the door-jamb and lit a cigarette, studying the doctor carefully.

"Do you remember a man coming to you with a pain, a pain so terrible that it almost drove him out of his mind? Do you remember me doctor, how I pleaded with you – begged you to ease my suffering? Do you recall how you chose to ignore my pleas, how you left me in agony for weeks and months? Well, my good doctor, now it's pay-back time for you – that's why I say you will never leave this cell alive."

The doctor's bottom jaw dropped in disbelief as he heard the words and was left speechless as the man slammed the door.

The doctor drifted in and out of sleep as the cell became warmer and warmer and he wondered if he would ever get out. Was it to become his coffin, he thought. Oh, dear God – What's happening to me – I'm never going to get out of here – and what is that nest? Oh, please...

He looked at the trays of half-eaten food that were scattered round the cell and on the bed. Whenever the man had brought food, he just placed the trays on the bed without bothering to collect the empties. There were now seven trays in the cell and as he looked at them, he pondered ominously over the huge amounts of red jam on each of them.

There was no fresh water in the cell and the doctor moaned inwardly that he couldn't bathe. He was sweaty and sticky and the smell of urine was becoming unbearable. The light-bulb glowed *continuously and he was completely disorientated.*

The doctor layed on the bed, idly staring at the huge nest when a sudden movement caught his eye – a movement by the entrance to the nest. The doctor's heartbeat began to race.

He rose from the bed and moved slowly towards the grill. Near the entrance to the nest was an insect, nearly an inch long, black, but with faint yellowish colouring under the thorax. It was cleaning it's wings, spreading them, readying itself for flight. Suddenly, another one appeared at the entrance then flew to the ground, landing carelessly. They were too big to be wasps, he thought, too black – a sudden fear went through the doctor when he realised they were hornets.

As if by telex, the jam registered in his brain and he touched his body, feeling the stickyness.

There were now several hornets hovering round the entrance to the nest and many more were on the floor. Panic began to set in for the doctor as he moved back to the far end of the small room, watching the hornets intently.

He turned to the door and banged his clenched fists on the bare metal. "Let me out! Let me out of here! Help! Help! For God's sake let me out!" But the only sound he could hear was the echo of his own voice – then buzzing wings.

The doctor slowly turned round and gazed, open-mouthed, at the mass of hornets. The over-heated cell had incubated the nest and the hornets were already foraging for food on his side of the grill.

Several of them had settled on each of the trays, hunting, tracking the sweetness. In desperation he grabbed the remaining blanket from the bed, sending a tray crashing to the floor. He draped it over his head and shoulders and groaned as he felt the jam on his neck and arms, and he trembled with fear.

The far end of the cell was now one mass of deadly, stinging, hornets. All seven trays were covered with crawling insects, eager to feed after their hibernation. He saw several being stung to death as they crawled over each other – and a few had become stuck to his blankets.

When the light went out he thought he was hallucinating. Then he heard a soft voice whisper, "Goodbye doctor – have a pleasant death now."

The doctor cried out, "Oh God no! No please!" When he felt the first sting on his leg, his sphincter muscle collapsed and he passed into unconsciousness.

"Daddy. Daddy. What are these?"

"Those? They're honeysuckle,"

"And these daddy?"

"Those are antirhinums – we call them bunny-rabbits."

"Bubby-rabbits?" The boy laughed. "Why, daddy?"

"Because look – " He bent and plucked the small flower from its stem and pressed it between his finger and thumb. The little boy laughed as it opened and closed like a small rabbits mouth.

"Is that a bumble-bee daddy?"

"Oh, John do something – "

"Hang on, I'll get it – "

"Ouch! Mummy, it bit me."

The small boy began to cry as the father shewed away the wasp. It had bitten him high on the forehead and now it began to swell. His whole body began to swell. He was a balloon – hundreds of them flying across the sky – red ones and blue ones and yellows, all mingling together – but now they were black, dropping into the sea...he was on the bridge again, searching for mines – there they were, hundreds of them with their spikes pointed skyward – mustn't touch the spikes – but slow down or we'll hit them...no...slower not faster...no...look out...!

The doctor woke in panic, sweat running from his body. The light had come back on and he stared at his legs in horror, unable to grasp the situation before him.

His brain wasn't registering the deadly hornets covering his lower body – it was too busy sending a self-destruct signal to his heart. But it was a faulty signal and the doctor wriggled for another hour before it was finally rectified.

The man pushed open the door, catching the cold air on his face. The cell floor was covered with hornets that had failed to return to the nest. He looked down at the doctor, searching his face, imagining his death.

Not a pleasant death, he thought...

- RETRIBUTION - TITLES
'NAIL ME TO A CROSS' +

It was a time on the
Earth when men could talk
with animals and call upon
the birds of the sky.
Tolkien middle Earth —
9.51PM

TO-DAY — DAY TWO —— 9.55AM

I have checked my parcel
and find that I have
an ample supply of the
necessary ——— .

Right

How to write a book —

Chapter ONE

Death came quickly
for the unsuspecting
chicken

CREATIVE!

Reality-killers ©
Fantasy-fighters ©
Image-eaters ©
"— gimme a bag of image-
eaters will ya — and make
it ~~like-to-us~~ lively! —"

"Yessir, of course. Would you like a big bag or a small bag?"

"A big bag!" (What's this fuckin' idiot on — a big bag or a small bag!)

"Of course — and what about some fantacy-fighters — we do a very good line"

"What are fantacy-fighters?"

"They are the ones that gobble up the walls —"

"— gimme a carrier-bag full of those quick"

"Yes of course I will sir.

~~~~~~~~

Three pipes in a line means — wrecked

A.M.
10.40.

Chapter One

Page 1.

This is the story of a man who thought he could write a book. He had some kind of vision

25,000 copies

TITLE

A Nomme De Plume

Eye Dunnit

Once upon a time, when men could talk with animals and call upon the birds, a wizard set out from the village of ~~Ashhydale~~ ashdale

Queen Fintella
Morlene AND THE TWELVE SISTERS
OF THE GARDEN

Hey, mushbrain — hows the book
going? It aint you asshole,
Hey mush ------- What??}
PRON HUSH}
MUSH} &
Perhaps a ,000,000 Copies
Comedy?
'as in Mushroom
Okay Brain, lets get going then.
Let's get some stuff out here —
... it was running deep now,
surging forwards towards the
gates. A huge mass of brown
semi-liquid shit had taken
control — There was only one
thing he could do — send
for A. N. DREK, the shit-shifter...
(.. come on Mush, you can
do better.)
Governor: (HEARAFTER - GUV.) (NOR)
Good Morning.
MR. DREK: Good Morning. I've come
about your shit problem.

– 247 –

GOV'NOR: Good. You're just in time. There's shit everywhere.

MR. DREX: Okay. Lead me to it. – Um, smells like you've got some good shit here man.

GOV'NOR: Pardon?

MR. DREX: This shit – it smells okay.

GOV'NOR: I Don't understand. Would it be a problem if it didn't smell okay?

MR. DREX: YES. It makes it harder to ~~take~~ if it doesn't smell right. How long's it been out?

GOV'NOR: ARE you taking the piss?

MR. DREX: I don't know about that. All I've got on my ticket is a prison full of shit.

GOV'NOR: CHIEF!!   CONT. P. ~~~~

– 248 –

CHIEF: Yessir, please sir, three bags full sir

GOV: Take this man across to the wing will you. He's come to ~~take away~~ the shit but he's not taking the piss. See to it will you.

chief: Yessir three bags full sir.

GUVNOR: (Thinking) Mans a fuckin' idiot!

(MR DREK was becoming impatient)

Mr. Drek: Come on then let's get to it..

CHIEF: Right. Where's your equipment?

Mr Drex: What equipment?

CHIEF: The equipment for
getting rid of all this
shit.

Mr Drex: I'm going to eat it.

CHIEF: Eat it? Are you
taking the fuchin' piss?

Drex. No I fuchin' aint
takin' the piss — and
for that you can get
rid of your own shit.
Goodbye! }   }
                    →   →

Nexi Day

Gov'nor: CHIEF!!

        ...to be continued.

Now hear this! Now hear
this! Clear all main
brain cells and prepare
for rapid fire intake.
Clear all main cells!
This is no drill!
Repeat, this is no drill!
Mushbrain coming through
on wave loon loon
victor one!
Okay Mush, take it..

You ain't gonna wake 'it, baby 'cos
Nills are laying 1000~1   TIME-LATE

MORNIN' ALL

Hi Jo, I haven't seen you
for a while — please don't
worry aboot the book will
you — I've just put it
on hold for a while.
I'm just wondering if
I can draw pictures,
but it seems that I can't.
As with the book — I can
see the words but th
sentences come hard — in
the drawings, I can draw
the faces and the trees, but
a picture will not come ...
dead Jesus — stop tormenting
me ...
maybe I should practice ..
and practise in earnest! Yes! AN ARTIST!

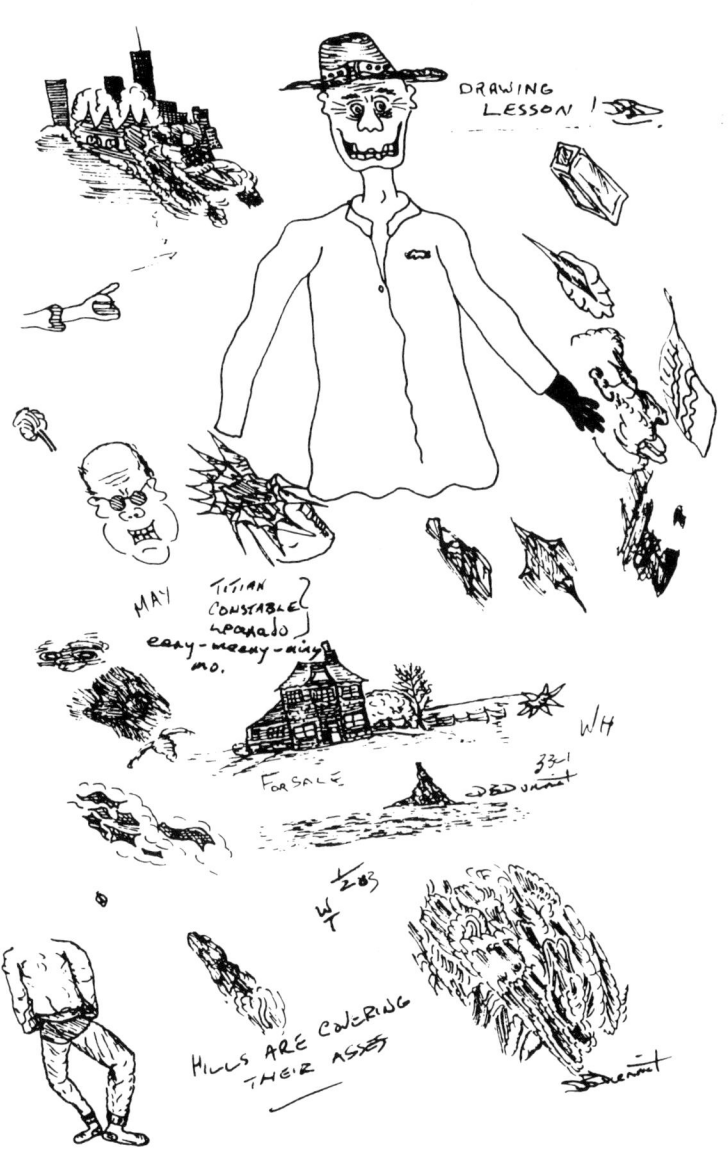

DRAWING LESSON !

MAY
eeny-meeny-miny mo.

TITIAN
CONSTABLE
LEONARDO

FOR SALE

HILLS ARE COVERING THEIR ASSES

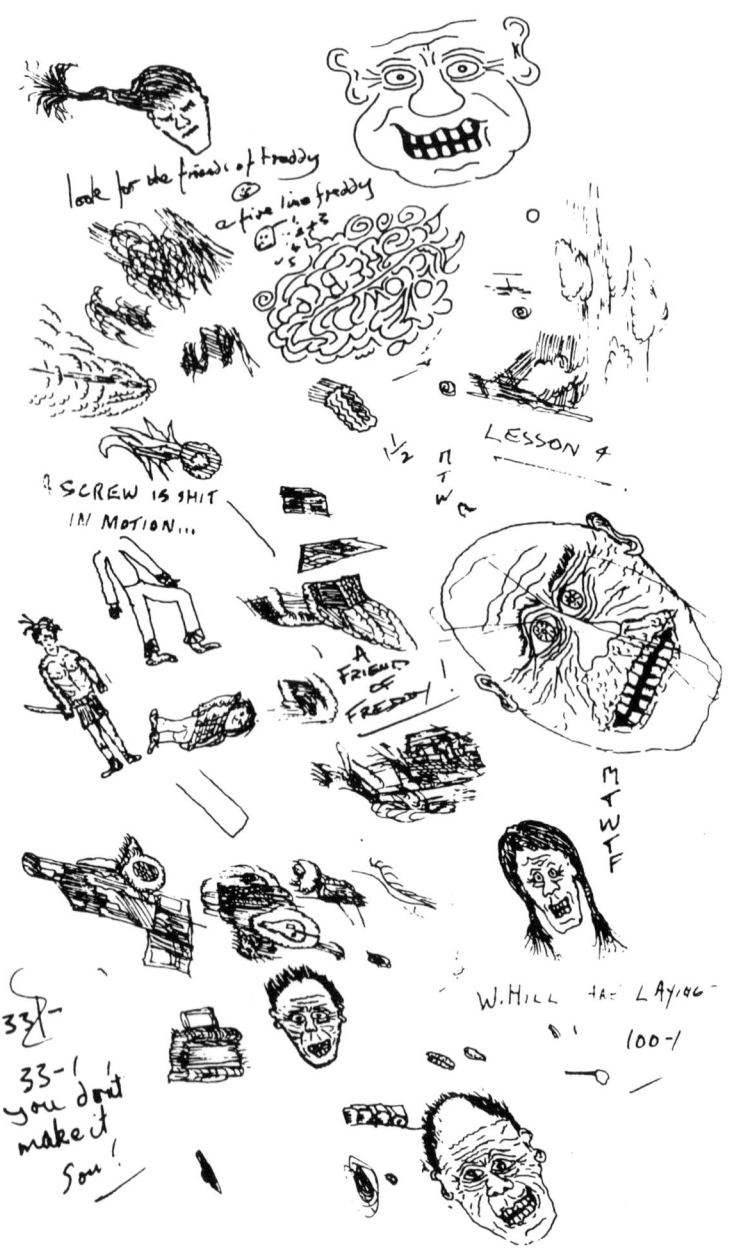

look for the friends of freddy

a fine line freddy

LESSON 4

A SCREW IS SHIT
IN MOTION...

A FRIEND OF FREDDY

MTWF

W.HILL the LAYING
100-1

33-1
you don't
make it
Son!

From the Book of Bong

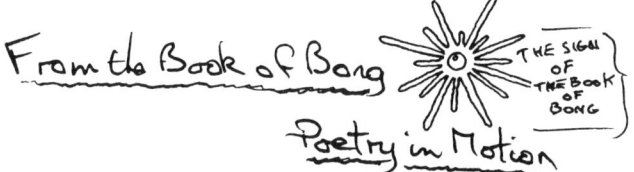

THE SIGN
OF
THE BOOK
OF
BONG

Poetry in Motion

I can see white beards dancing.
Blue black bodies with legs running deep.
I can see bodies rolling,
Changing colour as they meet.

Come and watch the surfers breaking
On the shore in jagged lines.
Pick out shapes as we're dancing
Carve an image in your mind.
Now I see a rainbow forming —
Here it comes now, shining through.
Can you see the colours, baby
Ruby red and indigo blues...

...to be continued

Dennit

FROM THE BOOK of Bong

"Society must be protected from violent criminals — you will go to prison for twenty-five years."

"Do I get straight out if I produce a get-out-of-jail-free card?"

"No."

"What if I throw two sixes?"

"No No."

"Fucksake — you aint makin' it very easy are ya?. Can I at least nip over to Fenchurch Street station first?"

"Why."

" 'Cos that's where all my stash is man — an' I'll need a whole lot if I'm gonna do a twenty-five."

"Well, that sounds reasonable — officer, take this man to Fenchurch Street will you."

"Yes M'Lud."

PTO

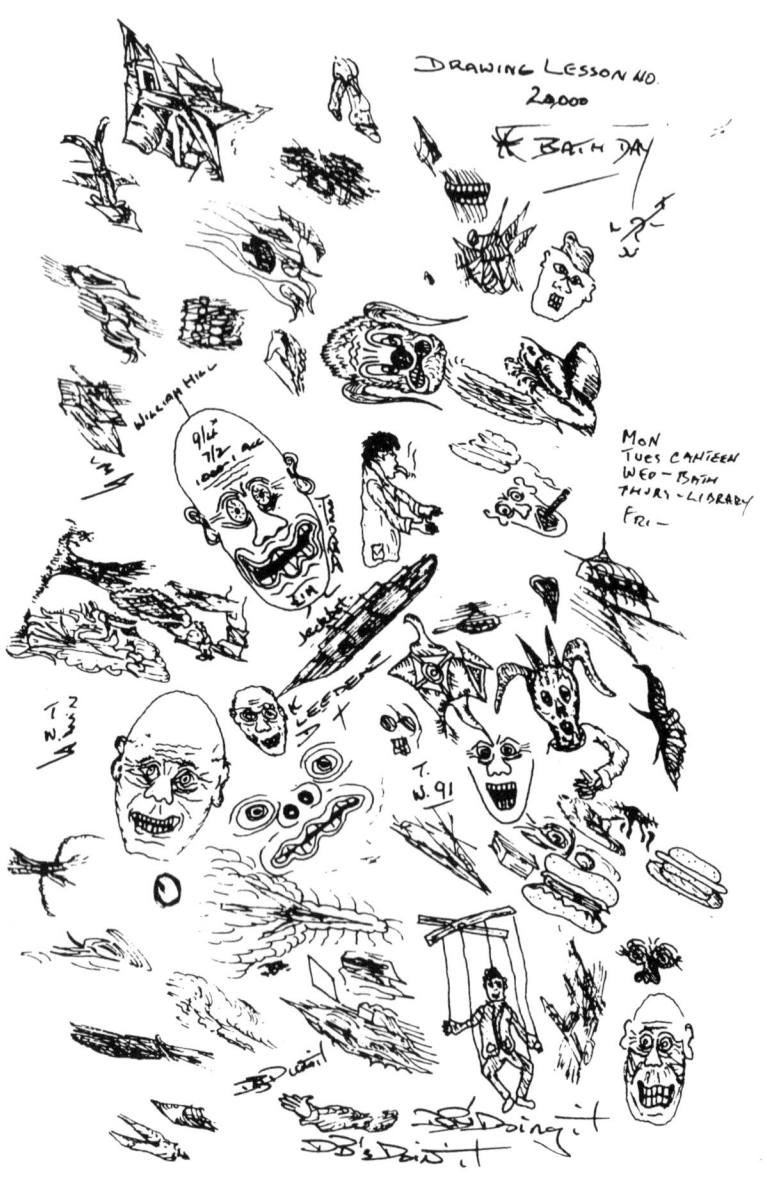

DRAWING LESSON NO.
20,000

BATH DAY

MON
TUES CANTEEN
WED — BATH
THURS — LIBRARY
FRI —

"Hang on, can we go the long way round so's I can collect my £200 before going directly to jail?"

"Do you need £200 before you go to jail?"

"With dope the price it is, and with the current rate of inflation I'll need about ten grand I should think."

"As much as that?"

"Yes. And that's without counting all the incidentals."

"What incidentals?"

"Well, I'll need uppers, downers, inside outers and about two hundred-weight of black."

"Not all at once surely?"

"No, but I want to make sure I've got it just in case – you know what it's like."

"Yes. Yes of course. So what are you asking of this court?"

"All I'm asking is for you to give me permission to go and get my stash, I promise to come back."

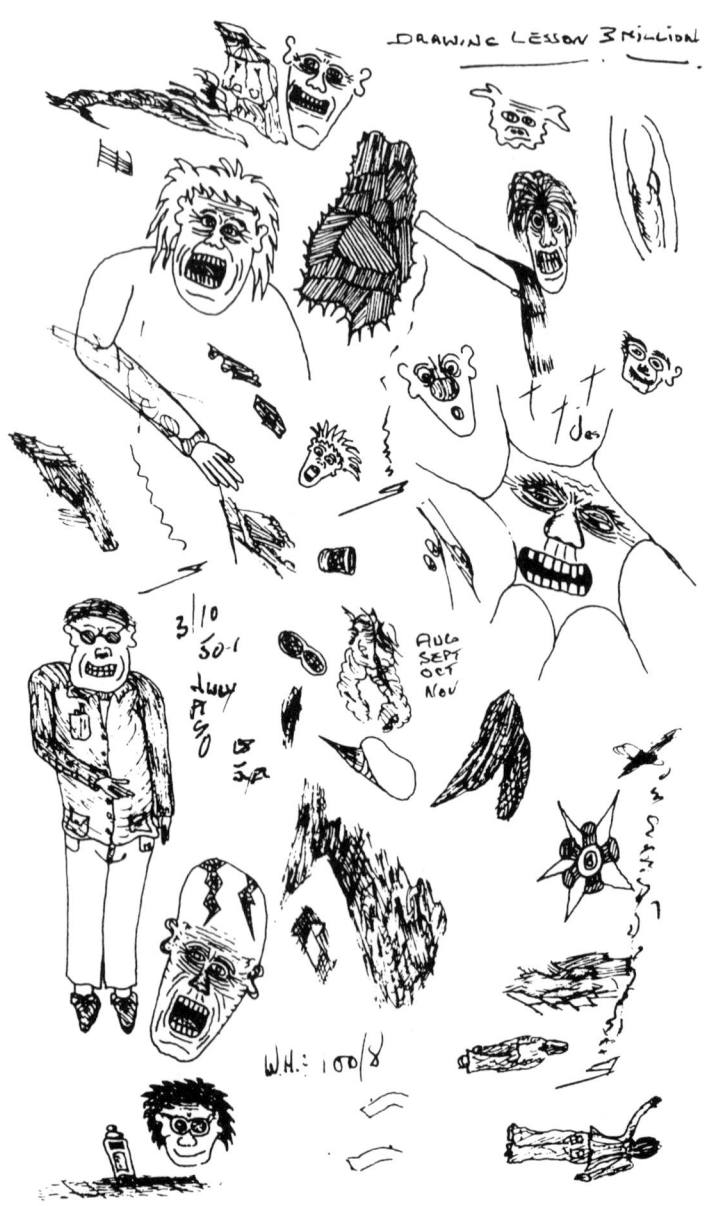

"You promise?"

"On my honour your honour."

"And your stash is at Fenchurch Street?"

"No — it's still in Thailand."

"Oh —"

" But it's alright — Chief Muzilowa is minding it for me. If I could nip to the station, I'll make do ship and be back before you know it"

"Why can't you go by air?"

"I've got a doctors note saying no flying, I'm afraid"

"I see, well, this is most unusual. I think this would be a good time to stop for a smoke. This court is adjourned for a week"

"But I'll miss the boat — an it'll soon be the rainy season."

"Oh dear, in that case you'd better go straight to jail. We couldn't hold ourselves responsible if you were to drown in Thailand —"

"— No it's alright cos, I'm protected

by Lloyds, against drowning and besides, nobody has drowned in Thailand for nine thousand years."

"Really?"

"Honest."

"So. You want to go to Thailand, pick up your stash, and then come back and do twenty-five years?"

"Yes."

"Um... oh, alright – but you will be accompanied by an officer of this court and be handcuffed at all times."

"Tch..."

"What?"

"Why have I got to be handcuffed?"

"Because I said so."

"Oh yeah — well fuck you – just take me straight to jail."

———

94 DAY IN

looking good   Look OUT!

—don't look down—   TFFOF

Lôôk lively

2 08
2: 208
25 00.
10

1 HARE!

WRECKED

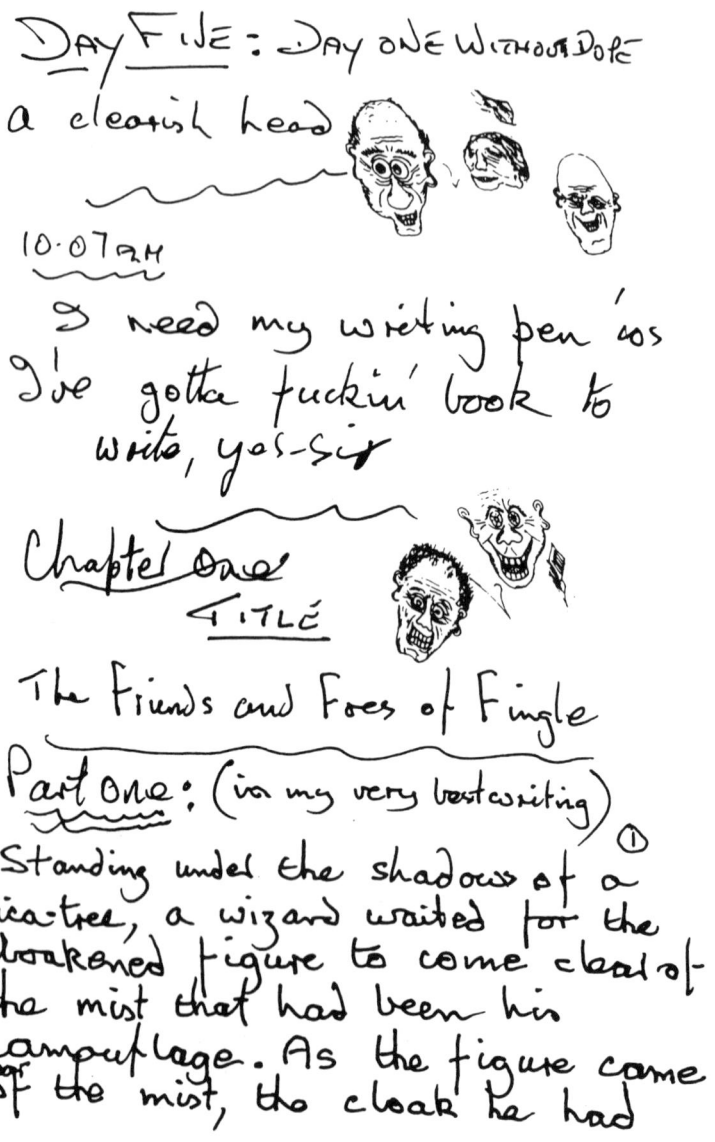

Day Five: Day one without dope

a clearish head

10.07am

I need my writing pen 'cos I've gotta fuckin' book to write, yas-sir

Chapter One
TITLE

The Friends and Foes of Fingle

Part One: (in my very best writing) ①

Standing under the shadows of a Pica-tree, a wizard waited for the cloakened figure to come clear of the mist that had been his camouflage. As the figure came
clear
ⁿof the mist, the cloak he had

about him changed from the colour of grey-white smoke to that of subtle greens and browns of the terrain he now stood on.

As the figure approached, the wizard stepped out from under the shadows...

---to be continued

Help.

The tunnel was long and narrow. It was dark in the tunnel but he could see a dim light that seemed to be coming from the end of it, but he couldn't quite reach out...

one forever striving to cast out the other...

CHR

The Friends and Foes of Freddie

TAWNY-OWLS — ha.

The F's and F's of F

PART 3 OF — THE EFFS AND EFFS OF EFF

"Greetings, Fingleweed — at last I have found you," said the wizard, opening his arms.

"Taynan! By the gods..."

The two wizards embraced for a moment until Fingleweed stood back a pace and looked into the ageing eyes of his teacher and mentor. "It is good to meet with you again after so many years, Taynan. I much missed you when we had to set about our seperate tasks but why do you seek me now, after so many ~~moons~~, Suns and Moons ~~have crossed the skies~~?"

The old wizard pulled his purple cloak further round him and adjusted the hood against the increasing wind...

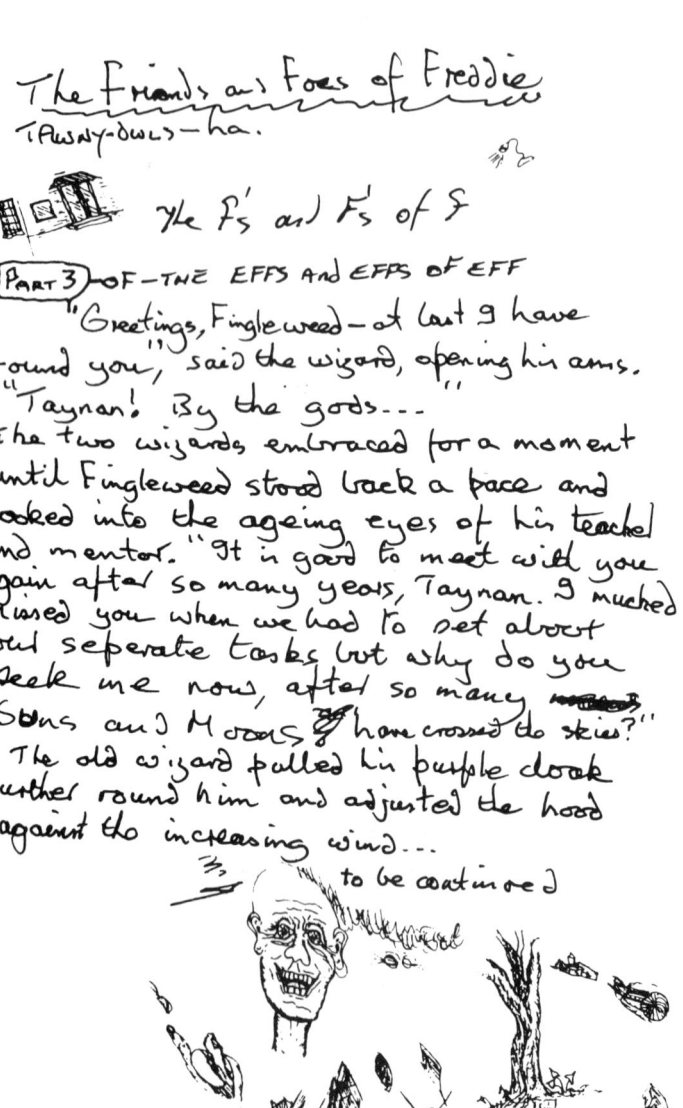

to be continued

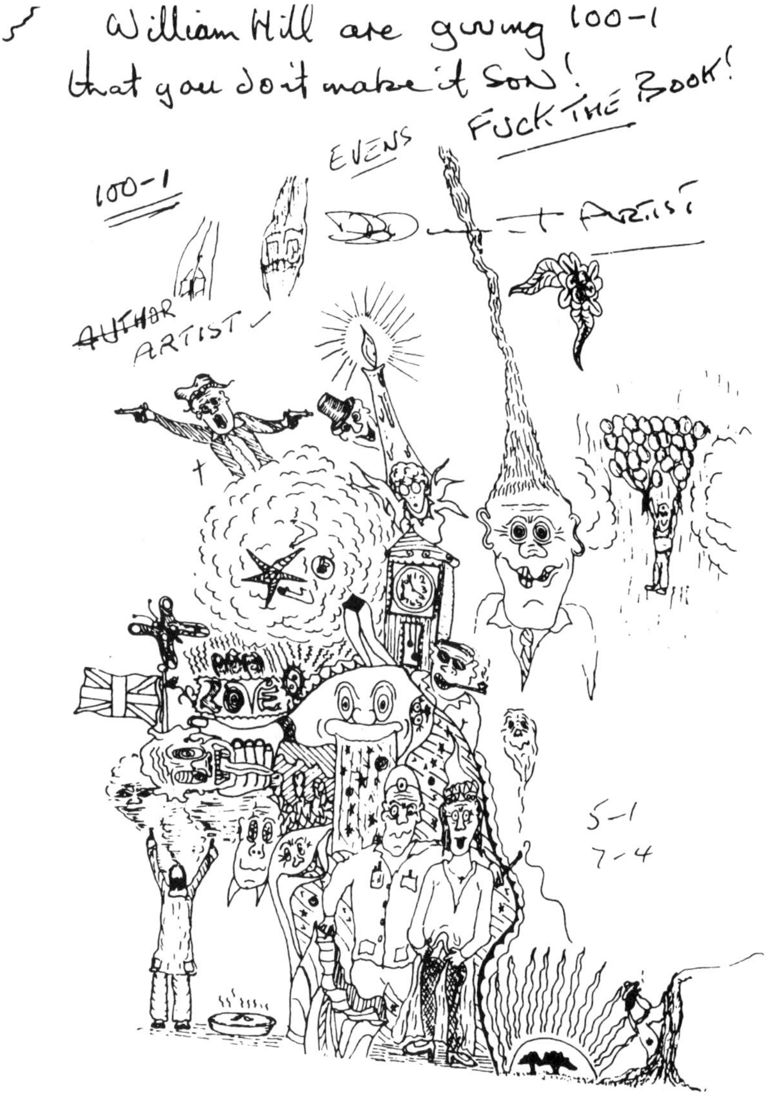
William Hill are giving 100-1
that you don't make it son!
FUCK THE BOOK!
EVENS
100-1
ARTIST
~~AUTHOR~~
ARTIST
LOVE
5-1
7-4

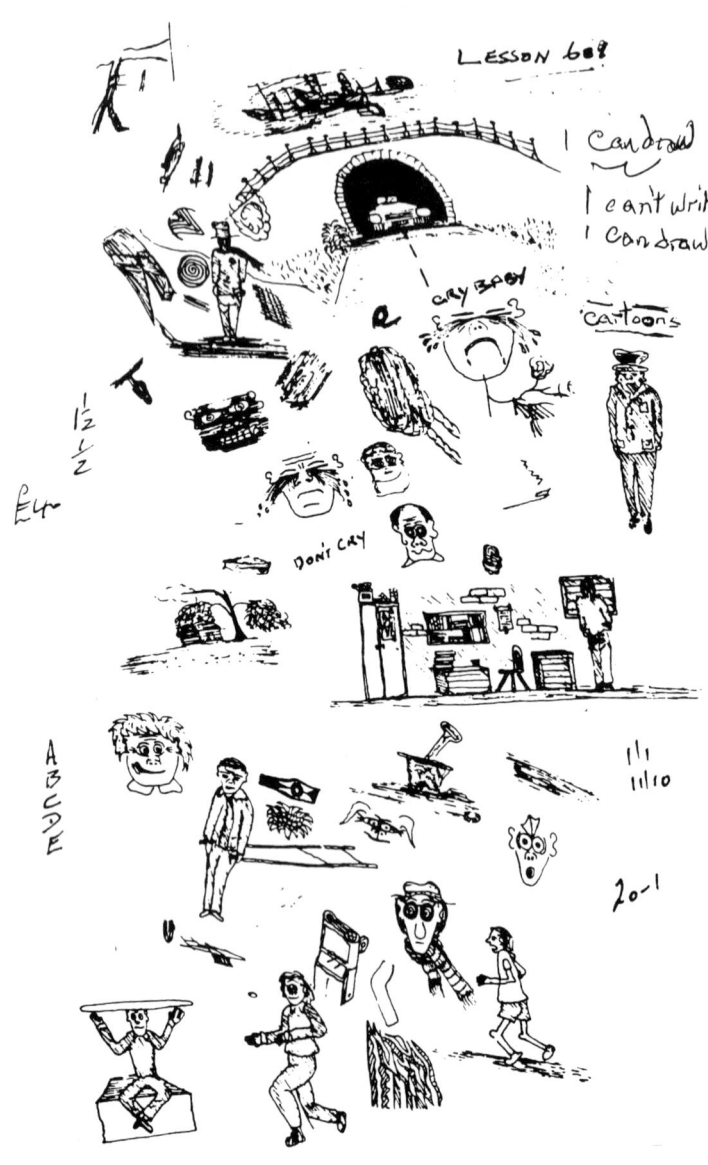

The friends of Freddie

Part 4 With his staff to aid him,
he and Fingleweed made their way
along a twinty path that led to a
small cave.

Once inside the cave, seated
together on the remains of a Woolly-
Sagmus, with a fire burning brightly
before them, the wizard began to speak.
"Much is happening, Fingleweed – or
should I call you by your more
Earthly name, Hagen – feared by men
and more than a few magicians, I
hear," chuckled the magi.

"Aye, but not to you, Fumblemonklox –
or should I call you by your more
Earthly name – Taynon, I believe,
also feared by men, sorceress to if
what I hear be truth."

"Indeed what you hear is truth – but
fear only seek out those souls who
threaten the harmony of the Kingdom."

...to be continued

Once upon a time...
2 B continued...

MAN

WOMAN

D Dummit
D Dummit
D Dummit Production

LESSON 71

$\frac{8}{10}$

NEWS AGENTS

VID
NEW
FILMS

MONEY

D Dummit

Come, sit here with
+

D Dummit

magic in motion

W.H — 25/1

$\frac{9}{10V}$

D Dummit

Chapter One

Page 1.

This is the story of a man
who thought he could write
a book. He had some
kind of vision

25,000 copies

TITLE

A Nomme De Plume

Eye Dunnit

Once upon a time, when men
could talk with animals and call
upon the birds, a wizard set
out from the village of Ashhydale
ashdale

Queen Fintella
Morlene AND THE TWELVE SISTERS

One deal a day will keep 'em away while two deals instead will take care of the head.

P.M. - F.S. RC

E.s. Fc. C. SPT.
3x3

FINGLEWEED

!DOCTOR!

Please explain the following,

He stands there in blue with a
white jacket on, ▇ a smirk on
his face, telling me, no no no.

But if I get out and my health
comes back, I'll see you ▇▇▇
again, and then you will ▇▇▇▇

He keeps me in pain when
there is no need - doesn't
listen to me, ▇▇▇ ▇▇▇ - but he
will one day ...

Beta.) Rev.✓
pump.
/ Back
pain very
deadly

left

1998
Serious
spread
Pain

40 + 25   65
        25 MINIMUM.
AND I WILL RECOMMEND TO THE
HOME SECRETARY THAT YOU SERVE
A MINIMUM SENTENCE OF 25 YEARS
BEFORE YOU ARE CONSIDERED FOR
RELEASE

Pain Spots.   ●
Numbing Sensation
Stabbing Pains
Muscle Spasms
Dull Ache

HA!

x Sciatica x

The static — ▇▇▇▇▇

The need for Bong increases....

D.B. v REGINA   HAIL DRUGY — LORD OF THE BONG.
HAIL DYNAMO — Lord of Pain
    Beta-endorphin, send to me the secret of
your waves.

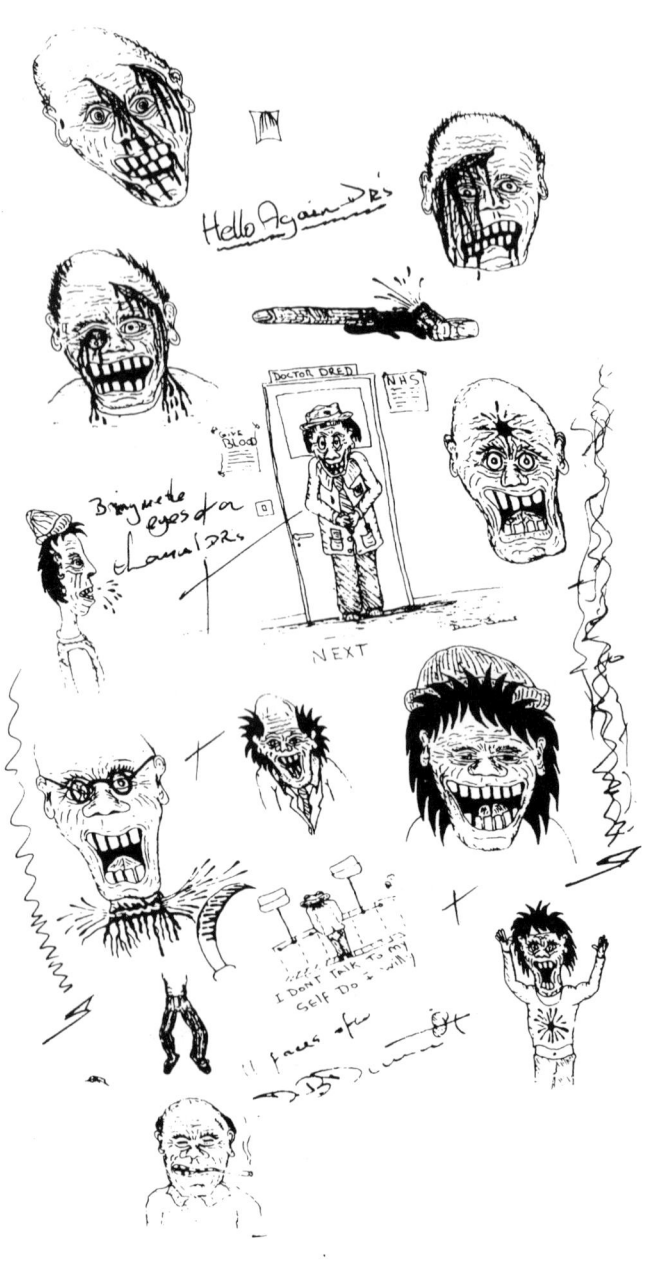

Come, come closer — that's it,
sit right there while I tell you
a story. If you're smoking a
joint, well, that's okay — but
try not to let me inhale the
fumes because I'll need a
clear head if I'm gonna
tell you this story.

N.B.
5000-1

Come over here, man — I've
gotta story to tell and
you better believe it 'cos every
fuckin' dot and comma
is the truth

Nine doctors and a needle
A needle full of doctors.
    "Good morning, Dr. Sorry to hear
you've got a headache — here, take
some of this," said Hegen, pumping
10 grams of dia-morphine straight
into his jugular.
                ...to be continued

– 277 –

Day Four —

When Jo regained consciousness, he lay ~~ed~~
still. ~~His throat and mouth~~ was completely
dry

"Sir, a report has just come in about
a missing prison officer

"Let me see it" said the inspector,
taking the sheet of paper.

Death in a Closed Room Continued

— 4000 jag. 25,000 House. 3000 F.
THE Doodlemaster General.

Help!

HELLO
I AM THE:
HONOURABLE
DOODLEMAN
△ MASTER △
GENERAL

STONE

A 5 STAR DOODLEMASTER
GENERAL - ★ADHI
& BART

A.M.
"Hello JOHN — How are you?"
2000
Cartoons —
"— Dunno — I aint got a brain —"
— And this is me celebrating leaving school — 1957 — FROM Family Album
DEAR MR DUNNIT,
YOUR CARTOONS ARE SHITE.
I know you asshole — I'm working on it!

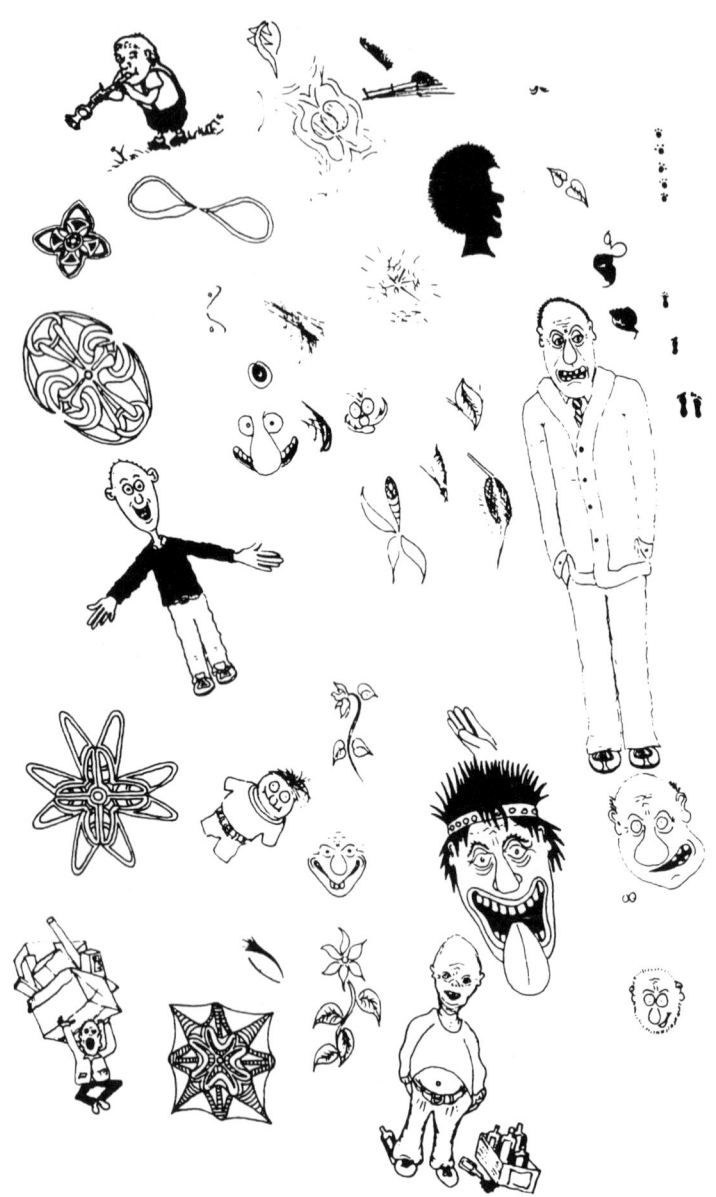

9:59 am

MAY SUE.

ballot

Hey man. y'av had enough

2:42 PM

Dunnit

MOON

IT'S NOT A BALL

SO DON'T TREAT IT LIKE ONE

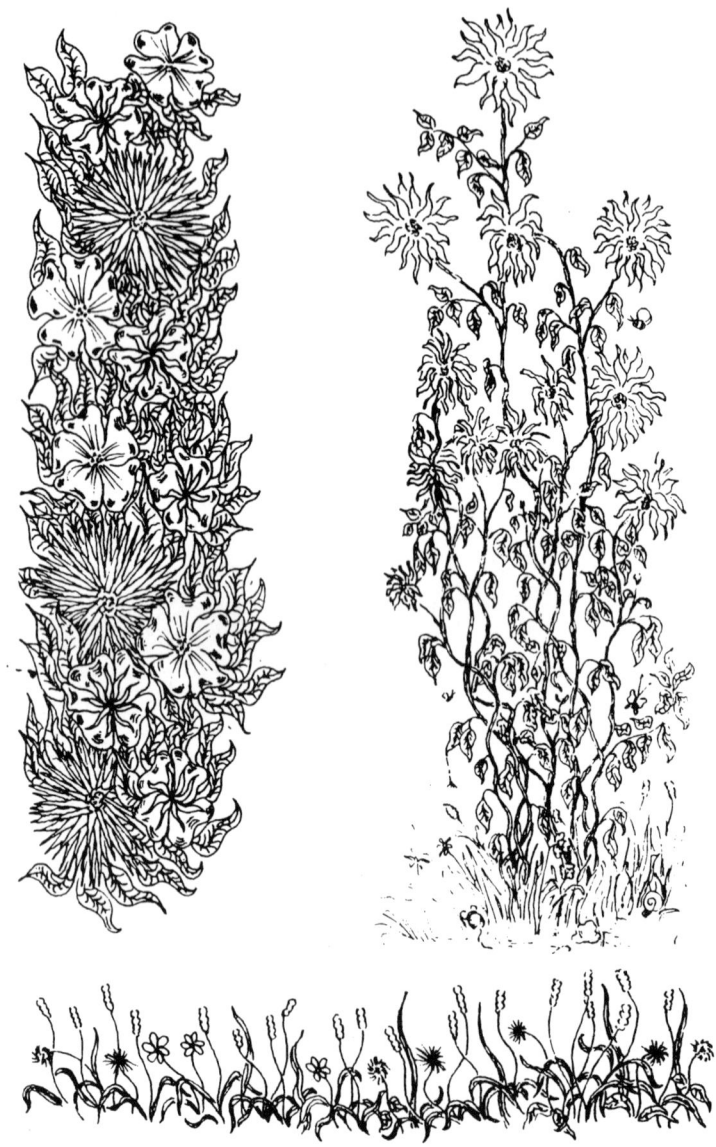

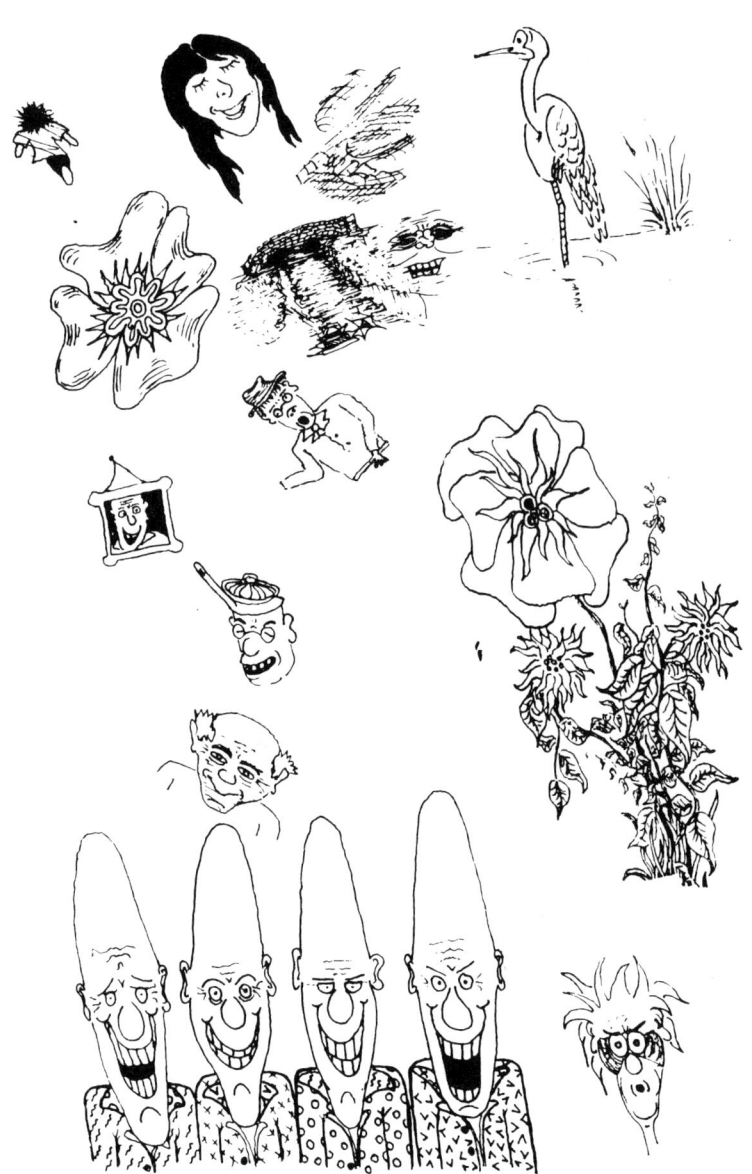

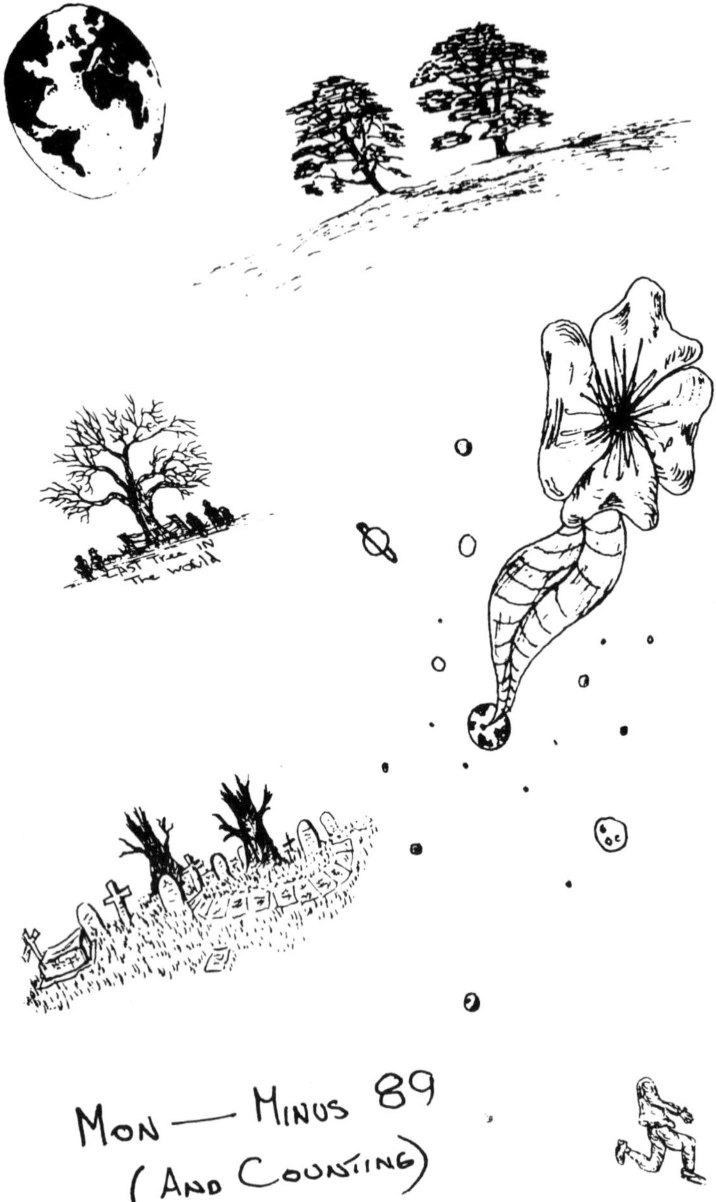

MON — MINUS 89
(AND COUNTING)

The Friends of Freddy †

Part 5 — "We are two of the Five,"
continued Taynon, "and we must seek
out our friends, Hagen. Queen Fintella
has laid upon me a heavy mantle,
a prophecy that must be fulfilled
be it good or nay lest the Kingdom
decay into a barren desert of lost
souls. Let me tell you what I know
and give you concern. The Line has
begun to crumble beneath the
Northern Rafters —"

Fingleweed rose to his feet and
stood by the entrance to the cave,
casting his eyes over the green
rolling hills that lay to the West
Kingdom.   ...to be continued

9/10

9/10

8/10

Deal Christine,

Hi baby - hope everything is okay with you and the kerbets.

William Hill are going to lose a million. — 1000-1

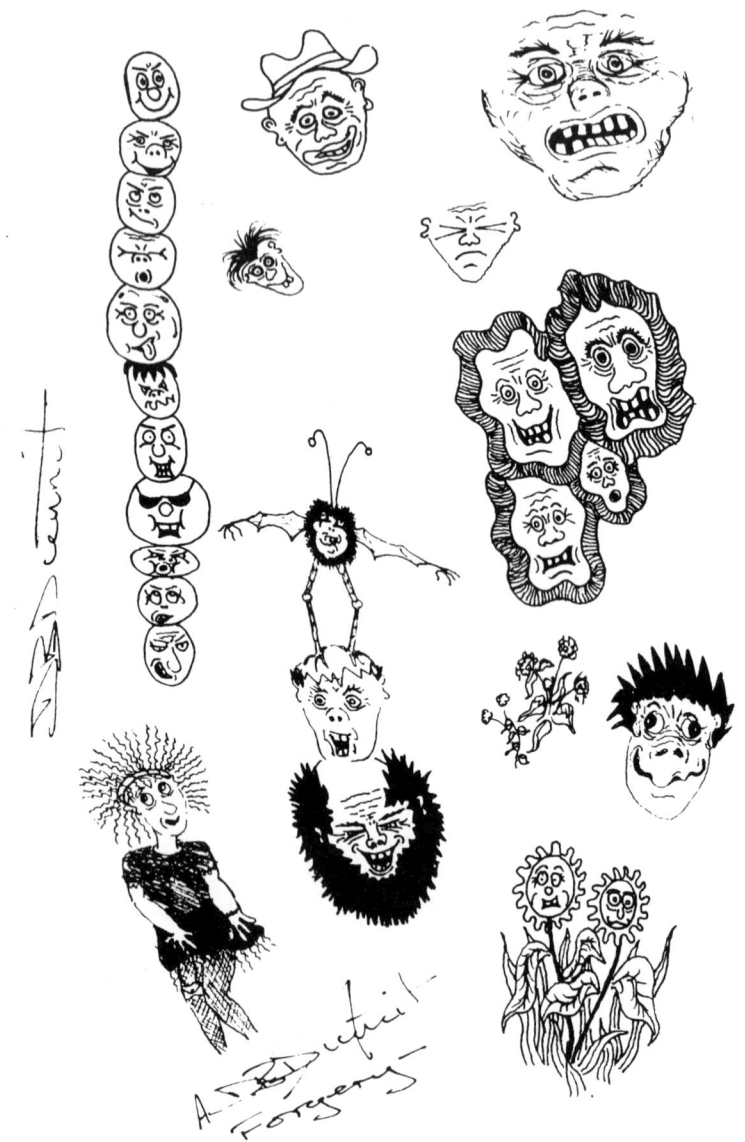

HAVE A NICE J

2:20   Laser Radio

♪ dream baby dream —
— coming to you from,
do loins —!

TITLED
   'A SCENE FROM,
A LOWER PLANE

3:15 LAZER

'THE LADY
   IN NETS'

'THE NETS IN
   THE LADY'

Artist

IN THE CARE OF —
      Look out —
      there's a screw about
      —.

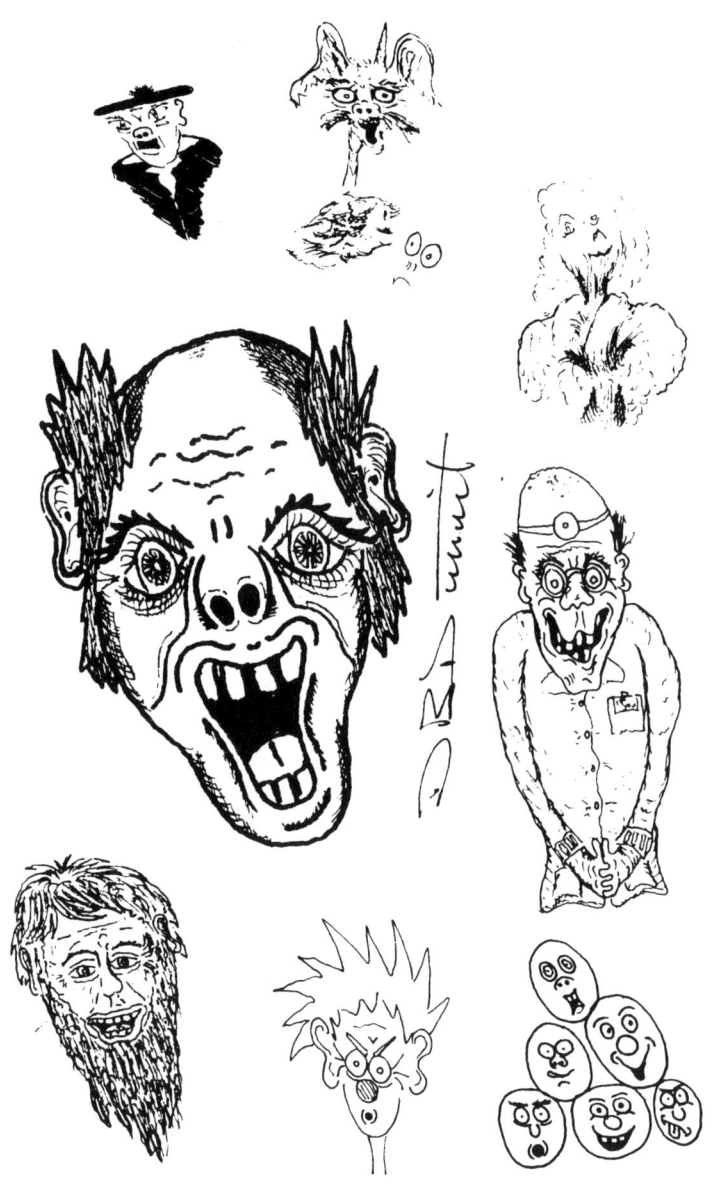

Fuckin' Game innit

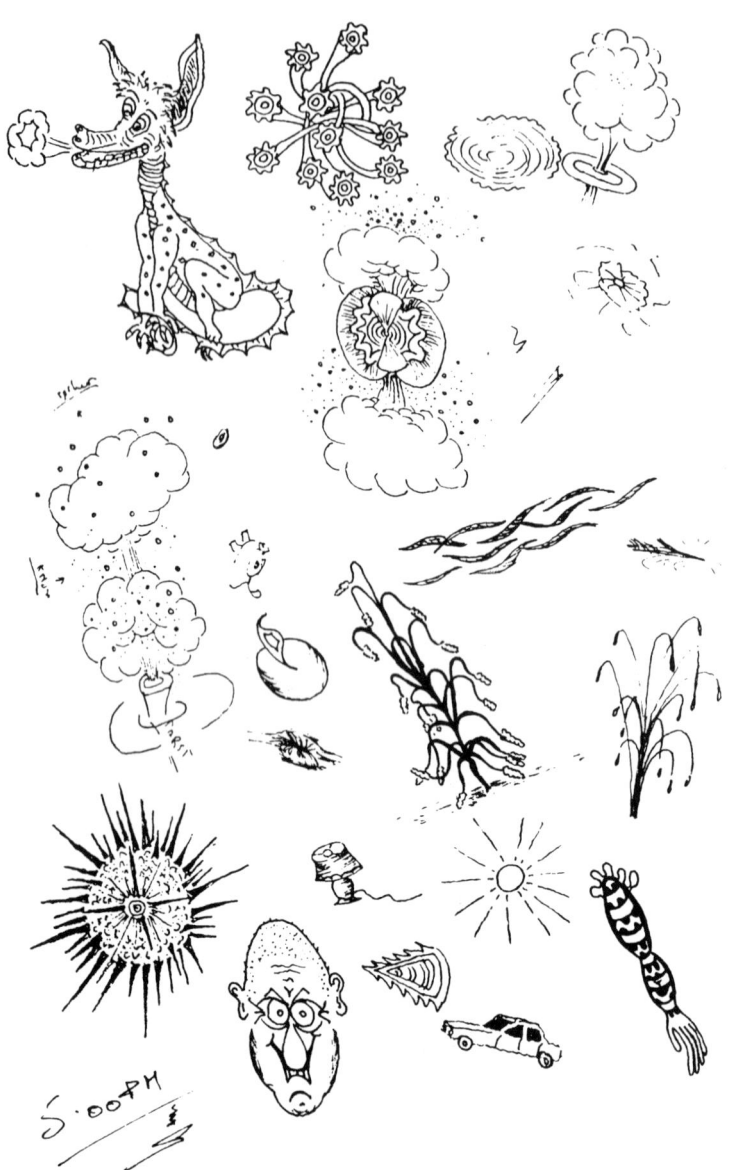

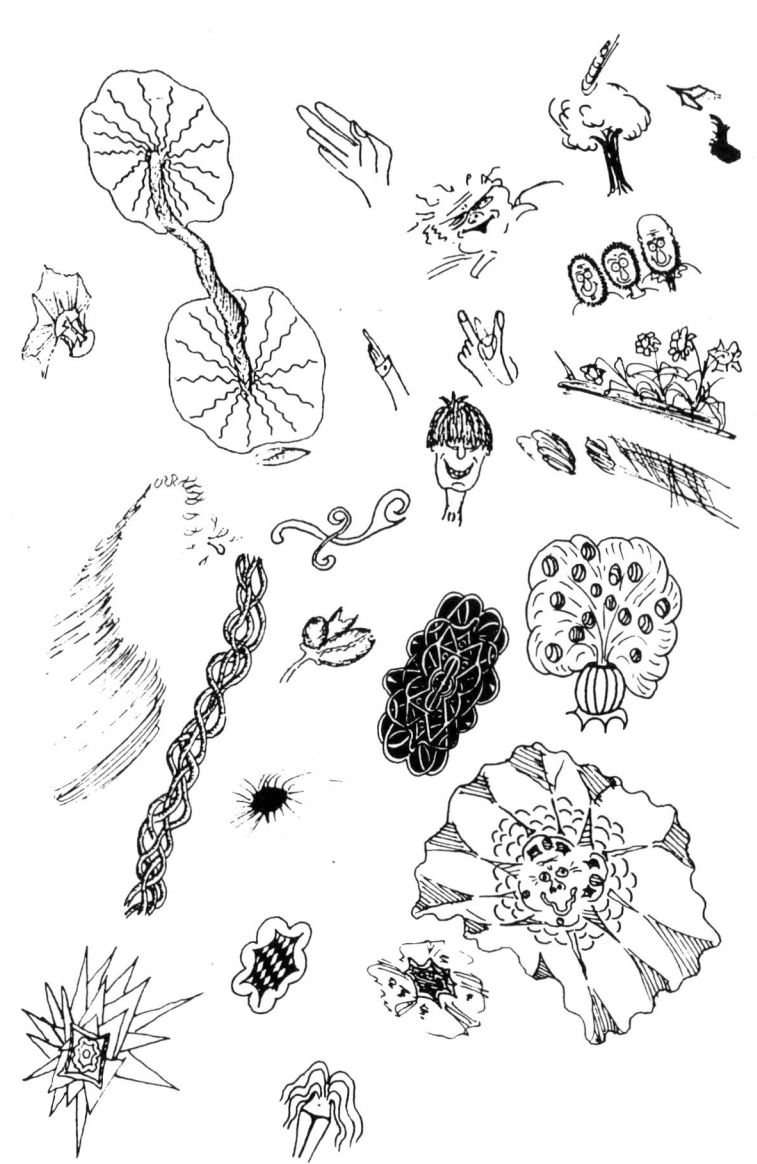

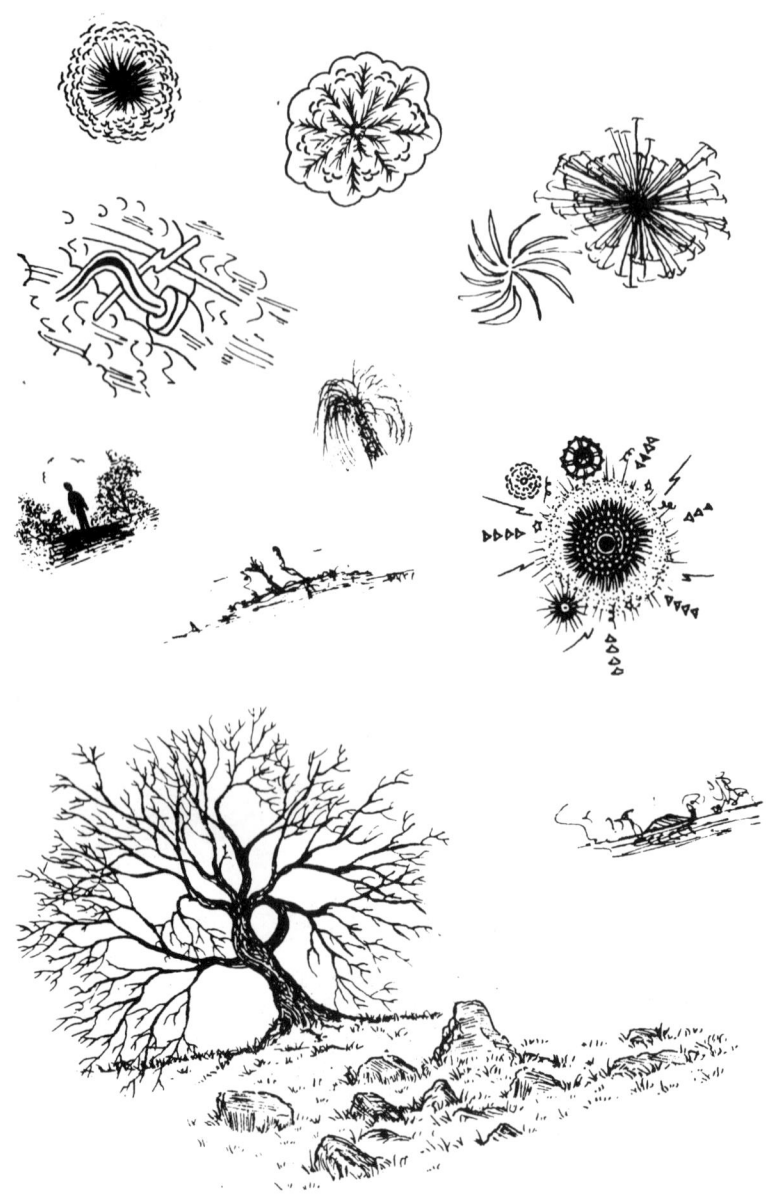

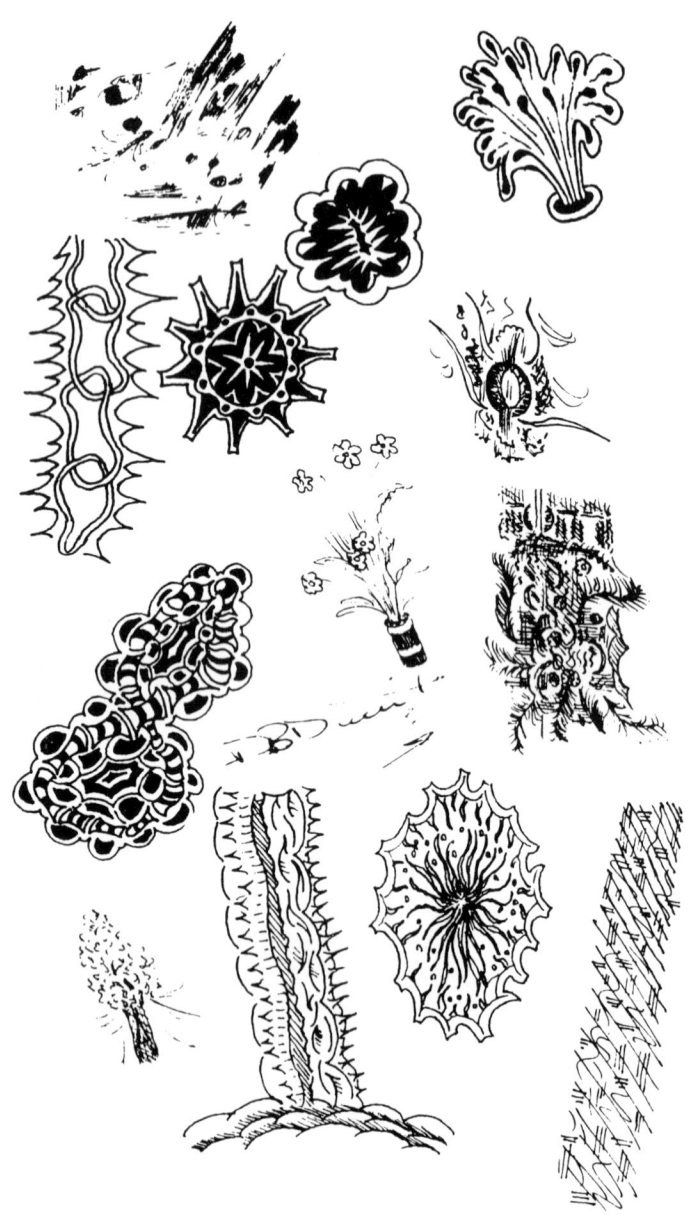

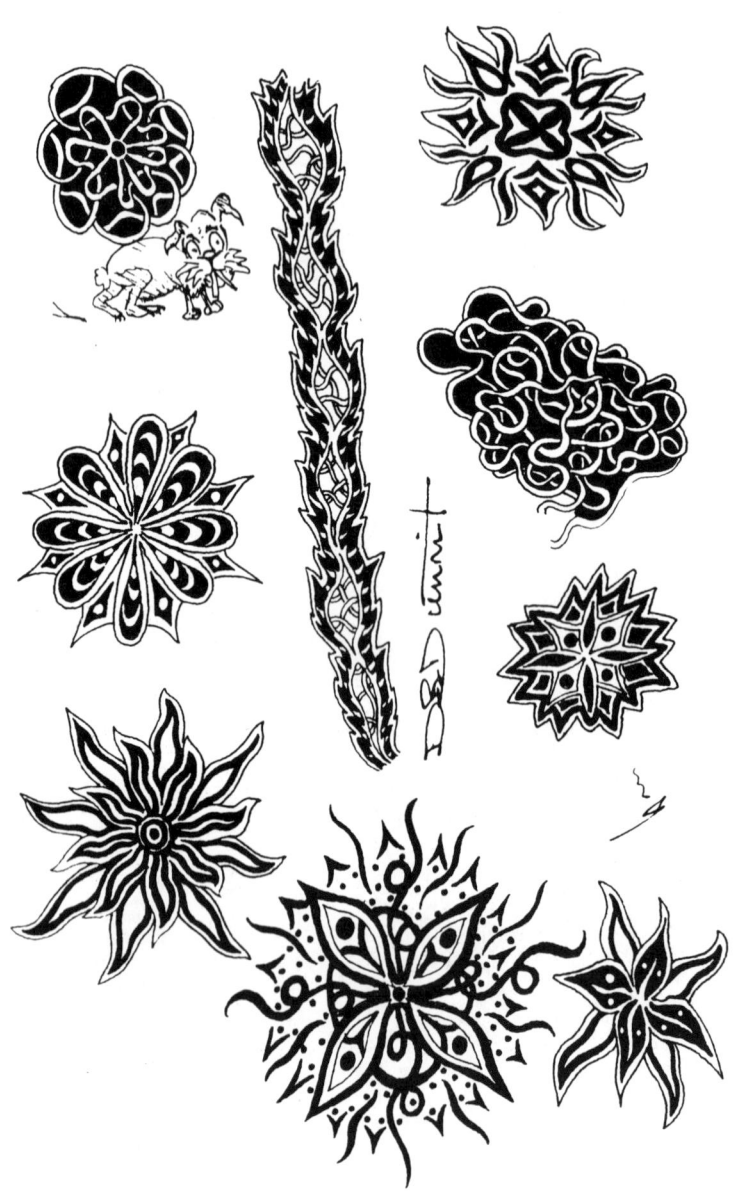

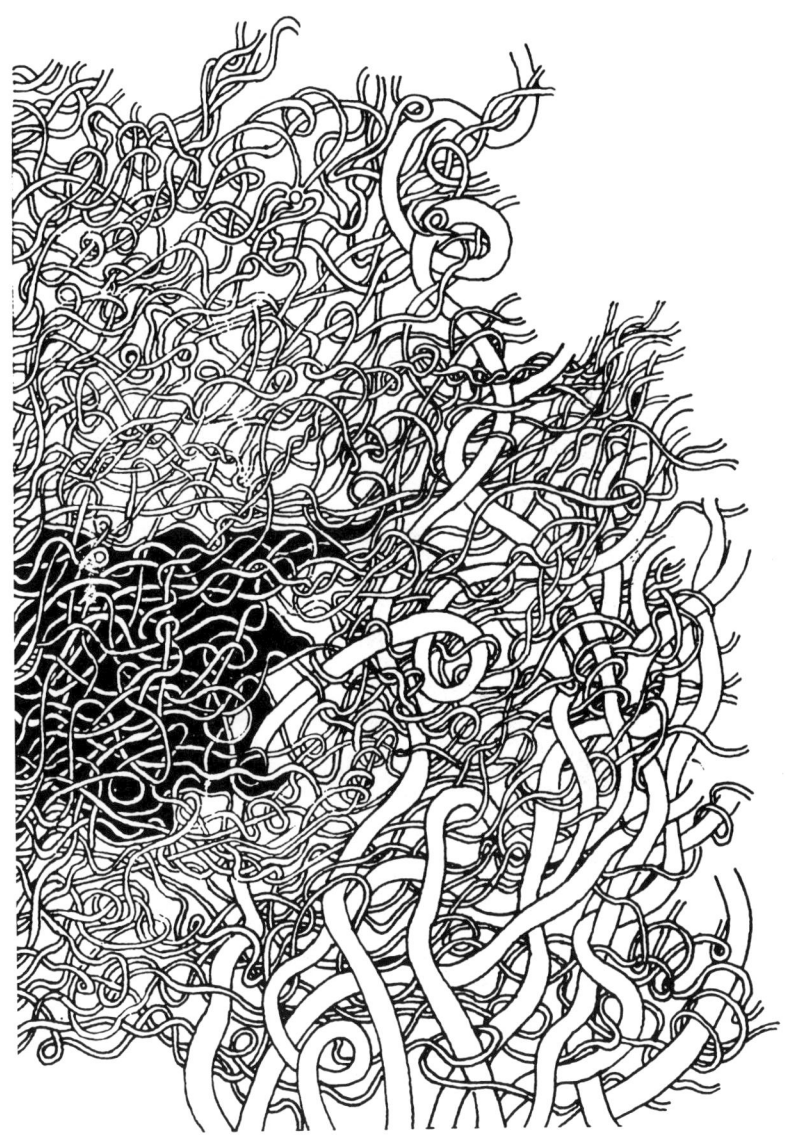

After serving the remaining two hundred and twelve days of his sentence under constant observation and in total isolation, Jo was finally released from prison on a warm spring morning in early May.

He gained no parole.

He won back no lost remission.

He served nearly seven years imprisonment.

Jo could taste the salt in the tears that were running from his eyes as he looked down on the charred remains of two catering coaches. After a few minutes, he closed the bathroom window and began to wash the dust and soot from his hands.

Soon, he was back in the bedroom stretched out on the bed, smoking a joint, and staring blankly through the ceiling.

Taking a long pull on the joint, Jo again caught sight of the front page of the local rag. He took hold of the paper and gazed at the picture that ran with the headline…

FIRE WRECKS FAMILY'S LIFE

Five years of struggle to build up a family business went up in smoke on Saturday as two catering coaches were wrecked by fire.

The roadside snack bars, parked in Malins Road, Newbury, were engulfed in flames after a gas leak blew up in one of them.

Now the family that owned them have lost their livelihood.

Jo Sullivan, 40, and his wife Christine, 40, their sons, Jason and Steven, started with a small burger van.

They spent thousands converting two coaches and had official pitches on the A34 and the A303 where they served passing traffic with snacks and drinks.

But at lunchtime on Saturday one of the coaches exploded into flames and was gutted. The fire spread to the other coach parked in front of it, severely damaging it.

Steven said, "We heard a bang outside and thought there'd

been an accident but when we got out there we saw flames jetting out the back of one of the coaches."

Jo and Christine had been away and only returned to find the gutted coaches yesterday afternoon. "I couldn't believe it, I still can't," Jo said later. "It's taken us five years and so much hassle to get where we were."

The family reckoned the business would have been in profit soon after Christmas but because cooking equipment was stored in the coaches, the Sullivans were unable to insure them for fire, so they have lost everything.

"We'll start again on something," said Jason, "but it's too soon to work out what exactly we'll be doing."

The family said it was unlikely to go back into catering.

While reading the story for the hundredth time, the sadness Jo felt was beginning to dissolve among increasing desires for retribution but before they gained any momentum, Jo caught sight of his knuckles – the left one first, then the right. A twinge went through him as he looked at the faint black lines that should not have been there.

As his mind began to stir, remembering the thick black lines that mysteriously appeared while he bathed in the prison bath-house many years before, Jo licked a couple of fingers and gently rubbed spittle along one of the thin, faint, but undeniably visible grey-black lines. As his fingers followed the lines the marks began to disappear. There were three or four lines on each hand and as Jo continued erasing them, his mind was quickening with thought...

...black lines in the bath...mystery lines that came from nowhere and disappeared in the same manner...now these lines that should not be there...

come little one, a game we will play...confusion...yes, confusion I said it would be called...a rubber-round-the-head-man...yeah, I'll squeeze so many heads that by the time I've finished they'll be calling me the headache-maker-man...

...negative thoughts are not to be encouraged...Irene...it is a journey you are going on, a journey of life with a riddle here and there and a game or two just to keep everyone on their toes...

Without realising it, almost, Jo left the bed and knelt in front of a chest-of-drawers. Slowly, he pulled the bottom drawer out until he could reach in and take hold of a package.

Returning to the bed, he carefully removed the brown outer paper and took hold of several exercise books.

He began flipping through the pages in absent thought until his eyes fell on a page that stirred his heart...

I feel compassion so strongly that I have made a covenant, a very good covenant, full of love for the ones I love and the ones I can help and the ones I can't help.

I want to help so many.

I want to shower them with Frankinsence.

I want to plant a thousand trees and rid the world of hunger and pain.

I want to be a White Knight for those in need and who are without the strength to fight on alone.

I want to be a teacher of love and understanding.

I want to be a healer so that I might ease the suffering of those in plight, and so...

dear Jesus in the night
please,
stay with me...

if you can keep your head

if your aim is pure

if your aim is pure

if your aim is pure you will remember

you will remember

confusion

riddles and rhymes

> *head games are fun but hard to play*
> *follow the rules or be taken away*

…a name, there was a name…

if your aim is pure

…it is, it is…you must know that in my heart it is…

I will mark your hands

*If your aim is pure you will remember and now, dear unknown guardian angel, I **do** remember and here comes the name that will take me to dreamland…*

"Excuse me sir – would you mind telling me your name?"
"Of course not, officer – it's Monkbox."
"Christian name please sir?"
"Fumble"
"Fumble Monkbox – unusual name. You wouldn't be taking the piss by any chance would you?"

click,   click,   click,   click,   click,   click,   click,   click,

After different tears were shed and thought on, Jo found pen and paper and began to write…

Part One   <u>1963</u>

He moved the cabinet further
into the passage, lifting it steadily
over the lip of the carpet. He
grabbed the blue money-bag and
hoisted himself up until he
could reach the wooden frame of the
window-light, then climbed out
onto the roof. He waited a
few minutes, catching his breath.
When he was sure nobody was in
sight, he lowered himself from
the roof and walked quickly away.

It was just after.....!

Postscript — from the author

It took me nearly five years to get this book to you — getting on for fifteen if you consider I scribbled the first page way back in July '82.

Now, all I have to do is sell it.

You will remember of course, if you did <u>read</u> the book, the purpose of writing it was to find out whether I was capable — and would it make money?

The short answers are :–

I was

It did

Goodbye. J B Dunnit